# SKELMERSDALE

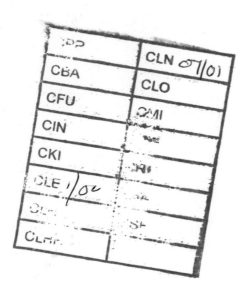

| CPP | CLN 07/01 |
| CBA | CLO |
| CFU | CMI |
| CIN | |
| CKI | |
| CLE 1/02 | |
| CLH | SK |
| CLHP | SF |

# *The* WHITE GUARDIAN

## Praise for *The White Guardian*

"An adventure on a grand and passionate scale. For readers of
science fiction, magic, and parody alike, this book has an appeal
as vast as the story within."
—*Realms of Fantasy*

"Characters both major and minor are sacrificed without
hesitation in this headlong rush of arcane intrigue
and earthly violence."
—*Publishers Weekly*

"A charming book, with the metaphysical playfulness and
inventiveness that have marked this series at its best."
—Arthur Hlavaty

## Praise for *The Eternal Guardians*

"Some writers write in deadly earnest. Others revel in satire and
parody or even simple buffoonery. But only a gifted few manage
to skillfully combine those flavors to deliver a spicy blend
that satisfies both appetites at once. Ronald Anthony
Cross pulls off that trick."
—*The Flint* (Mich.) *Journal*

"Cross propels his battered characters to the limits of their
endurance and mettle, never letting up for a moment."
—*Science Fiction Age*

"This is a fast-paced, action-packed story full of twists and
turns. I recommend this book to readers who
enjoy adventure and magic."
—*Mountain Eagle* (Albany, N.Y.)

# The
# WHITE
# GUARDIAN

## Book Three of
## The Eternal Guardians

*Ronald Anthony*
*Cross*

TOR®

A TOM DOHERTY ASSOCIATES BOOK
NEW YORK

07933728

This is a work of fiction. All the characters and events portrayed in this novel are either fictitious or are used fictitiously.

THE WHITE GUARDIAN

Copyright © 1998 by Ronald Anthony Cross

This book is printed on acid-free paper.

Edited by James Frenkel

A Tor Book
Published by Tom Doherty Associates, Inc.
175 Fifth Avenue
New York, NY 10010

Tor Books on the World Wide Web:
http://www.tor.com

Tor® is a registered trademark of Tom Doherty Associates, Inc.

Library of Congress Cataloging-in-Publication Data

Cross, Ronald Anthony.
    The white guardian / Ronald Anthony Cross.
       p.  cm.—(Eternal guardians ; bk. 3)
    "A Tom Doherty Associates book."
    ISBN 0-312-85863-9 (hc)
    ISBN 0-312-86839-1 (pbk)
    I. Title.  II. Series: Cross, Ronald Anthony. Eternal guardians :
bk. 3.
    PS3553.R5725W45   1998
    813'.54—dc21
                                                            98-11421
                                                            CIP

First Edition: June 1998
First Trade Paperback Edition: June 1999

Printed in the United States of America

0  9  8  7  6  5  4  3  2  1

To hybrid dogs and cats
(all bull and terrier breeds)
(Tonkinese and lynx points),
the very best.

And to what this implies
for us humans.

# A Note about Fighting Dogs (A Confusing Subject)

**American Pit Bull Terrier (APBT)**—The ultimate bull-and-terrier fighting dog.

**Staffordshire Terrier**—Another name for the APBT, but the show-dog version. Also the name of the ancestor of the APBT, a smaller dog.

**Bull Terrier**—Like the dog in this novel, Blackjack. The English version: These dogs are feisty, yet full of fun. Not commonly thought to be as great a fighter as the APBT, but I, like Corbo, am not so sure of that. I think maybe they are just better natured.

**American Bulldogs**—Nothing like the squat little bowlegged English bulldog, these are the American working farm dogs and hog catchers. Big, smart, but definitely still a bulldog, with none of that terrier nonsense built in, these are the heavyweight champs. For a while, when they first started using these poor farm dogs to fight, they were called pit bulls, confusing matters further. The Alapahas mentioned in this book are a distinct breed of these from the Alapaha river territory in Georgia. Some bulldog men love 'em and some hate 'em.

**Bandog**—Half bull-and-terrier, and half bigger dog of some kind, usually mastiff.

Other fighting dogs, such as the Presa Canario and the Dogue de Bordeaux, play no role in this book, and so I will not describe them.

# *Preludes*

# Prelude I

*SAXONIUS THE GIANT, torn by Demons in their awful rage." *Yeah, right.* "Texas" Jed Hinks, despite having acquired degrees in cultural anthropology, comparative mythology, and finally archaeology, and adding the image of learned professor to his identity, was still a cowboy at heart. And like all Texas cowboys, he loved to brag a little.

But he would not be bragging about this "find" in the journals. Maybe a little bit at the local bars, when he had a bit too much to drink.

"Lemme tell you boys about this little archaeological dig a mine," he might say, feeling the glow of booze light up that tall-tale gene that rode down the old Texas chromosome trail from father to son.

"It was over in old England, she was, when I was just a young cowpoke archaeologist cruisin' the local talent and maybe breaking into a few crypts." Something like that, perhaps. But he would definitely have to be well into his cups to mention it.

It had been in an old churchyard in Winchester. One of the locals in the Green Rooster pub had heard about Jed, about what he was doing there (small pub, big news), and offered to sell him some "very, very valuable relics." The poor old fellow was so completely lacking in conviction, but obviously driven by even the remotest chance at one more drink, that cowboy Jed almost didn't glance at the coins. But when he did!

All it took was a few more coins, English pounds this time, actually, trading hands in the other direction, to talk old Willie "The Worm" Burton (relative of Sir Richard's?) into leading him to his "secret place."

Two weeks later, and with full cooperation from the English, he and his small crew of hardly working Brits, as he liked to put it, dug up the myste-

rious, deeply buried crypt. SAXONIUS THE GIANT, it was labeled, TORN BY
DEMONS IN THEIR AWFUL RAGE.

It was obvious that this must have been a very important man, because
the crypt was huge and also highly unusual: a giant room built of stone and
buried deep in the earth.

There were more coins, all from the same era, and the few bits and
pieces of bone which were apparently all that was left of Saxonius. He had
been "torn" all right, but not by demons, for there was also, mixed in with
the bones, what was later identified as shrapnel from a World War II German
hand grenade.

But at the moment, Texas Jed was not noticing the bits of metal in with
the bone, nor was he zeroing in on the abundance of eleventh-century arti-
facts. It was the other object in the room that captured his attention, for neither the grenade nor the ravages of time had destroyed it—though really, that
could not possibly be the case, because what it was, unlikely as unlikely gets,
was an Ovation Custom Legend guitar. There was even enough coloration
left so that Tex could immediately identify it as that new Cadillac greenburst
finish that Ovation had just recently come out with. "Takes a licking but
keeps on ticking," he thought, confusing it with Timex. He recalled, in an
amused reverie, that he had once been amazed to see a salesman bang the
rounded plexiglas back of one of these guitars into a wall as a demonstration
of its durability, but even that guy wouldn't have claimed . . . would he?

So this had turned out to be one successful dig that even the British did
not want to boast about. It was definitely hush-hush here, and frankly, Tex
wouldn't have wanted it any other way.

Whoever this mysterious eleventh-century German was, damn it, if he
played an Ovation, Tex figured the best thing to do was cover it up. Sure,
some of your modern jazzy guitarists liked to tinkle around on those plastic
guitars, and all of your "sensitive" folksy people played mellow-toned Mar-
tins, but he was a Gibson man himself. All the yodeling cowboys of his
youth had twanged away on big jumbo Gibsons.

He himself lugged around a J-200 wherever he went, and one day he
looked forward to really getting good on it. It was a man's guitar, and that
was that.

He had to smile, thinking of big Saxonius playing his Ovation Custom
Legend to entertain surly King Rufus and his nasty court—everything in
the crypt which could be carbon-dated, including, preposterously, the guitar,
had been dated back to that period of time. *Maybe that's what they killed him
with,* he thought, *just whacked him out with that damn plastic guitar. Never
bought the hunting accident story myself.*

He often thought like this while he strummed a few simple chords on his old Gibson. He was one of those cowboys who never realized how dull it is to hear some guy strumming chords as if he's accompanying a singer, when he's not. Well, maybe he did realize it, because sometimes he would hold out the beautiful, fancy Tex-Mex-looking instrument and just look at it and say silently to all those he played for, "Well, damn it, at least it's a Gibson."

# *Prelude II*

G RAY, GRAY EVERYWHERE, and not a drop to drink," the fey young woman named Tippi said, maybe (maybe not) to herself. If she saw or otherwise sensed the existence of the other, obviously more together young woman watching her, she gave no outward sign of it. She simply sat on a colorless something-or-other—Violet could not tell what it was—and stared straight ahead. Tippi's eyes were huge and round, giving the impression of genuine (probably) astonishment.

"There's nothing to drink, all right," Violet agreed. "Along with all the many other charming nothings offered here: no food, no color, no noise, no people."

"So why are you here?" Tippi asked in her high sweet voice, which hovered on the edge of a dizzy fall into hysteria. "I thought you wanted to see me dead." She shrugged and smiled, but it was not a fun smile. "Well"—she shrugged yet again—"I'm dead. Again. Here in my own sweet world of gray." The smile went away. "Where nobody comes and nobody goes." A gray tear ran down her cheek. "Where I can take off all my clothes and nobody knows."

Violet, who was, though not tall, taller than Tippi, and saner, and whose very posture and demeanor radiated strength and purpose, walked over to whatever it was Tippi was sitting on and took hold of the crazy little bitch's plump little arms (Violet's were slender with just the most charming hint of muscle tone) and pulled her to her feet. She slapped her hard across the face and said, "Snap out of it, you crazy bitch. I haven't got time to wait for your moment of clarity to leisurely arrive."

Tippi did not resist her, simply staring into Violet's slightly slanted eyes with her own, which were even more rounded than before, if that were possible.

"Thanks," she said, straight-faced. "I needed that."

"That's not half of what you need," Violet said. "You need to be dead. But thanks to you, there are already too many people dead, many of whom are my loved ones. So, as much as I'm tempted, I'm not going to leave you here to starve to death sitting around on your crazy helpless little ass in this ugly fucking gray world you've either created or discovered. I'm going to take you out and dump you in the nearest nuthouse, and then spend the next few hundred years forgetting I ever met you." She waited for a reply.

After what seemed an inordinately long time, Tippi said, "You've taken up swearing. It does not become you, not with all that fucking makeup and that oh-so-military posture, oh no, not at all. Me, on the other hand, it becomes, like everything else." She smiled wickedly. "You see, in a certain way, I guess I'm kind of what you've been aiming at."

Violet twitched. The fingers of her hands, which were once again gripping both of Tippi's arms, bit in. *Was it true? For it was no secret to her that despite her good looks, there was something untouchable, foreboding even, about her. She had always assumed it was the aura of the power of the mystic stone she carried, but was it? Tippi also had wielded power and—*

As if reading her mind, which perhaps she was, Tippi said it for her:

"Everybody wants to fuck me." She smiled a full, effortless, happy smile out of nowhere. "And I couldn't care less. I guess that's 'cause I'm crazy."

Violet just shook her head, and let go of Tippi's arms. For the first time since all the violence, she felt as if she could almost smile. "That probably explains it all," she said. "Come on, let's get out of here. This place gives me the creeps."

She pointed, and a mystic doorway, looking like a tunnel with a light somewhere way up ahead, appeared.

"My, aren't we gifted," Tippi remarked. "Just like that."

"Yes, we are gifted," Violet answered. "I can modestly but truthfully say that I'm the most gifted to ever have wielded one of the stones."

"And I," said Tippi, "am the most gifted who has not."

The two women went through the tunnel, out of the gray and into the light.

# *Prelude III*

THE BIG STATION-wagon-sports-ute, GMC's latest model, which reminded Jimmy Running Deer of a pregnant rocket ship, rolled with surreal silence through dark empty space. It was not empty as in "nothing there," but in the sense that what *was* there seemed sparse and not quite real. A representation perhaps of what should be in a landscape. Just enough of it to evoke a sense of place. A big straight ribbon of highway out of nowhere headed nowhere. An obligatory tree here, an ugly little shrub there, and in the distance some phony-looking mountains that you couldn't quite make out. You could drive forever at any speed you chose (there was no speed limit here) and not reach them.

Occasionally you would rocket through some little town just to remind you that yes, this was planet earth, and humans did live here: a gas station-cafe, a tiny grocery store, maybe a bar, and a couple of nameless buildings.

Often they were forced to pull up at these road stops in order to feed the big hungry ute. Once in a while, Jimmy, who was the oldest among them, would wonder where all the gas was coming from, for despite all the warnings and protests and programs to "downsize,'" despite all the tiny Oriental sub-subcompacts you saw around town these days, even including those electric go-carts a handful of self-righteous masochists drove, everyone and his or her brother was driving trucks, utes, or vans. (It was getting harder to tell the difference between them.) Furthermore, due to the incurable social disease, nostalgia, big cars could be counted upon to make periodic comebacks. This seemed to be another one of those periods.

Ironically, the one area of progress that Jimmy actually enjoyed was usually, as on this trip, denied him. The Guardians did not like to travel in whirlybirds.

"No place to park, Jimmy," Raphael had jokingly informed him. But Jimmy felt sure that he knew the real reason. The ute-wagon was practically a tank. And of course it had airbags in the dash, doors, ceiling, probably in places he'd never dreamt of. (Ashtray? What ashtray? As if the Guardians would let you smoke around them.) If they ever had an accident, they would probably smother in balloons.

Besides which, Rafe had explained patiently, what was the hurry? Which was true if you were going to live damn near forever. But not as true for Jimmy. So the only breaks in this surreal monotony were these desolate pit stops.

And just as soon as the metal beast had guzzled its fill, they would rocket off again into that same endless highway through nowhere.

They had been driving too fast, or so it had seemed to Jimmy Running Deer. He remarked to Raphael, who was driving, "Slow down a little, kid."

But Raphael had argued, "Why? No one's on the road but us."

It had only been a minute or two later that the big, svelte new Caddie had jumped up on their tail, sounded the horn once, just to be sure they were awake, and then whipped around them, and, its large but streamlined shape outlined with little "safety lights," shot up ahead and out of sight.

"Must have been doing a hundred and ninety," Jimmy had said in awe. He'd always had the peasant's reverence for the Cadillac name, as well as whatever was the latest version of the humongous Northstar engine. As time went by, it got bigger, then smaller, then bigger again, then smaller, but always it got faster.

"This be Montana," Thaddeus said from the back seat. And they had driven on in silence. And on.

Jimmy Running Deer kept drifting off. It had started to rain. The monotonous *whick whack* of the windshield wipers was hypnotizing him. Outside, although it was still supposed to be afternoon, it had turned practically as dark as night. You could sure tell that you were a long ways from Arizona, and that in itself was enough to make him uneasy. Bad dreams, starts and fits, can't go to sleep, can't stay awake. And then you factor in the weird objective of this hunting trip and— That woke him up a notch. But not for long.

He focused in on the young man driving the wagon, and must have dozed off yet once more because, once again, he saw Raphael as he used to be, instead of as he was now. A young boy, so sweet looking with all that golden hair and those big, inquisitive green eyes. So much like his mother. Jimmy felt a surge of panic. Surely the boy was too young to be driving a car. He should shout a warning, but he couldn't speak, couldn't move.

With a start he woke up, and ten years went by just like that in between two strokes of the windshield wipers on the big ute-wagon. Raphael the boy became Raphael the man, albeit a far younger-looking man than he was supposed to be. For the first time it dawned on Jimmy how little Raphael had changed over the years. Lean. Delicate looking, even. Like a fag, damn it. Jimmy had tried to get him to get his perfectly straight little nose out of those damn books of his and get some damn exercise, but it was hopeless. He was doomed to live out his life, which let's face it was something like an eternity, as a skinny little wimp without enough muscle to whip your cat. And he was so intense. Always so damn intense; even as a child he had never gone through a period where he would have been thought of by anyone as playful. Just like his mother, Elena, God rest her soul. The Indian God, that is, not the pale, white-skinned masochist God. Jimmy grimaced. In some way, mysterious to him, he loved the boy, but did not like him. Same with Elena. Same with the rest of the Guardians.

Except for Thaddeus, whom he did not love or like. Yet the man had the burden of the stone, was a Guardian. Deserved that same cold respect. Were the stones of power not a curse as well as a blessing?

He turned and looked at the tall Black man sprawled out in the middle row of seats, sporting that ridiculous white cowboy hat, wearing shades. In the dark. Was the man awake or asleep? Unreasonably, Jimmy felt a surge of anger at the fool. He hated people who wore shades when they were, at least to his way of thinking, unnecessary.

Thaddeus moved, reached up, and with his long, exquisitely tapered fingers (manicured nails, even) took off his expensive sunglasses. He looked unblinkingly at Jimmy with his hooded, slightly slanted eyes, and Jimmy thought he was going to speak, but he did not. He simply buzzed down the window and threw the shades out into the rain. A burst of freezing air came in. He buzzed the window back up again. After a pause he said in his low, laconic voice, "If my shades offend you, cast them out, my man." Then, without waiting for an answer, he closed his eyes and apparently tripped off to sleep again.

Like Raphael, slender, elegant; yet, unlike Raphael, big, very big.

With another inexplicable surge of anger Jimmy Running Deer turned back around and looked out the front window into the rain. Definitely getting darker. Pretty soon you wouldn't be able to see the wonderful scenery—little joke there—just the freezing rain. He shivered.

"Wake you up," Thaddeus mumbled from behind him. "Lazy nigga," he added, whether addressing himself or insulting Jimmy's pure Apache blood, who knew?

There was nothing about Thaddeus that Jimmy found understandable, let alone comfortable to deal with. And, as sad as it was, there was one other person riding in this car who elicited that same confused, angry emotion in him: his own cousin Fatman, *one of the people*. Fatman—he had been named Billy Blackfeather in the tradition of his people (a large black feather, from a crow, no doubt, had floated down from the heavens to land at his father's feet) but since the age of eight had insisted upon being called Batman. Then as he grew and grew (at least as much outward as upward) the name had shifted to the more descriptive version. "Duh da duh da duh da duh da—Fatman!" as the kids had all sung to him many times.

Thing was, Fatman didn't care. That's what always got Jimmy. You could call him whatever you wanted. Push him around, he never pushed back: he was just too good-natured. And if pride had always been the mosquito buzzing around on the inside of Jimmy Running Deer's net, Fatman was the angel of acceptance. "Let it go. It's okay. It's just the way things are."

Last man in the world to be a bodyguard. Bodyguard got to be lean and mean. (Jimmy glanced down at what was just the beginnings of his own private little potbelly and made a resolution to go to work on that as soon as he got back from this worthless task they were all plugged into here. Which, of course, owed its origin to the brilliant mind of the inscrutable Thaddeus, conked out in the back seat.)

Of late, the two male Guardians had sort of formed a team, Thaddeus as the sensitive and Raphael doing all the magical enforcing. While the girl, Violet, the only one of them left with any common sense, as Jimmy saw it, had for the last few years simply withdrawn and gone her own way, accompanied by her own little personal schizophrenic traveling companion. What made this trip a sort of paradise, if you asked Jimmy, was the fact that, even though it meant riding in the ute all the way from eternally warm Arizona into cold, wet, loathsome northern Montana, at least Violet, who sat next to Fatman on the bench seat in the rear of the van, had somehow been persuaded to leave her little nutcase friend Tippi back home.

No doubt about it, the group had fallen apart without the earth-mother guidance of Elena, the only Indio in the ranks. And nobody was even sure what had happened to her. "Is Elena dead?" he had asked her son Raphael. A simple question, right? Wrong!

"Elena no longer exists on this earth or on any world or plane where Thaddeus can sense her," the angelically beautiful Raphael had answered, after a moment's contemplation, without a trace of emotion in his voice. "Which means that she's probably dead. Or might as well be," he added as an afterthought.

No, there was no question in Jimmy Running Deer's mind, this group was shot straight to shit city without any semblance of leadership, unless . . . unless . . . For the first time it struck Jimmy: was it possible that the leadership role had been taken over by that jive-talking ex-junkie hipster nigger? Suddenly Jimmy remembered: some of the Guardians could read your mind, at least part of the time. He remembered William, Violet's long-lost brother (another of the missing-presumed-dead around here), reassuring him, in what seemed to him now another era (the golden age?), "We wouldn't any of us do that, Jimmy. We respect your privacy. We've trained ourselves to block people's thought streams out. Besides which, there's too much of it; it's too chaotic. It would drive us nuts."

But that was William, and William along with Elena was gone, and what about Thaddeus? Who could tell what he would or wouldn't do? Jimmy shivered and again looked out the front window. What do you know? Rain.

It was just beginning to turn dark, or rather turn night, which meant even darker than before, by the time they finally pulled into the town, and it was still raining steadily. Raphael stopped the wagon, and for a moment they sat staring out the windshield at the blurry shapes of what appeared to be a row of old, deserted wooden shacks.

"This is it, though," Thaddeus said in his low calm voice. Thaddeus was the psychic locater of the group, the one who knew where it or he or she was. Just as he was never lost or confused in the streets of a major city, he was equally at ease finding his way around the psychic world; so if he said "This is it," then whatever it was, here was where they would find it. Unlikely as it seemed to Jimmy, looking at this dump.

"Looks like a ghost town," Jimmy said. "Cahee, Montana."

"Named after a small Indian tribe, now extinct," Raphael added.

Another thing about Raphael that Jimmy Running Deer could have lived without and not really missed at all, was his habit of telling you stuff you never knew if it was real or a joke. A dumb joke. So how did you act here, for instance?

"Cahee Indians," Jimmy said. "Sure, great name. Wonder why they're extinct, with that name."

Raphael smiled his innocent smile. "The sharp-tongued Apache warrior is hard on his red-skinned brother. Let's just mosey on into town and see what kind of vibes we pick up here." He started the big ute cruising slowly down the main and probably only street of Cahee, Montana.

Nobody home. It gave Jimmy Running Deer a creepy feeling. Jimmy was a warrior pure and simple; no blood of the shaman was running through his veins. And all of the weird mumbo jumbo that the Guardians practiced back at the ranch produced results that were apparently invisible to mere mortals like himself. The same was mostly true of these occasional psychic trips they found it necessary to make in order to guard the world from—what? Almost all the time, when stuff happened on these trips, it was stuff too subtle for him to perceive, but the few exceptions had been spectacular enough to make any skeptic worry. And each time had been unpredictable and different. Fatman, however, had not shared in any of these experiences.

"It's a ghost town, all right," he snorted, as if to say, "Montana is a long way to go for this."

"They are all in that building up ahead," Thaddeus explained patiently.

"Huddled around the campfire," Violet added, "figuratively speaking, of course."

Jimmy Running Deer visibly started; she was so damn quiet back there in the dark, he had actually forgotten her presence. She was always like that, quiet, composed, smiling that little Mona Lisa smile. But of the three Guardians left, she was the one could scare you the most. The silent fury, he thought, as the wagon pulled up in front of the only lit-up building along the highway.

None of them thought to consider what an odd entourage they must have formed, filing out of the big flashy ute and dashing through the rain to the sheltering overhang of the saloon. Perhaps only the tall Black man wearing the big white Stetson would have had some awareness of the scene: the slender Eurasian woman all decked out in decorator cowboy clothes and weighted down with Navajo jewelry; the two big Indians, both wearing headbands and necklaces, long coarse black hair glossy wet; and Raphael, the archangel, the beautiful one, slender, elegant, decked out in a floppy British tweed fisherman's hat and woolen sweater.

They stopped for a moment on the porch, where Violet fussed with her wet hair, then entered.

"Hi," the tall, laconic man behind the counter said. "Welcome ta Whiskey Bill's. I'm Whiskey Bill here. Sit yourself down and stay a spell. Name yer poison."

There were five other men seated at a big round table playing cards, presumably stud poker. The men cajoled and threatened the dealer while he slowly and deliberately dealt one card at a time, faceup.

"Don't give me no one-eyed jacks," one of them howled as he was dealt to. "Ace me, dude, match the one up, not ta mention the other down here in my hidey-hole."

"He's bluffin'," one of the others said, adding dryly, "as usual."
"As always," a third one threw in.

The Guardians, along with their bodyguards, led by Thaddeus, sat down on the tall wooden chairs at the bar.

"Bourbon and branch water." Thaddeus waved to Raphael, who said, "Beer."

"Me, too," Fatman said, and Jimmy nodded.

"And for the little lady?"

"The little lady," Violet said, "will have"—hesitated—"a whiskey sour."

The bartender put on an oafish, comic, puzzled expression. "What's a whiskey sour, boys?" he drawled sarcastically. "Been so long I done forgot." Which brought a round of chuckles and snickers from the cardsharps.

And right there, everyone knew there was going to be trouble. Only thing left to figure out was just how soon and how much.

Suddenly one of the men wailed from the table:

"She downed her whiskey sours
In a nightclub after hours
Where her memories of times gone by grew dim
And if you bought her a drink or two
She might spend the night with you
But she'd be dreaming that she spent the night with him."

A short period of silence followed this outburst of strangely sweet singing.

Then Whiskey Bill said in a soft voice, "You strangers here might want to prepare yourselves for the Visitation."

Another short but significant hush.

Thaddeus looked at Raphael, who looked at Violet, who shrugged, then turned her gaze back to Thaddeus.

Thaddeus broke the silence slowly and carefully in his low, soothing voice. "Uh, what Visitation are we preparing ourselves for here?"

Whiskey Bill rolled his eyes comically up toward the ceiling and answered, "From above."

"Uh, flying saucers?" Raphael speculated cautiously.

Whiskey Bill's expression turned sour. "How 'bout thet, boys. Sherlock Holmes here wants to know if it's flying saucers."

One of the men at the table laughed raucously, drowning out one of the others, who was speaking in a soft voice.

"What I said," the man repeated, "is, that which visits us hath no need of them flying saucers. Nor anything else, fer that matter. The Visitation is solely of the spirit."

"Amen," Whiskey Bill added.

This time it was Violet who broke the silence. "Where are all the women in this town, anyway?"

Whiskey Bill smiled slyly at that. "Why, I don't know. Where's your wife, Kevin?"

The big bearded man at the card table smiled back. "Killed her," he said.

"And yours, Jimmy Dean?"

The scruffy little man who apparently was intended as the second coming of that most charismatic star of stars waved his drink in a salute to the strangers at the bar and took a swig of it in toast. Then he announced in an emotionless voice:

"Bitch nagged me once too often and I hed ta kill her. Damn fuckin' shame, too. Not a clean fuckin' dish in the whole damn filthy fuckin' kitchen. Gotta eat out all the time. Here. Only fuckin' place in town still open. Awful food," he added, for the first time his voice showing concern.

Whiskey Bill nodded sagely. "I say kill the bitches afore they cut yer dick off, throw it in a vacant lot or something, right, boys? That's what we done here."

To which he added, after a moment's reflection: "Can't live with 'em, can't live without 'em. But at least there's revenge."

The horrifying thought hit both Raphael and Violet at the same moment, but they hadn't time to utter it. Perhaps the "Visitation"—whatever that was—had bestowed upon Whiskey Bill the ability to read their thoughts; perhaps it was only instinct that caused him to interject before they could say it:

"The children? What could we do? There was just nobody hangin' around to take care of 'em." He brushed an imaginary tear from his eye and sighed dramatically. "I sure do miss the little tykes, though, the pitter patter of their fuckin' little feet."

Laughter erupted from the group of men seated around the card table. Whiskey Bill grinned a wicked toothy grin and added, "Psych."

Thaddeus spoke, his voice even calmer, if anything, and more soothing than usual. "Sorry, but I'm not getting this. You killed the kids, yes? You killed the kids, no?"

More laughter from the card table.

"Hey, listen up, boys," Whiskey Bill said, the grin leaving his face to be replaced by a sneer, which in his case was not all that different. "The nigger speaketh, and he will not be denied." He seemed to be mimicking a comic fundamentalist preacher now. "Inquiring minds wantith to know. Well, let me give you the nitty-gritty, nigger.

"We killed the little bastards, all right. Right along with their bitch mothers and their fuckin' little dogs and parakeets."

One of the cardplayers raised his hand as if in a schoolroom. "Least we didn't torture 'em," he said somberly.

"We was in a hurry," Jimmy Dean tossed in, bringing another round of laughter from the cardplayers and putting a hint of a smile back on the dour countenance of Whiskey Bill.

"So now we live here all alone, all together, a society of holy men, dedicated to the Visitation, untainted by the corruption of women—or Injuns." His smile disappeared. "Till now," he added. Then he lifted the shotgun from behind the counter and laid it on top, the double barrels casually pointing toward Raphael, whom he apparently considered to be the leader of the group. But his squinty, pale-blue eyes were focused on Violet.

"Which brings us to you, babe. Which one a these sorry menfolks you belong to?"

Violet blinked, but said nothing. More laughter from the cardplayers.

"Fess up, boys," Jimmy Dean proclaimed. "Which one of you owns the squaw?"

It was Thaddeus who recovered first from the revelation that these "cowboys" had mistaken Violet's Chinese blood for American Indian heritage. And really, when you took into consideration the way she was dressed—all that Navajo jewelry and cowboy clothes—and the darker color of her skin, it wasn't really all that far-fetched.

"The squaw's mine," Thaddeus offered in his most relaxed, friendly tone of voice, no idea where this was going, just playing it by ear.

Whiskey Bill grunted, looking even more displeased with this turn of events, if that were possible.

"Shoulda got yerself a white woman," he suggested, "raise yourself up a notch, right, boys?" The boys agreed. "Make somethin' outta yourself. Be somebody."

"Or not be," somebody added.

As if on cue, the one named Jimmy Dean stood up, spread his arms wide, and finished, " 'Whether 'tis nobler in the mind . . . to take arms against a sea of troubles, and by opposing end them?' Or . . ." He gave up and sat down again.

The cardplayers gave him a round of applause.

"It's not so simple, see," Whiskey Bill elaborated. "After all, nigger,

Injun, or whatever, you're still men, and as such have certain rights." He turned his head toward Violet, whose narrow eyes were open wider than one would have thought possible, and said, "Except for you. That part's simple."

Then back to Raphael, "The Visitation will tell us what to do with you. And I wouldn't be surprised if it wants us to welcome you into our hearts with open arms, regardless of your creed or color."

"Amen," said one of the men from the table.

"So what we do now," Bill finished, "is wait."

Thaddeus looked from Whiskey Bill, with his shotgun on the bar, over to the men at the table, and there were guns there, too. He had not noticed when the men had taken them out and put them on top of the table, but they were there now. Handguns, though not auto loaders like the nine-millimeter combat model he carried. These were old-fashioned revolvers. Probably personally handed down from Wyatt Earp or John Wayne.

He knew that Fatman and Jimmy Running Deer were also carrying, and that Violet and Raphael were not, and that the two Apache bodyguards were watching him for some sign of what move to make, and when to make it. But it's one thing to have a handgun packed away in a shoulder holster and another to have a shotgun lying out on a bar, or a revolver on a table with a hand on it.

And there was more bad news. The worst of all. Thaddeus had observed Violet glaring at the woman-hater a moment ago, and was well aware of what she had been trying to pull off. He could feel the effort she had put into her mental assault: and the bad news was that for some reason, it had not worked. The shotgun was still there, and Whiskey Bill was not down on his knees whining about the pain in his head, so Thaddeus had to conclude that something about what these cowboys called the "Visitation" had altered Bill's consciousness so that he was now impervious to Violet's arsenal of psychic assaults. Probably true for the knights of the card table, too. He turned toward Fatman and Jimmy and shook his head. "Let's wait," he suggested.

They did not have to wait long. Apparently the being they called "the Visitation" had established the routine of appearing every night shortly after sundown. Perhaps like some of the earlier crossovers from other dimensions that Thaddeus had heard of from the other Guardians, this creature came from some cold dark place, and could not survive the heat or light of the day. This speculation was reinforced by the coldness in the bar. It was a freezing rainy night coming on in Montana, and nobody had even turned on the heat.

While Thaddeus and the other Guardians were busy analyzing and anticipating the situation, Jimmy Running Deer and Fatman were simply waiting for some kind of sign from one of the Guardians—probably Thaddeus, Jimmy figured—that it was time to fight. Or maybe, like the cowboys in the bar, they were just waiting for the Visitation—whatever that was. The funny thing was that when it came, Jimmy never even noticed it.

At first there was just a good feeling in the pit of your stomach, just the feeling of being alive, only stronger—almost like an itch, only you didn't want to scratch it, really. And good kept slowly getting better. And better.

This was accompanied by an odor, a very familiar odor that Jimmy associated with his childhood. A few sweet memories floated to him suffused within the smell: a black spider shining in her web, which was decorated with sparkling drops of rain. A few white clouds in the clear blue Arizona sky. A marble made of agate, dull, not bright, but with a strange depth to it, sinking into a clump of living, moving, green blades of grass. The dark velvet of his mother's breast. The erect black nipple calling to him. And clearly, he once again tasted the first cookie from a big yellow cardboard box—what were they called?

Surely there was nothing alarming about a few memories, a feeling of well-being, or that soft glow that emanated from the ceiling. Rosy and yet cool, it made perfect sense to him as he looked up at it. And, strangely enough, the more he looked at it, the more he could see in it. It seemed to be made up of small moving particles, rather like a pointillist painting. And if he concentrated—

Suddenly, in some inexplicable but totally meaningful manner, up became down and down became up. And he was falling into the moving, living light.

And now, as he fell, hundreds—no, thousands—of memories flashed through his mind and heart, faster than he would ever have conceived as possible. And yet, and this was the oddest part of all, somehow, he fully experienced them all, relived them all, the good along with the bad; he relived his entire life in the flashing of a few instants, and this time it was filtered through the overwhelming bliss issuing from his stomach. Which, yes, he realized now, was the light. Through this bliss he reaffirmed his entire life, the bad along with the good, and with this reaffirmation came the final revelation. That he was God! That all men were God. That you can do anything you want. Anything at all. Because how can they stop you or hurt you because you are alive now, living out your entirety now, and there isn't anything else but now. I am God!

At first he did not even feel the hand on his shoulder; he just felt the bliss drain out of him like the river of light it was, and disappear, leaving him to exist in a void so terrible and cold that he could not stand it, that he cried out in pain, realizing that it was the confines of his ordinary everyday consciousness to which he was returning. The self-constructed prison of his ego. Then, just as suddenly as it came, it was over.

"Shit," he said, shaking his head and registering the hand on this shoulder as belonging to Thaddeus.

"Shit is right," Thaddeus mused. "Got me, too, for a minute. Takes my magic twanger here a few minutes do its thing. Same way with dope or booze. But eventually, wear one of these rocks, and you got no choice but to be sober."

The stone he was alluding to was a piece of ordinary-looking black obsidian set in a simple silver amulet, attached to a chain around his neck, which he now held in his left hand. He must have been wearing it inside his shirt earlier.

Apparently Jimmy Running Deer was still suffering from the effects of his Visitation, because for the first time the stone did not look so ordinary to him anymore, but pulsing and alive with some kind of energy that you couldn't call light because it was the darkest of the dark, too dark to see, but there was a way you could look and—

"Better you don't look at it right now," Thaddeus said in his soothing voice. "In fact, don't really look at anything close up for a while or you'll get sucked in. Just sort of glance around, keep your eyes moving. You'll come out of it in a moment."

On the other side of Thaddeus he saw Fatman, who had gotten off his chair and was now standing on the wooden floor, openly weeping, apparently being dragged out of his reverie by Violet, who had her hand on his arm. For a moment, before Jimmy remembered to avert his glance, he could somehow see the power flowing from her hand and spreading. Then he blinked and looked away.

Suddenly he remembered where he really was and why, and whirled his head around, only to find Whiskey Bill, blissed out but alert as ever.

"I'm an old hand," Whiskey said, as if reading his mind, which, Jimmy figured, was what he probably was doing.

"Some of these youngsters here, they lose control a mite under all that good, good feeling. But you get used to it. And the more you get used to it, the quicker and the stronger it comes on, like a bigger and stronger dose of some wonderful drug, cleansing you, making you stronger in your convictions. But it don't affect women, do it, missy?"

Violet glared at him. "It only kills them," she said evenly, still holding on to Fatman, who was now blinking and looking around.

Whiskey Bill shook his head sadly. "You girls just don't get it, do you?

You just keep pecking away at everything without any regard for what it might mean to a man and without no regard for the consequences which you are bringing down upon your own heads. Such as death," he added as an afterthought. "And no, it does not kill you. Nor does it force us in any way to harm a hair on your pretty little heads."

"Well—not so pretty anymore," one of the cowboys from the table commented, breaking up everybody with raucous laughter.

"Can you shut it off for a minute over there? I'm trying to explain something to the little lady."

He turned back to Violet, who let go of Fatman's shoulder and was now standing erect, facing Whiskey Bill with her arms folded, looking more angry than afraid, but feeling more afraid than angry.

"No, it don't kill women. No, it don't kill nothing. It just gives us the power and the freedom to act. Fact is it don't concern itself with women one way or the other. It simply reveals to us"—long pause here—"that we are gods. And as such, have the power to be free to do what we want. Anything we want."

A chorus of "Amen" from the knights of the round table.

"But women don't have that power?" Violet said in a tight, controlled voice.

Whiskey Bill gestured around him. "Apparently not," he said dryly, bringing another chorus of guffaws from the local knights.

"Or we'd be all dressed up in suits and ties, sittin' around here watching ballet," Jimmy Dean further elucidated for her.

At this point, Whiskey Bill took a step forward, and, as if on a string, Violet also took a step forward to meet him. The two stood face to face, Bill puffing on his cigar like a dragon.

Slowly and deliberately, he took his cigar out of his mouth and blew a stream of vile, putrid smoke into her face, but she did not flinch or turn away.

"Do you mind if I smoke?" he said, drawing more laughs. "Hope you're not afraid of the big C."

Violet actually smiled, a small tight smile. "No, I'm not afraid of that at all."

"Well, good thing," Whiskey said, "being as that is not how you are going to die. I guess we don't have to worry about that either, boys, what with the Visitation affording us its holy blanket of protection."

But something about the way he said it . . . Violet shut her eyes, and then opened them again.

"What the—?" Bill started to say.

"Wrong," she said. "You've got the big C right now, Bill, and if you live long enough, which in this case doesn't have to be very long, you'll die of it. The Visitation doesn't care what happens to you. There's more where you came from." And now she smiled again, this time a broader smile.

Bill blinked and lurched for a moment, then quickly regained control, as if he had tripped over something or been struck.

"Thanks," he snarled.

"Hey," she said, "it's what I do."

Whiskey Bill took his cigar from his mouth and regarded it sourly, then threw it at her. It sizzled briefly as it made contact with the skin on her forehead, and then bounced off and fell to the floor, where it continued smoking furiously as if it, too, were addicted to itself. But once again she did not flinch.

"A little late to give up smoking," she said.

"Yeah, that is what you do, all right," Whiskey Bill said from between clenched teeth. "It's what all females do, over and over, picking away and picking away. Always looking for some way to drag a man down or drive him over the fucking edge. Which is why we were forced to take such desperate measures. Which brings us to you."

Whiskey Bill held out his right hand with the thumb pointed up, and then slowly and deliberately turned it thumb down.

"And I have further bad news. I have consulted that aspect of the Visitation which calls itself the Light on the Path, and I have been informed that none of you fellas have been accepted into the inner circle. Along with some of our other unfortunate brothers from this little town of ours, the spirit has judged you as real losers in the footrace of cooperation, and demands that you be dealt with compassionately, yet expediently." He paused. "Very expediently," he added. "My heart goes out to you. But, all the same, don't go makin' any suspicious moves. Don't want to get blood all over everything. No females left to clean it up. 'Cept you, missy. And you got the look about you a some woman never cleaned up nothin' in her entire life."

He turned toward the men at the card table, two of whom sat there with their upper bodies lying across the table, heads in their arms, moaning in ecstasy of some sort, and shouted to them.

"Get your act together here. The Visitation wants you to master your ecstasy and learn to function under it. Like your high priest and leader—" He turned back to Raphael and smiled, this time a full smile which spread across his face and changed his appearance utterly, made him look like a happy man for a moment. "Which is me," he finished. "Let us now depart this holy place," he announced.

Outside it was still raining hard, and it was bitter cold now. They paused on the sheltered porch, sandwiched between Whiskey Bill and his shotgun on one side and the cardplayers, who were all sporting revolvers, cowboy style, on the other.

Peering out into the rain, Whiskey Bill said, "First things first. That's a fancy wagon you got yourself there. Too fancy for keys, I reckon. Don't suppose you make it easy on us all and gimme the combo, open her up?"

Thaddeus shook his head.

"Well, that's fine," Bill continued, unabashed. "I'll get it outta ya soon enough, one way or another. If not, we'll just tow her off and use Joey's blowtorch on her. One he used on his wife, right, boys?"

Laughter.

"After we use it on you, that is."

He turned and pointed at one of the men, a short, pleasant-looking guy.

"Little Bill, whereabouts your little old yellow pickup? I don't see her here. And she ain't all that hard to see."

"I walked," the little plump guy in the slicker answered. "Needed the exercise. Don't want to let myself get fat like these two Injuns."

Guffaws from the men. Jimmy Running Deer just stood there with his mouth open, stunned, silently shouting for all to hear, "Me, fat?"

Whiskey Bill shook his head in amazement. "In this rain, you walked?" he said, more to himself than to anyone else. "Okay, looky here," he continued after a moment's reflection. "Here's what we got to do. We can't just shoot 'em and leave their bodies laying in the street, so either we got to walk 'em over to Little Bill's, shoot 'em there, and throw 'em in the truck, drive 'em outside of town, dig a hole and bury 'em, or send Little Bill off to get his truck and stand around waitin' for him to get back."

Little Bill looked puzzled. "But why not just shoot 'em and leave 'em lie? Least till the rain lets up."

"Sure," Whiskey Bill agreed sarcastically, "why not? Some station wagon chock-full of family and kids gets lost and figures it's late and maybe they's a hotel and a restaurant in some little town called Cahee, Montana, they never heard of till now. Headlights shine on a bunch a corpses laying in the street. Quick U-turn and then what, Little Bill? You get it now, maybe?

"What you guys want to remember here is that this thing we got goin' is just getting started. The Visitation is small, but more of it is pouring through to us each night. What we got here is only the beginning. And as in any relationship, gentlemen"—he paused for effect—"beginnings are fragile. So may I suggest a mite little walk in the rain, boys? Walk in the rain don't feel so bad oncet you got all a that mystic energy up there a-sizzlin' away in your brain, do it?"

Apparently no one disagreed. They moved off the porch and into the pouring rain, Whiskey Bill prodding Thaddeus with the short barrel of the pump shotgun, singing out in a twangy tenor:

> "Get along, leetle doggies,
> You're leavin' Wyoming
> Don'tcha know Montana gonna be your new home?

"Forever and ever," he added as an aside that brought guffaws from the cardplayers. But once in the street he called out, "Whoa, boys, know what we forgot? We forgot to search."

"But they're tourists, Bill," Jimmy Dean complained. "They ain't gonna be packing guns."

"Well, you're probably as right as rain here, Jimmy Dean," Whiskey continued. "Except there being no reason to take no chances at all, why take 'em?"

Jimmy Dean nodded reluctantly. "Yeah, I guess so," he agreed.

"So," Whiskey continued, "you folks are just gonna have to lay right down in the mud and all, sad as that sounds, right now, on your bellies, with your arms spread out up over your heads, while my man Jimmy gives you the old once-over."

For a moment everyone just stood staring at each other in the rain. Then Whiskey said, "I mean it. Now."

To which Thaddeus responded, "Look, Violet, do it, will you? What the fuck are you waiting for, anyway? We can't control these guys. Whatever's got into their minds is protecting them somehow, so do it. Okay?"

"What the fuck?" Whiskey Bill muttered, glancing at Jimmy Dean, who shrugged.

Violet held out her hands as if pleading, and said, "Please put down your guns. I don't want to hurt anyone. Please."

"What the fuck?" Whiskey Bill repeated. "The squaw's gonna hurt us?"

"Yeah," Thaddeus said, "the squaw's going to shoot you with the big arrow from the sky. Now, come on, Violet, will you?"

"Shit," Violet sobbed.

Whiskey Bill felt his hair rising up and vibrating. All of his hair, not just the hair on his head. That too, but also the hair on the back of his neck, on his arms, legs, hands, and under his shirt, chest hair moving about like feel-

ers. He even felt it in his crotch. This weird feeling was the last thing he ever
felt, because the charge flooded up his body to meet the charge rushing down
from the clouds. The flash of light and the deafening crash of thunder were
simultaneous, followed by the nauseating odor of burnt flesh. Shazam! Only
Whiskey Bill didn't turn into Captain Marvel. He just turned into dead
Whiskey Bill.

Violet, who was clearly on the edge of hysteria now, still standing there
with her hands out, palms up into the rain, looked so fragile.

"P-p-p-please," she sobbed, "your guns, put them down."

Jimmy Dean looked from Whiskey Bill's smoking corpse to Violet.

"Sure," he said, raised his revolver, pointed at her, and fired.

But Fatman, who along with Jimmy Running Deer and Thaddeus was
struggling to get out his gun, simply gave that up, stepped in front of Violet, and took the bullet, which, luckily for her but not for Fatman, was a
hollow-point coming from a .38, so that instead of punching through him and
into her, it broke up inside of him. He stood right there and took two more
of them before a fourth bullet from one of the other revolvers, this one an
old-fashioned, ordinary lead bullet, plowed right through his head and out
the back, still barely missing Violet but spattering her face with brains and
blood.

By now both Thaddeus and Jimmy Running Deer had their nine-
millimeter autos out, but had yet to get off a shot, and Raphael was already
hard hit and going down.

This time the lightning fried them all, and for a much longer period of
time: Violet was making sure. Even so, it couldn't have been more than a few
seconds, but it was a few seconds all of the survivors would remember for a
long, long time. A few seconds of blinding light and deafening sound, to
which the five possessed cowboys danced their last sickening, twitching
dance. Their mouths were open and they probably were screaming, but who
would notice under that wave of crashing thunder?

Perhaps it was only in Jimmy Running Deer's imagination that the man
nearest to him, the one called Little Bill, reached out his hands desperately
to him, and that, just before he burst into flame, his eyes bulged out and then
exploded. God knows catastrophes of that stature free the imagination along
with all of the other senses, so that in the end you're never sure what part of
your memory really happened and what part was just an hallucination born
of terror. But that would always be Jimmy's memory of it.

And afterward, the silence, the ringing in his ears, so that he could only
see Violet weeping and not hear it.

She was down on her knees now, with her face hidden in her hands. Not looking so chic, with all that mud plastered all over her, the posture grief had inflicted. It had curled her up in a shell, upon which the indifferent rain spattered.

Jimmy was aware that he was shouting something at her, but he couldn't hear what it was. Inexorably his gaze was drawn back to the men, what was left of them. The expression "ashes to ashes, dust to dust" ran through his mind. That was pretty much all that was left of them. Except for Whiskey Bill, who hadn't been fried so long.

Suddenly he remembered Fatman and began screaming something again, but he couldn't hear and so he couldn't be sure if it was coming out, which was like another weird hallucination.

Then he felt hands on his shoulders and the force flowing through them calmed him, and quite swiftly the pain in his head and the ringing in his ears dissolved and he could hear again.

"Calm down," Thaddeus was saying. "Fatman's dead. There's nothing anyone can do for him. And we've still got work to do."

Still in a daze, he watched as Thaddeus went over and took Violet by the arms and unceremoniously dragged the slender woman to her feet.

"Pull yourself out of it now," Thaddeus said, and then, apparently not finding the response he was after in her eyes, shook her with such force that her head whipped back and forth like that of a puppet.

Violet muttered something incoherent and tried to collapse back down to her knees, but when Thaddeus held on to her arms, jerking her back up, she snarled, "Don't touch me," and pulled loose. But this time she kept her feet.

"Why didn't you get all of them in the first place?" Jimmy yelled at her.

She was still holding her face in her hands, one on each cheek, swaying in the rain.

"I've never killed anyone before," she said between sobs.

Again that odd feeling, as if someone else were speaking, as Jimmy Running Deer heard himself say, "But now you have. You've killed Fatman, haven't you?"

Violet howled something into the rain. You couldn't understand it. But now Thaddeus caught hold of her arms again and once again shook her.

"Now, you listen here. You get control of yourself, Vi, and right now. Jimmy's right. You've already caused one death that you could have prevented, and damn near two. If you haven't got what it takes to use your stone, why don't you give it to that little psycho you brought home, my old pal Tippi. I guarantee you she'll use it quick enough. But for right now—snap out of it because we're not through here, and Rafe's had it."

Suddenly they all remembered Raphael going down with a bullet in his shoulder. Everyone turned to where he now sat in the mud, hand over bloody wound, but with eyes wide open and staring at them.

"No, I'm not out of it yet," he said in a low, slightly harsh voice. Then he cleared his throat and closed his eyes, but blinked them open again, as if fighting off sleep. "I've been hit in the shoulder, but the bullet went clear through. Clean—doesn't feel like it snagged anything important. Sure, I'd rather go to bed and let the stone work on healing it while I sleep, but I can't. So you guys stop squabbling and get me over there and I can still do the job. I hope," he added poignantly.

So Jimmy and Violet supported Raphael, and with Thaddeus leading they made their way back onto the porch and back into the late Whiskey Bill's saloon. Prepared to continue what had become a grueling, all-out fight to the death.

But the fight was over. The thing which might have been a cloud of consciousness still pulsated and swirled above their heads as if emanating from the ceiling, but the images and feelings which invaded their consciousness were not those of anger or resistance, but those of anguish, of loss, a flood of pictures of what might have been, mixed in with what could best be described as some sort of weird, silent eulogy for the dead cowboys. All of these images and surges of grief were flickering through their minds so fast they couldn't really sort them out or even begin to understand them. But they were there. And one thing was suddenly and completely clear to Jimmy Running Deer for the first time in his life, and it was so unexpected that it astonished him: a eulogy for one man is a eulogy for all men. Like everyone else in here except for cool, calm Thaddeus, he was crying unashamedly as a barrage of sentimental images from the six cowboys' lives was thrown at them.

Only Violet was immune, and held on to Raphael, who let go of Jimmy and lurched sideways. Violet helped him lower himself down to the floor, where she sat him up, leaning back against the bar. There was some blood on his shirt, but due to the miraculous healing power of the stone he wore, the wound had already stopped bleeding. And now once again the stones released Thaddeus and Raphael from the effects of the Visitation.

"I don't get it," Violet said. "Why not women?"

Jimmy Running Deer, who was still under the effects, mumbled something.

"What?"

"Because it's not time for it to mate," he repeated.

Violet wrapped her arms around her chest and shivered. "Jesus, get it out of here," she said in a low, disgusted voice.

But Thaddeus held out his hand. "And why not the other men in this town?"

Jimmy Running Deer continued to be the spokesman for the creature, whatever it was: "Because they weren't ready. They weren't worthy. Nobody here was prepared for the Visitation, but you have to start somewhere with someone and then build until you have the perfect world. They weren't prepared for higher consciousness and they couldn't really function under it. But you and Raphael . . ."

Raphael, sitting propped up with his eyes still closed, smiled. "I'll pass," he said in a whisper.

"Better get back," Thaddeus said, looking up toward the ceiling, apparently talking to the amorphous creature hovering there.

The swirling increased, the flickering images slowed, and although Jimmy Running Deer tried to hold on to it, the bliss seeped out of his heart for the second time that night. He felt the sorrow and isolation of his old normal self coming gradually back into command again.

And soon it was gone. The room was exquisitely empty. You could almost hear that cowboy singing his lonely song in it. What was it? Some sad lament about the hopeless plight of some woman totally dependent on men.

Thaddeus went over and knelt down next to Raphael and put his hand on his shoulder, careful not to jar him. Raphael opened his eyes again. Groaned.

"It's gone," Thaddeus said. "Can you do it? Better be now."

Raphael nodded, then groaned again. It obviously hurt him to nod. The pain operating upon his beautiful, pure features gave him the look of some martyred saint. Maybe he was.

He said, "Yeah, I can do it, but this is going to hurt me worse than it does you."

He fished his stone, which he wore around his neck on a silver chain identical to Thaddeus's, out from his shirt, and held it in his hand. Closed his eyes again. Waited a moment, gathering psychic strength.

When it happened, they all felt it as an explosion, silent but immense. Even Jimmy felt the collapsing of immeasurable planes and dimensions, and the ripping apart of worlds.

And when it was over, Raphael slumped over unconscious, but still breathing. For the first time, Jimmy understood the unimaginable powers that the stones conveyed, or perhaps only augmented, but augmented to such a degree that Raphael was able to break down connections between worlds, smash them apart so that they could never be found or used again.

Thaddeus looked worried.

"Is he okay?" Jimmy asked him.

"Yeah, I think so," Thaddeus answered, "but I don't think he'll be going to the dance tomorrow night."

Jimmy looked at Violet, who was now standing and staring at nothing in particular. She looked worse than Raphael to him.

"Vi, about what I said outside—" he started, but she interrupted him.

"You were right," she said. "So let's not hear any more about it. Let's get Raphael home where he can sleep it off. Start over. I'll try to be tougher next time. Or maybe I'll give the stone to Tippi. Why not? I can just see the headlines: 'Girl Gives Up Immortality, Lives Normal Life.' "

Only you're no girl, Jimmy said to himself. You look like a girl, but you're not getting any older, while I . . . Involuntarily he glanced down at his stomach. Pretty fucking big—for the first time he saw it like that.

"I don't think so," he said in answer to Violet's proposal. "But one thing's for sure. If you decide to give it up, you won't have any difficulty finding an army of takers. Me, for one," he added, and then, after a pause, "Fatman would have been first in line, if he were still alive."

"Yeah," Thaddeus said, "but he's dead, so he's last in line. We've got a long drive ahead of us and we're all knocked out, so let's leave Fatman here and split this ugly hillbilly scene, dig?"

After they'd made the arrangements over the car phone with the organization's pickup crew, and Jimmy had been suitably reassured that Fatman's body would be delivered to the ranch for burial on his home territory, and they had begun the long drive back to Arizona, Jimmy immediately dozed off again in the front seat.

Dreaming—reminiscing. Scenes from his boyhood and Fatman's. Another eulogy. It was almost as if the creature were still at work on his mind, which caused him to turn and look into the back seat. He was trying to see Violet, but she was lost in the dark. What was she going through? Was she really so different from him? He thought so, but how could you ever know? It was a puzzle. And since they were still in Montana and it was still cold and raining on the windshield, and he was still Jimmy Running Deer, he didn't try to solve it. He just drifted back into sleep and out again while Thaddeus flogged the big ute-wagon steadily and swiftly down the wide, straight, empty highway.

# Prelude IV

---

IT WAS RAINING along the Gulf Coast at Chickasala, Florida, too, but not the cold, steady, remorseless downpour that you got in Montana, something altogether different. Something much more dramatic and artistic, like a rainstorm in a Walt Disney film. A veritable symphony of a storm, complete with thunder and lightning. One sudden overwhelming cloudburst, over within an hour, followed by a myriad of heavenly rainbows arching up out of the dazzling green-blue sea. But the thing was, this happened here every day this time of the year, over and over, with stultifying regularity. And when the summer storm had run its way, the heat would dry up everything in a matter of a few minutes, and you would not even know that it had rained at all. You were hot and sticky before the rain, and you were hot and sticky after it. And you were bored—if you were anything like Melissa Sue Mellinger, that is—before it and after it. Yes, during it, too. Bored yes, but on your sweaty bare shoulder touched, perhaps, by a finger of sexual tension, only to turn around and find nobody there.

It was the same day after day after day. Until one day you would be too old. And being rich would not help you at all. Might even hurt.

What was perhaps the saddest thing of all about it was the fact that that fickle finger of sexual tension did not seem to touch anybody else the way it did Melissa. Take, for instance, her husband Rudy. *(Please take Rudy? Whoa, don't think that way.)*

Yet, dare Melissa be honest with herself about it? Was it that the hand which bore the finger that tickled Rudy's fancy did not belong to her? Nor to anyone else in particular, but beckoned to him, perhaps, in his mind's eye, from a shadowy figure wearing a veil? For Rudy, Melissa was pretty sure, cheated with strangers, and did not really want to know them. Was that such a price to pay for all this? Melissa looked over the balcony's wrought-iron railing, with its little angels and flowers and curlicues, to the broad expanse of brilliant green lawn, with the driveway cutting through and disappearing into those distant trees. She could go for a walk on her own front lawn. Or ride majestically up the escalators in her own mansion, from floor to floor. And then down again, home sweet home. Of course you could not expect to complete the journey in one day. You would have to break it up into several day trips, like Disney World.

Melissa could not help but smile at this. She was lovely when she smiled; after all, loveliness was how she had earned all this in the first place. Wanted: Gracious hostess to grandiose estate, occasional sex required. The ugly need not apply.

She began to chuckle. Melissa was so charming that she actually chuckled.

"What are you giggling about, out here by yourself, all alone?" He was chuckling himself as he said it.

Melissa started and turned around to find—surprise, surprise—Rudy, with his shirt off, in the doorway, watching her watching the storm.

"You're wet," he said, still in his bemused mode. "Have you been standing out in the rain?"

Rudy was quite handsome in a standard sort of way—rugged, conservative-looking, but handsome.

"I'm almost dry—here, feel my shoulder."

She could see the look of evasion instantly, that furtive alertness, scanning the territory for the quickest escape route. It was the main knife in her heart. Oh, there were plenty of slings and arrows in their marriage, but this was the killing blade.

He looked at his watch. It was a beauty, a Huer that glowed brightly in the dark, underwater.

"What time are the ladies due?" he said in his refined southern drawl. "Thought it was about now." (Misdirection.)

"No, that's not until later on. I'd almost forgotten about it." (What a lie!)

His turn: "Sounds like a helluva party to me. Wish I could be there with you girls. Ha, ha."

Melissa Sue knew he was just stalling, looking for an escape route. Still, why had he come in here in the first place? With his shirt off! Melissa sensed that the idea of this all-woman party had him stirred up, interested.

"I sure doubt it's anything to get excited about," she said, but as usual, she was lying, too. All they ever did was lie to each other these days. (*These days?* That was another lie.) And the fact was that the upcoming lingerie party had filled her with glimpses of erotic images at once both fascinating and terrifying. But she knew better than to attribute this excitement to the party. She knew that these parties were commonplace nowadays, and probably no more erotic than a Tupperware get-together. Sure, they would talk a couple of the more impressionable women into strutting their stuff in a negligee or a sexy pair of panties and a bra—big deal. The excitement was in herself. But the question was, why Rudy?

He looked at his watch again. It was a beauty, all right.

"Listen," he said, "I've got to get a move on, got to meet Ted and catch the plane. I only wish I could stay and we could cancel this fem fest and"—he searched for the word—"make love. But I'll be back Friday and we'll, uh, make love then."

Melissa Sue said something then that she would never have dreamed of saying before and could not imagine why she was saying now.

"Oh, let's not make love, Rudy," she said. "It's so difficult to make. Let's just fuck."

Rudy looked stunned. His jaw actually dropped open wide. But he said nothing. He was no longer looking at his watch. Instead, he just stood there, staring. Definitely staring. At her.

Later on, when night had fallen on her castle and the ladies of the negligee began to arrive, the first one to appear was Rudy's secretary—no, she was an administrative assistant, as Rudy was too important to have a mere secretary—Brenda Lake. And this was the oddest thing, because Melissa would have sworn that this business trip of Rudy's was really nothing more than a means of getting off alone somewhere with Brenda. But at least that vision had proved to be untrue.

According to Rudy it had been Brenda herself who suggested that the party be thrown at his home while he was out of town. And now here she was in the flesh, big and brassy and confident, strangely attractive in an almost masculine way, with that short-cut blond hair and those broad shoulders. And right off the bat, right there at the door, she did a very odd thing.

Without so much as a hello, she reached out and very tenderly touched Melissa on the tip of her nose. "The little princess all alone in her castle," she said. "Tonight's the night." She smiled.

For the first time Melissa noticed the woman behind Brenda, all in black. Whitest of skin, blackest of hair; even in the porch light you could be sure of that. Reddest of lips.

"Elspeth," she said, and for a moment Melissa didn't get it.

"My name," the woman said. "Elspeth."

"Sorry," Melissa answered. "It's such an unusual name. But I like it."

# 38                    Ronald Anthony Cross

"Sometimes it's Elspeth the Especial, Elspeth the Unholy, Elspeth the Priestess of the Undying One, but tonight I shall be Elspeth of the Flaming Panties, shall I not?"

She fished a pair of nasty-looking, scarlet crotchless panties out of the bag she was carrying and held them out for Melissa's inspection. But if the panties were nasty-looking, Melissa thought, they were insignificant in comparison to Elspeth's lascivious aura. She was one of those women men find simply irresistible but practically all women abhor.

Not knowing what to say, Melissa reached out and touched the silk panties, then drew her hand back as if from the flame their color implied, and said, "Who's the Undying One?"

Elspeth shrugged. "She's dead," she said with finality.

Others arrived later. The ladies drank champagne. Bubbly talk followed by more bubbly brew. One of them shed an Armani sheath to model a Victoria's Secret negligee. More bubbly. More chatter. Two more launched their modeling careers. And finally the main event.

Melissa experienced the champagne high as a numbing, sizzling form of paralysis, as if the bubbly were actually curare. All this as she watched (was unable to look away) Elspeth break out the latest sex toys and slowly start off what was to snowball into the most wanton, earth-shaking demonstration imaginable of girls just having fun.

First came the sex toys. These were the latest models, of course, and in Melissa's drugged state (*Yes, they drugged my drink!*, she realized triumphantly, but immediately forgot), these plastic wonders seemed to become infused with a life force. The little bright yellow-green plastic lizard seemed to be vibrating in time to the ladies' laughter. But it was staring at her.

The incredibly detailed, glowing, spotted ladybug with the wicked little elf rider, complete with whip in hand, vibrated with such speed and fury that its edges began to blur, and as she zeroed in on it, suddenly it grew. Became immense. "I'll grab your clit," the little elf shouted ecstatically. And Melissa shuddered and sighed because she could feel it just by thinking it. She could hardly stand the wave of pleasure that flooded her. Surely she would drown!

Even the old-fashioned straightforward dildos were wonderfully alive and seemed to her more cleverly wrought than anything by Cellini. Wouldn't he have loved them, though? Brightly colored plastic snakes who lived only to please, who longed to writhe all over her most sensitive parts, and undulate down, at last, to that mystic entrance into her secret damp tunnel. Peek in, chattering and clattering, and part the vegetation and slither in. "We love you," they rattled.

She remembered to blink and everything returned to normal. Yes! Blinking was the secret, if only she could remember to . . . ?

What was Elspeth doing? Was that normal? Why didn't any of the other ladies stop her? She couldn't see them, but she could feel them. They were as helpless as she. And that was so funny she almost laughed, because no body had even bothered to drug them, and yet they were just sitting there, like her, burning and watching Elspeth.

Elspeth had now taken off her dress and, in the most lascivious manner imaginable, was demonstrating the sex toys, along with the many advantages of crotchless panties. Right there on the gray furry carpet where all of them huddled around on couches and chairs.

"And you can do this," she said, smiling in unabashed joy, "or even this."

Whitest of teeth, whitest of flesh, reddest lips, blackest hair—was this what Snow White had finally come to?

But even the giggles and guffaws of the boldest of her friends grew first compulsive, and finally stifled, under this assault of sensuality. And Melissa, riveted to the couch, unable to turn away, cursed with a steady increase in all of her senses, could hear them swallowing, clearing their throats. But all she could see was Elspeth, whose wicked eyes were locked on hers as she shuddered and moaned and . . . as she . . .

An arm went around her shoulder; she could feel the warm soft flesh on her own. (Had she taken off her dress? Had they talked her into taking off her dress?)

The voice she heard whispering in her ear was that of her husband's secretary—oops, sorry, administrative assistant—Brenda. But the thing it was saying, surely she was only imagining that. *Oh God, let it be only my imagination,* she thought, followed wildly and irresistibly by a thought that couldn't be her own, could it? *Dear God, please don't let it be my imagination. Let it be real.* And it was real!

For some reason she experienced time differently in this high. Instead of rolling along steadily, it passed by in chunks like floating clouds driven by feverish gusts of wind. In quantum units.

Quite suddenly the girls (why did she insist on thinking about them that way? they were women.) had somehow dressed and were giving their good-byes. She barely understood them. But in the spirit of the quintessential—archetypal?—administrative assistant, Brenda seemed to have taken charge of the situation so skillfully no one really seemed to notice or care too much that Melissa could not take her eyes from Elspeth.

Flash: In the next time frame she found herself still seated on the couch, and though her eyes were still locked on Elspeth, her legs were spread and drawn up, and her bare feet were on the couch. Her toenails were painted red. How odd, she thought. How very odd. And she could feel everything through them: the couch, the soft wine-red rug; softer yet, Elspeth's body on the rug, then the walls, the ceiling. If she wiggled her toes, she could feel all the air in the room moving, swirling, readjusting. Everyone was gone except, of course . . . She felt Brenda's fingers on her bare breast. Luscious, luscious, she thought, both the hand and the fruit therein. One thing, really. The sensation, like a slowly pulsating charge of electricity, rippled outward from her hand-breast through her body—no, *bodies*—causing her to whimper out loud. Yes, she had a voice like Brenda's, who was whispering to her still, promising her terrible, wonderful, utterly unimaginable things. She was aware of her toes clenching and unclenching in all that wonderful air. It almost seemed to her as if they were causing it all.

She licked her lips—she still had a tongue. And said with her new voice, "Where did all the girls go?"

Laughter. Rich laughter that was almost as thrilling as the fingers pinching her dark nipple, as Brenda's strong but soft body pressed against her side. Then the whispering again.

"But you can't do that to me," Melissa said triumphantly, "because my panties aren't crotchless." At the time it seemed like an irrefutable argument to her. And she was suddenly suffused by a different, calmer kind of joy. *I've won,* she thought. *Everything I was afraid of will go away and I can go on and on, bored to tears until I die.*

But it wasn't the figure on the couch, of course; it was the one on the rug that, white and slender as a snake, turned over and crawled to her and raised up and yes, bit her on the thigh. The sound she made was like steam escaping from a kettle.

And Elspeth's face down there, smiling wickedly, wickedly like the Cheshire cat, as she said, ever so slyly, "I can move them aside."

Then she heard a strange noise, and lips soft as clouds on her mouth, and she simply melted into another dimension, and the steam from the kettle was Yes!

In the morning, she felt no guilt, no remorse. *Strange,* she thought, *that I would be capable of this.*

"You drugged me?" she asked Brenda.

Elspeth smiled.

"Of course," Brenda assured her. "Makes it easier. We're experts at it, right, Elspeth?"

Elspeth winked. "Yea, verily," she said.

"Again?" Melissa wondered softly. Last night she had learned first-hand all about the superiority of female sexual endurance.

"No, this is something else again. Just relax and enjoy." They pushed her back down on the bed again and were anointing her body with some kind of aromatic oil. Smelled like cherries.

"It's a beauty treatment," Brenda informed her. "Two weeks from . . . Tell you what, do me a favor. Stay away from mirrors. You know, don't scrutinize. Two weeks from now take off all your clothes and examine yourself in the mirror. Closely. Totally. I'll give you a call. Here, pop this." Round yellow-white pill. "Take care of your headache."

"But I haven't got . . ."

"You would have, but won't," Brenda interrupted as she swallowed the Percodan. "You'll feel swell."

"Speaking of which . . ." Elspeth was smiling that nasty smile, pulling off her panties, which were all she had on.

Later that morning, as they went out the door, Brenda handed her a mini digital videodisc.

"I want you to have this," she said. "I was supposed to give it to that sweet hubby of yours, Rudy. This was his idea, of course. Probably fire me when I tell him I didn't record your big porno debut. Guess I'll just have to go out and pound the pavement for another glorified secretarial gig."

Elspeth laughed out loud and shook her head. And they were gone, just like that. Melissa felt some strong emotion, but she wasn't sure what. And when she popped the disc in a player, sat down on the couch, and cranked up the TV wall, she realized that her dear hubby must have had a camcorder installed in the ceiling. For this? How long had this been going on?

She watched in a state of woozy wonder as the figures on the huge TV played out their perfect roles once more. At first, she had to remind herself who the sex-crazed one on the couch in between the other two was. Finally, she turned it off. She was nodding off, too tired to watch it anymore right now, but she knew she would watch it again. And again. *At last I'm a star,* she thought.

When Rudy came back that night, she acted as if nothing had happened. In fact, in some strange way she felt as if nothing *had* happened. Surely she couldn't believe something that incredible and dreamlike had ever really occurred. Except when she watched herself on TV. Then she believed. And every time she watched it, she felt that same strong feeling that she couldn't define, couldn't quite put her finger on.

Strangest of all, life with Rudy was the same as always. Except that the sex was better. She cared so much less about it, about him, but *it* was better.

He was dumbfounded. Hot as a firecracker for a while, but soon enough, he grew bored again.

"Had to fire Brenda," he announced out of the blue, trying to sound regretful, in his soft drawl. "Couldn't cut it." He shook his head, watching Melissa slyly all the time. *He's wondering, did we or didn't we?* Melissa realized. He really doesn't know.

"She seemed competent to me." Melissa could not resist throwing that in. He had not mentioned Elspeth.

So life went on, and Melissa felt herself slowly sinking back into the same mire from which she had been so miraculously rescued. Except that she had the disc. Watching it had become the main thing. To see herself like that and feel that feeling that she could not name.

And then she got the card in the mail. *"Remember the mirror,"* was all it said. And of course she had forgotten. Had it only been two weeks? Just *"Remember the mirror."* No signature, no salutation, no little x's on the bottom.

She took off all her clothes and locked herself in her bathroom and scrutinized herself in one of the mirrored walls. Not really expecting anything at all.

But little separate things brought themselves to her attention: first, wrinkles which had just begun to weave their web at the corners of her eyes—gone. On her forehead when she frowned—gone. That slight droop when she relaxed her mouth at the corners—gone. Flesh tauter, and—was it true?—paler, more translucent. This was some skin cream!

Now she began to notice other things. Breasts a little smaller, rising pertly, nipples a little lighter in color. Could this be true? She could not allow herself to believe this. Not at night. She tried to sleep but could not, and when she did, she descended deliriously into wild, feverish dreams which she could not remember.

In the morning, in the brilliant Florida sunlight streaming in through her bathroom window, she examined herself again. It was true. This was no beauty cream. She *was* younger.

When the call came, she didn't even bother with small talk. "What do you want?" she said.

She could almost feel Brenda smile over the phone. She thought she heard a faint giggling, but could not be sure.

"You will be one of us," Brenda promised. " 'Do what thou wilt' shall be the whole of your law. You will live forever."

"But Rudy . . ."

Melissa wondered if Elspeth was there with Brenda, smiling her nasty smile.

"Well, Rudy won't, you see. And it's such a shame to have to watch him grow old and wither up and die. Perhaps we should—well, help him along a little."

Melissa could hear the laughter in her voice. More giggling. Elspeth had to be there with her. Probably right there in the phone booth doing something incredibly wicked.

"You see, this way we get all his money without having to go through one of those drawn-out divorces. Believe me, there's nothing for you to worry about. We'll supply you the proper medicine. As I've said before, it's our area of expertise." (Sure enough, she could hear Elspeth's voice pipe in with "*My* area of expertise.")

"We'll send it to you in a ring. Like Lucrezia Borgia. Instruct you how to use it. He'll simply have a heart attack. May I suggest a nice restaurant, a wave of the hand over his Jack Daniels, and then—kaboom, right there at the table. No way for anyone to tell. Of course Elspeth and I will be obliged to drop by and console the widow in her grief. But no macho males, nothing suspicious."

She paused.

"And . . ." Melissa prompted.

"And we live happily ever after. For real!"

Melissa was so choked with emotion she could hardly speak.

"What?"

"Yes," Melissa hissed again, and this was the same emotion that she felt when she watched the disc, only now it was stronger and she could identify it. And identifying it made it stronger than ever and clarified everything that she had never understood about herself. The emotion was the ecstasy of freedom absolute.

# 1

I T WAS SOMEPLACE in New Mexico or maybe Arizona that the old man said good-bye to Elena. This happened in a period of time much earlier than these other events. But to those few for whom what we think of as time is only another sort of space to move around in, there is no continuity. One event is as close as another. They are all floating around out there in chunks, and they are all touching each other. So it was not really far away, or long ago, when the old man said good-bye to Elena, back in the days when she was "for real" young and they had first started traveling together. She had thought of him as Sanchez then, and it would be a good many years before she would find out his real name was Corbo. If he had a real name. If anything about him was real.

He was standing in front of the grungy little mirror that Elena had insisted on hanging on the wall so that she could examine herself before going out. He seemed to be examining a tooth.

"Good thing you have this mirror hanging here so I can see my tooth," he said. "Otherwise I would have gone my whole life without knowing what the little sucker looks like."

"Why don't you just use your great mystic powers to sense it?" Elena asked caustically.

The old man, as always, laughed. "Well, that's pretty good," he said. "Particularly for you, because as we both know, humor is hardly one of your strong points. You know, Elena, if you ever resort to one of those ads in the personal column of the newspaper, it should read something like, 'Pretty but humorless young woman seeks handsome but humorless man. The witty need not apply.' Right?" More laughter.

"But seriously, mirrors have their purpose. It was while I was looking in the mirror at my tooth that the idea came to me. And you know what, Elena? I like that idea."

He paused and regarded her seriously. Then he widened and narrowed his eyes exaggeratedly. "Good-bye, Elena," he said, and waited for an answer, but got nothing more than a frown from his apprentice. Still, he waited. But nothing.

Now he went into the kitchen and came out with a big brown paper bag—he saved paper bags. Still no answer. He went over to a cardboard box in a corner of the room, fished something out—Elena could not see what it was—and put it in the bag. Then he disappeared back into the little kitchen. Soon he reemerged.

"You know what, Elena, I was thinking that maybe I should pack myself a little lunch. So I did."

He held up the bag. Nothing from Elena.

"Maybe a cheese sandwich and a little pineapple. Did you know that pineapple is my favorite fruit?"

Elena frowned. "You said that bananas were your favorite fruit," she snapped back accusingly.

The old man nodded, thinking it over. "That's true, Elena, but that was yesterday."

"So today something else is your favorite fruit?"

He nodded. "Yes. So if I ask you tomorrow what's my favorite fruit, what, I wonder, will you answer?"

He waited. And waited. Elena shut her eyes and shook her head. *You would think I would get used to this kind of stuff,* she thought, *but you would be wrong.*

"Grapes," she said.

The old man thought about it. Nodded, looking pleased.

"That's not bad," he said.

Elena looked stunned. "You mean I'm right?"

He frowned and shook his head.

"Of course you're not right, Elena. What do you think this is, a guessing game? It was a little better than usual is all. But not right."

Elena did not even try to hide her crestfallen expression.

"So good-bye, Elena. I've got my lunch." He held out the bag and waited for an answer. Nothing. He sighed. "Do you know why I said good-bye to you?"

Elena thought it over. "Because you're going away for a while?"

He nodded. "Of course," he agreed. "But this is the funny part, Elena. You see, when I return—if I return—it may be that only a very short time has passed for you, but that a great deal of time has passed for me. Do you know what I mean when I say that?"

Elena thought about it and started to nod, but then shook her head. Her beautiful strawberry-blond hair blossomed as her head shook, and the old man could not help but smile at that.

"You're like a shampoo commercial, Elena, did you ever know that?"

Elena shook her head again, even more furiously, to greater effect, and the old man laughed, a sharp, piercing cackle. Long after it had died out, it seemed to echo in the little room.

"Well, you're getting better, Elena, because for once you are right. You don't know why that would be. I'm talking about the question of the passage of time and not the shampoo commercial here, though either would do. Of course you don't understand it, that I could go away for a long time, but be gone for only a few minutes. It's such a curious fact. But if I tell you that it's possible, then you had better believe it. So what I want you to do here is to think about it. Contemplate, Elena. How would something that odd ever occur? *How?!*" He widened his eyes like an owl.

*He should be saying "Who,"* Elena thought, and now it was she who was smiling.

"It would be a good thing for you to think about, Elena, instead of just sitting around here cross-legged on the floor, grinning like an idiot."

"But you said sitting cross-legged on the floor was good for you," Elena protested. In vain.

"Yes, of course it's good for your body to sit like that, but not necessarily for your brain. The grinning is no good . . ." He paused, getting it straight. "The grinning's okay, but it's not enough, you see? So go ahead and grin, but think about that curious thing I told you. About how could that be."

As he was going out the door, he paused once more, and said, "You know, like you are a secret agent for the government and your contact tells you it's on a need-to-know basis? In the movies? Well, that's what we've got here, Elena. We're on a need-to-know basis, and what you need to know is"—he widened his eyes again for emphasis—"everything." He went out the door.

Now Elena could not see him, but somehow she was still aware of him, where he was, what he was doing. He was doing something she did not like, something that frightened her so much that usually she would try to suppress and ignore it.

Today, however, curiosity was just too much for her. So she deliberately focused in on him. She was astonished at how easy it was:

He went around the back of the little shack, and in the shade of the overhanging roof he began to use the powers of the mystic stone he wore in the amulet around his leathery, weather-beaten old neck to open a doorway into another world.

He took his time with it, fooled around getting it just the way he wanted, and then he spent some time psychically exploring it for any sign of imminent danger. Yes, she could even sense him doing this. Finally he went inside, and the doorway dissolved, and he was gone. Where to? she wondered, not really wanting to know. There was nothing to do but wait. She waited.

Meanwhile the old man made his way cautiously across a scorched landscape decorated with a sprinkling of human skulls, all of them grinning like idiots, reminding him somehow of Elena, to the small green oasis where one found the creature he liked to think of as the demon Ketoko.

A deep voice which actually was several voices at once, coming at him from all sides, said, "I protest. I'm not a demon but an angel who abhors all forms of mischief."

The old man ignored Ketoko's protest and continued on his way, concentrating on the problem he was trying to solve.

A few hundred years ago, he and Popillius, another of the four Guardians, had found it necessary to subdue and dominate Ketoko in order to make use of the demon's ability to move effortlessly through time and space. They had even had the help of a younger and brasher version of Corbo himself. He smiled to remember this. But Ketoko had pointed out to him that he would take his revenge after Corbo was dead, and up until a week ago, Corbo had paid no attention to the threat. Why bother?

Then, the dream: Elena standing on a street corner in some great future city, covered with grime, green eyes vacant. Drooling. And he had known it was not just an ordinary dream but a portent of what would surely come to pass. The idea which had come to him while staring in the mirror at his tooth was to force the demon to take him back in time once more, in order to consult with Popillius and the younger version of himself. To put their heads, and mystic powers, together and figure out some way to reach out to Elena from the past. But this would be tricky. He did not like to use Ketoko because he knew the creature hated him and would be waiting for him to make the slightest mistake.

In fact, right at first, the idea had seemed more like a foolish urge, and he had almost let it fly away back to wherever it had flown in from. But all of a sudden, for some reason it had started looking better to him. After all, it was the only idea within reach of his brain, the way he looked at it. "You got to hook them like fish as they float on by," he said aloud to no one in particular.

Now he sat cross-legged in the lush grass that circled the small round pool of water, and waited.

A head popped out of the pool, but you could not see it clearly because all the features that made up the face were in rapid flux. It could make you sick to look at it.

"Ah," Ketoko said in his multivoice. "It's my old enemy, Corbo. How did you like the dream I sent you?"

The old man could not help but smile. Perhaps Ketoko had unwittingly just given him the answer.

"You can initiate dreams through time and space?" the old man tried.

Now the features began to change even faster.

"For me to know and you to find out," Ketoko chanted. Over and over. The old man sat patiently, waiting him out.

The chant grew fainter, faded out, and there was silence. Welling up from within this silence the old man felt that he could hear the hum of activity—the rising of the illusions of time and space, of centeredness and multiplicity. Of the world. He never tired of listening to it.

"I don't understand," Ketoko said, breaking the silence at last, obviously tuning in to Corbo's viewpoint somehow.

"It cannot be understood," the old man answered. He rubbed his hands together and said, "Ah, we now begin anew. Let's see, where were we? Enemies forever?"

"We had no choice," Ketoko chanted solemnly in his multivoice.

The old man nodded. "Good. Then let's play it through to the hilt. I command you to take me back to Constantinople."

Naturally Ketoko sang the song. To which the old man replied, "Oh, yes you can. Enough foolishness. You will do it now."

And even as he said the words, Ketoko reached out and took ahold of his arm and the world fell away and there was . . . absolute darkness. Suddenly a flash of light. Then darkness again. This time cleaving through the fabric of space-time was more like being in an incredible storm than it was like movement of any kind.

Between flashes of light, Corbo remarked, "The last time we did this, it was like walking along a road in the country." He could not hear his voice, either due to an absence of sound or too much of it—he was too disoriented to tell—but Ketoko apparently could hear him fine, or read his mind, or perhaps even understand him by some other unimaginable means, because he answered, "I can make it appear any way I want. Since at that time I was bargaining for the life of my only true friend, I made an effort to make it bearable for your human allies. By the way, it isn't dark with flashes of light, either. That's your puny mind's attempt to disguise it. It isn't anything at all, you see." Then, laughter.

The old man was hearing it, but from inside his head, he felt sure of that. "Hardly allies," he murmured.

"Oh, had a falling out? Too bad." More laughter.

And suddenly the old man knew that something was wrong, and at the same time what that something was.

"Stop here," he commanded.

But Ketoko answered, "Too late. We've already gone beyond the point where you can bully me, and I'm free to do whatever I wish. I will soon be free of you forever. Before you were even born. Oh, long before." More laughter, and this time it went on and on. Apparently not using a real voice and therefore not needing to stop to breathe, he was prepared to laugh forever. It was eerie moving through the flashing dark and pounding, steady laughter. More than eerie.

The old man could have laughed himself. Or maybe cried. *If only Elena could see me now,* he thought, *then she would realize who the fool really is.*

Corbo had ordered Ketoko to take him back to Constantinople, but he had forgotten to specify how far back. It had been in Constantinople that the old man, with the help of Popillius and his younger self, had first taken control of the demon's mind and subjugated him. What must have happened was that Ketoko had just now taken him back in time past that point. And now it was Corbo who was the victim.

"We're a long ways past your 'good old days,' " Ketoko pointed out, "and what do you know, we're still moving fast." More laughter. In fact, somehow he no longer needed to interrupt the laughter in order to communicate with words; it was a constant, harrowing, steady ground.

Corbo did what he had always done whenever the pressure was most intense: he consciously allowed himself to relax. Then again. Then again. It was like letting yourself go limp and fall out of your tight, troubled body, finding yourself in another, lighter, looser form, and then letting it go, and then again. Only each time some tightness or weight fell away, his consciousness billowed outward like a cloud. This was simple, choiceless awareness. He wasn't looking for anything, just touching everything, letting it pass. It was in this state of heightened awareness that he found the strange, incredible, unexplainable thing that Ketoko had been hiding from him. But it was necessary for Corbo to come back into what, for him, passed as ordinary awareness in order to exploit it.

A zillion years, or no time at all, later—it was all the same here—Ketoko dropped him off somewhere, somewhen, and simply disappeared.

The old man blinked, for the sun was bright here. His eyes took it all in at once, of course, but he couldn't process the information that fast—it was too different from what he'd expected.

Steamy heat, weird and wonderful creatures in the distance, strange fernlike trees and bushes, a biting smell, like sulfur or ammonia, a loud, thunderous noise—unidentifiable. And right there in front of him? It was the odd coloration that threw him. That, along with the creature's plumpness and almost comically awkward stance. Who would have thought that a Tyrannosaurus rex would turn out to have a smooth white body with a patch of black on its back and, the crowning touch, one black circle around its glistening, hungry little left eye? That it would look so much like a gigantic, fat ostrich, with weird little grabbing arms instead of wings, and a goofy bill-shaped mouth full of enormous white teeth ("The jaws that bite, the claws that catch"—was this the frumious Bandersnatch?).

This all was, in fact, so weird and unexpected that for a moment it was impossible for Corbo to classify the creature as dangerous. But dangerous it was. And that moment almost cost him his life, as the huge but somehow almost comical creature bent over, thrust its neck forward, mouth open, and, letting out a bellow that was a cross between a steamboat whistle and the angry honking of a gigantic goose, charged.

# 2

RAPHAEL FLOATED LANGUIDLY, enveloped in his airbed like an angel on a cloud, half awake, half asleep. He was still recuperating from the effects of having a small piece of hot metal driven through his shoulder at high velocity. And of having to force himself to bite the bullet (ha ha) and stay conscious long enough to finish his part in the fight. Then, of course, riding nonstop all the way from Montana back to the Blackstone Ranch in Arizona in a sports-ute, however fancy a model, was hardly conducive to healing.

But then again, Raphael had his stone, which meant that the healing was miraculous. Or was it?

Raphael had inherited from his mother Elena that down-to-earth peasant practicality that drove him to stubbornly demand, as perhaps a token of war, some little insight or advantage from every sock in the teeth fortune dealt him. Perhaps, even without his knowledge, he also carried some of his father's gritty tenaciousness.

For whatever reason, instead of just allowing himself to pass out and heal, he had forced himself to stay conscious and monitor the effects of the stone with a relentless concentration.

And he had concluded that it was not miraculous. Just fast. He could actually sense the effects of his speeded-up immune system, practically feel the flesh grow back, the white corpuscles racing to the attack.

Then sleep was forced upon him, and of course he could not keep track of that, but coming out of it, his relentless observation revealed several conclusions that were to open the door into a whole new level of understanding:

1. These periods of healing sleep were so intense that they were closer to a coma than to ordinary sleep. And although a severe

trauma might require an initial period of several hours, this would be followed by several short, intense periods of healing sleep, most of which lasted only a few minutes at a time.

2. The purpose of these "naps" seemed to be to allow the healing process to accelerate even more, by removing all the efforts to monitor the senses which consciousness demands.

3. He also intuited that each brief period of healing sleep would equal, for a normal person convalescing from a similar disorder, several nights' worth of rest.

4. In short, nothing was different, only all was faster—with the added benefit that the faster a wound healed the less chance you had to bleed to death from it. That the sooner and quicker your system attacked an invading bacteria or virus, the less chance it had to establish a foothold or induce some kind of confusing complication.

From these conclusions came an idea—awesome, frightening even, but filled with wild, unpredictable possibilities. He would have to check it out. Now.

He awoke fully and sat up in the bed. There was still a faint twinge of pain in his shoulder. A little stiffness. But it was clear that even as he lay there thinking things over, the dramatic healing power of his stone had been working away on him.

Resting against the back wall of his rather stark room was a stretching machine, one of those torture devices in which martial artists sit in order to crank their legs apart to master the splits. He climbed out of his ultracomfortable airbed and ambled over to it.

Back when Violet had first taken up yoga (she now did tai chi), Raphael had bought the device. He had borrowed what he considered the few essential stretches from her routine. (Violet, of course, had pursued hatha yoga by working on every asana known to man, before quitting to take up tai chi.)

From her vast workout Raphael had picked one asana where you stretched forward, one backwards, and one sideways. After struggling with those for a bit, he had then cranked himself out to a light stretch in his splits machine. He had not become exceptionally limber, but he was limber enough, he had figured. In fact, he sometimes had wondered why he bothered at all, since if he injured himself from being too stiff, his stone would certainly heal him.

And now it struck him that this was exactly the attitude that all the Guardians had taken. The stones protected them physically; that was strength and health. After all, they were immortal, or nearly so. Surely that was enough, wasn't it?

But Raphael had asked the question, and now he intended to have the answer, as soon as possible. He knew that what he was planning to do to himself would hurt, so perhaps that was why he stood there in front of the torture device for a while, just looking at it. Not thinking.

Finally he said aloud to himself, "Okay, no pain, no gain," sat down in his stretch machine, and cranked it out. He quickly came to the place where he attained a good stretch—just slightly uncomfortable. Normally he would have stopped here, and after his muscles loosened up a bit, cranked perhaps another turn and a half and then remained in it for thirty seconds, then considered it done. But today he just cranked on by, ignoring the pain. He cranked until a loud popping sound issued from his right hip. Then he stopped, all right. He felt an excruciating pain, hot like fire, flare from his hip down the outside of his right leg all the way to the outside of the knee, causing him to let out a high-pitched whine.

"Oh God, oh God, oh God," he said out loud, trying to fight the panic that drove his hand toward the crank to relieve the pressure.

The pain let up and then hit again, a terrible pulsing, almost electrical feeling. *I've injured a sciatic nerve,* he realized. *I never would have thought of that.*

His hand hovered over the crank, fighting against his will to grab the handle and set himself free. The pain went away, but immediately came back. This time it was even stronger, hotter.

"Oh God, oh God, oh God," he continued to pray, until suddenly he felt the healing power of the stone kick in, and the throbbing pain dulled to where it was bearable. He closed his eyes, leaned over the crank, and sure enough, he found he was able to will himself to sleep.

A few minutes later he awoke to find himself still cranked out but no longer feeling the pain. In fact, he was amazed to find that it really wasn't all that much of a stretch for him anymore. He felt exhilarated, ecstatic even, but also terrified by the results and what they implied.

Once again he hesitated. Then once again, surprised to find that he had it in him, he cranked the machine right through the pain until this time it was an agonizing groin pull that forced his hand off the handle. He was actually crying as he fought to keep from releasing himself. But once again, he stuck it out until the pain receded, and he nodded off into that mysterious healing sleep which only one of the four stones could bestow.

And this time he awoke with the realization that the sleep was not just the removal of pain, but the arrival of an ecstasy which exactly equaled the energy of the pain it replaced: as a further inducement, he was becoming more and more aware of the process.

Sometime later, when that hallucinatory day of unbearable pain and pleasure had ripened into evening, he cranked down the splits machine and got up out of it and turned on the lights. Feeling as if he were still in a pain-induced vision, he beheld the stark room as if for the first time, and wondered about the man who inhabited it, as if he were a stranger to himself.

The walls were white—he had insisted upon that, he knew not why—and there were no paintings or decorations upon them. The floor was covered with a simple rug made of hemp squares. A door led into the small kitchenette. A plain brown chest of drawers. A small generic writing desk. A closet. Another door, which led to a bathroom. That was it. Nothing about himself at all, as if he were waiting to be born.

It made him think, with a smile, of Violet's room, and then, with a wider smile, of Tippi's. How those rooms spoke. Shouted, even.

Violet's room was on the third floor. You had to ride the escalators she recently had installed to get to it. (While Thaddeus, for God only knows what reason, had insisted their little guest duplex remain spartan, Violet saw to it that the main house kept up with the latest fads in interior decoration.)

Inside Violet's room the walls were covered with paintings, mostly hers. Some were oils, some watercolors, and some pastels, but all were precise drawings of pretty scenes in soft colors. Young, pretty people and flowers predominated. Where there weren't paintings, there were mirrors.

The matching chest of drawers, bed frame, and makeup table were of shiny bright red lacquer. When he focused on it in his mind's eye, he saw Violet sitting before the mirror, wearing a dress patterned with lovely pastel-colored flowers, smiling at her image—"Hello, me." One of the pretty young people on whom a blemish would be an affront, an astonishment even. There was never anything out of place in Violet's room, or about her person. She was always smiling, but only sort of. A lonely smile, that one.

Tippi's room was Tippi naked. There it was. Raphael knew that he was (apparently) rendered impotent by the mysterious powers of the stone he wore. He could not lust. But there she was in his mind's eye, naked and unabashed. Pissed off at something, no doubt. Small, spicy, half crazy and half free, with those huge dark angry eyes and that little pouty mouth, as she wandered about in the wild disarray of her room, talking to herself. Every other word was "fuck." "Where did I fucking throw my fucking panties?" Something like that. Sure, Raphael was not allowed to lust, and yet he was amused to see how Tippi drew him inexorably to the edge of that cliff he could not climb. Or could he? Today, or tonight, rather, he felt that he could do anything.

Like a hero in a kung fu movie, he drew his knee up to his chest and threw a very high kick to the side, effortlessly straightening out his leg. Then he sank down into a full Oriental sideways splits on the floor—no problem. Thing was—the thing that left him blistering with feverish excitement was— this was just the beginning!

He got up and went into the little kitchenette, seeing it as if for the first time. After all, he had never paid any attention to it before; he ate all his meals at the main house. With a quizzical expression he opened the door of the small refrigerator. Whoa—he almost slammed it shut in revulsion. But instead got control. Began clearing it out. Putting stuff, both identifiable and not, down the garbage-disposal unit. Luckily there was not much of it. Actually, he enjoyed using the disposal, making the bad stuff disappear. *I should have done this before,* he thought, and resolved to clean up the kitchenette— no, the whole apartment—and keep it clean. Strangely enough, the thought of this was like the removal of a burden rather than the addition of a tiresome bunch of chores. It had been avoidance that was the real unpleasantness here. *Yes,* he silently exclaimed as he walked back out of the kitchenette and over to the little desk, luxuriating in the newfound revelation that even just walking around the room felt wonderfully different, ecstatic even, when you were as limber as a world-class gymnast. He opened the top drawer and took out a sheet of blank paper and a pen. Slowly and with much deliberation he made a list. The first thing he wrote was: *"#1—kitchen cleanser."* He thought for a while, then continued:

2. 6 quarts of milk
3. bananas (big bunch)
4. 6 quarts cottage cheese
5. 2 jars peanut butter, 2 jars jam, 2 loaves white bread

Crossed out the last part and amended:

1 loaf white bread, 1 loaf squaw bread
6. small table and chair, and a couple of knives
7. blender
8. some of that high-protein powder that Jimmy Running Deer uses (Muscle-Up? Muscularex?)

Then he paused again, and finally wrote: *"As soon as possible have Jimmy purchase and install resistance training machine (after consulting with me) and also exercycle. Best model. You pick, Jimmy."*

Avoiding the others, he made his way from his apartment to the kitchen of the main house, where he delivered the list to Mary Red Boots, who was, he noticed with a pang, getting old. But not diminished in fire.

"I'm sorry, but I don't know what is this 'squaw bread.' I never heard of no such thing in my time. And why is it called squaw bread, anyway?" She gave him a suspicious look. "And this'll have to wait. Jimmy's got plenty of chores to do first. He's out flying around somewhere in that copter thing of his."

Raphael shook his head and smiled at her. He knew he was still her baby, and that she could not really ever be mad at him, so she had to pretend all the time to pick a fight, so he wouldn't know. Didn't want to spoil him. He waited politely for her to finish, then said, "Call him on the phone, Mary. Tell him to drop everything until he's finished with my list. I mean it. This comes first—okay?"

He was smiling, but Mary could tell he meant business. She had to remind herself that this slender, almost pretty, boyish man who hadn't got any older-looking since he was eighteen was actually one of the Guardians, and not her kid. He had the power. Without understanding why, she shivered. "Cold in here," she explained, causing his smile to widen. Then, "Violet will be madder than a hornet."

Violet had elected herself boss of the ranch as well as of the Guardians. Raphael had to smile at that. The only one around here she hadn't been able to dominate was her nutcase friend, Tippi. If you could call that weird, antagonistic relationship friendship. Actually, he wasn't sure what to call it. But his own relationship with Violet, that was not so complex. When he was growing up, Violet had simply been an older sister to him—a very bossy older sister. She had actually been fairly dominant over her brother William, too. So at first his mother, Elena, had run things, and then later, when Elena had . . . Violet had taken over the reins. And Thaddeus, who seemed to have been amusedly accustomed to being pushed around a little by Tippi, pretty much always demurred to Violet these days. After all, it had been she who gave Thaddeus his stone in the first place. Made him one of the Guardians.

But this time, Raphael figured, he was asserting himself. It was a start, he thought, and then when he realized where that thought was headed, blocked it off for now, before it got there.

He shrugged, looking calm, as always. Serene, even. "If I tell you to do something, Mary, you don't need to worry about Violet. You need to worry about me."

Now Mary looked openly shocked. Change was not her element.

"You've never talked to me that way before," she complained, obviously on the verge of tears. But as she looked into his enigmatic green eyes, so much like his mother's, for consolation, she saw that what she had once thought of as serenity and maybe just plain sweetness was really very similar to detachment.

And she also saw there the same implacable stubbornness that had made his mother the leader of the group.

"Yes, sir," she said, not sure if it came out sincerely or sarcastically. Whatever, Raphael smiled at her.

"No need to get obsequious, Mary. Just do the deed."

He turned and left. Her baby no more, just like that. No good-byes, just do it or else. *He may not know it,* Mary realized, *but something is really happening here. He's taking over.* Then she wasted a few moments wondering what "obsequious" meant, and finally, deciding she didn't really want to know, called her son Jimmy Running Deer on his cell phone.

"To hear is to obey," he said, a few minutes later coming through the door. Mary could not help noticing that whether Raphael was or not, her son Jimmy Running Deer was definitely getting older. *Just like the rest of us mortals,* she thought wryly.

"Jesus Christ, God of the paleface," he said as he studied the list, "the kid has finally flipped."

"Thinks he's taking over," Mary grumbled.

But to her surprise, her son nodded. " 'Bout time," he muttered.

# 3

IF, IN THE past twenty years or so, the streets of Santa Monica had become so festooned with colorful beggars and exotic foreign visitors as to seem unfamiliar, menacing even, to its citizens, and if its skies were bright and rattling and stuttering with the vibrations of the blades of myriad copters whirling through the smog, imagine how it must have appeared to the tall, broad-shouldered warrior from another world. Yet if he felt awestruck or astonished, he showed no sign of it. In fact, it was with a certain amount of obvious disdain that he stopped, spread his arms, and emoted dramatically:

"O City of the Angels, meet Morgan the Dominator, your future master. Do you not owe me . . ." He paused to think, arms still spread, massively muscled back and chest emerging from the loose gray tank top. Leggings and boots? Well, why not? After all, this was LA.

Beside him, Elspeth monitored his theatrical display with a look that could have been interpreted as either disapproval or just plain boredom.

". . . reverence," he tried, without conviction. "No, not strong enough." He gave the problem another moment's thought. "Submissive awe," he settled on.

The old—but then, they all looked old—street lady decked out in an outfit made up of brightly colored but filthy patches, who normally mumbled solely to the sidewalk at her feet, suddenly found the courage to stare at his face. Apparently impervious to the brilliant Santa Monica sunlight, she did not blink. At all. Which after a moment made even the tall, fierce, black-bearded warrior uneasily shift his gaze.

"We don't owe you shit, Morgan," the old lady said in a dry, cracked, but ferocious voice. "Know why?"

No one answered.

"Because you're an asshole, Morgan, and you're already full of shit."

Morgan's mouth opened wide, and his hand went to his side, but fortunately he was not at the moment wearing his sword.

"Do the beggars in LA dare to . . . to . . . to . . ." he sputtered.

"Yea, they do," Elspeth informed him, and turning to the bag lady. "My name's Elspeth. Yours"—she closed her great dark eyes and then opened them again—"is Abigail? How charming. I'd offer thee my hand, except— who would? I need some info from you, so . . ." She closed her eyes again.

"You ain't gonna get shit from me. Wanta know why?" Abigail continued, obviously on a roll here and knowing it.

But Elspeth did not answer. She just stood there, eyes closed, decked out in black short-shorts and skimpy red halter top, slender as a willow, skin white as snow (in LA?), etc., etc.

"By the blood of the Goddess," Morgan proclaimed, "let me beat it out of her."

Eyes still closed, Elspeth shook her head, raised one finger, and pointed it at him.

"Nay, great oaf, thou wouldst get nothing from her, as much as thou might enjoy it. Her thought stream is too confused."

Morgan fairly groaned with pleasure at the thought.

"You won't get shit because you're already . . ." The bag lady continued her line of reasoning, undaunted.

Elspeth opened her eyes, and fixed her gaze on the old woman. "But enough is enough," she said, and doubled up her delicate fist. The thought of what her pretty, slender hand would have to make contact with, however briefly, must be credited more for her decision not to throw the punch than any feelings of mercy. The effect, however, was, pleasantly enough, almost exactly as if she had thrown it.

At the sight of the doubled-up fist, Abigail's eyes and nostrils flared as she threw up her arms to ward off attack, backed up, stumbled, and sat down hard on the sidewalk, where she froze, staring down. And soon she began mumbling to the dirty concrete, rapidly. "Worry worry. Hurry fast. Everybody's . . ." Her voice lowered to an inaudible steady mumbling as she tuned them out.

"There," Elspeth said to Morgan with obvious satisfaction, "back to normal again. The lady I seek was in her thoughts, the image was clear, but alas, the flow was too incoherent to learn anything from. Clearly we are red hot in our search for her. Abigail has seen her often, and I daresay Abigail rarely travels far from this corner.

"We must simply walk up and down this street until we find her, or perhaps through my magic ring"—she held out her snow-white hand to show him her little ring—"we shall be able to track her down, as the hound follows the scent of the wrongdoer."

Morgan looked doubtful. "Thy magic ring doth nothing," he said.

Elspeth shrugged. "Whilst 'tis true my magic ring hath lost much of its power . . ."

Morgan snorted contemptuously.

"Very well," she amended, "it hath lost all its power. Nonetheless, it resideth here on my lily-white finger, eagerly awaiting its chance to glut itself once again on that most delicious of all food of the gods, the mysterious force some call ether. And mark me well, sirrah, it shall find and it shall feast. And once again . . ."

She trailed off. Stopped walking. Closed her eyes. The plan she was about to initiate had been floating around in her consciousness for some time now, but it had been just recently that she had decided to put it into action. To say it was not without risk was putting it mildly. But after all these years—nay, centuries—of being patient, Elspeth was beginning to feel that the time was right.

When the head of the Wicca, old Dame Beatrice, had summoned Diana (aka Brenda) and Elspeth to the meeting at Ironwall Castle and informed them that she would not be accompanying them on this journey because "I'm getting too old for this sort of mission," Elspeth had been hard put to keep from replying, "About a thousand years too old."

"Of course one needn't remind thee," the aggrieved ancient one had complained, "of the myriad missions, both tedious and dangerous, that I have accepted. Accepted when, with my high office, I might easily have delegated to my many minions, such as thee, for instance. Missions which the very survival of our order . . . blah, blah, blah . . ."

Elspeth had almost passed out from boredom. As usual, once started, the old hag went on and on, mercilessly assailing them with tales of her past glory. Elspeth blocked out what she could of it, which thankfully was a lot, but it was obvious that the senile old toad was running on a full tank of gas. Then the Lady Diana, next rung up the ladder, took her turn.

Lady Diana/Brenda had petulantly complained that she needed to dedicate more of her precious time to recruiting powerful new members to the cult (a fun job, to say the least). She made her case. Then she made it again. Then again.

Elspeth had awakened from her near swoon only to hear:

"Well, then, let Elspeth supply the sacrificial victim. Any foreign female will do. Surely she can manage that without getting into mischief."

She had almost argued. Her first emotion had been outrage at the way the two high muck-a-mucks always stuck her with all of the unpleasant chores—pardon me, *missions*. For these swollen-up bureaucrats in the Wic-Org, every menial chore was transformed into a crucial mission merely by passing through their scaly hands.

It was then that she had remembered the burnt-out street lady with the magnificent aura of power whom she had encountered on the streets of Santa Monica only last year. Elspeth had been stopped in her tracks by the sight of that aura. In fact, on the spot, she had involuntarily closed her eyes and gone into a semitrance, as she was doing now.

Elspeth was not always sensitive to auras, but this one had sang to her, told stories of a glorious past. Of immense, incomprehensible power, followed by incomprehensible ruin.

Suddenly she had become aware that she was standing in front of the grande dame, queen of the witches, Lady Beatrice, with her eyes closed.

"I say to thee once more and only once more, wake up and open wide thine eyes when I am speaking to thee, foolish woman. Oh, I shall not soon forget this."

*But thou shall,* Elspeth said to herself, *just as thou dost always forget everything else.*

Then Dame Beatrice had done a most unusual (even for her) thing.

The old bat, standing in the midst of the glory of the great hall of Iron-wall Castle, had glared at Elspeth and farted. Had that been intentional?

Not knowing how to respond to that, Elspeth had simply taken the offensive.

"The City of the Angels is a most dangerous place. I will require a bodyguard."

"Very well, I will—"

"A most efficient bodyguard," Elspeth continued. "I would chose Morgan the Maleficent to accompany me."

"What?" The ancient hag's face had immediately colored to a darker gray. "The commander in chief of my army? But he is not—it is true that upon occasion, when it is absolutely necessary, that master of the sword doth accompany me or the king, but only because our safety is of such enormous importance." She trailed off lamely.

But Elspeth's lucky star was riding high and, after a long argument with both her superiors, she had won out. The next step had been simple—as simple as Morgan himself.

The moment he had arrived in Los Angeles and looked around him, the dunce had said, "Why, this place is immense. You would need a horse to get around in it. What I wouldn't give—"

"If I were queen of the Wicca, I would grant thee complete freedom to do what thou wilt with it."

The great oaf had blinked and said, "Then, much as I despise thee, thou must be queen."

So here she was, in the City of the Angels, with Morgan, daring to pursue her destiny. The thought made her shiver. Now if only her instincts were true, and the bag lady with the grandiose aura could withstand the flow of destructive power from the royal scepter—

She opened her eyes and blinked to suddenly see Morgan's fierce countenance. (If there were only some way to open your eyes more gradually!) "But what point was it I was about to make? I am ashamed to admit I've just forgot myself."

"Dizzy wench," Morgan muttered. "Thou wert about to remind me, unless I am mistaken, that even though thy ring hath lost its powers, thou still hast left those with which thou wert born."

"After all, I am a witch," she said, jumping right back on the horse, Morgan having thus guided her foot into the stirrup, so to speak. "And a good one, at that."

Morgan now tuned her out. He disliked Elspeth intensely, but sensed that his only real opportunity to rise to his rightful position of power lay with her. The fact was, he reminded himself, that he had been reduced for quite some time now, from general to lackey, at the whim of that senile old bat Dame Beatrice. In her language, the term "general" translated into "glorified bodyguard" for not only her but also that stuttering fool of a king, or the brutal Lady Diana, and now even the lowly witch Elspeth. But future dominators could hardly afford to throw tantrums of pride. *Grin and bear it for a while longer,* he told himself. *Once I take over, everybody else can grin and bear it and see how they like it.*

Elspeth used her magical power in just the manner he had assumed she would. Hand to forehead, excited outburst, "I can sense our prey up ahead, just around the corner."

This mysterious bag lady they were seeking was, it seemed to Morgan, always just around the corner. Much like his longed-for promotion from general/bodyguard/lackey to king. Then, LA!

Elspeth had advised him, quite without his requesting any advice, that due to the Los Angelenos' possession of guns and those ugly stinking vehicles they rode around in, let alone their metal—what had she called them, "whirlybirds"?—it might be foolish of him to try to take the whole city.

"Why not be satisfied, for instance, with the kingdom of Canoga Park, whilst cooling thy boots? I tell thee for thy own good, this place is immense."

But he was not so certain. One could always wear armor and keep the visor down. Shoot down the metal birds with arrows (he would need to recruit the most accurate of Wiccingham's archers). And see how these cowardly people liked a taste of the blade.

"Just look at their nasty little dogs," he now pointed out, glaring at a too-pretty young man walking what was apparently the result of the depraved coupling of a monkey with a hairless rat. "Have they no dogs of war?"

The ugly little dog's owner looked at him with good-natured curiosity. "What planet are you from, anyway?" he said in passing.

"Why, thine own, of course, more's the pity!" Morgan shouted after him.

Elspeth shook her head and went "tsk, tsk, tsk" at him. "Methinks thou shouldst keep thy great trap shut and let me do the talking. Thou hast not yet mastered the speech of the modern as well as have I."

Morgan snorted. She was right, of course. Although it didn't seem to him she spoke very differently from the way he would have, plainly the results were better. Perhaps it was because of the fact that she was a luscious wench who always showed a lot of flesh. He was aware of the effect that sort of thing had on most men, and he despised them for it. Also the women who utilized the tactic. But then, he didn't like the ugly ones either. He grimaced, still wondering, as always, why the Goddess had not made his world more palatable. But then, he would have eaten it.

"Do thy stuff, Oh modern maid," he grumbled. Elspeth stopped and curtsied saucily.

" 'S'fuck's that?" a tall young Black man said. "Fuckin' square dance?" He was also walking his dog, an old-fashioned Colby-style pit bull terrier with a lot of white showing.

"Nice dog, for a change," Morgan said, sounding sincere. "Does it bite?"

The guy pulled up and looked Morgan over insolently. "Hope so," he said. The dog began straining at the leash, growling a little.

"He's too small, though," Morgan continued. "My bandoggies would chew him up, I assure thee."

The guy looked interested. "Your bandogs be okay right at the start. But they run outta gas, you see? Pit bull terriers be fly. Don't never quit."

"Run out of gas?" Morgan wondered.

"Listen up, here," the Black continued. "You be pimpin' the bitch?" He was looking at Elspeth intently, but with a cold interest.

"Pimpin'?" Morgan wondered.

The man shook his head. "Fuckin' dumb honky,": he grumbled, and turned and walked away.

"I don't know what a honky is," Morgan complained.

"But methinks thou dost know 'fucking dumb,' " Elspeth tossed in innocently.

By the time they found the wench Elspeth sought, it was twilight in the City of Angels. Twilight here turned out to be the glint of a dying flame through smoke, and the angels all turned out to be demented, filthy beggars.

The woman they had searched for was one of these. Except she was too far gone to even beg. How did she manage to keep herself alive? Morgan wondered. And there were others like her. Perhaps this was one of those miracles the religions were always going on about. "And then the Goddess saith, 'Let there be miserable beggars, a ton of them.' And there were beggars. 'And now let there be ugly stinking smog.' And there was smog."

"Why dost thou—I mean, why do you stand there grinning like a fool?" Elspeth snapped. "I tell you this is the very lady we seek."

Morgan had to admit that as the day wore on, Elspeth's speech grew more and more like that of the weird Los Angelenos. He reminded himself to copy it.

"What an ugly pig," Morgan said, staring at the drooling, dirt-caked bag lady seated on the sidewalk. A very sad-faced raggedy man of indeterminate age stood beside her, looking quite apprehensive.

"Nay," Elspeth said, forgetting all about her speech patterns in her excitement, "I tell thee she is a fox. We can take her to our safe house, take off all her clothes, and bathe her. Anoint her body with oils. You will see what a fox she is then."

Morgan shook his head. "Oh, how I despise thee," he muttered. "All witches, for that matter. Save our most gracious Dame Beatrice," he tossed in, looking around nervously.

"Yea, do not forget thee to kiss the old hag's ugly buttocks," Elspeth shot back. "Groveling so becometh thee."

Morgan became aware that the raggedy man had been babbling in a voice too low for them to understand.

"What say thee, O hideous creature?"

The raggedy man motioned them to come nearer. Then, leaning forward as if to whisper a secret, he shouted at the top of his lungs, "I said you're not gonna take her anywhere or do anything to her. I take care of her. I protect her. I feed her. She'll eat if you put it in her mouth. Knows how to go to the bathroom. Most of the time, anyway."

Morgan shuddered. He had no use for the insane. Apparently the citizens of LA agreed with him, judging from the way they treated them here.

"What do they do with you when you die here, anyway?" Morgan had to ask.

Elspeth shot him an angry glance. But the raggedy man took the interruption in stride, answering with enthusiasm:

"They eat us. Grind us up into hamburger. Sell it at McDonald's, places like that. Tastes pretty good, too. Every once in a while you be chowin' down on a fatburger, goin' 'umm, umm, umm,' and you bite down on somethin' and find a—"

Morgan held out his huge hand. "Cease, enough."

"But they ain't gettin' the boogie lady here, and neither are you."

He held out his skinny arms in a bizarre, old-fashioned boxing stance. He was already wheezing heavily, apparently from the thought of all that huffing and puffing to come.

Morgan looked interested, but a glare from Elspeth stopped him before he got started. He merely looked at her and shrugged, causing the enormous mound of muscle between his shoulders and neck to swell up out of his tank top. And this in turn caused the spindly, raggedy man to flinch and back up a step. But his guard was still up. Way up.

"Why do you call her the boogie lady?" Now it was Elspeth who could not resist asking.

Once again the crazy denizen of the street adjusted effortlessly to the change of pace. "Know how you gets boogies in your nose?" he explained. "Know how some folks likes to—"

"Cease and desist." This time the order came from Elspeth.

"—do weird things with their boogies?" he trailed off.

Morgan moved toward him.

"You ain't gettin' her." The raggedy man milled his fists around in a threatening manner. "I'll fight to the death."

"Why, you—" This time Morgan's whole body began to swell, but once again Elspeth waved him silent.

"Let me explain the situation to you, Mr. . . . ?"

"Rags," the shabby fellow replied.

"Well, Mr. Rags, this fair lady thou knowest as the boogie lady is, in reality, the queen of a distant land. She has, uh, lost her memory. She did fall from a great height, upon her head, and thus . . ." She gestured. "Two holy men were sent to search . . ."

Mr. Rags's mouth was open wide. "Ya mean you two are holy men?"

"Nay, Mr. Rags, the two holy men came, they saw, and they sent us to deliver the reward and safely escort Her Majesty back to her kingdom. The great oaf here to guard her royal body and myself as a guide and ambassador, as my knowledge of thy fair realm is legendary."

People were beginning to gather. A macho, outdoors-type young man wondered aloud, "What is this, a movie?" He began straightening his hair, running his fingers through it. Then he mussed it up, just so.

"You ain't touching her."

"A reward of five hundred dollars."

The raggedy man swallowed and cleared his throat.

"You ain't . . ."

"Five hundred dollars and knighthood, of course."

"This is a movie, right?" The macho guy was trying to contain his excitement; it did not enhance his image. Still, maybe this was his big break.

"Knighthood . . ." the raggedy man muttered. "What the fuck?"

"But where's the cameras?" The crowd was buzzing now. Asking questions like "What are we supposed to do?" and "What's the sexy brunette's name, haven't I seen her on TV? What's the name of that soap?"

Elspeth turned around and visibly started at the size of the crowd. In a theatrical gesture she held one slender hand to the place where her white breasts threatened to billow out of the low-cut, tight halter top, and for a moment looked as if she might faint.

Morgan watched her interestedly, but at the same time with a good measure of visible contempt. *I'll catch her on the bounce,* he said to himself, not specifying which bounce.

But Elspeth, being Elspeth, swayed dramatically, then came right out of it. Smiled a lovely smile, and said, "Yes indeed, it is a film, and you are all in it. Play well thy roles and thou will all be well pleased with thy rewards."

"But where are the cameras?" Everyone began looking around and mumbling to each other.

"They are hidden," Elspeth continued. "Never shalt thou find them. This is Los Angeles," she added. "All things are being filmed all of the time." She paused, perhaps realizing how ridiculous that might sound, then continued, "By hidden cameras."

One man shook his head and walked away, followed by another, and then two teen-aged Black girls. But the rest of the crowd stuck it out, buzzing excitedly. The macho would-be star explained to those nearest him that this had been his theory all along.

"No use even trying to spot the cameras," he pointed out, as they were nowadays so advanced and miniaturized they could be anywhere—in her ring, her belt buckle, planted inside the traffic light, or perhaps even far away on the rooftop of a distant high-rise.

Morgan wondered whether or not this was true. It struck him as totally absurd; still, the people here seemed to be believing it.

"Must be a low-budget flick?" the macho lead male asked, hoping against hope.

Ever on top of the moment, Elspeth answered without hesitation, "It is of the highest budget ever. We have spared no expense with this—blockbuster."

The crowd now was humming like a swarm of bees. Morgan wondered what a blockbuster was. Elspeth had briefed him on movies and TV shows— some way of capturing the images of people acting out a story and then showing them to other people. He could understand the idea, but not the point of it.

He was also amused by Elspeth's lapses of language. One minute it would be all Los Angeles slang, and then suddenly all "thee's" and "thou's" again. He actually was learning it faster from her hopping back and forth like that. Or at least he thought so. When she looked to him for help, he merely said, careful to omit "thee's" and "thou's," "You are the director of this extravaganza, are you not? Well, direct."

He had asked her earlier, "What do we do when we find this woman? Kidnap her in broad daylight in the middle of town?"

And she had answered, "It isn't ever broad daylight here. It's a smoky haze, and it's no town. It's . . ." She had shrugged, at a loss for the word. "It's just Los Angeles. No one cares whom thou abductest in Los Angeles. They won't even notice."

Now here she was, surrounded by a crowd who thought she was making a movie. But the strangest thing about it was that she seemed to be enjoying herself. How could one so wicked be so happy? He would surely never figure it out.

Now he spotted the big minivan that one of Elspeth's new-world lackeys was driving around and around the block. All day long, following them and then circling. He waved her to pull over. Unnecessarily, of course, since who would miss the crowd Elspeth was directing here?

Right now Elspeth was explaining to Rags about knighthood. The queen, whom he knew as the boogie lady, would give Elspeth the authority to knight him.

"You mean everybody will have to call me 'Sir Rags?' " he said, clearly tempted. But then he shook his head.

"Now," Elspeth shouted to the young man, "grab him. Hold on tight. He'll pretend to put up a good struggle. The two of thee had better help. Don't worry about the sound, we'll dub it in later."

The three young men held Rags down while Elspeth commandeered two more from the willing crowd to drag the boogie lady over to the shiny, brand-new Mercedes van and stuff her into one of the luxurious, wine-colored, velvety captain's chairs in the back row. Morgan forced himself to get back there with her, while Elspeth jumped in front and slammed the door.

"Now we must drive off swiftly, but never fear, we shall be back to give to each of thee thy well-earned rewards," she told the crowd. "Wait thee here."

But about halfway up the block she had Melissa, who was driving, stop the van, and she leaned out the window and gestured back to the waiting crowd with her middle finger. "There's thy reward for being knaves, fools, and lackeys!" she shouted. Then she turned back around, settled comfortably back into her plush seat, and paid no heed to the furious crowd surging into the street after them.

"Drive like the wind," she suggested to Melissa, who was already driving as much like the wind as you could on as busy a street as Santa Monica Boulevard. For a moment Morgan thought they were not going to make it. But then a signal changed and Melissa found the room to punch the big Mercedes eight-cylinder engine (yes, eight!), jetting the lux-sport vehicle around the corner, momentarily panicking Morgan as he realized how fast they were traveling.

But soon he was back in control, staring at the dirt-caked wonder in the seat next to him.

"Dost thou actually expect me to believe that this wretched creature can withstand the power of the royal scepter and live?"

"I tell thee, she has done it before. Even greater psychic power than thou canst imagine has surged through her wretched form, and she has survived it." Elspeth considered for a moment, then added, "Sort of."

Morgan shook his head. He wanted to believe Elspeth just to get it all over with, but a kingdom was riding on this. And for his ambitions, a kingdom was a pretty good start. One day he would take LA. But the thought struck him for the first time as he glanced out the window at the smoky sky littered with ugly helicopters: why did he—or anyone else, for that matter—want to be king of—he shuddered—LA?, doubtlessly mirroring the thoughts of a myriad of previous stars of rock and cinema. The answer, of course: because it's there.

# 4

THE DINOSAUR WAS faster than any human—in a way. The first thing Corbo did when he realized his mental command to drop the beast in its tracks had failed was, naturally enough, to run like a bat out of hell. It was almost comical to see how fast the skinny old man could sprint, still stubbornly holding on to his lunch bag in one hand, with a T. rex breathing down his neck. Except, of course, there were no human beings alive here to see it. Only one sleepy-looking little fat thing with a very long neck, sort of a miniature brontosaurus, which popped its head up out of a low mass of spiky ferns and tracked him like a periscope. It opened its mouth wide and gave a loud ululating cry, uncannily like laughter, as the old man streaked on by, legs churning like a loony victim out of a cartoon. The little creature's hysterical laughter seemed to contain a sad, echoing quality, but Corbo had no time to waste contemplating this.

Just as this little creature wasn't an actual brontosaur, the one chasing him couldn't actually be a Tyrannosaurus rex—could it? If it was, it was a small one, although bigger than any carnivore Corbo had ever dreamed of encountering. And it was awkward, but fast—too fast. First it casually watched him sprint off. Then it raised its head, pointing its nose straight up in the air; and stretching its wretched little arms straight ahead, it settled back onto its big, thick hind legs, using its long tail for balance. For a moment it hovered there, bouncing a little as if getting in the mood. Then it tilted its head down and turned it sideways, again very like a bird, sighting in on the rapidly disappearing form of the old man. Finally it took off, springing from leg to leg, taking enormous leaps, and accelerating to what must have been the speed of a freight train. So it was fast in that straightforward way. But once it reached Corbo, it just barreled right on through, knocking him head over heels, finally separating him from his precious lunch, and abruptly (for a creature that large) pulling itself to a stop.

Now, as Corbo rolled over and with surprising agility somersaulted up onto his feet, the beast went into fighting mode. It rocked forward and lowered its head down until it was close to the ground, balancing itself once again by sticking its tail up in the air. Then it moved toward its prey, swaying its neck back and forth like a goose and clacking its enormous mouthful of teeth open and shut. At the performance of this awkward finishing routine, it was not nearly so fast. And now the old man began to circle it, forcing it to stand up every once in a while and tilt its head in order to zero in on what it was chasing.

At one point it seemed to Corbo that it completely lost track of him and simply stood there looking confused, wistfully clacking its teeth together.

One choice was to just stand there, keep very still, and hope it would forget about him and wander off. The other was to run.

The old man ran. He ran so fast that his long puff of white hair-beard was streamlined as if he had combed it. But here it came again. This time Corbo threw himself down and to the side on his belly, from where he watched the tyrannosaur charge by, stop, and go into its search-and-identify mode.

Suddenly the giant, machinelike creature just crashed down and lay there, inert. Apparently Corbo's psychic command had done its job, but it had taken this long for it to register. Or perhaps it had programmed itself to charge after the old man, and had carried this out on automatic pilot until it was completed, then reacted to whatever was the next command to penetrate its pea brain.

The old man went over and examined it. There was something comical about the way it lay there with its great mouth open, tongue lolling out, little eye wearing a black mask. There was something indefinable about it that the old man liked. "Reminds me of my bulldoggie," he said aloud. What had been the name of that dog? Old Jiggs? How many hundreds of years ago had that been?

This creature wasn't really unconscious, just lying there obeying its psychic orders. Its eye, the masked one, was open and trying to track, bulging and wiggling. Could this silly-looking, gooselike creature really have been the dreaded T. rex? Maybe an allosaurus or something like that? Leaping lizard? Stumbling lizard, more likely. "Duckbill dinosaur" would really work here, except that the damn thing didn't have a duckbill. But it sure as hell had the mannerisms of a duck more than those of the dreaded T. rex, at least in the imagination of the connoisseurs of giant lizards, to which, to some degree, the old man belonged.

He had, somewhat soberingly, lived through the age of awesome mythical beasts, these having all turned out to be, disappointingly enough, figments of primitive man's imagination, only to then see them discovered again, for real. Add to that his love of fighting dogs, fighting men, fighting women even (but dogs first), and it had to add up to something of an interest in the world's largest and most vicious land predator. Nothing fanatical; he did not sit around in a room with posters of dinosaurs all over the walls or anything like that. But he had occasionally been known to point out to Elena, "You know what a brontosaurus is, Elena? Big fat thing like the Loch Ness monster? Well, did you know that it had two brains, little tiny ones, one in its little tiny head and the other, which must have been a little bit bigger, in its spine? Yes, it's true. You would be better off talking to its butt than its face, you see. Do you know who that reminds me of, Elena?" Or, "Sometimes I wish there were still Tyrannosaurus rexes running around here for me to throw you to, Elena. Lions just aren't enough."

But what difference would it make if it were an allosaur, anyway? The old man knew from his experience with fighting dogs that the small ones were often more ferocious and, yes, even stronger somehow than the larger ones. It was quite possible, the old man figured, that the "leaping lizard" would have kicked the shit out of its bigger cousin. But for some reason, he wanted it to be a T. rex.

Must have been about fifteen feet tall, maybe a little more, if you counted from its toes to the top of its head. Of course if you added in the tail . . . Maybe that was it, the old man figured—they were adding in the tail when they told you how big those T. rexes were. Which was misleading—the tail went clear the hell off in another direction. Corbo frowned and shook his head. The way he saw it, scientists didn't have a lick of common sense. So it was probably a T. rex after all.

While carrying on this conversation with himself, he had walked back to look for his lunch. Happy to find it still intact, pineapple and all, still musing about the "king of tyrant lizards," he returned to where, sure enough, the great gooselike beast still lay.

After a while, Corbo knelt down and held the back of his hand near the creature's nose.

"Hope you can smell that, Jiggs." He paused and closed his eyes, trying to recapture his feelings toward his old bulldoggie and psychically broadcast them into the consciousness, such as it was, of this antediluvian version.

"Do you mind if I call you Jiggs? You'll have to earn the 'Mr.,' " he informed the T. rex, "like the dog did."

Mr. Jiggs had been what the English called a butcher's dog. Short-legged and heavy, but a lot more athletic than the sorry creature people called bulldog nowadays. The old man liked to differentiate by thinking of the earlier dog as a bulldoggie.

"Jiggs was a good dog," he said aloud. After a moment's silence he clarified the statement. "Though not a great one. He had the heart, plenty of that, all right, but he lacked the quickness and athletic ability that the later, more specialized bull-and-terrier-mix fighting dogs were bred for. A somewhat primitive model, like yourself."

He was silent for a while, and in the silence found to his surprise that a solid feeling of relaxed well-being was settling in. Here he was, isolated, lost in primitive times, perhaps forever. And he was just lying around with his T. rex, feeling fine. He amazed even himself!

What the hell—he let himself sink on into that bliss. His eyes closed momentarily, and he was aware of a low, reedy, vibrating sound. Was Jiggs purring like a cat? Seemed to be.

Corbo continued to stroke the gigantic head and talk to the creature. "Bozo was the great one," he said. "Quick as a snake, stubborn as a mule. Handsome. Debonair."

Jiggs raised his head and twisted it sideways, sighting in on the old man, looking skeptical, as if he were saying, "You talking about a dog?"

But then he laid his massive head back down and resumed purring.

Maybe he was just having trouble breathing lying down, trying to support that enormous belly. It could be more like snoring.

Yet there was a definite connection here, a sense of camaraderie that seemed to occur often between man and the most vicious beasts: After all, what could be more vicious than a cat? Or a dog, for that matter? And the old man knew what those who had never owned a fighting dog could not know, which was that the love of a dog for its master was strongest in the most brutal of the canine family. In fact, all the features that people romanticized in the noble collie were magnified a hundred times in a good, game pit bull terrier. Corbo grimaced a little to think of a wimpy collie receiving all those unwarranted accolades.

"All you'd have to do, Jiggs, is give him a whiff of Bozo and he'd run for the hills so fast he'd take his master's arm along with the leash."

Jiggs made a small, birdlike, cawing noise, as if in agreement, and the old man chuckled.

"Sorry," he went on about the cowardly collie, "but I've got to herd me some sheep, you know. The old call of the unwild. Bozo, on the other hand, would never have backed off from you, even."

After a while he added, "Of course, that's why he's dead." And then, "Of course, he'd be dead anyway, like everything or everybody else I've ever known. Might as well be a splendid brave creature for the little bit of time you have on this earth. Or whatever earth you're on. But I do not need to tell you that, right, Jiggs? Just like my Bozo, you're an all-the-way kind of critter. When you live, you live; when you die, you die. You don't mix them up."

That strange sense of contentment grew even stronger, and the old man knew that this was only possible because it was shared. He had felt it many times before, even with killer whales. It was a mystery. Totally a mystery. Killer whales would ravage everything from polar bears to whales, but they would not attack a human. They actually liked humans, and had often befriended them. There was not one case ever known of one of them hurting a human. Why was this? It made no sense at all. He shook his head in wonder.

He had released the T. rex a long time ago, but for quite a while it seemed content to just lie there and have its head stroked while the old man chattered away.

"Getting late," Corbo observed. "Let's have some lunch." He opened his paper bag and peeked in it. "It's not time for the pineapple yet, but I have a nice peanut-butter-and-lettuce sandwich. Half for me, half for you." He popped the tiny morsel in Jiggs's enormous mouth. The creature continued to purr, but did not bother to either chew or swallow. The old man relished his half. "So good," he remarked softly. "It's the mayonnaise that does it." Then, frowning, he added, "Maybe. You know, who the fuck knows? It's a mystery. But it's a great sandwich." Then he added, shaking his head, "Corbo the gourmet."

Then finally Jiggs sighed as if thinking of an obligation, got up and bounced around on his big hind legs, getting in gear again, made a strange chirring noise, then turned and bounded off.

The sun was just starting to set, and the old man figured it would be feeding time for Jiggs and the other carnivores. "T. rex must take a lot of food," he said, still talking aloud.

He took a stone out from the pocket of his jeans and held it in the palm of his hand. It was a black stone in a simple silver setting, identical to the one he wore around his neck. But it was not the one he wore around his neck.

For a while he sat there in silence, staring at it. Then he said, "Pretty much everything dies—but even Germanicus? What happened, little stone —

you got tired of crazy Germanicus and decided to run away with crazy Ketoko? *Quién es mas loco? Germanicus o Ketoko?* It rhymes. It would make a nice hit song, I imagine."

He crooned it out loud in a sickeningly sweet imitation of Frank Sinatra:

"Quién es mas loco?
Germanicus o Ketoko
Ketoko or Germanicus, the swine
Please tell me which, so I can still this heart of mine."

Suddenly the old man emitted a burst of high-pitched laughter that was answered by another screaming cackle, probably from that same little brontosaur-type creature he had glimpsed earlier.

When both their voices had died out, as if from a great distance, the old man heard the triple voice of Ketoko.

"Neither of us is as crazy as you."

Corbo held up his hand with the stone in it and said, "Missing something? You know, they were right, two stones are better than one. But why don't you come on out from wherever you're hiding, and let's see if we can make a deal. As one crazy to another."

There was no answer. Night came on, and naturally enough was filled with strange noises. But the old man slept. Sitting up. In little bits and pieces. Yet he was aware of the strangely silent approach of the big T. rex behind him. Of the creature standing there all bent over, tail up in the air for balance, head turned sideways, watching him in its birdlike way. And when it went back, turned round and round like a dog in the nearby bushes whence it had just emerged, made itself a nest and lay down and went to sleep, the old man sighed and let himself fall into a deeper and far more restful period of sleep. He figured his watchdog was nearby and, in its own way, at work.

# 5

———◼———

WHAT THE FEM-WICCA Society (or Wic-Org, as Elspeth liked to call it) thought of as their safe house in LA turned out to be, simply enough, a big expensive house in Palos Verdes with walls around it and a cliff protecting the rear part of the big backyard. Melissa viewed this with some irony, since she had recently been informed by the strict commandant of the new-world chapter of the Wic-Org, Mistress Brenda, that her own sweet mansion in Chickasala, Florida, had now also been designated as such. Was she supposed to feel honored? Elspeth had smirked as the pronouncement was being made, but had instantly put on a comically straight face when big Brenda looked around with that fierce expression of hers.

What also made this house safe was the presence of the two goons, their big American bulldog, the automatic weaponry, and the shotguns and handguns that had arrived along with them.

Melissa had been designated housewife/welcoming committee/maid, which in the Wic-Org was signified by the title "Hearth Lady." This title had been bestowed upon her like knighthood—no shit—like "I dub thee Melissa, Lady of the Hearth." Elspeth here, trying hard, as always, to keep a straight face.

"Which means get thy sweet ass to LA, buy us a good big fast car, set up the house—I'll give thee the address—for seven people. Which means groceries—a lot of groceries—maybe buy a freezer. Get the place cleaned up, linens; you may have to buy a couple of beds. Oh, and give thee the royal boot to the two old people living there. Look not at me like that; they shall still receive their stipends, great enormous ones, I might add—they simply have to check into a motel and enjoy there for a while the wonder of modern satellite television. I would recommend to them highly that they search out reruns of *Bewitched,* or perhaps they will even be able to receive straight porn." When she saw how Melissa was still regarding her, she added petulantly, "After all, this *is* kidnapping—sort of."

"How long?" Melissa had mistakenly asked.

"How would I know, fool? Dost think I've researched the average time it takes for a kidnapping? Simply inform the two decrepit old knaves to get out until someone tells them to get back in again."

Here Melissa had pointed out to Elspeth that it wasn't actually a kidnapping, strictly speaking. Since no one was asking for anything in exchange, it was simply a straightforward abduction. And Elspeth the Unpredictable had surprised her again by, instead of snapping back at her, nodding her head in agreement. She said, "You are wise to remind us of that. Indeed, words are important. It is quite necessary when engaged in a risky enterprise such as this one to keep a clear concept of what we are actually trying to accomplish here. It is not an abduction either. Indeed, it is an opportunity, new life for the Wic-Org and for the chosen one herself."

At this point her expression turned quite serious for the first time since Melissa had met her. It lent a grave dignity that added immensely to her already considerable beauty.

"I am tempted to follow my heart and trust thee, my sweet. But I must not go too far at this point. No need to burden thee with knowledge thou wilt not be able to use. But believe me when I tell thee that this wretched creature we have just stolen from the streets has just about run out of opportunities. It's this way: if she fails in the task we have chosen her for, which is most likely, she will lose all. As will Morgan, myself, and possibly thou as well."

Suddenly Melissa was all eyes.

"If she wins, she will win all, for all of us, but perhaps for herself even more so. After all, if she wins—she shall be queen."

Melissa looked at her like, "Will be *what?!*"

Elspeth had merely shrugged. "It would not help thee to try to understand too much just yet."

"I'm too stupid?" Melissa had dared to retort.

But once again Elspeth had merely shrugged. "Too unimportant," she had corrected. "Too vulnerable. For now, just keep thy trap shut around Brenda and keep thine eyes open."

Melissa dared, "You can trust me. I want to know more." Though she was not really sure she did—yet.

Elspeth smiled her old lascivious smile, and the moment of dignity was gone.

"Hey, lady," she said, "grit thy teeth and do thy chores. Thou hast an eternity to work thy way up through the ranks. And in case thou hast not figured it out with thy pretty little mind"—she had leaned over and French-kissed Melissa—"the way to my heart is not quite through my stomach." She had looked down lovingly. "But almost."

Later on that day, they had the burnt-out bag lady in one of the lavish bathrooms, stripped down, soaking in the oversize sunken tub. Melissa was watching from the open doorway, reluctant to go in yet hesitant to just take off. Elspeth, naturally, was right in there with her, naked as a jaybird, making a big, sensual deal out of bathing the woman. They had already changed the water once, and now that some of the grime was melting off, you could begin to see what she looked like, even though, of course, the slack quality of not only her expression but her entire body misled you.

Something about the woman was fascinating. Melissa shuddered to realize it. *How morbid,* she thought to her rich little self. But it was true; she could almost put her finger on what it was, but not quite. Elspeth's babblings about how this burnout could somehow become a queen seemed strangely appropriate. Melissa's consciousness started to float off, but then drifted back to the woman again and again, ignoring the nagging banter that went on constantly between Elspeth and Morgan, who was supervising the affair. Until Melissa was almost hypnotized, staring over Elspeth's kneeling form into the bag lady's enormous green eyes. Beautiful, enormous eyes the color of the shallows in Tahiti.

"These are nifty titties for a lady of this many summers," Elspeth said, running a soapy sponge over them. "What wouldst thou guess, thirty-five, forty?"

"I would say a trifle more than that," answered Morgan, who was seated on the marble steps leading down into the tub. "But for God's sake, witch, how would one be expected to guess the age of a demented peasant? We're probably off by as far as I could throw thee."

To which Elspeth replied with a smile, "Take care, sirrah, I may turn out to be heavier than I appear."

To which Morgan replied, "True, but I would be much inspired for the task at hand."

This was probably the friendliest exchange Melissa had yet witnessed between the two of them. They were basking in the afterglow of their successful mission, Melissa realized. But about the woman's age, Melissa, still staring into her eyes, had a sensation that they were farther off than either of them realized. Once again, she shuddered.

"By the Goddess's garters, Elspeth, dost thou have to make such a sensuous job out of bathing a demented peasant? Her 'titties,' as thou dost so poetically name them, are positively gleaming with cleanliness by now. So what is the point?"

Elspeth, who was sitting waist deep in the lukewarm water, turned to face Morgan, who now had his boots off and his enormous feet in the water.

"The point is, Morgan, that bathing, like most of the simple pleasures of life, is a sensual experience, meant by the Goddess to be most fully enjoyed. By both she who is bathed and she who bathes her. My Goddess, man, dost thou not ever have sex? I would hate to be thy partner."

"Actually," Morgan said, flashing a wicked smile, "we would both hate it, but yes, thou art correct, thou wouldst hate it more than I. And yes, I do have sex. But like everything else I do, it is controlled, carefully measured. Mostly I prefer to share it with enemies whom I have conquered. I care not a whit for whether they are male or female—it matters only that they once had the audacity to oppose me."

Elspeth grimaced. "They must enjoy that," she commented caustically.

"I certainly hope not," Morgan retorted. "Anyway, I do my best to make it unpleasant for them—that's where my pleasure doth lie."

"Sorry I asked thee." Elspeth shook her head and tried to get back into her thorough cleansing of the bag lady. But it was just before she turned back that Melissa, still in her dreamy state, staring into the woman's haunted green eyes, sensed whatever it was that happened. It was to her as though a presence beyond the reach of normal senses rushed through the room seeking something here but unable to zero in and thus stop. It just roared through, leaving a low humming in her ears. And causing Elspeth's left hand to flare up momentarily as though it were on fire.

Melissa blinked. Nobody else seemed to have noticed anything, so she kept her mouth shut. She had probably imagined it. Only, outside, she could hear the giant American bulldog barking excitedly—it was more like the roar of a cannon than the bark of a dog—and one of the goons with the guns was shouting, "What the fuck are you barkin' at? Will you fucking shut up, Willie?"

Whatever it was, it seemed to be over. Which was when the very weird thing happened with the bag lady.

# 6

D AYBREAK. THE OLD man was still sitting cross-legged, waiting, in the
shade of the same palm frond. He was so completely a part of that great
silence from which later arises the hum of existence that two exquisite little
dinosaurs came out from a small clump of fern bushes to examine him. He
figured maybe they were babies, but for all he knew they could have been
adults. They were two-legged and sported horns on top of their heads, and
they were both colored a bright lime green with tangerine circles on their
cheeks and bellies. They were very birdlike and delicate, and their move-
ments reminded Corbo of quail. They darted up close, sniffed him, trilled excitedly to each other, and then darted back a little ways, where they continued
sniffing the air. Suddenly one of them squawked, froze, and then, amazingly, blew a loud blast on its horn, a shockingly bright and plaintive sound.
Then they were both gone. A slight trembling of fronds and the faint rever-
beration of the horn blast were the only evidence that they had been more
than a vision.

After a while, Corbo sighed and said aloud to the empty air, "Do you
think I do not feel you watching me? It is my particular talent to pay close
attention to events, mostly after they occur, but, if necessary, before they
occur as well. So why bother to hide? What will that accomplish? I don't
know how you ever managed to pry the stone away from Germanicus, but I
will try to hold back my tears for that poor fellow."

Another laugh here, from the fat little brontosaur somewhere in the
distance.

"I have it now. In fact, I have two of them—see?" Corbo held out his
open hand, displaying the twin black stones nestling there, and waited.

At first only a minor turbulence disturbed the air behind him. He did not turn around, but he was aware of it. In fact, he was aware of so much more now.

"I didn't get it from Germanicus," Ketoko said in that same triple voice, only now it had lost its grandeur. It was sort of sad-sounding, even. "A friend gave it to me. But did it once belong to Germanicus? How extra-ordinary." He said it as if it were two separate words, making the old man smile.

"Yes, it once belonged to Germanicus. You can't tell that? Interesting. Only Popillius and I seem to have developed that sort of sensitivity. Not that I compare to him in these matters. He could probably tell you something about everyone who's ever touched the damn thing."

Ketoko came out of the mystic doorway which had formed behind the old man in the heavy, steamy primordial air. But hesitated, with one leg still inside.

"Popillius is dead now," he said lugubriously.

The old man's smile widened at that. "Who isn't?" he said. "Everyone except you and me is dead or unborn, whichever way you like to think of it."

"It's the same before and after their puny little lives. Same nothing-nowhere state," Ketoko agreed. "But let us not waste more precious time. Let us . . . transact." He drew the word out, obviously relishing it. "You give me back my stone, and I'll take you to wherever you want to go. There it is—I give up. You win."

He walked around in front of the old man and held out his hand, all innocence and surrender. Except that his face, which was constantly and regularly changing features, suddenly shifted into high gear until it was churning and writhing.

"Well?" he said, still holding out his hand.

The old man answered with another bout of high-pitched laughter. Which lasted entirely too long.

Ketoko withdrew his hand.

"Anne Marie is getting tired of hearing your laughter," he complained after a while.

"Who's Anne Marie?" Corbo asked, when he managed to get some control over himself. He was actually wiping tears from his cheeks.

"I don't know," Ketoko said in his somber triple voice, sending the old man into another fit of gleeful howling. "A being from another dimension?" he guessed in a monotone. "Maybe a fairy? Or an angel?"

"Or," the old man got in, wheezing and choking, "she could be the queen of France." More laughter. And in the distance the little brontosaur joined in.

"Do you think she could be the queen of France?" Ketoko said, his face shifting into its excitement mode again. "The name sounds like it."

The old man cleared his throat and took on a very serious demeanor. He then recited in his most pedantic tone of voice:

> "Anne Marie was queen of France
> But never changed her underpants.
> For this, just why I can't explain,
> The people crowned her queen of Spain."

"Or," Ketoko continued, undaunted, "she could be just about anybody, anywhere—that's the trouble with being telepathic."

Which of course sent the old man off into another cackling binge.

"Or she could be . . ." The humanoid with the changing face stopped in midsentence, took two quick steps, and threw himself on the old man, or at least tried to. But he never managed to get ahold of him anywhere, let alone snatch out of his hand the mystic stones.

Corbo, who was obviously very much at home rolling around on the ground, dropped the precious stones, effortlessly grabbed hold of one of Ketoko's wrists with each hand, planted a foot in his stomach, and toppled over backwards, taking the demon with him and of course adding to the face-changer's momentum—so much so that a piddling little kick sent him flying on over for a crash landing on his stomach. Corbo, having somersaulted backwards onto his feet and turned around to face him, all of this in one graceful movement, thus ended up standing behind him. Here the old man patiently waited for the demon to figure out where he was, panic, and try to scramble up to his feet. Obviously enjoying himself, Corbo bent down and playfully took hold of both of Ketoko's ankles, straightened up, and tossed Ketoko forward onto his face again. Then, without taking his eyes off the floundering demon, he beckoned behind him and shouted, "Come on, Jiggs. Sic him, boy." While at the same time picking up the stones again.

It was, of course, not the words that controlled the beast, but the thoughts behind them. But the old man had, over the years, developed the habit of speaking in order to focus his psychic powers.

From a large clump of fronds directly behind Corbo, the T. rex or allosaur, whichever it was, suddenly popped into view. Apparently Jiggs had been lying there on his legs like an ostrich, hiding. He quickly turned his head sideways, zeroing in, then hopped forward on his powerful legs. Two quick hops, and he was there. His prey was just once more scrambling to his feet when Jiggs moved his head sideways again and then swept it back, knocking Ketoko down, hard. Then the T. rex opened its enormous jaws and scooped him up. All of this was much more effective than the giant carnivore's original attack on Corbo, and Corbo assumed that Jiggs must have done a lot of his hunting from ambush. Right now the T. rex reared up to its full, terrifying height, swiveled back its head, and thrust Ketoko up to the skies, as if in offering. But did not bite down. Yet.

"Let me guess," the old man said. "Anne Marie doesn't want me to let my little pet here eat you?"

"Yes indeed, sir!" Ketoko shouted from up there.

"Too bad," Corbo shouted back at him. "Chow down, Jiggs."

The happy T. rex chomped and chewed and ground with its enormous teeth, all the time snorting and belching.

Whatever it was he was eating, he was enjoying it, the old man figured. And in just a few minutes, it was all gone.

Content, Jiggs followed his tail around and around in a circle, then lay down. Purred. And slept.

The old man sat down near him. "Let's see what we can accomplish on our own here with these two little stones," he said to the sleeping dinosaur. Then he closed his eyes. "Take me," he said aloud, and then to himself, "to where I want to go."

For a moment, nothing. Then a sensation of rushing movement through a series of multidimensional planes which just kept opening up and opening up into greater sensations of space.

Suddenly, in what must have been the blink of an eye, he was moving through a room. Elena was in it, along with other people, but there was something wrong, and he was moving so fast he missed her. Couldn't hold on, but the other woman was wearing a ring. Something about the ring called out to him as he whipped through the room. He threw a flash of power from the stones into it, and tried to catch hold, but no, he was wrenched back, bursting through the planes. Everything closed up like pieces fitting into a jigsaw puzzle, and he was back where he had come from, Jiggs snoring at his feet. He shook his head. "Sorry, Elena," he said, "but I don't think I can do it on my own. Everything seemed to be happening too fast for me."

Jiggs's only answer was to open his big mouth and sigh.

# 7

ELSPETH JUST HAD time to notice, along with the barking of the dog, a slight tingling in her ring finger, when the woman she was bathing lurched forward, grabbed ahold of her left hand, stood up, and was suddenly jolted backwards, twitching as if hit by a lethal charge of electricity. Then she fell back down into the tub, where she spasmed once more and submerged.

Elspeth stood up and sloshed backwards herself, dropping her sponge and muttering something unintelligible.

Morgan jumped up, brushed Elspeth aside, waded in, clothes and all, and fished the bag lady out of the enormous tub.

Suddenly her green eyes opened wide, staring into his, and she spoke for the first time.

"Sorry, Elena," she said, "but I don't think I can do it on my own. Everything seemed to be happening too fast for me." But she said this in what surely was not her own voice, but the voice of an old man.

This was so eerie that it caused the hackles on the back of Elspeth's neck to dance like snakes, and even Melissa, who was standing way back at the edge of the deck, moaned as if hurt. Morgan reflexively tossed the woman back into the tub and watched her submerge. But this time she sat back up of her own accord and slumped there, brilliant green eyes still wide open but no expression whatsoever in them, face and body slack.

"By the Goddess's luscious thighs, what just happened here?" Elspeth muttered.

Morgan looked at her and shook his head. "If thou knowest not, what on earth art thee here for, wench?" he snapped.

For a while Elspeth was silent, obviously thinking it over, as Morgan waited patiently for her answer.

Finally she nodded and spoke: "This we do know. Something beyond our understanding hath happened in this room, and I did not cause it, and thou didst not cause it, Morgan, and certainly innocent little Melissa did not cause it."

Morgan looked puzzled. "So?"

"So, this boogie lady caused or somehow was the cause of it. I don't know what it means, but obviously it's a sign of some sort."

"But what good is a sign if thou canst not read it?" Morgan groused.

"It may become clear to us later. For now, we know this much; something mysterious was in the room with us. Power hath caressed my ring, but jumped from there to her."

"What?" Morgan complained. "I saw no such thing."

"Of course thou canst not see power, fool, but what dost thou think was pinning her to the wall whilst she was jerking about like a frog on a spit? One may only discern the result of it. Dost thou not yet get it?" she continued. "It means we have got who we wanted to get. It means I was right. It means she is or once was a lady of power. And if the goddess of luck will blow us her sweet kisses, it means that so shall she be again."

# 8

THADDEUS, AS USUAL, was working the vibes, as Raphael perceived by the eerie blue light which illuminated the door to his apartment. Working as in "No, I don't play the guitar," or "I don't play the vibes, I *work* the vibes. It *is* work." Or sometimes, if his roots were upon him, "It *be* work!"

Raphael got the point, as had Violet. When, upon acceptance as a Guardian, Thaddeus had inherited William's room in the main house, he had wasted no time testing out his new position.

"I don't like William's room," he informed Violet as soon as he had unpacked. "In fact, I don't want to live here in the house, you dig? Be best you build me a little guest house out back, give me a little room to stretch my limbs. I don't care what it looks like, but it's got to be soundproofed so's I can dig my sounds loud—I do mean loud. We put a blue light on the porch; when I turn that light on it means nobody knock on the door or interrupt me. Just come on in, wait till I'm through with whatever."

To Violet's question, "What if the door is locked?" he answered, "Don't install a lock on the door. That solve that."

And it had. Then, taking them all off guard, he had suggested, "Know what, make it a duplex. The kid here want to be movin' out there with me. You women can have the house."

And to everybody's astonishment—especially Raphael's—Raphael, who had in those days been *the kid*, had accepted. Had jumped at the idea. Could that much time have passed? It struck him now, as he paused at the door, reminiscing in the blue light, that the reason so much time had gone by so fast was because essentially nothing had happened to him. Except for now. Things were starting to happen now, and best of all, he was causing them to happen.

He opened the door and went in. Softly, careful not to disturb Thaddeus—if Thaddeus, thus enthralled in his music, could be disturbed, that is.

It occurred to Raphael, watching Thaddeus gliding through the icy blue
light (yes, blue lightbulbs inside as well as outside), wailing away on the
vibes, mixing it up, that of them all, only Thaddeus was unique. Only he had
developed his own style. Even his appearance was stunningly different.

A tall, slender, and very elegant Black man, Thaddeus, before he became a Guardian, used to be something of a clothing fop, but had now taken
on more of the appearance of a Moorish pirate. He dressed most often in
loose shirts with oversize pointy collars and three-quarter-length sleeves
made of some brightly colored satinlike material. He had them especially
made, and wore them either with loose-fitting shorts and sandals or with
jeans and track shoes. He dressed no other way, and he always wore shades,
big round ones that made him look like some kind of bug. It struck Raphael,
and not for the first time, that Thaddeus's odd style of dressing would not
have been unsuitable for a superhero in the comics. And now, watching him
moving quickly and athletically back and forth, actually dancing as he
pounded on the vibes, Raphael was again reminded of how odd he was and
how ordinary the rest of them were. Violet with her "fashion sense," and he,
the good-looking all-American boy next door. Boring! This could not have
been said of the Guardians of old: the German giant, the dapper playboy, the
gorgeous Italian goddess, and the crazy old man, Corbo. It was as if they had
been imported from different planets.

They had died before he was born, but his mother Elena had told him
stories. Particularly about Corbo. Even the stones were different, had their
distinct qualities. Had they reflected the persona of whichever Guardian had
wielded them? Or, as the old man had suggested, were the stones the masters and were the Guardians, over the course of the passage of centuries,
molded by the differing forces of their stones?

Yet, how could that be? Had they not once been one stone?

"Maybe they felt it necessary to break up and go their own ways," the
old man had suggested to Elena. "Maybe they don't even like each other.
Particularly Yawtlée, here." (He had actually called his stone Yawtlée.) "He's
a little cranky, aren't you, Yawtlée? He doesn't really like anybody too much.
And I don't want to hurt your feelings here, but Yawtlée isn't exactly in love
with you, Elena." Here, according to the story, he had leaned forward to
emphasize the punch line. "Unlike your many other admirers," he managed,
before breaking up into laughter.

Raphael did not know whether his mother had believed Corbo or not.
But she had acted as if she did, one day introducing Raphael to her stone as

the old man would have. As if it were a person. He could still remember it vividly. His mother, with those beautiful green eyes so like his own, sitting cross-legged on the Navajo rug where she had been meditating, and then drawing his attention to the stone she wore in an amulet around her neck, introducing him to it. "Its name is Yawtlée," she had said by way of introduction. "Yawtlée, meet Raphael. He's only a little boy but maybe one day he will be a warrior."

Raphael had kept himself from asking questions, but Elena had answered him anyway.

"Because Yawtlée only likes warriors. If you are not a warrior, it would be better if you did not come near him. Or touch him. He will punish you if you are lying."

Raphael had touched the stone. He had been afraid but he had touched it anyway. He had felt its power, as perhaps it had felt his. So fierce and forceful: Yawtlée, the warrior's stone. How different it had seemed to him from the power of the stone his mother had given him, the stone that had once belonged to Popillius. The difference seemed so dramatic to him that when the survivors had come back from what he had later named the war of the stones—Violet, and with her Tippi and Thaddeus—when they had described to him their perception of what had happened to his mother, and Violet had tried to give him back his stone, he had refused to take it.

Violet, who had never seen him behave like this before, had naturally enough interpreted it as a way of dealing with shock. But it was not.

"I want Yawtlée," he had said. "Let this guy have the pimp's stone."

But Thaddeus had only smiled and held out his hand. "Fine with me," he had answered. "Us African-American gentlemen all be pimps or basketball players anyway. Only jobs you let us have," he had added as he hung the amulet around his neck and tucked it out of sight under his fancy white shirt.

Raphael had never forgotten that, and it had colored his future relationship with Thaddeus. It had been, he felt, the right thing to do in a difficult situation. And best of all, Thaddeus had done it with style and panache.

From then on, Thaddeus had been *the man* to Raphael. He had always gotten along with Vi's brother William, but he had never been drawn to him, looked up to him. Let's face it, the guy was a cold fish. And Mary Red Boots's kid, the big Apache, had been too full of himself to ever take over that role. Still, in the female-dominated world in which Raphael had grown up, he was the best you could do. But once Thaddeus had shown up, that had been it.

The incredible thing was, and he still could hardly believe it, Thaddeus had accepted his new role without complaint.

"Only thing," Thaddeus had solemnly informed him, "you be hangin' out with me, you will have to respect jazz, you dig? You don't have to respect me, you don't even have to like jazz, but you have to respect it. Jazz is religion, only it's *real* religion, not all that wishful-thinking sentimental bullshit. Jazz is love, only it's real love. Not that 'I-love-you-but-what-if-you-hurt-me-so-I'll-hold-back love,' but all-the-way let-go love. Jazz is mysticism. And it is a true way of power. Jazz is creation."

After a long time of waiting in the awesome silence which followed (which also was jazz, as Thaddeus had explained to him later), he had asked haltingly, "What about other music?"

Thaddeus had laughed, a low, rich, melodic sound—jazz? "There is no other music," he had replied.

When Raphael had mentioned that his mother had liked romantic Mexican ballads and that Violet was devoted to classical music and opera, Thaddeus had laughed until there were tears in his eyes. "Not laughing at your mama's music," he had explained. "Romantic Latin music is fine. Sometimes the best of it becomes mysterious and fluid. Particularly the Brazilian. Then it becomes jazz.

"But classical music and opera . . ." He shook his head. "What a sad way to fool yourself into believing you be cultured. Take my word for it, classical music another word for some very stiff shit from the past. And opera? Good gracious, my man, if you can't laugh at opera, what you got is no sense of humor. All that silly, dead, lifeless shit. My, my, my."

He was wearing shades (always), so you couldn't really see his expression, but you could tell how serious he was about his "sounds."

Which was why, even though Raphael had some of the most exciting news of his life, he was standing here waiting patiently while Thaddeus flowed along the river of bells his mallets summoned from the vibes, till the inspiration ceased. Could be a few minutes, could be forever.

# 9

WHAT THADDEUS USED the vibes for, mainly, was to allow the melodic lines flitting just beneath the surface to form themselves with the least amount of intrusion from his consciousness. He had found that when you composed on the guitar, the music was shaped a lot by the properties of the instrument. It became *guitaristic*. He figured the guitar and piano were probably the worst offenders, but was not sure in which order.

He had chosen the vibraphone primarily because of the sheer simplicity of the instrument. The layout—totally linear. He also loved the delicate, bell-like tone. An added benefit he had not expected was that when you played it, you moved around, swung your arms. Actually doing all this in rhythm: truth was, you danced it.

The dancing, and the ease with which the instrument drew out that stream of music which flowed through deep within him, beneath his thoughts, helped him to sink into an even deeper trancelike state than he had ever been able to attain with the guitar. And the deeper you got, the clearer the sounds came through. Until all there was was sounds. Then gradually, little quickly darting thoughts like electrical charges began to buzz in, like now. More and more of them, until the music was farther away, harder to keep up with. This was when you stopped.

Thaddeus swayed there, mallets hovering over the vibes but no longer touching, eyes closed, breathing slow.

In the silence that followed, he gradually became aware that he was looking at Raphael, who, silent as a statue, was looking back at him.

He smiled a big, slow smile. He liked Raphael, who was always surprising him. And now, talk about surprises, he could hardly recognize the boy. In just a couple of weeks, the kid had blown himself up like a balloon.

Every day now Raphael looked like a new person. Thaddeus knew the theory behind the incredible gains, knew that probably it had even been he himself who had inspired it, but when you saw the results, it was magic. How could anybody get that big that quick? What's more, the effect seemed to be snowballing. The more muscle mass he built, the more he was able to summon forth. Faster and faster. Three weeks ago, Raphael had been a slender, sensitive-looking youth. Now he was unmistakably a warrior, bristling with muscle. He had stopped combing his beautiful red-gold hair, which fell to his shoulders, and started growing a goatee, giving him the look of a young Viking. His formerly languid green eyes now quite often flashed a wild, aggressive gleam. Just a trifle manic, Thaddeus felt. It was as if he had grown overnight, not so much boy into man but boy into swashbuckling superhero.

On top of all this, Raphael had now started dressing almost entirely in tank tops and shorts, obviously emphasizing the effect. It did not occur to Thaddeus that the boy's looks complemented his own, and that the two of them looked like a couple of B-movie pirates.

"Yo," Raphael said at last, sounding like the kid he used to be. Last month.

"I was in my room, working out. Suddenly, I—I don't know, I just felt weary. Incredibly weary, like I just couldn't go on. Like I had to sleep, you know?"

Thaddeus nodded as if he knew. "Yeah," he said, interested.

"Okay." Raphael started to pace back and forth in front of Thaddeus. "I went into something—not sleep, but like a coma. It was so weird. Nothing like that has ever happened to me before. I had no control over it—it just came on and on."

He looked troubled, all right. But with all his recently acquired muscle mass, Raphael's expressions had to be reinterpreted. He was like a stranger to Thaddeus. It was with some amusement that Thaddeus noted that what used to look like "sensitive/confused" now came across more like "aggressive/aggravated."

"Anyway, I blacked clear out. It was scary because I tried to fight it but I couldn't. For a while I wasn't aware of anything. Then I heard a soothing sound, like splashing, moving around in water. A dog was barking—big dog. There were voices—excited—but I couldn't tune in on them. Suddenly I was aware of what had drawn me there."

He stopped talking, as if here even he was doubtful about what he was working himself up to say. Then he blurted it out.

"My mom was in that room. Alive. She was the one in the water, I could sense that. But somehow, and this was the weirdest part, the old man, Corbo, he was in there with her, and we all know *he's* dead. It's like he was somehow mixed up with her. Speaking through her, seeing through her eyes."

He paused again, staring off in space.

Thaddeus was definitely getting interested now. "Anything else?"

"There was some kind of power in that room. Real power. All this was just for an instant—I think." He frowned. "And then it was over and she was gone. But totally gone—off-the-face-of-the-earth gone. Like before. Like dead."

But Thaddeus shook his head. "No, I don't buy it. She was alive then, she's alive now. She's just hidden, like before—wherever she was all this time. Or I figure you would have tuned in on it. Don't you dig?"

Raphael nodded. "Yeah, she's alive," he said. "Only we don't know where."

But Thaddeus shook his head. "Don't be so quick to give up on me, studly. You found her, so you know where she is, dig? Now where is she?"

Raphael, clearly puzzled, said, "I just plain don't know."

Thaddeus shook his head. These Guardians were such ingenuous fools. Probably because they had come by their powers through the gift-curse of their stones, while he and Tippi had been forced to work hard in order to develop their mystical powers. Not for the first time, he wondered how Tippi was handling this "hanging around" the Guardians without being able to lay her eager little hands on one of the stones. The reason he was wondering was because she was the only one not naive enough to think he would be too "nice" to invade her thoughts. And she guarded them ferociously. He did not know how she did it, but he was not surprised. Perhaps she had been able to siphon a little of the power from Violet's stone. While Violet was busy looking in the mirror, putting on her fucking makeup, he added cruelly. Something like that had to be going on, because Tippi, along with the rest of them, was not aging. He wondered if Violet had picked up on that. If so, she had never mentioned it to him.

"What are you smiling at?" Raphael asked, looking a little miffed.

"I'm just essentially uncluttered, dude. You know, happy darkie after a hard day's work in the field: 'All I needs be the sun and the moon makes me happy, massa.' " Thaddeus threw in the Blackspeak for flavor. The neighborhood he had grown up in, you surely had to disguise being smart. But when you were as smart a kid as he was, you had to learn to hide it in your damn sleep. From your damn mama, even. He had learned that well, as had he learned everything else. Fact was, he still enjoyed throwing that curve ball around from time to time.

"Look, studly," he continued, getting into his zone, "close your eyes. Come on now, do as I tell you."

Ever the obliger, Raphael closed his eyes.

"Now, you got to concentrate here. What I want is, you picture an elephant, you understand?"

Raphael mumbled, "An elephant?"

"Yeah, but he pink, you dig? Bright pink, like one of those flamingos at the zoo. Picture him carefully, you know, right down to the curly tail. That's right, he got a tail like a pig. But he pinker.

"Now, picture him moving along this cartoon road, bright colors, bunch of trees, flowers. Crows be singing. Like in a Disney film. Crows be Afro-American gentlemen like myself. Right? Crows be singing, he be dancing along. A cumbersome saraband, right? Quick—where's your mother?"

Raphael's eyes opened wide and he blinked, but said nothing.

But Thaddeus had caught the thought as it popped in and out of Raphael's mind.

"LA," he said. "The beach. Right, muscles?"

"I don't really know," Raphael said, "do I?"

"Yeah, you know," Thaddeus said, "but you got to learn to trust yourself. These things pop into your head, you got to grab 'em quick or they be gone. First thought's always right. And LA's what that was. You go pack—hey, just a toothbrush, you dig? You guys can't seem to remember, you're rich. We get there, we buy us some fine threads, California style. You know—laid back."

"Unlike formal Arizona?" Raphael suggested wryly. "Yeah. I'll be right back."

"Catch you in . . ." Thaddeus examined his watch. It was a Cartier, and it was wafer thin and *très élégant*. But you could hardly tell what time it was by it. "Well, sometime soon."

Thought to himself, as Raphael went out the door, *Kid looks different, talks different, walks different. Damn near ripped the door off the hinges. And all of this practically overnight. What else can those stones do that nobody ever thought to try?*

Outside.

It was early evening, hot, sultry. Maybe summer, Thaddeus figured. But then, it was always like this in the Arizona desert. It could have been winter. He checked his watch. Couldn't even see it in the dark, but if you could, it still wouldn't tell you the fucking date. October, maybe? He chuckled as he undid the snakeskin or whatever-poor-creature strap around his wrist. A bird cried out. He could hear some insects buzzing—he guessed it was insects. It was a loud, steady drone.

So if he remembered right, it was fall or winter, but what difference did that make here in Cheerful, Arizona? If these Guardians were going to live forever, you would figure they would have at least wanted seasons. But no. He tossed the useless, ridiculously expensive wristwatch into the darkness. To the night bird.

"Tell you what time go to sleep," he said lugubriously. "What time wake up." *Problem with being rich,* he thought, *is expensive shit is mostly even worse than economy shit.*

He strolled across the space between the little guest duplex where he and Raphael lived toward the main house. It was a lot of space. Everything was big out here—big house, big space.

Sure enough, as he had half expected, shadowy figures were moving on the wooden platform Violet had installed earlier this year. Tai chi. Violet and her instructor, Mrs. Lim, were practicing a Yang form. *Slow-motion lemurs,* Thaddeus thought, and smiled. Violet was very, very good, as she was at most everything. But she would soon abandon tai chi, as she had abandoned yoga, as she abandoned everything.

As he got closer, he made out Tippi sitting cross-legged in a corner, sketching them. She was not the type to practice tai chi, and she was even smaller than Mrs. Lim, but she could probably kick both their butts if she got mad enough, Thaddeus figured.

He climbed the wooden stairs and without a word went over and sat down cross-legged next to Tippi.

"They be tough, but they be too slow," he whispered. Tippi giggled in reply.

Thaddeus forgot to breathe for a moment as he saw the quality of her drawing. You could almost feel the figures moving across the paper. Even her style had become elegant, smooth, and swift. She drew as if the picture were already there on the paper and she was rushing to fill it in. When she finished, she would rip out the page and toss it on the pile beside her, and immediately dive into the next one.

"That's fantastic, Tippi," he said. "I mean it."

But she didn't seem to pay much attention to him, just kept that charcoal moving on that paper.

Having finished their slow-mo, the two women walked over to Tippi and Thaddeus, moving as gracefully as snakes.

"We have now become invigorated," Mrs. Lim said happily.

"I'm sure you have," Thaddeus answered. "Violet, I have some important news. We need to talk. Mrs. Lim, could you please leave us?"

Refusing to give up her smile, Mrs. Lim said, "I would much prefer to eavesdrop."

Violet laughed. "Oh, let her stay."

"Why not?" Thaddeus replied, looking wryly amused.

When he finished briefing her, Violet said, "I'm not sure that's such a good idea, you and Raphael going out there alone."

Tippi stopped drawing, looked up, smiled, and said, "I don't think he's asking you, Violet. I think he's just telling you."

Thaddeus nodded. "That's it," he said.

"Is a power struggle?" Mrs. Lim said happily. "How interesting."

"Very well," Violet said icily. "I'll make the arrangements."

"No," Thaddeus said. "That's the point. You give me the names, phone numbers I need. Then you through making arrangements for everybody. I make my own, right? When *you* want to do something, that's when you make arrangements. You just hang out here where we can reach you if we need to. We may need some real help, you know."

"Wouldn't that be a surprise," Violet said, giving Mrs. Lim a jolly laugh. But she borrowed a pencil and a piece of paper from Tippi, wrote on it, and handed it to Thaddeus.

"That's all you'll need," she said. "He'll take care of all of it."

The three women watched as, without a good-bye, Thaddeus stood, turned his back, and walked away from them. But then, just as he was moving out of hearing range, Violet called out to him and he turned back. "What now?"

"Do me a small favor, will you? You know that watch I just gave to Raphael for his birthday?"

Thaddeus nodded. Right, he was thinking, Raphael's birthday. That meant it wasn't winter at all. Spring had come to Arizona without his even noticing. *Have to get me out more,* he told himself, *commune with nature.*

"See to it that he wears it, will you? For luck?"

Thaddeus was puzzled. This was a side of Violet he had never seen. He shook his head. "No such thing as luck."

"Yeah, thanks," Violet snapped. "Forget it."

Thaddeus waved his big hand as if performing the tai chi movement "ward off" and said, "Chill, okay? I promise. Any other sentimental, uh, bullshit 'fore I go?"

They watched until he was gone.

"I sense that he is embarking upon a great adventure," Mrs. Lim commented. And then, "I hope he will not be hurt."

"Me, too," Tippi responded from where she still sat cross-legged on the wooden floor, still drawing.

Whatever Violet was thinking she kept to herself.

# 10

——✦——

THE CROWD THEY moved through consisted of a bewildering array of people of all ages and conditions, in bizarre costumes, few of which had any relationship to the Renaissance—which was, after all, the name of this fair. There were barbarians, African tribesmen, wandering Arabs, wizards, fairies, elves, early Brits with genuine blue faces, medieval peasants, and even a little group of Elizabethans in full regalia. There were a few morose knights in hot, heavy armor. Mostly the ambience was that of classic Disney.

Through this bizarre, noisy crowd Elena moved in silence, looking neither to the left nor right, not responding to anyone, but keeping up with Elspeth, who held her arm. Morgan walked in front of them, and for him the crowd parted. Melissa, who walked on Elena's other side, was decked out in a simple green frock which was cut low enough to expose a lot of cleavage and long enough to cover her knees. Elspeth's dress was similar, also a deep green, only more elaborate. Unlike Melissa, she wore jewelry: dangling silver earrings in the shape of the crescent moon, and another, longer crescent moon in her hair, also silver. Silver rings on her fingers, and probably her toes, Melissa figured. It had been explained to Melissa that where they were going, the color designated Wic-Org; the style and jewelry, rank. Elena was dressed in white. "Green is the color of those who choose the Goddess," Elspeth had commented, "while white is the color of those whom the Goddess chooses." *Sacrificial victims* was what popped into Melissa's mind.

Every so often someone from the crowd would call out to Elspeth, something along the lines of "Blessed be, sister," and then fall in behind them. These people were invariably dressed in green.

"To enter the other world," Elspeth had explained, "more power is needed than one alone can supply. It doth call for a full coven. And verily they had best be good. Six shall be men, and six ladies. And one shall be an especially powerful and high-ranking witch, such as myself. After we have raised up the cone of power and broken the barrier between worlds, then shall we enter the old country whence came Morgan and myself. Then shall we light bonfires and make merry until sun-up. Well, perhaps not quite, but almost, almost."

Knowing Elspeth, Melissa had no doubt of that, and in fact she felt that new but oh-so-familiar stirring inside her at the mention of "making merry," but as is common with the few humans among us who take their fill of sexual pleasure without associating it with love or fear or right or wrong, there was no real urgency to the feeling. It was merely an itch that would be scratched and then be gone for a while—momentarily but completely gone.

Melissa knew by now that this was the way it was for Elspeth, only more so. When it was time to play, Elspeth's capacity to enjoy sex had no limits. But she was not in the least driven. She could drop it in a minute, and forget completely about it, should it become necessary. This was the way for a person of power to gain control, not by futilely striving to suppress the necessities of the physical body. "The only way out," as Elspeth had remarked on one occasion, "is all the way in. Which leadeth through."

So tonight, after raising the cone of power, they would enter another world, and possibly party all night, or, should Elspeth change her mind, travel all night. As so often was the case with Elspeth, though, Melissa observed, sleep would not be an option. You got used to it. In fact, when you lived an exciting, thrilling life, you found you craved sleep a lot less than when you were married to some goon like the late Rudy and playing the role of the big winner's little woman for a living.

"Now doth she smile like an angel; it maketh one to wonder why," Elspeth remarked.

"This other world we are going to is real?" Melissa responded. "I mean, a real place, different from this one?" She figured "other world" was probably some kind of witch slang for "seeing things differently," or being part of the group, but didn't know how to put the question.

"How many times must I say thee yea?" Elspeth groused.

"And will I be part of the coven?"

Elspeth pulled up so abruptly that one of the witches in the entourage bumped into her from behind, causing her now to do an about-face and glare at the culprit and swear, "By the devil's great green dickie, wilt thou

watch thy humongous feet. We are aiming our little darts at higher awareness here.

"And as for thee, Melissa, fie on thee for a fool. We shall be in need of
great power tonight, and thou hast none and are nothing. Best thou shouldst
enlighten thyself most fully in this area before thou movest on to the next."

"And Brenda is your boss?" Melissa asked innocently, striving for total
awareness of the pecking order.

"Brenda is not here," Elspeth snapped. Then stomped off. Everybody
followed.

"Brenda is my superior in age and in the organization, but not in talent.
She is a highly ranked bureaucrat, and was so before I was born. But I am a
real priestess, and that she shall never be."

"Before you were born?" Melissa mumbled. "Uhh, just how old . . ."

"No one knoweth," Elspeth said in a softer voice, this conversation all
being spoken across Elena as if she weren't there at all, which, in a way, she
wasn't. "But the bitch has lived a very long time."

Though Elspeth did not say it, Melissa seemed to catch the thought
*Much too long. Maybe I'm gaining some psychic powers after all,* she
mused.

"Smiling again!" Elspeth commented. "Methinks it may be time to enlighten thee in yet another matter. The one thou callest Brenda cares little
what name doth mark her enterprises in this world. She hath chosen the
name Brenda for use here, because the name Diana is too striking. She wants
to be low-key."

Fat chance of that, Melissa thought, but kept it to herself.

"In the old world, to which we now are making our merry way, she demands to be called Mistress Diana. It is not so much a name as a title. And
she hath well earned it. Before thou wast born, she was Mistress Diana."

Melissa looked confused. "So?"

"So, if thou wishest to keep thy smile, thou must remember what to call
whom when. Best not forget the mistress part, either."

They continued to walk along in silence, Melissa obviously as confused as ever.

"Listen to me, pumpkin," Elspeth continued. "Nobody understands it.
But those of us who survive learn to live with it. To use it, even. This affair
of which we speak is a long, long story. A fairy story even. And it taketh
place in two different worlds. Over too many years for me to count. And I
am not the young maid I appear to be." Here she paused, apparently waiting
for Melissa to disagree, but Melissa said nothing.

"Nay," she continued, "in truth, I should have been sleeping the sweet sleep beneath the grass for many long years now. Instead, here I am a young fox, spry and lissome, attractive to all who possesseth good taste, regardless of race, creed, color, or sex."

Again she seemed to be waiting for some response from Melissa, and again she got none.

"As to Diana, the woman is no goddess, merely a mortal like myself, who has been alive a long time. And she herself subordinate to an even older, even more unpleasant hag than herself."

Elspeth sighed as the image of Dame Beatrice popped hideously and unbidden into her head—another talentless bureaucratic slut with seniority in the Wic-Org.

"But, as to the Goddess who founded our order, she who presideth over all of us"—looking a trifle confused here—"if she were still alive—this goddess of love, our lady of the night, the queen of the witches—that would indeed make for another story."

Melissa did not look very convinced. "If she's a goddess, how could she die?"

Elspeth shrugged. " 'Tis a rough world."

She stopped walking abruptly, and everybody stopped with her, except for Morgan, who stormed on ahead and disappeared into the crowd. She turned to face Melissa, and now spoke to her in a reverent whisper, as though she was fearful to speak the words aloud.

"There were four of them, or so she told us. I don't even know if they are alive or dead. Humans or gods. They had powers that I could not explain even if I did understand them. For instance, my own powers seemed to mainly originate from this ugly little black stone, which shineth not at all, in my ring." She held up her slender hand for Melissa to scrutinize. Indeed, the little piece of black volcanic quartz in her ring didn't seem to be doing much of anything.

"But it was she, the queen of the Wicca, who filled it with power by holding it next to her own gem of magick and willing it to be so. The power it required for this to be accomplished, she explained to me, was so piddling that she could not even detect the difference in her own magick stone.

"So, of the four of them, this is how she explained it to me: First came she who must be obeyed, the Goddess of the witches. Of beauty, of love, and of deceit. Drusilla."

Melissa must have looked puzzled again because Elspeth stopped here and nodded as if agreeing with her, before she continued.

"Yes, thou sees it too. Perhaps thou dost wonder why a goddess should wish to be called Drusilla? Why should that make her—comfortable? Someone must have called her that as a child. Someone she loved. And that would indeed make her out to be an ordinary mortal." Again she paused, staring at Melissa, who looked as if she were about to say something. And this time she did.

"I was thinking," Melissa said hesitantly, "that Drusilla is a Roman name."

"Gadzooks." Elspeth slapped herself on the head. "Why did I never think to question the origin of the name? Well, it's too late for me to make use of that information now, for she has been gone away for many long years. Officially she is in some otherworldly abode, increasing her powers by ceaseless meditation. Unofficially"—here Elspeth cupped her hands and pressed them to Melissa's ear, but unfortunately, when she spoke into it, she seemed to have forgotten to lower her voice, so that Melissa twitched and jumped back away from her—"she is dead. At least that's the conclusion I've come to.

"Next comes a god who takes the form of an old man, Corbo the Trickster. Like the others, he was subordinate to her."

Here again Elspeth paused while interpreting Melissa's expression. She shrugged.

"Again, I must agree with thee. It doth sound most doubtful to me also. Particularly when one studied her expression as she told the story. Methinks I did detect the distant whistling of the wings of fear when she mentioned his name. But this is the story, as she told it to me.

"Next was the god of brute strength or the god of the skies, Germanicus. Yes, I see it, thou needs not point it out to me—Roman again. But what about Corbo? What kind of name is that? And what of Pop? For Pop is the last of them. A sort of celestial pimp and party organizer. The ambassador of the gods, as Lady Drusilla often put it. All of them her servants, but our bosses, should we ever, any of us, encounter them, which as far as I know none of us ever has.

"Here is the big secret. I confess I was not going to tell thee of it. But I find myself impressed with thy quick wit. I may soon need to ask more of one such as thyself than simple sex games."

Once again she cupped her hands and made a funnel to Melissa's ear. Melissa winced, but hung in there. This time, to her relief, the witch remembered to whisper.

"Though we were to do the bidding of the other gods, should ever we encounter them, we were not, under any circumstances, to reveal the existence of the old world. They knew not of it. Dost see? Of course not, how couldst thou? It is because of the loch—lake? You see, it is in the old world that Drusilla found the lake of the wondrous healing waters. Well, not so much found it as killed those who found it, and then took it away from them. It is the waters of this lake in the magick ointment we gave to thee which gave thee back thy youth. Dost thou see it now?

"No? Though they were gods, and despite the great power of their mystic stones, they were aging. Because of the waters of the lake, she was not. Oh, they were aging slowly, but since our lady aged not at all, she had only to wait, and then, when they grew old and decrepit, take their magical gems. Or, if they gave them over to their apprentices, use her vast experience to rob them of the stones."

Here again she fell silent. Melissa waited, but nothing came out.

"Well, what happened?"

Elspeth looked glum. "I don't know, but methinks that while she was waiting, one of them killed her. Probably the tricky one. She always seemed to fear him the most."

Now it was Melissa who looked irritated. "So if she's dead, then what's the point?"

"The point is . . ." Elspeth said, looking angrily back at her, just as Morgan made his return.

"By the Goddess's teats, woman, where in the world hast thou got thyself to? I have been combing the Faire grounds for thee. Canst thee keep up?"

Elspeth gave Melissa a look, and said, "Let us try once again. Pray thee, show us the way, and though it may be too much for us maidens, we shall try to cleave to thy boot steps, shall we not, ladies?" Amidst much giggling, they were off again, with Morgan plunging resolutely into the crowd as if parting the Red Sea.

"The point is," Elspeth continued, "that Dame Beatrice was the Goddess's next in command, followed by Lady Diana, though I was her fun thing, as thou art mine. That the world for which we now are headed is ruled by Drusilla, who methinks is dead, through Dame Beatrice, who is almost dead, and next through Diana, who is far too alive to suit anyone who knows her. The major purpose of that entire world, or at least the part of it we know, is merely to protect the waters of the loch for Drusilla."

"Who is dead?" Melissa tossed in.

Elspeth shrugged. "Long time, no see. Besides, the trick for us is to

make use of the magick of the loch for ourselves, obviously, but also to keep
up on our pretty little toes."

They walked on in silence for a while, Melissa striving to make some
kind of sense of all this bizarre information, while Elspeth found herself
caught up in empty reminiscences—unusual for her.

Suddenly the crowd parted as a small, plump man dressed all in green
and wearing a silly (especially on him) red cap with a pheasant's feather in
it was jerked through by a goofy-looking white dog that seemed to be something of a cross between a dog and a pig. The creature was wearing a cruel
choke collar, but paying not the slightest heed to it as he dragged his owner
behind him, barking happily in the voice of a much larger dog. Completely
certain of its destination, it ran straight over and crouched way down in
front of Elena, as if getting ready to leap, and wiggled there on the end of its
tail.

The man on the other end of the chain—yes, the dog was on a chain and
not a mere leather leash—was short and stout like his dog, but obviously no
match for him. Now that he had the chance, he jerked viciously on the chain,
but the superpowerful creature, focused in on Elena, totally ignored him.

Elena came to life, if you can call screaming coming to life. As easily
as a child might toss aside a toy which has suddenly become unbearably boring, she tossed aside Elspeth and Melissa.

Everyone else stared in astonishment. And finally, the morose Morgan,
who had been quiet all this time, said, "What the devil does she mean by
'peet bowl,' anyway? Some kind of gardening term?"

The short stout dog owner gathered in a little of the ridiculously long
chain and finally managed to jerk the dog away. The short stout dog jerked
the man back. Then it stood up on its hind legs and, still wagging its whole
body with wild, passionate joy, placed its front paws on Elena's stomach and
tried to lavish her with its tongue. This resulted in a head butt starting from
its superbroad, cube-shaped head and delivered through its long but squared-
off snout, knocking Elena over backwards so that she wound up sitting in the
dirt.

"What a strong doggie," Morgan exclaimed. "Though too small. I fear
it would be no match for my champion bandoggie, Nighthawk."

"I'm really sorry there, ladies," the little drunk with the dog was saying. "Damn your ass, Blackjack. Bad dog!" The dog wagged even more furiously at this epithet. And barked some more.

"You're right there, buddy, he's no fighting dog, he's just for show.
He's one of them English bull terriers. People get all confused up about

'em—ain't never been no real fightin' dogs. Them's yer Staffordshire terriers. Wish I'd figgered that out before I bought him in the first place."

He seemed to have established some control over the pig-dog now, but you wouldn't know it to look at Elena, who sat in the dirt, face in hands, crying like a child—in fact, more like a machine than a person; she was merely acting out one of her strongest conditioned reflexes.

This particularly nasty little psychological land mine had been buried in her subconscious, waiting for someone to step on it, many long and mostly painful years ago, on the hot sunny day (weren't they all) in the dusty (sometimes muddy) little town where she had been born and raised in old Mexico. The memorable day that nasty little Emiliano had used his pit bull on her to extract revenge for her tattling on him to Señora Alatriste, the new teacher.

You had only to glance at Señora Alatriste to recognize that you had better do something to get on her good side right away. True, you also only had to glance at Emiliano to see that the same law of physics applied to him. But, in Elena's eyes, he didn't seem to occupy a position of such awesome power as did teachers and other adult authority figures. As so often turned out to be the case with Elena, the fates were eager to prove her wrong.

Emiliano's pit bulldog had bitten down on her leg more like a giant pair of pliers wielded by a demon craftsman than like a mere dog, and she still bore a scar from it. But the dog had not stopped there. It had squirmed ever forward, trying to cram more and more of her flesh into its oversize mouth.

Fortunately for her, an old man whom nobody thought much of, called Don Pedro, who was strolling by at the time, simply opened up his shabby white coat and took an enormous but very ancient-looking *pistola* out of his waistband, rushed over, and despite Emiliano's shouts of protest, casually held the gun to the dog's head and blew him away.

"You are fortunate it was not you, Weely," he said to Emiliano, who was now coming to his senses and backing away. "For I would just as soon kill you as I would step on any useless cockaroach." Emiliano ran for all he was worth.

The old man turned back to Elena, who of course was bawling her heart out, as well as bleeding a lot.

"You are afraid of my *pistola?*" he said. "She makes a loud noise, but fortunately she still has some of her bite left." (As if the gun were losing a little of its vigor with age, along with him.)

"Listen, don't cry, little girl. You must be brave, because life is vicious, you see? You're not nearly brave enough, I am afraid." Then, shaking his head, the old caballero casually put his *pistola* back in his waistband, closed his coat, and walked away. This was Elena's first experience with a crazy old man, but unfortunately, it was not to be her last.

Well, she had lived through that. And here she was now, down in the dirt, bawling again, living through it for the second time.

But that was not even close to being the weirdest thing that happened at the Renaissance Faire that balmy afternoon in May.

The voice of that other, even crazier old man cackled and then spoke.

"Ah, Elena, you are such a fool," it said, "to be afraid of such a magnificent animal. The white cavalier, we called him in the old days. A noble warrior and a gentleman, both at once."

Everyone was totally silent. Shocked out of their wits, for grotesquely enough, the voice was coming from Elena.

"And you too, sir, are a fool to compare this dog with one of those ugly little mutts from County Staffordshire. Why, James Hicks himself pitted a small bitch of his against a much larger Staffordshire bull-and-terrier and the white bitch killed him easily. As easily as you might . . ." Elena paused, searching for the most appropriate simile. "As easily as you might down another dram of ale."

The little drunk stared at Elena, but if he thought it odd that her voice had just changed into an old man's, he gave no sign of it.

He simply snorted in derision and shot back, "You don't know diddly. This noble"—he gestured grandly with surprisingly elegant hands—"white grand dragon or whatever the fuck you want to call him couldn't even whip your cat. Furthermore—" He swayed. "Hicks musta made that up. Everyone knows these dogs can't fight. Their miserable little hearts just ain't in it. Clown of the dog world, is more like it. These white bull terriers ain't—I hate to say it—but they ain't dead game." He said the word "game" with immense reverence, as if indeed this was the secret holy name of God.

Elena fairly jumped to her feet, and spoke softly in Corbo's thin voice. But the softness had at its core an edge of anger Elena had never heard in it before, if indeed she were hearing it now. "You dare to insult this, this magnificent animal, as well as the man who not only was an acquaintance of mine but who had the genius to engineer the breed? A drunken oaf like you? Be careful I don't just swat you like the bug you—"

Silence. Except that by now everyone in the crowd was saying something to someone, so that only Elspeth and perhaps Melissa heard Elena remark in her own sweet voice, softly, "The old man was always a fool about fighting dogs." She reached out her hand and, to the immense joy of the dog, tenderly touched his broad head. "Sorry, Fido," she managed to say before her expression went slack and her eyes blank again.

"God's blood," Morgan swore. "What manner of . . ."

"How would I know?" Elspeth started to say, but switched in the middle to: "It most surely is a sign: within the Maid of Los Angeles dwelleth a wise old man." But she looked quite puzzled. "Who loveth white doggies," she added, looking even more puzzled.

"Maid of Los Angeles," Morgan groused. "She's forty if she's a day. God's blood, woman, you can tell by her nipples that she's borne a child."

Everyone in the crowd shut up again, and this time stared in shell-shocked attention at Morgan, who shrugged.

"If you ask me," the drunk with the dog said, "she sounds like a fuckin' old man. And furthermore, she don't know shit about dogs. And further even more, she ain't no friend of James Hicks, because that clown invented *this* clown"—he pointed to the dog, who wagged himself happily in answer—"about a fucking thousand years ago, and then, as most of us do"—he gestured around to those in the crowd—"he fucking died. And furthermore"—he was wheezing now in his effort to blurt it all out—"while he ain't no fighter, don't mean I ain't no fighter. I can take this bitch."

He started to put up his guard, and then, as if for the first time, truly saw Morgan, and quickly put it down again.

"But I won't, because I'm a gentleman."

"Best take thyself away," Morgan suggested.

"I could use a beer," the little dog owner shot back hopefully, as if Morgan were about to buy him one. Then he sighed and pulled on the chain attached to the pig-dog's choke collar. "Come on, Blackjack, let's go get us a beer."

At the mention of the word "beer" the white dog pranced about excitedly, going nowhere, and with a couple of whiny complaints allowed himself to be led away from Elena. Then he and his owner were swiftly swallowed up by the noisy crowd.

"Well, wasn't that a pleasant diversion?" Melissa said to Elspeth as they continued their march through the Faire.

But Elspeth chose not to answer her directly. "Something is happening here," she said, more to herself than to Melissa, "something fey and invisible, but it giveth off a great smell, and what it doth indeed smell like to me is magick. Magick of the grandest and most complex variety. For over a century now have I prayed for this blessing from the Goddess, for when the pot is stirred it must be time to add the new spices and hope for the best."

She glanced slyly at Morgan, who was moving steadily up ahead, parting the crowd, and said across Elena in a lowered voice that she felt would not reach him, "In these turbulent times that are rushing to meet us, I shall indeed have sore need of someone whom I can trust with my very life. That one could rise most quickly through the rank and file—nay, veritably leap over it—a hundred years in a day. Could that one be thou, Melissa?"

If Melissa knew one thing in life it was not to hesitate at a time like this. You didn't rip yourself free from the vile web of poverty by responding to Rudy's marriage proposal with something like "Aw, gee, let me think on it for a few days and I'll get back to you." When the merry-go-round of life offered you that brief glimpse of the gold ring, before it swept you on by, you had to jump off your horse and grab it, and worry about where you would land later. After all, the gold ring would pay for a Band-Aid or two.

"Elspeth, I swear to you, I am that one," she answered back, perhaps a trifle too loud. "I swear it upon . . ." but she couldn't think what to swear upon.

Elspeth nodded. "We shall see," she said.

Morgan had stopped and turned around. "I say, what's she swearing about?"

"Just swearing for the fun of it," Elspeth answered him. "Like 'Fuck thee, thou great fool.' Like that."

Morgan said, "Oh," and shook his head in puzzlement. The ways of women had always been a great mystery to him. And he thanked the Goddess for that.

An hour later and they had gathered the entire coven, and the Faire was shut down for the night. Another hour and Melissa had learned what it meant to summon up the cone of power and enter another world for real.

But could this be real? She caught glimpses of the flesh in flashes of light from the bonfires, heard the little sighs and cries of the dancers and lovers. Smelled the intoxicating rush of sexual orgy. Felt the touch of hands. It was more like something from a fairy tale than from "real life," as she had once called it. Like a naughty dream. But if it was a dream, she did not want to wake up. She wanted to dream forever.

"Don't pinch me," she mumbled. But amidst much laughter, pinch her they did. Many hands pinched and stroked. And the wild laughter and the strength of the wine—everything was coming in loopy waves. "Hashish wine," Elspeth had called it.

"Is this all a dream?" she murmured, as beautiful nude Elspeth came into focus. Those eyes, you could drown in those eyes.

"It is simply a different kind of dream," Elspeth whispered before their lips and tongues met. And the hands and the hashish wine came on in another wave, making everything beautiful but out of focus again, like the ripples in a pond.

# 11

---◈---

THE OLD MAN snorted and woke up. It was night, and the biggest moon he'd ever seen illuminated the eerie landscape. "The good old days," he groused to himself. The shrub in front of him trembled (in the breeze?) as if it were laughing. "I must have drifted off, even though I was trying not to," he said, keeping an eye on the shrub. Then suddenly he realized—"Oh no. Was I only dreaming, or did I reach Elena, only to fail her again? All that effort, and then when I drifted off to sleep—the results." He seemed to remember people dressed up in medieval costumes, Elena, and a white bull terrier. Arguing with somebody over bulldogs.

The old man shook his head sadly. "What a fool my dream self is. Don't you agree with me, little shrub? Or should I say, 'Don't you agree with me, Ketoko?' "

His vision of the shrub grew hazy and disappeared. It was Ketoko who was there, sitting cross-legged in the dirt, staring at him.

"How did you know?" Ketoko demanded in his booming triple voice. "I was controlling the part of your mind that interprets what the eyes bring in."

The old man smiled. "I do not have to see to know," he said. "In the same way, I knew it was not you that my faithful pet Jiggs gobbled up for lunch, but rather some kind of double without any real life in it. Like a Tibetan *tulpa*. Where did you pick that trick up?"

"I have a few secrets of my own," the demon answered. Ever in movement, Ketoko's arms were now stretched up over his head and his fingers writhed in the hot night air. "You sleep sitting up," he remarked.

"I don't really sleep," the old man said. "I meditate like that, and now and then I drift off for a bit."

"Ho ho ho, you lie to me and to yourself, Corbo. You do really sleep, and just at the wrong time. So here we are. We both have our tricks, and you have your pet dinosaur. You have the stones and can't get back to where you came from, and I can get back, but have no stone. What do we do now?"

For a while they were silent. Finally the old man sighed and spoke. "We have to compromise. We have to make a bargain of some sort between us. And we have to trust each other to some degree. There is no other way."

"This is sad but true, old man. But I will not take you back to where you can take control of me, because now that you know I have one of the stones you weel surely take eet away."

For a moment the old man was startled by Ketoko's sudden accent. Later, much later, he might allow himself the luxury of wondering about that, but now was not the time for it.

"No, no," the demon continued, "if I must trust you that much, then here we must both stay. Forever."

Silence. The old man was weighing whether it would be wise to try to take control of Ketoko now, using the new power supplied to him from being in possession of both of their stones. But the demon obviously was still packing plenty of residual power and probably, he feared would, at the very least, be able to escape.

"I am not a demon," Ketoko complained. "I wish you would stop thinking of me that way."

Causing the old man to smile.

"To start with, send your dinosaur away. Then at least I can relax my vigilance in that area."

Without getting up, Corbo turned to take in the giant form sleeping behind him, and sighed. "How's this?" As always, speaking aloud to focus the force of his thoughts, he said, "Sleep deep, my friend, for you have served me well and deserve your rest. Nothing shall wake you up until the first rays of the sun strike you. Then you will wake up, and only then, refreshed from this deep, rich sleep. And you will hunt and kill and eat. And though I will not forget you, you will forget me."

He sighed and turned back around.

Ketoko was comically snoring, and for a moment Corbo thought he'd put the fool to sleep. "Oh, for God's sake," he said.

Then Ketoko opened his eyes and said clearly in triple voice, "Ho, ho, ho. Who says that Ketoko lacks a wonderful sense of humor? Not me."

The old man shook his head. "Being a fool does not imply having a sense of humor," he explained patiently.

But Ketoko only laughed again.

Then suddenly his voice changed utterly. It became an exact imitation of the old man's voice: "Oh, for God's sake." Then back to his own weird triple voice again: "Don't tell me you believe in God, Corbo. You of all people."

Corbo said, "I have no need of beliefs. I go as far as I can go, but no matter how far I go, there is always something beyond that I can't see or understand or touch, or even realize, but it's there. That's what I mean by God. But let's get on with it. I've spent enough time with the dinosaurs."

Ketoko nodded so vigorously his head seemed about to pop off. "Me, too," he declared.

"Okay," Corbo said, "let's try it this way. We trust each other. You take me back; you can keep your stone. I have no need of it."

Ketoko's sonorous triplex laugh was deafening. "Oh, come now," he protested when he could speak again.

"Okay, okay." The old man held up his hand. "How about this? For now, I keep the stones—Wait, hear me out. I keep them and you take me back to close to where we started from. Then I give you your stone. But I hold on to it. You have your hand on it, see. Then, when we arrive, you take it. And don't worry, I swear to you I'll let you keep it. All right?"

Ketoko said nothing.

"Believe me, there's no other choice. No other way to do it."

Silence. At last Ketoko spoke. "Your word of honor. Swear to your God, the Beyond."

"Cross my heart and hope to die," the old man said, trying to keep from laughing out loud.

"All right," Ketoko said, "let's go."

# *12*

───◈───

I T WAS SUNDAY, another early morning, already coming on too hot. At least it seemed early to Raphael, who hadn't gotten much sleep last night. His mother was here somewhere, he was sure of that now, but where?

For a few moments yesterday, in the late afternoon, he had almost gone into a trance, the awareness of her had become so strong.

They had been in a taxi, just another one of those ubiquitous van-sports-utes, painted a garish yellow, driving from the airport to downtown Santa Monica, when the spell had come over him.

"It's Mom," he had stammered, when it was past. "She's really alive somewhere. And it's like she's herself and the old man. You know, the *brujo* Corbo. Both at the same time. It's all mixed up. And I get glimpses of people dressed real funny. A white dog—some kind of fighting dog, all that muscle. People dressed like—I don't know—Robin Hood? But she's gone now. Clear gone, like before. I don't know. It doesn't make any sense."

He half expected the taxi driver to jam on the brakes, jump out, and run for it, freeway or no freeway. But hey, this was California, and the driver, a tough-looking young woman, turned around and casually stared at him with a pleased expression.

"Uh, don't you need to watch the road?" Thaddeus suggested uneasily.

"Uh-uh," she said. "I'm pretty psychic, too. When I'm not singing, that is. I plan to be a singer. Folk songs. But like rockabillyish too. Sort of. I write 'em."

But she turned back around, and now was driving using the normal senses. She whistled a few bars from a strange tune. "Recognize that?" she said.

"No," Thaddeus replied tersely.

"That's because I wrote it," she said. "What about you, dude?"

"What about me what?" Thaddeus snapped.

"Kind of songs you play. Wait a minute. Let me guess. Use my psychic powers. I got it. You're into jazz, right?"

"Yeah, right. You're very gifted. Now will you leave us alone and please shut up for a minute or two." Thaddeus was more than a little annoyed at being constantly distracted right when he needed to concentrate the most, but this *was* California.

"Yeah, sure," she said agreeably. "I'm not really psychic, you know. Or yeah, really I am, but that's not how I guessed about your sounds, dude. Pure deduction. Ovation guitar, right? You can always tell them 'cause they're round-backed. And you're Black, so it's got to be rhythm and blues or jazz, and don't nobody I know play R and B on an Ovation. So . . . I deduce."

Thaddeus tried to block her out.

"Yo mama's still gone, right?"

Raphael nodded.

"And you got no idea where to, right? Or where from?"

Looking miserable, Raphael shook his head. His face was so expressive that he looked at the moment like a massive, muscular man with a face more suited to an eight-year-old boy. A sensitive one, at that.

"Myself, got me a Martin D-thirty-five. That's the sound you gotta have—you know, the songwriter/singer sound—that's yer D-thirty-five. Well, I'm going to have one, anyway. Those fuckers cost a fortune. Got me a Yamaha jumbo. El cheapo. What kinda Ovation you got in that great old hard-shell case back there?"

"Why don't you either shut up or use your great psychic powers to help us locate his mother, okay?" Thaddeus snapped at her.

"Shit, that's easy," she said. "Santa Monica off-ramp coming up here. Dressed up like Robin Hood, that's the Renaissance Faire. Just gots to be, baby. And the white fighting dog—well, that kinda fits in, don't you think?"

Silence from the back seat.

"Don't you? Think, that is?"

"How fast can you get us there?" Raphael practically shouted.

She shook her head. "That's clear the fuck in Santa Barbara, like about a thousand miles in the hot sun. They'll have the Faire all locked up for the night. But hey, first thing tomorrow morning and it's 'sirrah' and 'my lady' and the whole bit all over again. All fucking hot day long. On and on. I went there once and played a couple of my songs. Didn't interest nobody much, I have to say. They like that Old English crap, I guess."

"Tomorrow morning," Thaddeus said. "What time do they start up?"

"Let 'em outta their cages like ten o'clock. Something like that. I don't know it makes any difference how soon you get there. She's either there or she's gone, right? And—"

"She's gone now," Raphael echoed from the back seat.

"So tomorrow it is. I could use the fare, you know. Saving it up for my Martin. Get that sound, babe—that old Martin D-thirty-five heavy bass-line twang. So, where to now?"

After a moment's silence, Thaddeus said, "Tell you what, you drop us off at the best guitar store in Santa Monica. Then you pick us up tomorrow. At what hotel? What do you recommend around here? The Crest? Okay. Then you pick us up tomorrow, let's say around noon. Give us a couple hours to get there. The Faire be in full swing."

He held out his hand to ward off Raphael's protests before they were uttered. "I know you be all excited. Who wouldn't? But listen up here. There is no point in getting there too early. Your mama's been there, but she's not there now. Besides which, we need to lay back. Got us a few chores to do. Have us a nice dinner. Get us a good sweet sleep, you dig? Then we ready for anything. We get there, the Faire is jumping, and we ready for it."

Raphael nodded wearily.

"Okay, then," Thaddeus continued, "let's say twelve o'clock sharp. This be afternoon, not the middle of the night, you dig?"

The musical cabbie nodded vigorously from the driver's seat. "I think I can tell the difference," she assured him.

"Twelve o'clock it is, then. Crest Hotel. You be out there, okay? You do know where there's a decent guitar store, right?"

"I should hope so. Look, I could wait for you. Even go in with you." She was starting to get excited now.

"What's your name, anyway?" Thaddeus asked her. "Can't keep calling you 'you.' "

"Cal."

"As in California?" Raphael asked in disbelief.

"Like in Calvin," she said, shrugging at the wheel.

"No, Cal," Thaddeus continued, "I want you to drop us off at the store. We going to fool around some. Eat some dinner. Got to score us some California-style threads. Think things out—you know. So you go home, practice on your jumbo whatever. But we owe you. You show up tomorrow, you hear?"

"Sure thing. Know what? Let me sing you my earthquake song on the way, okay?"

Raphael and Thaddeus looked at each other and grimaced.

"Earthquake song, right," Thaddeus remarked.

"Everybody got to have an earthquake song out here," she informed them, and then burst into song. Raphael rather liked it.

"You guys connected?" she asked hopefully when she finished.

Raphael smiled. "Only to ourselves," he answered.

The next day, twelve o'clock sharp—"noon, not the middle of the night"—as they stepped outside the sleazy little hotel, all decked out in their "California threads," Cal was there waiting at the curb in her big yellow taxi-van.

The first thing she noticed this time was that the tall Black guy was lugging two guitars: the rounded one from yesterday, but also a flat case, a good hard-shell like the other, but no Ovation in this one.

"Bought a new guitar at Orville? What kind?"

"Get out the cab for a minute, why don't you?" Thaddeus said as he lifted the tailgate and stored his Ovation inside. "Come around here and have a look for yourself." He set the flat case down gingerly on floor of the ute, next to his own, opened it, and took out the guitar. What was this?

At first it looked to Cal like some older Martin, maybe one of the triple-0 models from the late thirties—not all that fancy, like, say, somebody's Ovation Custom Legend infested with fuckin' abalones, but pure Martin all the same. Then she got up close to it and everything stopped for her, including her breathing.

It was the most beautiful guitar Cal had ever seen. Up close it gleamed with delicate yet elaborate inlay work. The markers on the fingerboard seemed as luminous and magical as moonlight on water. She could barely make out a signature there in pearl. "What the fuck is this?"

Still wearing his ever-present sullen expression, the tall Black dude related his experiences at Orville's Guitars. She was aware of the other dude, the pint-sized Arnold Schwarzenegger with the sweet face, watching it all with something of the same wonder that she was, but maybe that was just his everyday expression.

"They didn't have a D-thirty-five in the shop. Can you dig that? I don't think so. I'd change shops, I was you. Anyway, I told the guy waiting on me, Larry what's-his-name, 'Where's the most expensive guitars you got here?' So he sneers and tells me you can't judge guitars that way, like he knows, right? So I told him, if I need spiritual or philosophical advice I'll go to someone smart, so where your most expensive guitars?

"He takes me to where they got them locked up in a case. Chairs in front of it. Poor fools go there and sit in the chairs and stare at guitars they can't afford.

"They had a couple of guitars in there I would have personally preferred. Particularly the latest Taylor Anniversary. Anyway, I figured you're a Martin freak. This here is their brand-new Ani DiFranco signature model." He grimaced at the thought that someone would name a guitar after a folk-style fingerpicker, no matter how good she was. "It's a little brighter than a D-thirty-five, but anyway, here it is. It's for you. Another thing, I don't need any thank-yous or anything like that. Why don't you pack that away for now and drive us to San Bernardino? You can sit around and play that thing all afternoon while you wait for us to come back from the Faire."

Cal was so shell-shocked that for once she was totally silent as she drove. She heard but did not register when Thaddeus in the back seat remarked, "At least that guitar be good for something."

Raphael laughed. "A lot of money just to shut someone up."

"Hey," Thaddeus said, "best possible way to spend you money, Rafe—believe me."

"Oh, I'm a believer, Thad," Raphael said in a low, serious tone.

"You can use my earthquake number, you want," was the only thing the singer-cabdriver managed to mutter as she drove.

"I might do that," Raphael had answered.

Still in a daze, as the two men got out of the taxi, Cal thought to ask Thaddeus, "Why are you gonna lug that Ovation guitar around the Faire? Plan on playing?"

The blond muscleman had smiled innocently and answered for him, "It's a special-made case. He carries his guns in there, too."

That had not even registered. Cal had just sat there and played that fantastic Ani DiFranco guitar for the rest of the afternoon. Until her fingers were so raw she wouldn't be able to play at all for the next couple of days.

But later on, much later on, she began to realize these guys were gone. They had gone into the Renaissance Faire and they were not coming back out.

Furthermore, they must have had some inkling of this possible turn of affairs, because the Black guy, Thad, had given her a fifty and told her, "We're not out of here by—what time does the Faire close? give us about half an hour after that—don't hang around, you dig?"

Something about the way he said it had alarmed Cal; calm, determined, but resigned, as if he were entering enemy territory. This was the Renaissance Faire, for Christ's sake!

"You want me to call someone if you don't show up?"

The tall laid-back Black man had smiled his soothing smile and said, "Not to worry. We fine. We don't show, we be someplace else. But we take care of it. You just forget about it. Go home. Live your life and work on your guitar."

*So there it is; despite all the money, power, and generosity, these guys still have that dumb macho male thing going on underneath there. Probably wreck 'em,* Cal thought sadly.

"Most singer-writers can't play for shit," he had rambled on. If he could read her mind, he gave no sign of it. "I'd recommend jazz. That means you really got to know some stuff about chord structure. The scales are just hidden in the chords, so don't worry about scales at first. Just work on understanding chords for a while. The time for scales will come soon enough. Course, if you really want to get serious, you'll have to get a cutaway. This guitar's beautiful and it's got a beautiful tone. Yeah, I'll admit it, it's a sweet guitar. But it's too slow up the top end of the neck. Anyway—later."

And that had been the last she would ever see of that strange pair: the tall, sour-tongued hip one, and the smaller, superbuilt one with the beautiful face and the sweet, sweet smile. The smile of someone who was perennially good-natured. Only thing was, something about the smile reminded Cal of Bon Bon, her big fluffy cat. Bon Bon also was perennially good-natured, but he was happiest when he could catch and torture to death some poor creature smaller than himself. She shivered. Had he been joking about the guns in the guitar case? But they were gone, and though she did not yet know it, she sensed that they were a long time gone, and she was driving back to the city with fingers so sore that her eyes were tearing. And feeling—what was it? Feeling frightened. Because this gift, like all gifts, was a double-edged sword. Because what was the excuse now? Was she going to really do it, or had it all been talk? An act?

It was a couple of weeks later that she went to Orville's shop and found out what the guitar had cost. She actually felt faint upon hearing it. And later that afternoon she called in to work sick. She spent that night sitting in her small Hollywood flat, staring at that beautiful guitar, and her eyes were tearing again, and this time it was not because her fingers were sore; it was because her fingers were not sore enough to justify owning a fifteen-thousand-dollar guitar. That night she sat there, determined not to move from that chair until she made the decision: *either pawn the guitar and face what you really are, or live the dream for real with all the pain and pleasure that decision implies.* It took clear until dawn before she made her choice, and before that night was over she could damn well see how you could hate someone or love them, see them as a saint or a demon, depending on what you had hiding there deep down inside yourself.

# *13*

As per THADDEUS's prediction, the Faire was in full swing. An amazing throng of rowdies was making merry here. Thaddeus, in his shades, faded green Quicksilver T-shirt, black shorts, and gel-cushioned track shoes, was dressed so incongruously for the Faire that nobody seemed to pay any attention, save once in a while to throw them a request to perhaps "play a sweet pavane for me with thy lute, O minstrel." But Raphael, who was wearing a pair of red ersatz-Scottish plaid shorts, seemed to be riling up everybody. A fact he was apparently either unaware of or totally unconcerned about.

"This does not trouble the wise," Thaddeus remarked, to himself really, quoting the Upanishads.

"What?" Raphael wondered.

"You're pissing everybody off with those shorts, but it doesn't seem to bother you any."

"Why should it bother me?" Raphael said. "If they're pissed off, that's their problem, not mine."

"You've got a point," Thaddeus answered. This was definitely a new Raphael. He had always been amazingly even-tempered, but wasn't there a hint of mischief peeking out from somewhere deep inside there now? Maybe even a touch of macho devil that was definitely new? Did it come as a side order with all that muscle? All those scare stories about the evils of steroids. Had no one ever pondered whether they were really the effects of the 'roids or maybe just the effects of the muscle itself? Thad had.

At one point Thaddeus and Raphael came upon a group of sullen, drunken men who waved them over. Apparently these were descendants of

Scotsmen, for they began to viciously denigrate Raphael for wearing a phony tartan. They seemed really to be feeling their oats around Raphael, though from the furtive glances they threw Thaddeus, he deduced they were a little wary of him. After all, though not very muscular, Thaddeus was well over six feet tall, and Black. He himself considered their judgment a mistake. The three great fighters he had seen in his life—Rocky Marciano, the only heavyweight champion who had never lost a bout; Mike Tyson; and the greatest of them all, Rickson Gracie, the Brazilian jiujitsu expert— were all guys who said they were five-foot-eleven or so, but were really adding on a couple of inches, and were loaded with muscle. In short, they were guys exactly like Raphael. On the other hand, Thaddeus did have guns in his guitar case; maybe these drunks were psychics. Causing him to smile.

After what seemed to Thaddeus a long time of enduring insults from drunken louts, Raphael calmly reached out, put the palm of his hand on the loudest one's face, and pushed. The man did not go down, but did go quite a ways back.

"How about you wee laddies all shut your fucking bonnie little wee mouths or I'll kick your bonnie butts clear back to the fucking Emerald Isle?" Raphael said cheerfully. "Or is that Ireland? Oh well, close enough."

The sullen group was obviously thinking about it until Thaddeus chimed in, "I'd do it, I was you. Us niggas be mean."

Grumbling and throwing a few obscene hand signs, the Scotsmen retreated. Perhaps all the way to the safety of their beloved bonnie lochs and glens, Thaddeus hoped.

"Us niggers?" Raphael repeated, in phony awe.

"Not you and me, Rafe—me and some other nigga like me."

"Oh, shit," Raphael groused as they moved on through the crowd. "I thought I'd been promoted to honorary Black or something like that."

"You never make it, Rafe. But never. You the whitest of the white. You be the great white hope. They let you in the great white brotherhood. You be the white Guardian. Right? Champion of justice."

"Sorry to have to remind you," Rafe said, smiling, "but I'm half Mexican, dude. 'Fraid I'll never be the white Guardian. I could be the Chicano Guardian, maybe."

"Oh, yeah," Thaddeus said. "You be the Chicano Guardian, all right. You less Chicano than me, señor. In fact, it's impossible for me to even remember your mother was from Mexico, let alone you. Man, she was a beauty, though. Had her such an ugly kid."

For a while they walked through the Faire in silence. "Looking for the right place," Thaddeus explained. Finally they came to the base of a grassy hill. Although the Faire was filled with booths selling every kind of snack and drink imaginable, this appeared to be the place where the serious eating was done. People were buying everything from corn on the cob and kidney pie to Near Eastern treats like tabbouleh. There was a booth specializing in piroshkis, baklava, and other Russian specialties, causing Thaddeus to remark grimly, "If the Russians ever went through a renaissance of some sort, I've personally never seen any evidence of it."

The smooth, grassy hillock was filled with people sitting and eating and of course swilling down the ubiquitous ales and beers. Thaddeus examined it carefully. "I like it," he announced. "It's pretty much in the center of everything and a little quieter than down here. Let's see—we get us a place in the shade, sit down, do a little work for a change."

Raphael hesitated, then said, sounding worried, "You know, man, I'm not getting anything. But nothing."

"Hey, dude," Thaddeus answered, "who's the sensitive here? You let me tell you when to start worrying. You strictly an amateur. Trying to tune in while you're walking around this noisy place 'bout like trying to enjoy a gourmet meal same time you joggin'."

Raphael grinned. "When did you ever eat a gourmet meal?"

"Maybe not," Thaddeus informed him, "but I have sat down in the shade a lot. Let's head on up the hill, sit under that spreading chestnut, or whatever, give it a try."

"Are you kidding?" Raphael started to say. "There's no way we can get a place up there." But Thaddeus had already started up the hill. And sure enough, as soon as they reached the tree, a family of four, dressed as generic medieval peasants, rose and surrendered the choice spot.

"Got to get him some beer," Thaddeus remarked.

"Great luck we got this place," Raphael said innocently.

Thaddeus turned his head and stared at him in disbelief. "It wasn't luck," he said. "I pushed him. You know, 'Go get some more beer, you so thirsty.' Like that. You just concentrate on it and shove it at them."

Raphael looked startled. "Gee, I don't think that's right, Thad."

"Listen, you got to wake up," Thad snapped at him. "And I do mean now. We've got serious work to do and I need a place to sit, so they been sittin' here a while, it be time for them to move on.

"You know, Rafe, you just don't get it. Say you given the ability to play great music on the guitar. But you don't ever do it. Fine, but don't call yourself a musician. You got to practice. Polish your moves. Otherwise you'll never be able do your thing."

Thaddeus opened up the guitar case, grumbling to the people sitting next to them, "No, I'm not gonna serenade you. Got me some panties in here is all."

At which point that family decided it was time to move on.

"Did you push them, too?"

"Didn't have to," Thaddeus said, leaning over the guitar case, looking in. The gleaming latest-version Ovation Custom Legend guitar lay snugly resting in its oversize hard-shell case. Along either side of the guitar's neck, which was inlaid with enough abalone shell to momentarily blind any innocent thief should he open the case to steal a peek, the case widened out, sporting two narrow compartments, each just big enough to accept a slender Browning hi-power nine-millimeter handgun. At the bottom was another compartment for capos, spare strings, and several clips filled with hi-power hollow points. And caressing the strings of the guitar and sort of veiling the sound hole was—what? A pair of white nylon panties?

Thaddeus picked up the panties and examined them carefully. Seeming to like what he saw, he nodded and commented, "Tools of the trade."

"Uh, whose, uh . . ."

"They yo mama's panties, Rafe."

Not having any idea what to say to that, Raphael said nothing.

"See, Rafe, I touch something belongs to someone and it talks to me. Best of all is something they wore close to they skin, and haven't washed. Years ago I fished these out of your mama's dirty clothes up at Lake Wachala and used them to trace her. Found 'em in my pocket later."

"But why do you still have them?"

Thaddeus shrugged. "You never know. I plastic-bagged 'em and stored 'em. In fact, tried using them once or twice, but got no vibes at all. Figured she just had to be dead. But you say she's alive? Let's see." He lay down in the grass and placed the panties over his forehead and down a little, shading his eyes, sighed, and remarked, "Panties my favorite."

The people on the other side of them got up and left in a hurry.

Raphael sat cross-legged, watching intently for a while, but there was just nothing to watch. So he, too, lay down and closed his eyes.

A sudden feeling of sadness settled onto him like fog. Here they were, and where was she? He knew good and well that his mother wasn't here. In fact, that his mother wasn't anywhere.

Only for a few brief moments, lately, she had been. What could that possibly mean? It hurt him to think about it. And of course he found no trace of her. After a while he sat up and watched Thaddeus, who, mouth open, breathing shallowly, looked dead. Finally, he, too, sat up and rubbed his head and sighed.

"Tell you the truth, Raphael," he said, "I'm not getting anything. I don't believe she is alive. But if you say she is, then okay, she is. But even so, we're at a dead end. What do we do?"

Raphael was aware that Thaddeus was staring at something behind him, when suddenly a bark shocked him out of his funk. He swiveled to see a scrappy-looking white bull terrier down toward the bottom of the hill, squirming happily at the end of a chain. The dog barked again, this time a staccato burst.

"The dog," Thaddeus said in his low calm voice, only somehow sounding excited. He waved his hand in the air, using Elena's panties as a banner. "What you say to a dog? Oh yeah—here, boy!" he shouted.

A string of curses rose to them from the bottom of the hill as the dog, with one superhuman—or maybe supercanine—effort, broke free and raced up the hill toward them, dragging his chain behind him. Having climbed the hill faster than either of them had imagined possible for a dog, he trembled before them in supplication to Elena's panties, taking in great sniffs of air.

"The nose knows," Thaddeus commented, holding out the panties to the dog, who began to whine in ecstasy.

"Dog knows your mama. For real, Rafe. Don't you get it? Your mama's alive, and this dog is proof of it."

Raphael was totally confused. "How can you possibly—?"

"Hey, Raphael, this is Thaddeus, you dig? This what I do—know!"

"And that's why he's so excited about the panties? But Christ, Thaddeus, he can't—there can't be any odor left on these things after all these years."

"Don't use the palefaces' god's name in vain," Thaddeus said. "I don't know how. You got to be right, but somehow he's smelling something. Must be psychic. Like me."

"What?"

Thaddeus shrugged. "Why not? I come from the South. You didn't know that, did you?"

Raphael shook his head.

"Georgia. Along the Alapaha River. Farmers got them some bulldogs there, big ones, maybe twice the size these little English bulldogs you see nowadays. And they ain't got those little crooked legs, you know? They got long strong ones.

"Anyhow, one day I was a little boy. A little poor raggedy boy. And I was as Black then as I am now. I was staring in through the fence at this farmer's front porch. Wantin' to go in and ask he let me have a glass of water, or maybe just drink from his hose. It was a hot day, and in south Georgia—well, that's an ugly kinda heat you-all don't understand. I wanted so bad to go in there, but he had himself one of those big bulldogs, must have weighed over a hundred pounds, all muscle and teeth. I could see him up there sleeping on the porch. He was snortin' and twitchin' all over, having hisself a bad dream, I guess. Anyhow, I opened the gate, real slow, and took a couple of steps in.

"Bulldog woke up and scampered off the porch. I said, 'Good boy.' The bulldog made a whining noise that sounded friendly, but just stood there watching me.

"Anyhow, I got me a drink from the hose, and headed back. The dog keeping an eye on me, but in no way threatening, just interested, that's all. Only about halfway to the gate I caught sight of the shiny red Schwinn bike the farmer's kid rode around town. And the thought popped into my head, 'I could steal it right now, ride it up to Bristol, and sell it there 'fore they caught me. Use some of the money to get a bus home.' Well, the moment that thought entered my mind, the bulldog came for me. I just barely made it through the gate, but I swear, that dog was psychic—no doubt about it."

"No sech thing as psychic." The small, portly man pursuing his dog had finally made it up the hill and waited patiently for Thaddeus to finish his story. "Sure like to see me one of those big Georgia bulldogs, though. Betcha they could whip an American pit bull terrier."

Thaddeus shook his head. "Pound for pound, there ain't nothing on the face of this earth whip an American pit bull terrier," he informed him. "And there's some pretty big ones, too. Big enough to take care of any Georgia farm dog."

"Another expert. Glad to see the Faire's full of experts on fighting dogs," the portly dog owner replied sullenly. It was only noon, but like yesterday, this guy was positively reeling under the effects of all the available ale.

"Tell you what," he continued, "Blackjack here just plain loves panties, that's all. Know why? Because he's nasty. He's nasty and he's ugly and he's not very game—to put it mildly—and he's fuckin' near impossible to hold on to. Drive you nuts."

"Now my turn tell you what, though," Thaddeus remarked. "We going to buy that dog. Got to have him."

"What the fuck, are you insultin' me? This is my dog and a man don't sell his dog. Not for a million dollars."

"Really?" Thaddeus brought out a big wad of bills and began to count while both Raphael and the dog's owner watched in amazement. Finally he finished. "Twenty," he said. "All I've got on me right now. Give you twenty thousand for this bull terrier. Know he's worth more, but twenty buy you a lot of ale. You have a little left over, buy your girlfriend a little something."

"Fuck her," the little drunk said. "You tellin' me you got twenty thousand dollars in your pocket? Twenty fucking thousand?"

"I never carry more than small change. No point tempting the fates. But here it is, twenty big ones—you keep the change."

"Shit, I'd sell my sister to you for twenty thousand dollars," the little drunk said.

"But I wouldn't pay twenty thousand for her," Thaddeus assured the guy, forking over the money.

"Come to Daddy," the drunk whined.

"Take the chain off," Thaddeus said.

"I don't want the chain."

"Take the fucking chain off," Thaddeus repeated, a mean edge suddenly creeping into his voice. "I tell you what, I've got a couple thou I held back I'll give you, you let me put the chain around your neck."

The drunk swayed, looking uncomfortable. Almost went over backwards and rolled down the gentle slope.

"No way to fasten it," he said, looking edgy.

"I'll find a way," Thaddeus said, standing up. "You want the two thousand? Come on over here."

He took the chain and handed the little drunk the money, which the little man somehow stuffed in his "Renaissance" pants back pocket, then solemnly stood there, looking very frightened, while Thaddeus wrapped the chain around his neck once.

Holding two links together, Thaddeus said to Raphael, "Fetch me the combination lock outen my backpack, would you?" He fastened the chain with the lock and said, "There you go. That for what you been thinkin'. Got yourself an ugly little mind go with your ugly little dick. Piss me off."

The drunk fingered the chain around his neck. "Pretty tight," he said. "Wha-what's the combination?"

"Know what?" Thaddeus said. "I forgot. Now get the fuck outta here. Here, get hold of the chain, lead yourself somewhere. You like a nigga slave now. Go enjoy youself."

"Hey, fuck you," the little drunk got his courage up to shout as he led himself back down the hill.

"Careful or I sic my dog on you," Thaddeus shouted after him. The pig-dog growled menacingly. Looking back in amazement, the little drunk, still carrying his chain, now turned and tried to run, but tripped and rolled. Got up gagging, and stumbled off into the crowd.

"You were pretty hard on him," Raphael said softly.

"Oh, not really," Thaddeus replied. "All the time he was thinking like, 'What's a nigger doing with all that money?' 'Nigger' this, 'nigger' that."

Raphael shook his head. "He can't help it, Thaddeus."

Thaddeus smiled. "Me neither," he said cheerfully.

"So you give him twenty thousand dollars?"

"Hey," Thaddeus said. "You think twenty thousand dollars make a guy like that happy? He be drunk all the time for a couple months, buy some dumb shit he don't need, then wake up broke about a thousand times more miserable than he ever was to start with."

Raphael shook his head again. "Then it's cruel."

Thaddeus replied, "Look, kid, it's not cruel, it's not kind. It's instant karma. He could take the money, go to a night course in scriptwriting at UCLA, and support himself while he writes a screenplay, sell it and become rich and famous. See, it's up to him."

"I see," Raphael said. Then coyly, "Running out of nigga talk?"

"Sometimes I forgets me how," Thaddeus said, suddenly sounding weary. "And as for you, you keep using the N word, I'll have to give you a fortune. Wreck your life."

Rafe smiled. "Already has, only I'm used to it."

Thaddeus said, looking quite serious, "In a way that's got to be the truth." Then to the dog, "And as for you, Blackjack—that your name, right? As in"—here he imitated the voice of the dog's former owner—" 'What kinda dumb nigger wants to pay twenty thousand for Blackjack? Dumb fucking fifty-pound dog eats and shits like he weighs a ton.' " Thaddeus grimaced. It plainly had not been fun for him to read that dude's mind.

"Renaissance Faire to that turkey obviously had some kind of connection to white supremacy—don't ask me what—and as for you, Fido, you and me goin' to get along fine. I think 'growl,' you growl; I think 'jump,' you jump."

Blackjack whined and trotted over to Raphael and nuzzled his hand.

Raphael laughed, one of those happy free laughs only the eternally young at heart can possess, causing even Thaddeus to smile. Not losing sight of the fact that, as Prince, whom Thaddeus considered the greatest of all pop composers, had expressed it, "The beautiful ones, they hurt you every time."

"Okay, okay." Thaddeus held out his hand as if to push the two of them away. "The dog be yours. Suits you, you know. Just don't go fallin' in love. Love be cruel. I'm not so crazy 'bout dogs anyway, come down to it."

The white dog was already on top of Raphael, who was still lying on the grass, and he was licking Raphael's face.

"Damn, he's strong," Rafe said, trying to fend Blackjack off.

"So are you, so toss him off and let's get our act on the road here!" Thaddeus replied. He was down on his knees now, closing up the guitar case. But he still had the panties in his left hand. "Bring Fido over here and let's see what we can do." He tossed the panties down in front of the dog. "Sweets to the sweet," he remarked. The dog crouched down, sniffed at the panties, and immediately began to whine and writhe like a snake.

"Let me try to read him first, see what I get," Thaddeus suggested. He kneeled down and put his hand on the dog's thick, muscular body.

Immediately the dog jumped into his face with unbelievable quickness and abandon, resulting in another of his remarkable head butts. Like Elena, Thaddeus went down.

"Shit," he said, sitting back up and palming his nose. "Fucking thing can jump to the moon." He examined his hand. "Bloody nose, too. Great. Good dog, Blackjack. Got a handkerchief?"

Raphael was taking all this in with obvious amusement. "Sure, I've got a handkerchief, Thad. I use them instead of toilet paper. I've also got a couple of doilies I carry around in case we're invited to tea."

"Got me some Kleenex here in this backpack," Thaddeus said, treating Raphael's jibes as if they were not worth noticing, which was his way.

Holding the wad of tissue pressed to his nose, he said, "This time you hold on to him."

There was something inexplicably pleasant about the feel of the dog's body under Thaddeus's hand: the short fur, the muscularity, the heat of life— for this creature was very much alive.

"Wow," Thaddeus said, and sat back down in the shade again. Cautiously, he removed the bloody Kleenex from his nose. "Your mama's really alive. At least that's what I get from the dog. He's seen her here. He likes her, if 'like' is a strong enough word. At least that's the feeling I get from him. I get an image, but it's not really recognizable. Dog's don't see the way we do. It's all blurry and two-dimensional. I get a strong, strong odor, but it doesn't mean anything to me. But still, the overall feeling I get is that he's seen her.

"And I got to tell you the truth here, Rafe. I didn't believe there was any chance of that. Last time I saw her she was getting zapped by Ketoko, and you could practically see her soul fly out her nose, or whatever the fuck it does. But wham! One minute Elena, next minute empty shell, next minute he waves his hand and even that's gone. Thing is, I should have been able to sense her if she was alive. That's my thing and I'm good at it. And don't think I didn't try."

"Well, what now?"

"Well, what you think now, Rafe? You 'spose to be getting in your two cents' worth, too, you dig?"

Rafe shrugged. "Let's try the obvious thing first. See where Blackjack leads us."

"Okay, why not?" Thaddeus waved the panties in front of the dog, driving him to a frenzy of joy, much to the amusement of some of the over-the-edge bawdy Renaissance drunks lying around in the shade nearby.

"Go find her, Blackjack. Good boy. Let's go."

Blackjack took off down the hill so fast he was almost immediately lost to sight, disappearing into the crowd down below, giving the group of rowdy drunks even more reason for hilarity. Raphael shouted "Blackjack!" into the wind and then turned to behold Thaddeus standing there, eyes closed, with the palm of his left hand thrust out in the direction that the bull terrier had disappeared, obviously trying—in vain—to assert some psychic control over the animal.

"Hey," Raphael projected, cupping his hand over his mouth to imitate a microphone. "Earth to Thaddeus, earth to Thaddeus, come in, come in."

Thaddeus opened his eyes and let his arm fall to his side. "Gonna need us a leash, I guess," he suggested in a forlorn tone of voice.

"Well, at least he can't get out of the Faire, can he?" Raphael wondered.

"Hey, hey, I keep yelling at you!" one of the drunks shouted.

"And I keep ignoring it," Thaddeus replied.

"Hey, fuck you, too, Jack, but tell you what—I take you to the dog, you buy me an ale? A Bass."

This seemed to drive the group to even more hilarity.

But Raphael looked interested. "You know where he was heading?"

"Oh, I think so." More laughter. "Is it a deal?"

"Deal," Raphael agreed.

"And the dude plays us a song on his guitar there."

"No, the dude doth not," Thaddeus assured the guy.

He shrugged. "Okay," he said. "Name's Byron, Jack. Your name?"

"Jack, as you suggested," Thaddeus answered him. "Look me up sometime, why don't you?"

More laughter. *Group fortune cookie for today,* Raphael thought: *"All attempts at humor will succeed." Or: "You will be a fucking clown."*

"Or: 'Your attempts to get drunk will all work today,' " Thaddeus tossed in, obviously reading his mind.

"Well, let's get with it, Byron. Not *the* Lord Byron, is it?"

"Yeah, but my friends call me Lord." This time just blowing the drunks on the hill away. As the three descended toward the food stalls, Lord Byron's compatriots were all still rolling around on the grass choking with laughter.

"First I get you a leash so's we catch him, we can hold him," Lord Byron suggested. "If we turn out to be stud enough, that is." And he was starting to laugh at that one as he felt Raphael's hand clamp down hard on his shoulder. It was hard as a vice.

"You want to find out how stud we is?" Raphael suggested, smiling his open, friendly smile. But there was a hint in those cool green eyes of . . .

"No, no," Byron assured him. "You're strong enough for a fucking elephant. I just wasn't looking at it right. Shit, that was a sobering experience."

"Hey, don't worry about it. You just do your part, the dog, the leash, and you'll have plenty to drink. But let's quit fucking around and get on it."

"And if I . . ." Lord Byron was sobering up fast here.

"If you're leading us on a wild-goose chase," Raphael informed him, "I'll punch your fucking lights out. Just like that."

"Shit," Lord Byron murmured, blinking nervously. "I'm gonna need a lot of booze to get drunk again."

But he was moving with a purpose now. "Guy over here makes leashes and collars for regular dogs, but also for bulldogs."

"That half-pig creature is a bulldog?" Thaddeus asked in disbelief.

"Some bulldog people believe that yer original bulldogs was like all these bull-and-terrier types. And that it was from these that they bred the little squat ones with the pug noses. Others believe the original bulldog was more like your country-style bulldogs come from Deep South. They call all these dogs bulldogs."

"And they need special leashes and collars?"

"You fucking better believe it. You should have hung on to that chain, 'cept it looked good around Elmer's neck like that. At last he's wearing a necktie. Show us a little class for a change."

"Who sells these special bulldog leashes and collars, then?" Raphael asked.

"Who else but Elmer Ratger himself? That's what he's doing here with Blackjack, see—advertising. Lots of these Renaissance Faire folks go for mastiffs or bulldogs, so this is a good place for it."

"And what are you doing here?" Thaddeus wondered out loud.

Evidently Lord Byron was sobered up some by what was happening here, for he replied thoughtfully, "I don't know. Getting drunk in some different type of place, I guess. As opposed to getting drunk at home." He looked sad. "Dreaming I could score here, I guess. They've got a lot of women ripe and drunk. On the other hand, I got a TV at home."

Raphael looked at Thaddeus and shook his head as if to say, *Wow, what a life.* He turned back to Lord Byron and started to say, "You'd better buckle down—" when Byron interrupted him.

"Hey, here we are already."

But Elmer was no longer there, obviously off somewhere trying to get his chain removed.

The young man who was filling in for him in his stall handed Raphael a leash.

"It's for Blackjack," Byron informed him.

The kid's eyes widened. "Shit," he said, and, taking it back, gave him the thickest leash from the wall.

"And collar?" Raphael asked him.

"He's already got a good choke collar," Byron reminded them.

But now Thaddeus intervened. "Know what," he said, "how 'bout this one? Will it fit Blackjack?" He pointed to a spiked collar hung up for display on the wall.

"Needs a size bigger," the clerk said, finding a larger spiked collar. "Here you are."

Thaddeus took the formidable-looking piece of dog attire and said, "Well, pay the man, Rafe. I'm running out of cash here."

Looking amused, Raphael pulled a wad of bills out of his pocket and paid the clerk. Then Thaddeus set his guitar case down on the counter and opened it up. Put the new collar in the bottom compartment.

"Hey there," the kid who was minding store said, "you stash bullets in your guitar case. Cool."

Thaddeus silenced him with that hard look of his. He explained to Raphael as they moved on, following Lord Byron, "Could just picture me that snow-white pig-dog decked out in this black spiked collar, and figured I could always pack it away in my case, probably won't never need it. Like the guns. But you know . . . ?" He shrugged.

The next place Byron led them to—of all places—was back to the main food area where they had just come from, only a bit farther, to the big main beer, wine, and ale stall.

Medievalists galore, in lines comparable to those one might encounter at Disneyland, clamored drunkenly for more booze and shouted ribald jibes at the bawdy serving girls, who all seemed to have imbibed at least one for every one they dished out. No question which was the most popular booth at this faire.

"Renaissance Faire, my ass," Thaddeus remarked. "Dark Ages Faire would be more like it."

But here was the white bull terrier, leaping up in the air from time to time—jumping either for joy or for ale, for every once in a while, one of the jolly fellows with a medieval sense of humor would pour a little ale on his head.

"Turn him loose, this where he goes," Byron informed them. "Every time. Loves beer, stout, ale. Don't like wine, though."

"Me either," Raphael exclaimed. "Scrunches up your stomach."

"A consensus, I see," Thaddeus said, smiling. He was picturing Raphael at a wine tasting, rolling around the precious ambrosia on his tongue, then swallowing, then proclaiming to those eagerly awaiting his judgment, "Scrunches up your stomach. This stuff sucks."

"What do you figure we should do with the dog now? Come on, let's have a little input here, Rafe."

Raphael closed his eyes to show Thaddeus he was thinking, working real hard at it. But only for a moment.

"We give him some booze, you know, mellow him out. Then we try it again."

Thaddeus nodded. "I like it," he said. "Okay, Byron, I'm going to give you a twenty here." He gestured at Raphael, who fished a bill out of his shorts pocket and forked it over to Byron. "What I want you to do is buy yourself a pitcher and bring us one over there." He pointed to a shady spot on the hill. "What's Blackjack's favorite brand, you know?"

Byron shrugged. "Just as long as it's a hearty ale," he explained. "None of that American shit. And I must admit that I quite agree with him. Nothing beats a robust British ale."

"Okay, I'll take your word for it," Thaddeus said. "You bring the pitcher over to us there, and get a cup for the dog."

The white dog trotted jauntily up the hill beside Raphael, as if he understood he was going to get his beer.

"Some animals," Thaddeus shook his head, "I don't know what, but they have something people don't really understand. Some kind of ESP or some special powers."

Raphael stopped abruptly, widened his eyes, and feigned shock. "What the fuck is this, info you got from the *National Enquirer?* 'Chicken Sees

Jesus Hanging Around the Farm with Elvis'? Some hangover from your superstitious youth in Georgia? You want to remind yourself from time to time, there's these stones—four of them. That's where all the weird powers come from. And nobody knows why. But the rest of the world out there—hey, it's as normal as apple pie."

Thaddeus shook his head, and the white dog barked, reminding them he wanted to get to the shade.

"Wrong," Thaddeus informed him as they continued up the hill. "Wrong, wrong, wrong. How many times must I inform you, both Tippi and I were gifted psychics before we ever touched the stones."

"You seem to forget," Raphael tossed back, "that you were given pieces of crystal which had been powered up by our stones. That's where your powers came from."

Thaddeus stopped and raised his hands to the heavens in frustration. "Did I not tell you over and over that we were chosen in the first place because of the psychic powers we displayed?"

Raphael shook his head. "Sorry. The world is full of people think they have psychic powers. Any one of whom can get some crackpot scientist to validate them. And if I remember right, Thaddeus, your Dr. Lindquist was as nuts as they come. No, believe me, dude, you're kidding yourself. The world is a simple, ordinary place, subject to the laws of science. The stones are storage batteries for some kind of incredible energy we do not, as of now, understand. But they are also subject to the laws of science, and one day we will be able to explain them. There is no such thing as magic—these four stones are all there is of it. The rest is all wishful thinking. Sorry, but the truth is the truth."

"But, but . . ." Thaddeus was starting to sputter, then caught himself and calmed down. "How do you explain what we just went through in Montana?"

Raphael shrugged. "We know there are other worlds, alternate universes, but there's nothing magical about any of them. They are simply an expression of the laws of physics."

He started back up the hill. For a moment Thaddeus stood there staring at his back. Then he shook his head and followed.

Soon they were sitting in the shade again, watching Blackjack clumsily but eagerly slurp up ale from the paper cup Raphael held for him.

"Believe I forgot to mention," Byron informed them, "you can't get yourself a pitcher here. In fact, they'll only give you one cup of beer at a time. That's why nobody ever gets drunk here."

Raphael and Thaddeus exchanged exasperated glances.

"So's I had to get a friend of mine to get you that other cup of ale I gave to you. Had to bribe him. There goes some of the money you gave me, but hell, I'm on you guys' side."

Raphael fished out another ten bucks, commenting, "I'm running out of change fast, so this is it."

Thaddeus swilled down the ale. His mind reeled momentarily, but quickly the effects dissipated. His mystic stone interpreted the effects of drugs as if they were a disease.

"Why you drink that stuff, anyway? You know you can't get drunk," Raphael asked.

Thaddeus smiled. "I like the taste."

Byron nodded approvingly. *Same as me,* he reckoned, putting away the ten. And now that he had the money . . . He fidgeted from one foot to the other. "Well, gettin' late and I got me some other business. Just about time for them to shut this place down, I figure."

"Tell you what, why don't you go get really drunk," Thaddeus suggested. "Don't stop till you're unconscious. We all know you're going to do it."

"Pretty mean," Raphael remarked, watching Byron stomping down the hill muttering angrily to himself.

"Didn't your mama never tell you to always tell the truth? Which remind me, the dog's had his fill of booze now and this time we got a leash on him. Let's try him again," Thaddeus said, taking out the panties. "Ain't much happening here really, but on the other hand, it is getting toward closing time, and we haven't even got going. Guess I miscalculated a little."

"Time flies when you're having fun," Raphael pointed out. "No, seriously, I kind of like this medieval set."

"Yeah," Thaddeus agreed, "nothing like the fucking Dark Ages."

So they started down the hill once again, this time with Raphael holding on to Blackjack's leash as the dog surged against it, going somewhere with almost irresistible energy.

This time Blackjack took them out of the main food section of the Faire and through the crowd to the edge of a small lake, to a stall which sold crystal balls, swords, candles, and incense, along with other medieval witches' paraphernalia. There was a rather large tent set up behind the stall which apparently could be entered only behind the counter in the back. It was straight for this tent that Blackjack was headed. With Raphael in tow, he surged at the leash excitedly and hauled him straight to the counter and, to the consternation of the serving wench tending store, tried to drag Raphael around behind it and into the tent.

"Hey, you can't go back there," she snapped. "Get that dog out of here. I mean clear out."

But Raphael, who was already behind the counter, managed to pull the white bull terrier to a stop. "No dogs allowed?" he said. It seemed unlikely.

"No Blackjack allowed," she explained. "Both of you get back around the counter, and then you take that fucking mutt out of here and tie him up or something, and you can come back here. But out front with the other customers, not back here."

But not only did Raphael not move back around the counter, he moved farther in, obviously headed into the tent, and now Thaddeus had followed them back into no-man's-land.

"Hey!" she yelled, physically getting herself between Raphael and what was obviously his destination.

Two big men, both wearing green Robin Hood hats complete with pheasant feathers, emerged from the tent. Obviously they had been in there guarding the entrance. Which made this all start to look interesting to Raphael, but at the same time made him more than a bit apprehensive. Like all natural-born warriors, he was always looking for an edge, and this sure as hell didn't feel like it was headed that way. He was trying to think fast here. But what could you do? It was closing time, and a few of the booths were already shuttered up. Go away, and come back tomorrow? Same situation would be waiting for them. And in fact, it would probably be worse, because if they had something here they wanted to keep to themselves, Raphael's interest would surely alert them. But what was it they were guarding?

Thaddeus must have been monitoring his thoughts, because the idea pushed itself most forcefully into his mind, complete, almost like conversation: *A doorway. They took your mama through here and now they guarding their backs, you dig? Forget about tomorrow. It be now or never. Fresher the scent, the better. Both for me and the dog. Let's go for it, studly.*

Raphael took another step.

Now the woman got out of the way. The bigger of the two men took a step to meet him.

"You cannot come in here," he said in a casual, yet firm tone. Both men were tall and bulky; looked like hired muscle to Raphael, medieval outfits or not.

Thaddeus smiled. "Sorry, but we really need to get in there for just a minute or two."

The slightly smaller one turned toward the entrance to the tent behind him and said, "Will, come here, won't you?"

A third man came out of the tent and joined them. He was bearded and brawny, even bigger than the first two. And instead of a Robin Hood–style cap, he wore a simple, unadorned round helmet on his head. No ornamentation on it at all, but on second look, the thing was pure silver. At the very least silver-plated, Raphael figured.

"What seems to be the problem here, gents?" the man said with a marked British accent.

"Hey, no problem," Raphael answered him. "Me and my friend here need to take a look in your tent. Just for a minute. Please, it's very important to me. You see, my mother is missing."

The big man in the helmet nodded. "Know what?" he said. "You're breakin' me heart." He punched himself on the chest to show them that he knew where it was. "But tell you what, laddies, I don't think so. You have a search warrant, fine. You don't have a search warrant, bug off."

"Know what, laddie?" Thaddeus answered him. "We don't have a search warrant but we're not going to bug off either. Want to know why?"

But the big guy wasn't biting.

"Oh, come on, blade, ask me why," Thaddeus suggested.

Now the man shook his head. "Mary," he said cheerfully, "I know it's a little early, but be a good wench and close up the shop, will you?"

The woman from behind the counter said "But—," to which the helmeted man answered, "Now! Clear them all out of here."

Grumbling and arguing a bit, the few stragglers allowed themselves to be forced away from glass cases of daggers and swords which flaunted intricate, Celtic-style silverwork on the handles. Meanwhile, both groups waited, as if by agreement. No one gave ground. No one moved forward.

At this point the man said, "Fine, Mary, now you go up front there and make sure they don't try to get back in here. Go on up there, woman. Let men do men's jobs. You do yours."

"But—"

"No buts."

She stomped off angrily to the front of the store, where she occupied herself by putting out a CLOSED sign and pulling a curtain across the front of the stall.

As soon as she left them, the helmeted man smiled and brought his right hand out from behind his back. It took a moment to register on Raphael that what the big man in the silver helmet was casually pointing in their direction was definitely not part of his costume. It was a large, heavy revolver. And it had a big round cylinder, which Raphael assumed was a silencer, screwed onto the barrel.

"Gentlemen," the helmeted man said cheerfully, "I really don't know what you're after, but methinks I'd back out of here in a hurry if I were thee." He examined them warily through squinted eyes.

"And so you shall," Thaddeus answered.

Raphael butted in with, "Hey, wait a minute, Thaddeus, this is not—"

By the time he got to the word "necessary," Thaddeus was boldly proclaiming in the archetypal manner of the confident stage hypnotist, "You cannot move. Not a muscle. Your arms will fall to your sides and stay there and you will drop the revolver."

The other two men stood there with arms at sides, looking dazed, clearly obedient subjects. But the big one wearing the silver helmet simply smiled, pointed the gun at Thaddeus, and squeezed the trigger.

The gun bucked, there was a muffled popping sound, and Thaddeus looked down at his stomach in disbelief, dropped his guitar case, groaned, crumpled up, and fell on it.

Raphael was aware of the dog whining uneasily as he released its leash abruptly, took one very quick step forward, and leaped across the distance between them, crashing into the big guy and grabbing the wrist of his gun hand. Momentum carried them on into the tent, where Raphael took in but hadn't time to register, the large white witches' circle drawn in chalk the width of the tent floor. He just held on to the gunman's wrist for dear life.

Fists smashed into his head and body from everywhere as the other two came out of their trance, and Raphael went down, but even so, he held on to that wrist. Clamped down on it, in fact, and wrenched it with such force that he jerked the big guy down to his knees along with him.

These men were taller than he was, and they were muscular men, but Raphael had managed to pack more muscle onto his frame than was humanly possible, and furthermore, these men were not particularly good fighters. He was. He expertly wrenched the wrist again, so viciously that the helmeted man howled and a loud popping noise issued from his elbow. The gun flew and skidded across the floor of the tent.

Raphael let loose his grip and tried to go for it. But after all, there were three of them. The helmeted man, who, broken arm or not, was the fighter of the trio, threw himself on Raphael, wrapped his good arm around his neck as best he could, and shouted, "The gun!" One of the other men, the one wearing the sword, reached down and grabbed hold of one of Raphael's arms, and between the two of them they immobilized him long enough so that—

The third member of their group stood up, looking ecstatic. "All right," he said, holding out the revolver. "Now get away from him."

Raphael head-butted the big man suddenly and viciously, being careful to get below the helmet. Then he wrapped his legs around the guy's waist, and in a traditional Brazilian jiujitsu move pulled the helmeted guy on top of him into the guard position and forced the guy's head down and into his shoulder.

"Get the fuck away from him!" the guy with the gun yelled, trying to figure out how to get off a shot.

The other fellow, having lost his grip on Raphael's arms, now shuffled around the two guys on the floor, trying to figure out how to get to Raphael. Should he get down on his knees and punch at him, or stay on his feet and kick? He tried a couple of kicks. It was possible to land them into Raphael's ribs, but he couldn't kick too hard without taking a chance of kicking his buddy, the man in the helmet, who now, suffering from an obviously broken nose, which had already swollen enough for the tears and swelling to blind him, as well as a broken arm, was like a rag doll that Raphael was using to ward off the gunshot. The kicks in the ribs were enough to cause Raphael to grunt, but no more.

"Will you get the fuck away from him?" the gunman shouted. Then, "Right!" as the guy backed off. It had dawned on him that all he had to do was calmly walk over there and kneel down, put the gun against any part of Raphael's body, and pull the trigger. He was almost there when the sound of an unsilenced handgun being fired crashed through the tent like a clap of thunder.

All fighting paused and everyone except the helmeted man turned to see Thaddeus standing in the doorway of the tent, pointing a Browning automatic at the man with the silenced revolver. Both men were on their feet, pointing guns at each other, but both men were swaying.

Time seemed to slow, and the strange thing was that Raphael's awareness was drawn to the white dog, who was prancing back and forth as if someone still held his leash, whining nervously. *Poor dog's a pacifist,* Raphael thought, feeling sorry for him, inappropriately enough.

Then both men fired again, almost simultaneously, and both of them stood there for another moment, their shirts being swiftly tie-dyed with their own bright blood, and then they both crumpled and went down hard.

Raphael let go of the big man's head, released his legs from around the guy's waist, and in a typical Brazilian jiujitsu-style move turned a sort of back somersault, twining his legs around the guy's arm, which he still held on to. So swiftly that before you could figure what he was after, he had broken the poor fellow's other arm, and then rolled over, trying to get away from the kick which he knew was surely coming from the guy who was still on his feet. And come it did, and it was a hard one, right in the head.

This was as close to being knocked out as you can get. It was like crawling through a red fog of pain. Only the recuperative powers generated by the stone he wore around his neck kept Raphael conscious, and he could actually feel that power flowing into him, keeping him going. His arms were now automatically protecting his head so the next kick caught him in the ribs—yes, he could feel them crack. But there was more of a pause between it and the next kick. The guy was taking his time now, aiming carefully and trying to get his whole body behind his kick. Confident. Too confident.

Raphael rolled over into the kick, so that it caught him but was partially muffled. He was able to lurch up enough to grab the guy's leg.

At first his opponent went berserk, frantically raining punches down on him, but of course Raphael tucked his chin into his shoulder, and next he felt the man's knuckles slam into the top of his head. It hurt him, but not as much as it hurt the guy who threw it. "Oh, shit!" the guy hissed, obviously learning the lesson of not throwing wild punches, but learning too late.

Raphael let go suddenly, and the man lurched backwards away from him. Automatically, as he had been taught as a child in his jiujitsu class, Raphael back-somersaulted away from his opponent and came up on his feet.

The guy with the broken arms was down on his knees and somehow going for the gun. Either Raphael hadn't broken one of his arms well enough or the guy was a born optimist, because he was scuffling around on his knees and was able—God knows how—to partially raise his right arm and stretch it out toward the gun. Raphael faked a run at the other guy, then changed course and kicked the helmeted warrior very hard in the elbow of his out-stretched arm. Heard it break loud and clear this time. The guy did not so much scream as squeal like a pig.

Raphael knew enough to resist the temptation to go for the gun on the floor. Kicked the guy with the helmet once more, flipping him like a turtle onto his back, where he lay twitching, and immediately began to circle the last one of them who was still on his feet. The circling was just a fake, though, to get the guy moving. Raphael, who planned to immediately clinch and then take the fight to the ground, simply didn't want the guy to get off a kick or punch with his feet set. Once the man's feet were moving, Raphael charged straight in and, as the guy threw a weak overhand right that flew over Raphael's head, tied him up tight.

Just as he was getting ready to throw the guy, so weary that he was sick and dizzy, what should he see but Mary Mary Quite Contrary, flying through the door of the tent with—what? A big fucking sword? Yes!

The saucy wench in the low-slung peasant blouse charged across the tent toward the two of them, face distorted with a fanatical expression, and a long sword with an ornately engraved silver hilt held up over her head, reminding Raphael for some reason of the movie *Psycho*.

He and his opponent let go of each other and flashed apart like frightened fish.

But the peasant wench with the homicidal expression was fast and merciless, whipped that sword down, and at the last moment, realizing that he could not possibly get away, Raphael tried to step inside and brought his arm around in an inside circular block. But she was so fast that she caught him with his right hand somewhere around his left shoulder, just starting to sweep, and drove the blade down hard into his right shoulder, until it hit the bone and lodged there.

This was the magic moment. This was now or never. This was three seconds left in the game, and everybody knows the ball is going to Larry or Magic or Jordan, and they have to create the miracle or die, and the whole team dies with them.

Raphael was aware of this. Aware of everything all at once. More aware than he had ever been in his entire life. Aware of everyone and everything in the tent: the white dog, prancing and whining so loud that it was almost a howl now. Thaddeus on his back in his faded green Quicksilver Messenger T-shirt, with the brilliant red design of his lifeblood spreading, blinking in and out of consciousness like a red light in the fog. Of the impact of sword hitting bone, jarring back up the blade through the woman's arms and into her body. The man with broken arms and nose who was, amazingly enough, still struggling hard to get back up and get hurt again. And yes, the one who wasn't hurt was already down on one knee and had a hand on the gun. And still Raphael's awareness spread out beyond the tent in all directions, taking in the Faire, beyond the Faire, the world, beyond the world. But as Corbo had pointed out to Ketoko, no matter how far you go, inside or out, there's always something beyond.

*Now,* he thought, and his consciousness snapped back in and focused on the blade going in and stopping. Realizing that there was no time for pain or dizziness, he continued his circular block, and hit the blade, the flat of it— yes, things were that clear in this total now that engulfed him. Hit it so hard and with such concentration and exactness that he struck it up out of his shoulder and her hands—the force of the strike had already jarred it loose—

and sent it spinning through the air, spraying his blood. In one fluid movement he leaped after it, and it was like it was in slow motion, and yes, everything was in slow motion, everything except him, and in that same movement
he plucked the sword out of the air with his left hand, and spun and whipped
the blade around as he spun and caught the poor guy's arm coming up with
the gun and then there was nothing the guy could do but stand there watching his arm bounce off the floor and wait for Raphael to spin around again
and finish the job. As he fell, spouting blood like a fountain, Raphael was already turned, watching the woman they had called Mary run for the door of
the tent.

He heard Thaddeus trying to shout out something, but it came out like
some kind of hoarse, inaudible choking. But Raphael knew what it was,
didn't want to know but knew, didn't want to do it but knew he had to do it,
knew better than to think about it, and now felt the first wave of dizziness and
weakness, but fought it off and did what had to be done.

And she was fast, but she was slow compared to him, and he brought
her down before she got around the counter in the stall.

Back inside the tent, Thaddeus was breathing as if through gravel. His
eyes opened, but did not really focus, then closed, then opened again. His
heavy lids fluttered, fighting the good fight, but then lowered again. But the
bleeding appeared to have already stopped. The mystic stone was doing its
work. Raphael figured Thaddeus would either be dead or well on the road to
healing by tomorrow. If they could live that long. If they could get away.

He turned away from Thaddeus and threw up, hard. He was aware that
Thaddeus said something else, but again he couldn't understand it.

"What?"

It was clearer this time.

"I said, not yet. Kill them all first."

"Oh, shit," Raphael muttered. But he was up and moving again, somehow. And he knew Thaddeus was right, because he was almost ready to pass
out now. Blinking in and out like a light, like Thaddeus. He caught the poor
guy with the broken everything trying to crawl out of the tent, and wondered
if he should say something, but there was nothing to say.

"What?"

Thaddeus was trying to tell him something again. "Bring the helmet.
Uh, leave the head. My guitar case."

Raphael tried to summon up the strength to get mad or argue, but again,
he knew Thaddeus was right; Raphael's shoulder throbbed clear up through
his head, and he could not think why, but knew. Later he would remember

that there was another handgun and several clips of ammunition hidden in the case. He staggered back with the helmet, the case. Somehow he was still carrying the bloody damn sword.

"Pass out," he mumbled. She had gotten the blade clear through some of the bone. A little more to the right and she would have severed his arm; a little more to the left and it would have been the head or the side of the neck.

But he had done the great thing. The surprise move that won the game of life and death. And the high from that was still working, keeping him going. Well, the high and his stone. It suddenly occurred to him that *he* might be the one to wake up dead in the morning, and not Thaddeus. The thought caused him to laugh, but it came out as more of a choke.

"Don't blow your cool," Thaddeus suggested, eyes closed. "Now get me up to a sitting position and get that sissy white pig-dog over here."

It took longer than usual, and for a moment Raphael thought they were not going to make it. But Thaddeus was the psychic genius among them, the way Raphael saw it. Far more so than Violet or he. More than anyone except maybe—the thought made him uncomfortable—Tippi.

He kept dozing off more and more, sure each time that this was it, only this time, when he came to, there it was, the doorway into another world. Somehow Thaddeus had mustered up the strength to do the job.

"This the one." Thaddeus was weary, but quite certain. "Check out the pig-dog."

The dog was doing everything possible to indicate approval short of waving flags and shooting off fireworks.

"The nose knows," Thaddeus said once again, wearily.

"Why the helmet?" Raphael snapped. "I can't carry all this shit."

"Later," Thaddeus said, reaching out. "Gimme the damn helmet and guitar case. The fuck you want with the sword? Oh, okay, give me the damn thing. I'll carry it, too. You carry me. Come on, man, it's not that far. Hopefully no one will have any idea where we've gone or what we've done. Because, baby, if they manage to follow us—"

But they did not see the figure dressed all in black, blending into the shadows, watching them from just outside the doorway into the tent, and finally following them through the entrance Thaddeus had just created into another world.

# 14

T HEY WERE ON top of a rolling hill, and it was dark now, so that you couldn't see much.

"Your mama was here. Sitting around a fire," Thaddeus mumbled. He closed his eyes, but blinked them wide open again.

Blackjack barked once in what was obviously approval and wagged his tail, or rather, his tail wagged him.

Which seemed to cause Thaddeus pain. "Listen up, Lassie," he said cruelly. "You take off while we be asleep, fetch youself a partridge for dinner, you know, take care your needs. Oh, and don't bother bringing one for me. I hate partridge and all that gourmet shit like that. Hurry up. Then you get your ugly little white ass back here and defend your masters with your worthless butt while they be sleeping."

The dog whined in complaint and began to go around and around in a circle, working the grass down, before he curled up at Raphael's feet. It made Raphael even sicker than he already was to watch him. He closed his eyes.

Suddenly he became aware that his teeth were chattering. If it was spring here, it was freezing. Like springtime in the Rockies or some damn mountains. He had just started to worry about it when all of a sudden he was warm as toast. The stone must have turned up his temperature to what it considered ideal for healing. He started to drift off to sleep.

"One more thing." Thaddeus was whispering now, but still going on, "A bedtime story. This for you, not the dog, so don't you go to sleep on me. Gotta be told, so you listen up good."

Raphael was on his back, nestled down into the tall grass, like the dog and Thaddeus. And it must have turned warm as fire, or maybe he had a fever, but suddenly sleep seemed more necessary to him than life itself. But it also seemed essential to hear Thaddeus out, so he tried to do both at once. His eyes were shut now for keeps. You couldn't have pried them open with a crowbar. But as he drifted off, the story Thaddeus was mumbling to him took on a visual clarity like a little cartoon, like the stories his mother sometimes used to tell him to put him to sleep when he was a little boy. In a strange way it was like those stories, and in a strange way it wasn't.

"There were young knights among them who had never been present at a stricken field. Some could not look upon it; some could not speak. They held themselves apart from the others, who were cutting down the prisoners at my lord's orders, for the prisoners were a body too numerous to be guarded by those of us who were left.

"Then Jean De Rye, an aged knight of Burgundy who had been sore wounded in the fight, rode up to the group of young knights and said, 'Are ye maidens with your downcast eyes? Look well upon it. See all of it. Close your eyes to nothing, for the battle is fought to be won. And it is this that happens if you lose.' "

The picture faded for both of them, the teller of the tale and the listener. And in that intense weariness brought on by their wounds, by the power emanating from their stones, focusing on healing to the exclusion of everything else, including consciousness, they were, the both of them, unable to sense the figure in the dark, dressed all in ninja black, watching them. Observing, naturally enough, their helplessness. Nor were they able even to sense yet another dimensional doorway opening up, or the three people coming through it with murder on their minds. Ordinarily, of course, both of them, but particularly Thaddeus, would have been able to sense all three— the mystical power used to open the portal, the three people, and even the murder on their minds.

Strangely enough, though, Raphael did notice how the artifices of Blackspeak had fallen away from Thaddeus's voice, how even the tonal quality had changed. *Why, it's an effort for him to speak that way,* he realized. *It's the opposite of what I thought. And when he runs out of energy, he is forced to speak in classical English.* He could hardly believe it, but it was true. And though he wondered at this, he did not lose track of the story or its significance. The last thing he saw as he drifted off was that group of young knights, their innocent faces distorted with horror at the gap which had just opened up between their idealistic vision of the glory of war and the hideous reality which had just revealed itself in all its shoddy squalor. He understood these men completely, understood that it was not just this bloody fight which had shattered them, but the fact that the gap was now open in all areas of their lives, their world. For was not their world composed of ideals? This was the gap between the way the mind thinks life should be and the way it really is. Once opened, it could not ever really be closed. Oh, time would shut it partially, but it was a door that would always be open just a crack, waiting for the next attack of reality to blast it all the way open again. And each time it was smashed, it would be open wider, and harder to shut, driving some of them to hysterical fanatical religion, some of them to drink or drugs (most of them) or other desperate attempts—not to close the door, but to blur the mind so that they couldn't see it there waiting for them, out of the corner of their eye all of the time.

Sure, there were men who could stomach this, who would eagerly throw aside their image of what should be and go for the throat of the truth from then on, but these were very few and far between. This was true enlightenment, not some religious fluff, but the worship of reality in all its horrific splendor, all the good and all the bad, at once, without any attempt to pretend it wasn't there or to alter it in any way. It was not something you could read about, or train yourself for; you only had to want it. It was right there, in easy reach of anyone. In fact, all you had to do was to stop blinding yourself, and then walk right over there to that "crack between the worlds" and kick it open and leave it that way.

Yes, he could see it so clear—in fact, it was the only thing he could see—reflected in the faces of those young knights. And if he'd had the energy, he would have chuckled now, even in all his horror, at the thought of some aspirant begging a Zen master to tell him what he must do in order to "open the door." What could you tell him or her? "Want to?" Or perhaps, "Stop closing it?" For the first time, Raphael could see it all quite clearly, but he had not even the slightest desire to go there ever again. In fact, had he been able to summon up the energy, he would have shuddered in horror at the thought. That void had opened to him for the first time up in Montana, and he had quickly slammed it back shut again. But this time!

Yes, he could see all the faces of those innocent knights quite clearly, and his was there among them.

# 15

---

KETOKO AND CORBO, right hands clasped together over the two stones, staring fiercely into each other's eyes, hustled through time and space. Since time and space were expressions of the same living thing, as Ketoko explained it, the energy created by moving through time allowed him to emerge anywhere he chose in space. Corbo paid no attention to his prattle; he didn't care how it was done. And he knew he could not allow himself to be distracted even for a moment here.

*In fact,* he thought, *this demon is the very essence of distraction,* and then he realized that that thought was only more distraction.

Reading his thoughts, Ketoko grinned, but perhaps he only grinned because he was Ketoko.

Suddenly they were standing on land. "Don't move," the old man said, sending his psychic senses out but trying to keep control of his concentration.

Wherever it was, it was hot, but unlike prehistoric wherever, it was a fairly dry, comfortable heat. They were near an ocean; he could smell it, feel it. And there were people here; yes, his senses returned to him bearing the awareness of human consciousness, highly developed consciousness. Victory?

But the excitement of that discovery, momentary as it was, turned out to be the distraction Ketoko had been waiting for.

"Yes," he hissed in a voice like the north wind as he grabbed both stones. The old man tried to hold on with both his hand and his mind, but suddenly found that he was not really standing on solid ground as he had assumed. The shock caused him to lose focus and he simply fell away from the stones a short distance, and then tumbled down a steep hillside. Sat up bruised and dazed.

"Yes!" Ketoko shouted again. "I have them both. Now I will evolve into a god. Did you think that I could duplicate myself but could not duplicate mere earth?"

"I didn't think of that," the old man admitted sadly.

And then, with a howl—again like an angry burst of wind—Ketoko went, somewhere or -when else.

"On the other hand," the old man continued, taking his old friend, the mystic black stone Yawtlée, from his pocket, "I did think that if you could generate the illusion of another body, surely I should be able to generate the simple illusion of an extra stone." And he laughed long and hard, because to him, even though life was equally cruel and short and long and sweet and sad and funny, it was the funny part that he liked the most and saw the clearest. As he had once put it to Elena, "I laugh all the time because everything you do is so ridiculous. You're just like everyone else."

"Well, little Yawtlée, here we are again. Let's see if we can figure out what 'here' means this time."

He got up and dusted himself off. There was a dirt road, a path really. He walked along it until he met another man, a fellow dressed in robes. He spoke a language that Corbo had once spoken, such a long time ago. But this man spoke it quite differently, an earlier, more primitive form. Still, with the help of the psychic power of the stone, Corbo had no difficulty recalling it from the distant past. Sometimes he would have to hesitate for a moment and coax the fellow to generate an image along with the word associated with it, but he had no doubt that he would soon be speaking this tongue as fluently as he ever had. It was ancient Greek.

# 16

---

A N ARMY OF ants, no doubt activated by the sun, was conducting its early-morning marching drill back and forth across the hills and valleys of Raphael's face when he awakened the next morning. This unpleasant situation was compounded by the ecstatic white dog, whining and licking some of them off from time to time. Blackjack had obviously not followed Thaddeus's advice and fetched himself a partridge. As to whether he had been guarding them with his life all night, who could say?

Raphael's head ached and his shoulder was stiff and sore, but it was clear to him that already the most essential parts of the healing process had been completed while he had been asleep, if you could call that coma-like state sleep. The stone had done its work. Had an ordinary person been through this, not died right off, been rushed to a hospital, pumped full of antibiotics and painkillers, and then gone through a little surgery and a rehabilitation program, he would have reached this condition months from now, if ever.

But Raphael did not stop to wonder about this. He got up quickly and hurried over to check on Thaddeus, who was by far the more seriously wounded of the two. There again, it was clear that the magic of the stone had done its work. Raphael winced to hear himself think of it as magic. It was science, he reminded himself.

The bleeding had stopped, and the bullet wounds had healed. The bullets were still in there, but he would just have to carry around the extra weight for a while. He seemed to be breathing easily and he looked quite healthy, if you didn't take into consideration the bloody, torn clothes he wore. But he was in a state somewhere beyond mere "deep sleep," and obviously nowhere near coming out of it yet. There was no shade on the hill, so Raphael took off his own ripped-up tank top and did his best to shade Thaddeus's eyes with it.

It was a fairly large hilltop they were on, overgrown with tall, very green grass, but even so, he could see that something was wrong. Over on the far side, where the hill sloped down, he could see where the grass had been trampled, and involuntarily he shuddered. He could almost taste the violence that had taken place there. Surely he had not developed his psychic powers to that degree overnight? That was Thaddeus's level of perception. So it must have been the chill in the air that caused him to shiver.

Blackjack, of course, wanted to follow him. "You stay here and guard Thaddeus," he said, trying to mentally "send" the idea. "Stay." The dog seemed to get it. He whined to let Raphael know he didn't like it, but he stayed with Thaddeus while Raphael, lugging the heavy sword with his left hand and moving his right arm in a small circular motion in order to loosen up his sore, stiff shoulder, moved across the crest of the hill to the far side, where whatever it was he could glimpse lay among all the trampled grass. It turned out to be exactly what he had been afraid it would be: more dead bodies, three more, the life obviously ripped out of them by a sword.

Holsters, but no guns. A card on one of them, on his chest, pinned there by a—what was it, some kind of surgical tool? A very small, very sharp blade of some sort.

Raphael extracted the blade, wiped it off on the man's clothes, a callous gesture he would never have been able to picture himself doing, before yesterday. But some things had changed forever, and he wasted no time or energy on being shocked or sympathetic. They were dead, and that was that for them. The only value that they had left for him was in whatever information he could glean from this sordid little task. But searching their bodies turned up nothing of interest to him. Who cared anymore that one of them was named, according to his California driver's license, Efraim? Or that he carried in his wallet only five bucks?

The card that had been pinned to Efraim's chest bore a message written in a neat, precise hand: "Happy birthday to you, from one of your secret admirers." But did not, unfortunately, mention which one. Raphael shook his head, turned, and started down the hill.

There was a road. Raphael stood in it wondering what to do. Since there were no indications, he just stood there in it. After a short while, he began to drowse off again, right there standing up, when he was brought out of it by the clip-clop of horses' hooves. Off in the distance (for the road was

long and straight) he could see a carriage coming. He tried to wave it to a
halt, unsuccessfully, but as it passed him, he caught a glimpse of someone
inside peeking out.

The chariot pulled up, and a small, slender man jumped out and trotted
back down the road to meet him. The saucy fellow was dressed in gaudy,
brilliant red silk pants and a shiny yellow blouse, the sort with billowing
sleeves. He wore a bright green cap that looked to Raphael like some sort of
colorful dunce cap. In fact, the man looked to Raphael like some sort of colorful dunce.

"Let us immediately dispense with the formalities, my friend, perform
our duties as members of the human family, and go on about our ways. For
though, as thou hast discerned, 'Looketh the part of the Fool do I, and even
beeith the Fool am I.' Yet, I am the king of Fools." He pulled up in front of
Raphael and bowed formally and elegantly. Raphael shrugged and bowed
back.

"As well as the Fool of kings. My time is most valuable and I do not
normally waste it by stopping to jabber with strangers."

Raphael nodded. "Then why did you stop?"

The little Fool literally jumped for joy. A most ridiculous little hop,
while he made with his pursed lips a loud farting noise to go with it.

"Good good good," he chortled. "He asketh the Fool the wisest of questions, thus perhaps hoping to transform the half-wit into the whole. Let us see
if it worked." He bent over deeply from the waist and closed his eyes, and
then twisted his torso into an odd and somehow yearning posture. Cupped
his hand to his ear as though listening for something coming from a long way
off. Then once again he made that loud, rude farting noise and stood back up
straight again. Smiled happily.

"Oh, alas, it hath not," he said wistfully. "Let me think. Why didst thou
stop, O Fool?" Same loud farting noise again. "No no, thinking is not the answer. Let me just say it, then, without thought, as it occurred to me. I stopped
because as the carriage passed thee by I peeked out the window and I saw
thee, but I did not see thee alone."

The little Fool fluttered his eyes for effect and then added, "There was
something perched on thy shoulder." Clearly he was waiting for Raphael to
do his part in the conversation. Raphael swallowed. For some reason he did
not want to ask what it was that the Fool saw on his shoulder, but of course
eventually he did.

"What I saw perched on thy shoulder was the dark angel of death," the
Fool said. "Canst thou tell me, perhaps, was it for thee or me? Or perhaps

even for others that thou might encounter, that causeth it to smile so and beckon?"

The little Fool's eyes grew enormous and round with fear as he waited for the answer in that dusty road.

When Raphael got back, Thaddeus was awake and sitting up. But just barely.

"A little dizzy is all," he mumbled. "Good thing nobody came after us when we were helpless last night."

"Oh, they came, must have followed us on through, but luckily we seem to have a guardian angel," Raphael explained. "Here—a little Fool that I met gave us these rolls." He tossed one to the ecstatic Blackjack, who must have swallowed it whole, and the others to Thaddeus, who caught them and scrutinized them skeptically before tearing off a piece of one to taste. "Ambrosia," he declared.

Raphael grinned, but it was a weary grin. "Ambrosia is supposed to be liquid," he pointed out helpfully.

"Manna, then," Thaddeus agreed. "A little Fool, huh? That where you got the cute hat?" Raphael was indeed wearing the bright-green dunce cap.

He smiled. "Exactly," he said. " 'At last I've found someone who's more of a Fool than me,' the man said. And gave me his cap."

"You suppose to feel bad about that, blood." Thaddeus reminded him.

"Whatever." Raphael yawned. "These rolls have to do us for a while. I feel like I'm passing out. Guess I'd better lie down again for a bit. Supposed to be a town up the road a ways. Two towns, actually, but then, alas, beyond them, no more. Oh, by the way, I hate to tell you this, but, Thad, we seem to be in medieval England."

"Let me get this straight," Thaddeus said in his deadpan manner. "You met a little Fool who gave you his jester's cap and told you that we were in medieval England?"

Raphael nodded wearily, lay back down in the grass again, closed his eyes.

"Well, in that case," Thaddeus groused, "how could we be elsewhere?" And then, to the dismay of Blackjack, he, too, lay back down and immediately went back to sleep.

*1*

IT TURNED OUT to be a long journey to anywhere from the hilltop where the two Guardians and their dog awoke later that afternoon—early afternoon, but still it was already quite cool. The air was fresh and clear, and there was a feeling of immense quiet and solitude surrounding them, as if they were completely alone in this world. Raphael had to remind himself of the dead bodies a mere stone's throw away. And of the weird little jester he had met on the road.

Thaddeus had awakened to the sound of Raphael performing his daily exercises, endless push-ups, breathing hard. "We must be at a high altitude," Raphael remarked without missing a beat.

Thaddeus looked around. "Course it's high altitude, freeze you ass at night, mountains everywhere you look. What you be thinkin'?"

Moving stiffly, he rummaged around grumpily in his backpack until he came up with a bottle of bright red mouthwash. Gargled and spat out a stream of the nasty-looking stuff.

Still bobbing up and down like a cork on a fishing line with a fish on it, Raphael remarked, "Gee, looks like you got that mouthwash stuff all over your clothes, Thad. Hope we can find you a cleaners quick."

Thaddeus looked down the front of his savaged Quicksilver T-shirt. "Oh yeah, sure," he said. "Blood and bullet holes. Damn, that be my main shirt, too. Now I can't go to the hall. Ah, well." He took off the bloody rag, then grudgingly his shorts, underwear—everything except his track shoes— and tossed it all casually into the grass. Fished out a new very similar, if not quite identical, outfit from his backpack and put it on. Then he came up with a ball of twine and methodically tied the silver helmet onto the bottom of his backpack. Slung the pack on and stood up.

"Yeah, high altitude all right," he said. "Everywhere you look, mountains. And things smell different. Stronger. I can smell stuff I can't even see. Dog must be enjoying it."

Indeed Blackjack looked ecstatic, but then, when didn't he? He was running back and forth sniffing energetically at everything. He barked, but only once, as if saying something he was sure would be understood.

"Wants us to get going," Thaddeus interpreted. "You ever get tired doing push-ups, we be on our way."

Raphael shook his head. "Never happen," he boasted. "You actually feel up to it? Long walk to the nearest town, from what I hear."

"Longer the better," Thaddeus answered. "Need some time to recuperate. I can walk a little bit, then we have to pull over so I can take a nap. And you can do a few thousand push-ups. Let me guess—your shoulder's not sore?"

"It was when I started," Raphael grunted, still pushing himself up and up. "But it feels pretty good now. I guess it helps the healing. Gets your blood circulating."

"In that case, might as well walk," Thaddeus ventured unenthusiastically. "Get my blood circulating, too. If you can stop yourself from pumping yourself up like a big meat balloon. People have popped theyself, you know."

"Yeah, you're right about that anyway. Guess push-ups just ain't going to cut it for me anymore. Get to town, find me some weights or something."

"Only took you about a million push-ups to figure that one out, too." Thaddeus remarked, setting the tone for the day. And many others that followed.

The mountain air was fresh as spring water, and at first they couldn't seem to get enough of it. But in a short time they no longer had to stop every once in a while to catch their breath; this, they figured, was probably the work of their stones accelerating their powers of adaptation. They both agreed that they were probably on a wide plateau nestled somewhere in high mountains. But this was the only thing they agreed on. For as they traveled down that long lonely road, they passed the time by arguing about everything, the dog apparently agreeing all of the time with Raphael.

"You trying to tell me Leadbelly a better guitar player than Joe Pass? You gots to be either insane or more of a nigga than I am."

Raphael retorted, "You haven't really listened to Leadbelly, while I *have* listened to Joe Pass. He was a good all-around guitarist. Very glib. Did everything a little better than everybody else. Very boring. I never once heard him do something surprising or original.

"Leadbelly, on the other hand—man. Nobody could do what he could do. A lot of it was just pure physical strength. Everybody short-sells strength, endurance. And rhythm. You would have to say that Leadbelly was the greatest rhythm guitarist of all time. Man, you listen to one of those disks they got off his last session, that big old twelve-string pounding at you like a freight train roaring into the middle your head. He made Joe Pass sound like a little old lady at a tea party. That's guitar!"

Thaddeus shook his head and muttered, "Kid's a white nigga. Nothin' worse on the face of this planet. If that's were we still at."

He remembered vaguely that a couple years ago, right after Raphael had quit college ("fucking waste of time"), the kid (he would always be "the kid" to Thaddeus) had bought a guitar. Thaddeus had been hurt because Raphael had not consulted him about it. What kind of guitar had it been? Some kind of nylon-string, quite mundane. (Thaddeus thought of nylon-string guitars as learners' instruments.)

Thaddeus knew for a fact that Rafe did not take lessons. "I just play around on it," he had explained. Along with the standard qualifier, "I'm not very good."

This was the first time he had stood up for himself and argued his point with Thaddeus. Not backed up an inch. Maybe it was a side effect of the new muscle. Thaddeus was most pleased by this development. But decided it was time to one-up the kid.

"So Leadbelly is better than Joe Pass, right?"

Raphael nodded warily, well aware that something was sneaking up on him here.

"Then how 'bout Big Bill Broonzy? You don't be tellin me Leadbelly better'n Big Bill Broonzy?"

Raphael muttered something.

"Say what?" Thaddeus said. "I can't hear you, blade." Though he actually could.

"I said I never heard Big Bill Broonzy, but he can't be better than Leadbelly, can he?"

"You bet you white ass he is. How 'bout Blind Blake?" Thaddeus was grinning happily, convinced he had the kid on the ropes now.

"I've heard Reverend Gary Davis. He's more complicated than Leadbelly, but—"

"Blind Blake better than Reverend Gary Davis. Reverend Gary be overrated."

"What?" Raphael complained. "You're kidding, right?"

"I'm kidding, wrong," Thaddeus went on. "How you tellin' me all about

guitar, but never even heard nobody? What you think about Wes Mont-
gomery, back before he got famous, you know, when he was really going
somewhere?"

"Django was the only great jazz guitarist. The rest of them are like
second-rate saxophonists."

Thaddeus was too dumbfounded to reply here.

As they traveled down the long dusty road, they argued on and on about
the merits of various guitar players. And anything else they could think of.

"So you leave the guy's big mean three-fifty-seven magnum revolver
and you bring along a fucking sword? What were you using to think with?"
(Here Thaddeus would supply a humorous possibility.)

"It's a six-gun, Thad. Two of the bullets are in you. That leaves four. I
didn't see any clips or bullets and I was too wiped out to search for them."

"That's four people you could have put a cap in."

"I could stab a hundred and fifty and this sword would still be good
as new."

"But it's no good new in the first place."

"Okay, okay, so I shouldn't have brought the sword, but what's the
point of lugging along the guy's helmet?"

Thaddeus suddenly turned serious. As usual, his speech pattern altered.
"I couldn't reach the guy wearing the helmet. He just ignored my mental
commands. But that's not all. I couldn't read him, or even feel his presence.
I figured it was the helmet doing it. And as you know, it was just that."

Raphael nodded grudgingly. A while back when they had been resting,
Thaddeus had untied the helmet and handed it to him. "Try this on, blade."
And he had.

Immediately he understood what it was like to be without the stone. At
first he couldn't put his finger on it—just a sort of dulling of the world, like
stepping from a color movie into an old black-and-white. No, more like
from a three-dimensional world into a two-dimensional model. Everything
lacked the unexplained depth it normally had for him. It had taken him a
while to figure it out. Then he got it.

"What all of us experience is not, as we like to think, the world, but only
a model of what filters into us through our senses. We don't see—out there.
What happens is that light waves bounce off what we are seeing, and our
eyes, using their sense of touch, filter these waves. Then our brain makes up
an image of what the eyes have just processed. So the world we see is really
only a picture we are showing to ourselves inside our head!"

Raphael's world picture was no longer being animated by a constant influx of information from what might have been his most colorful sense, the psychic one, amplified by the mystic stone he wore in an amulet around his neck. Objects formerly brimming with life, telling him some things, suggesting others, were now truly *inanimate*. He took the helmet off as fast as he realized this. He had not had any idea that the norms lived in such a dull world, because, even if on some rare occasion he took off his stone, there was still a lot of residual power left over from it that would linger for—who knows how long? But this "magic" helmet cut him off instantly. He shuddered. This was really depressing.

"No wonder they grow old and die so quickly," he had remarked to Thaddeus. "Take away my stone and I wouldn't want to live that much either."

But Thaddeus had only smiled knowingly. "Believe me, blade, we human beings very adaptable. We get used to everything *tout de suite*. And we all want to live forever."

"Is it because it's silver? Is it something else in the helmet? What the fuck is it?"

Thaddeus had only shrugged. How would he know?

They had not talked about it since then. "One other thing about about it," Thaddeus said to him now. "It's not just that it blocks off our psychic abilities. It's that the dude was wearing it; he knew what it would do. I could tell by his expression when I was trying to push him. He thought it was funny. Either he's from someplace where they use these helmets for just that reason, or he knew about us—our stones. I don't really think he knew about us. Just a guess, maybe, but I don't really think so. So that probably means that we are headed into someplace where people other than us have psychic powers of some sort."

Raphael looked doubtful, but couldn't argue with that logic.

"So this helmet may be important."

Raphael shook his head. "I still don't get it."

"Oh, for cryin' out loud," Thaddeus said, for the first time since Raphael had known him, causing the kid to grin. "Say I want to kill you. I'm psychic, you're psychic. I attack you psychically, you use your powers to defend."

Raphael nodded. "Right. A stand-off."

"Yeah," Thaddeus continued, "would be, only I got a friend wearing this helmet and he attacks you while I keep you busy. What you do now?"

" 'Oh, for crying' out loud'—is that what your mama used to say, Thaddeus?"

"Matter of fact, it is. What your mama used to say, blade?"

Raphael closed his eyes, then his grin grew wider and he opened them again. They were as pure green as ever, but somehow this always surprised Thaddeus. "Criminy crow crumbs," Raphael revealed.

Thaddeus stared at him openmouthed. "Are you putting me on?"

Raphael shook his head.

For a moment Thaddeus remained silent, staring off into space. And through on it into somewhere else. Then he said, in an unusually soft voice, "We gonna find your mama, blade. Put that in the bank."

Raphael was touched. Until now he had just been swept along, and had not stopped to reflect on how far Thaddeus would be willing to go for him. But suddenly he was aware that the guy was carrying around two slugs and had never even considered turning back. And he hadn't even known Elena. Had he always been this way? Raphael couldn't be sure, but he didn't think so.

"Thad, can I ask you something?"

Thaddeus looked mildly amused. "No," he said, "I don't think so."

Raphael ignored this jibe and continued: "Has the stone changed you?"

Thaddeus chuckled. "The inability to get high off drugs has changed me some."

"But I don't get it," Raphael persisted. "Why did you take them in the first place?"

Thaddeus thought about it. "Jazz," he said, and shrugged.

It was one of those rare occasions when Thaddeus had succeeded, however slightly, in striking a nerve without a great deal of digging. The kid spread his arms out in a strange gesture of irritation that spread his lats out like the wings of a bat. *More like a flying squirrel,* Thaddeus corrected his original vision, and couldn't help but grin at the image this conjured.

"Jazz is somehow linked to dope? I don't think so."

Thaddeus continued to prod. "Who the best tenor ever?"

Raphael looked thoughtful for a moment. "Coltrane, naturally." He had a wary expression, as if he might be stepping into a trap.

"I like Dexter myself, maybe Johnny Griffin, but let's say, okay, Coltrane—most everybody agree. Now, alto?"

Without hesitation: "Bird."

Thaddeus nodded. "Nobody argue with that. Somebody might throw Sonny in there with the Trane. I'm the only one crazy enough to prefer Dexter, so let's rule him out. So you left with Bird and Coltrane. Let's see what they got in common. Genius, jazz, saxophone, now what else? Can't get it? Okay, it start with *h.*"

Raphael looked as if he'd swallowed a lemon.

"Not going for it? Okay, let's throw Sonny and Dex back in. Uh-oh, big surprise, same thing. What you think? It's an astonishing coincidence, or something, right?

"Well, don't look so pissed off," he continued in a softer voice. "It's the price they paid, and I was willing to pay it. But it's a heavy one. Jazz the only thing worth that. But on the other hand, I'm pretty happy to get out of the deal. Power of the stone give you that special concentration without all that confusing ecstasy. Biggest plus of all is all those extra years to work on your chops. The big H masked the pain of living and open them up a little, but robbed them of a good third of their life. While me—who knows how long I'll be hanging around working on my chops?"

For the first time it was clear to Raphael how much wiser this revelation of Thaddeus had been than his own. After all, you could only build so much muscle, then you leveled off, and that was it. But you could get better and better at the guitar for as long as you lived. Which would be . . . It was too much for him to comprehend—too many paths opening up into all directions for him to begin to follow through on this now. He would have to store this magnificent revelation for when this . . . he couldn't think what to call it; after the horror of the first battle they had barely survived, "adventure" was hardly the word—"war," maybe. Yeah, he would have to store it until the war was over, and then go to work on it.

"I never would have thought of the power of the stones as being like dope," he mused.

"It is dope," Thaddeus answered in a low voice that was almost a whisper. "And we are addicted. But at least it be primo."

The first day they were still weakened and recuperating from their injuries, so they were only able to hike down the dirt road for short periods before they felt the need to stop and rest. This usually resulted in another brief interlude of almost comalike sleep. But as long as they were conscious, they argued.

"This be medieval England, you figure?"

Wary nod.

"Because he say 'methinks' and 'thee' and 'thou' like some Errol Flynn movie, and got hisself all done up like a court jester?"

"He was a court jester," Raphael replied. "And who is Errol Flynn?"

"Let me see, can I assume that in your brief but charming interlude with education, history was not your forté?"

Raphael smiled. "Nor French," he replied. "But I see you've lost your Blackspeak again. This must be where you tell me how good you were at history."

"Good at everything," Thaddeus responded. "In fact, I was fly at school, but at history not so fly."

"To be fly, or not to be fly," Raphael declaimed.

Ignoring him, Thaddeus went on, "But you don't have to be good at history to understand that we cannot be in ye olde England because of the changes which have taken place and are even now still taking place in the English language. If you went back to England before the time of Shakespeare, you wouldn't be able to understand the locals' English any more than if it were French. It wouldn't be just a little odd, it would be a totally different tongue. Like take the adjectives 'fly,' 'boss,' 'def' all meaning the same fucking thing, all usages that have occurred during your lifetime. Some words like those—of which there are hundreds—will die out. Others will hang in there. The language is not only changing, it's changing so fast that older people can't understand the younger ones."

They had stopped walking, and Raphael, clearly amazed by this whole notion of constant flux, said, "Well, those words are because of the influx of Black culture, though, right?"

"What you think 'Anglo-Saxon' means? It means you got the language of the Brits—you know, the savages who painted their faces blue?—mixing with the languages that the Angles and Saxons, Viking tribes, spoke.

"Then come the Danes. Give them a big area in the north called the Danelaw, still got some Scandinavian place-names and speech patterns going on there.

"Now come the Norman Conquest. You dig? The Normans are Norwegian Vikings whose language is now French. But it's got to have some of their original tongue slipping in there, right? Then they take over England.

"Those languages all be stirred into your Anglo-Saxon stew. Hundreds of years, all the time, dig? So what I'm trying to tell you is that it has always been this way, Blacks or no Blacks, and no way could you understand someone from merry olde England. If you don't believe me, we get back, go get yourself a copy of Chaucer in its original form, and dig in. I'd like to see that one."

"Maybe the stone?" Raphael suggested. "Mom said old man Corbo could use it to understand foreign languages somehow."

Thaddeus shook his head. "You'd know it. Be aware it was happening. No, I guarantee you, we someplace else."

But Raphael wouldn't buy it. "No way. This is ye olde England, all right, and you'll realize it soon enough. Got to be somehow the stone that lets me understand the language. But we're in England, I guarantee you that."

"England," Thaddeus muttered under his breath, "the mountains of jolly olde England. Right!"

"Well, there are mountains in Wales, aren't there? Scotland?"

That night they slept by the side of the road, really hungry and really cold. But in a short while they could feel the power from the stones rev up their metabolisms, and soon they were comfortable enough, with the white dog curled up between them, against Raphael's side,

"Do you realize," Raphael was explaining to Thaddeus, "that all this time we've been putting on warm clothes and sleeping under blankets, if we'd just waited a few minutes we wouldn't have needed them? We could probably walk around naked in a snowstorm."

"Do look that way," Thaddeus admitted grudgingly, obviously searching for a way to argue and not finding it here. "All those stories about Tibetan lamas who spose to be able to melt the snow with their bodies and sleep outside in the Himalayas in below-zero weather. Maybe they true."

"What stories?" Raphael looked astonished.

"Oh, come on, Rafe, even you must have heard stories about Tibetan monks: Red Hats, Yellow Hats?"

"Red Hats, Yellow Hats?" Rafe repeated in his standard amazed fashion. "You're putting me on."

"No, I am not putting you on. Yellow Hats the good guys. Red Hats the Nying Mapas, they the bad guys. You know, you really have to pick up a book or two and have a peek at them, we get back."

Rafe shook his head. "Red Hats are the bad guys, huh?"

"We talking really big hats here." Thaddeus demonstrated with his hands.

"You're putting me on," Rafe insisted. "Listen, we get back, I'll make you a deal. I'll read whatever you want me to. You come with me, we'll go to Tibet and see for ourselves. Nying Mapas," he repeated in awe.

And Thaddeus was still telling him stories of the frightening magical Red Hat priests of Tibet when they encountered the first group of fellow travelers on the road.

There were seven of them, all men, all on horseback. They came down the middle of the road, moving at a leisurely but steady pace. Two of them sported falcons on their shoulders, and one of them was holding on for dear life to the long leashes of two very large, very ferocious-looking dogs that somewhat resembled the modern great Dane.

When the dogs saw Blackjack, they growled and surged at the end of their leads, causing their handler to pull his horse to an abrupt stop and, even though he was of slightly more than average height and quite stocky of build, almost jerking him out of the saddle. One of the other men, dressed in what looked like a dark red velour Robin Hood outfit, complete with cap and feather, shouted:

"Get thee thy ugly cur off from the road before I loose my doggies on him. And on thee as well," to which he added, seemingly as an afterthought, "Or I shall trample thee and take much joy in it." At this, his crew of merry men had a great laugh; even one of the horses pranced and whinnied happily as the whole group pulled to a stop and let their leader move out in front.

These men had come down the road from behind, and Thaddeus and Raphael had not heard hoofbeats until they were almost on top of them, so the whole affair was rather startling. Not startling enough, however, to send them scurrying off to the side of the road shivering in awe. In fact, they looked at each other, obviously more amused than afraid, and Thaddeus remarked, "No silver helmets, right?"

"Nor big red hat," Raphael answered.

"Though he do have a funny-looking little Errol Flynn one with a feather in it."

The man facing them from the back of a tall chestnut stallion was quite handsome in an aristocratic way, with long blond hair, a silky reddish-blond mustache, and deep blue eyes. He had very pale skin, or at least had started out that way. It was quite red now.

"Bitters," he shouted in a crisp, rage-filled voice, "loose the dogs!"

"Beg your pardon, my lord," the pleasantly homely, stout man minding the dogs said. "It's just 'at I hates to see a doggie get 'isself hurt. Mayhaps we can—"

"I said loose the doggies, imbecile. Now! And consider thyself demoted to—"

"I know, I know," the man called Bitters said, and dropped the leads.

The pale-faced man's horse reared dramatically as he shouted in his theatrical voice, "Slasher, Demon, at them! Kill!"

The two big dogs immediately whipped around and ran away as fast and as far as they could run. Which was surprisingly fast, and very far. Thaddeus nudged Raphael with his elbow and winked.

"What? What . . . ?" the handsome man in red stammered as he wheeled his horse around and watched his dogs rapidly disappear from view.

Thaddeus, unable to hold back any longer, broke up laughing, and Raphael quickly followed suit.

The aristocrat turned back to them. "You dare?" he choked in a low whisper filled with rage, "to laugh at me?"

This caused them to laugh even harder. Shaking his head and regaining some of his control, Thaddeus informed him innocently, "Man, I never did see no sissy dogs run that fast in my life. Right, Rafe? They just took one look, and . . . whoosh! They gone! Pretty big, too. Be afraid this little white dog. I don't know, man, they always say, 'Like master, like dog,' you dig?"

Now the picture of icy rage under control, the man in red dismounted slowly and deliberately. When he stood facing them in the road, he said, again in that hoarse whisper, "I swear by the Goddess's teats, the two of you shall taste my blade. Prepare, varlets, to die."

"He call you a fartlet or something, Rafe. You going to let him get by with that?"

Raphael spread his arms wide. "Okay, okay," he said. "I admit it, I'm a varlet. But can't we just forgive and forget?"

More laughter. Even the sturdy dog handler, recently reduced to stable boy, started to chuckle, then quickly clamped his thick hand over his mouth. "Sorry, your lordship, but they are funny," he mumbled.

Hand on sword hilt, his lordship tossed a glance back at the man he had called Bitters and informed him, "For thy inept training of my dogs, thee shall be horsewhipped. For your giggling—" He paused, thinking it over, and then shrugged. "Thou shalt be horsewhipped again. But very hard. And as for thee, the two of thee, it may dismay thee to realize that thou hast just offended the finest swordsman in the land, none other than myself. And know thee that whenever I draw my sword, it refuseth to go back into its scabbard until it hath tasted the blood of my enemies."

"But what difference does that make when your sword is stuck in your scabbard and you can't get it out?" Raphael wondered. "When it sticks in there like it's glued?"

And indeed, the elegant master swordsman did seem to be straining. His aristocratic face was now a deep red, with a purple vein pulsing across his forehead like a miniature fork of lightning. Unable to pull, he jerked and stumbled, but could not for the life of him get the sword out.

All at once he simply gave up and relaxed. "So be it," he said surprisingly. "Thou hast won. Indeed only by the fiendish use of witchcraft most foul, but thou hast won. Do not think for a moment, however, that ever shall I forget or forgive thee. I shall keep my eyes and ears open, and one day I shall come upon thee with my sword out. Then I shall carve thee up like two fat partridges for my table. And as for thee, Bitters . . ."

"Horsewhipped, sire," Bitters reminded him.

"Exactly," Sire agreed. "It shall be my first task when we arrive home. It will refresh me and I shall keep up the whipping until I am inspired with a plan for my revenge on these two knaves. Alas, this may take me quite a while."

"Uh, sire, all due respect . . . I . . . I quit," Bitters stammered. "There, I said it, and it's glad I am. No more kicking around poor Bitters. And all that horsewhipping, you'll have nothing left for the horse. I never hired on to be a whipping post. Nor a stable boy. Nor a dog handler, either, for that matter. So, I quit. I am giving your lordship notice as of . . . right now."

Bitters's former lord and master rolled his eyes to the heavens, mumbling something on the order of: "Oh, dear Mother in heaven, how you must hate me. But thy will be done, painful as it usually is for me."

Then he addressed his former servant again. "Oh, no, no, my good man Bitters, I shall not horsewhip you. As a reward for all the service you have given me, I shall slice you up like . . ." Then he was back struggling with his sword again, jerking himself around as if doing a comic dance in the road. ". . . a pie. A big, ugly—very ugly—meat pie."

Two of his men were now busy experimenting with their own swords, with similar results. One of them jerked about so frantically that his horse reared, throwing him off.

The man got back up and dusted himself off and then remarked casually, "It's no use, sire. I'm afraid it's something in the air. One simply can't take one's sword out here."

At this the man in red whirled on him and fairly shouted in his face, "It is not something in the air, fool, 'tis witchcraft most evil, and these two are its source! Canst add two plus two together?"

For a moment the poor fellow looked as if he were busy working out the mathematics in his head. He clearly mouthed the word "four." Then he shrugged and got back up on his horse again. He seemed to be saying, "If you can't get it out, get on with it."

The lord and master turned back to Raphael again and said, "Very well, then, I am forced to go my way, but I shall not forget the two of thee. Nor shall thy insolence go unpunished, Bitters." He bowed elegantly. "Gentlemen, as I take my leave, allow me to introduce myself. I am Hugh Marshal, the Baron of Renbourne, known far and wide as Hugh Redblade, and I swear on my proud name, we shall meet again."

That said, he took hold of his horse's mane and vaulted into the saddle, causing a series of exclamations from his men such as "Best I ever seen him do it," or "Ain't he athletic, though."

Unfortunately, the horses wouldn't go anywhere. Two of them whinnied and pranced, and one of them reared up—the same one, throwing off the same rider—but none would move on down the road.

Sir Hugh held his forehead with his hand and closed his eyes. "Surely 'tis all a dream," he muttered under his breath. "A most terrible, hideous nightmare."

"But which one of us is dreaming it, my lord?" the one who kept getting unhorsed said. "I do hope it's me."

Thaddeus and Raphael were still trying to get control of their laughter, but not really trying all that hard, and finally Thaddeus managed to calm down enough to say, "Looks like your horses been bewitched. Just like your dogs. Luckily, I can remove the spell for you. Cost you, though. Bunch of coin of the realm, whatever that be."

Without a word, Lord Hugh of the red blade untied his money pouch from his belt and tossed it into the dirt. Then the riders immediately broke into a gallop down that long, empty road. All except one, that is.

"Gentlemen," Bitters said slyly, "now that I'm to be working for you, I regrets it, but I must ask for a small advance on my salary. Just a pittance. Enough perhaps for a few pints—which is why they calls me Bitters—a whore, and a bath when we gets to town. Oh, and a meal. A big meal if it please you, kind sirs."

Raphael started to protest. "We don't need—"

Thaddeus interrupted him with a hand signal. "We hire you, just what you do earn your keep?"

"Many things, sire. I can take care of your ugly white dog, though he certainly has the look o' someone gets in a bit o' mischief now 'n again. I could take care of your horses, if you had horses. I could instruct you in the art of speaking the English language properly. Beggin' your pardon, sire, but your way o' speakin', it is most base. Or I could—"

"This is England, then?" Raphael butted in.

"Most certainly. Where else? You goes straight up that road there till pretty soon you see Greenstone Castle, way up on top a high hill. Well, a little way up a hill. Then you keep on hoofin' a bit and you find yourself in Sou Wiccingham Village. 'At's where I come from. And then a ways further you cross the Wiccingham River, and you come to Nor Wiccingham. That's posh, that is. Live there meself. Well, used to before I up and quits."

He shook his head sadly. "Only one in me family to make it to Nor Wiccingham. Then I had to go and quit. On the other hand," he said, suddenly looking a bit happier, "he'd've probably beat me to death, I hadn't quit. Guess I made a pretty smart decision, when ya take that one into consideration."

Thaddeus nodded in agreement, waited along with Raphael for more. But no more came.

"Ah, I agree with you," Raphael tried. "So we're in Nor Wiccingham. We keep going. Then what?"

"Well, there's Ironwall Castle. It's on the other side of town. But I wouldn't go there if I was you."

"And . . . ?" Thaddeus gestured impatiently for him to go on.

"And what?" Bitters wondered, looking completely puzzled. "That's it."

"That's England?" Raphael and Thaddeus exchanged glances.

"That's what's left of it. Used to be bigger, they say. But I don't see how. Any way you go, you run into mountains. Can't get over 'em, under 'em, or through 'em. Ya see?"

"So," Thaddeus took over the questioning, "this is all there is. Then we must be the only strangers you've ever seen, right, Bitters?"

No answer. Bitters was still eyeing the coin purse that his former lord and master had been forced to abandon. In fact, he was practically drooling.

"Tell you what, time out," Thaddeus said. "You go pick up the purse over there and take what you want of it. Toss the rest to me, okay? Then you settle down and pay attention and answer some questions for a while. Right?"

No answer. Then, in a gasp, "Take what I wants? You must be daft. What if I wants it all?"

Raphael said, through gritted teeth, "Take it all, Bitters, but you'll have to treat us to lunch when we get to town, okay?"

Bitters, obviously restraining himself, walked casually over and picked up the purse from the road, peeked in it, and couldn't hold back a little moan of ecstasy. Tied it on his belt.

"You may ask me anything," he offered.

"Then we must be—"

"Pretty rich are we," Bitters finished.

"Yes, yes, we're filthy rich," Thaddeus conceded. "Money is nothing to us. Nothing at all."

"Then we, uh—forgive me fer not puttin' this in the delicate manner ta which I'm sure yer accustomed—we really are some kind o' wizards or somethin'? That stuff back there, they wasn't just . . . acting. Am I right?"

"Yeah, you're right." Raphael gestured impatiently. "We are wizards. The most powerful in the world, okay? Now—concentrate. Strangers? Wouldn't it shock you to see strangers, like us, for instance?"

Bitters looked puzzled. "You're strangers? No wonder as you don't talk proper. But I'll fix you up, I will. Thought you was maybe just some posh upper-class folk out of Nor Wiccingham, dressed up funny, wandering around on foot all over the place, lookin' at eagles or somethin like 'at. But we see our share o' strangers here, some of 'em talkin' even funnier'n you.

Fer instance, the witches bring 'em in sometimes from wherever they come and go from, with all their strange but, uh, religious doin's.

"And of course there was the dead uns you left behind you back a few miles in the road. That's one of the reasons the baron were in such a foul mood. Spooked the horses, they did. And the birds, can't get the falcons to hunt when there's all that good flesh to eat just layin' there. Mother forgive me for expressin' meself so openly." He rolled his eyes piously up at the heavens. "Expressin' meself at all, really." Looking a trifle bitter here.

Raphael and Thaddeus exchanged glances.

"Ah, you mean those bodies up on top of that big hill?"

Bitters smiled. "No, we found those, too. These was later on. The falcons, you see. Any dead bodies around, they'll find 'em for ya."

"The ones you found in the road, could you tell how they'd been killed?"

"All whacked to pieces with a sword, same as the others. How else?"

Thaddeus and Raphael exchanged uneasy glances again. Then Thaddeus kneeled down and unshouldered his guitar case. Opened it and took out a handgun. "Ever seen one of these?"

Bitters blinked. "Don't think so," he said. "Ugly, though," he added. "Nasty-lookin' thing, that."

"They"—Thaddeus paused, searching for the right word—"throw, they throw little pellets that can kill people."

Bitters shook his head and looked unconvinced. "They must throw them awful bloody hard, then. Think I'll stick w' old faithful here." He reached back and patted the simple, unadorned sword he wore strapped behind his shoulder. "By the way, I don't never brag or nothin' like that, but I have to tell ya that I'm just about the best swordsman ever tipped a pint o' good strong ale."

Thaddeus and Raphael smiled.

"Thought that was supposed to be your former boss, Hugh Redblade?" Raphael said.

"Well, he's pretty good, I won't deny that, but I'm better. I taught him everything he knows, ya see. When he was young. Then he demotes me down ta groom or some sech. Can't even remember anymore. Had so many jobs ya can't count 'em. Each one of 'em a demotion."

Thaddeus reshouldered his guitar case and they started down the road again, Bitters leading his horse as he walked beside them.

"Nice o' you ta carry all that stuff on yer backs like 'at so old Henry here won't hafta carry em."

Thaddeus studied the man's expression, but it was, as always, utterly deadpan.

"Bit of sarcasm there, Bitters?" he wondered, as he and Raphael shrugged out of their packs and tried to figure how to tie them on the horse.

"Here, let me do that," Bitters said, obviously at home with this chore. "As I told ya, I've been a groom, stable boy, you name it." He held up the silver helmet which had been tied to Raphael's pack. "By the by, you bein' strangers and all, let me tell you. This thing's illegal. Don't nobody allowed to 'ave one o' these things unless they be in the company o' Wicca. And since witches is all dressed up in green almost all the time, that pretty much leaves you out. If I may be so bold?"

Raphael gestured cavalierly. "Oh, by all means."

"We wrap it up so's you can't see what it is, and then maybe we can find someone fool enough to buy it. We gets richer and he gets dead."

"Witches wear these?"

"Actually, it's usually their bodyguards wear 'em. You know how it is, keep other witches from turning them on their masters, I guess."

"Yeah, that makes sense," Raphael admitted.

"Well, everybody knows that, 'cept you o' course. You two being strangers and all."

"So you *have* seen strangers here before," Thaddeus continued, as once again they started down the road.

"Every great once in a while someone makes it over the mountains. Lowers themselves down with ropes, see? You can get down here, but ya can't get back up. Mostly they don't even speak English. Not even all chopped up ugly like you speak it. They jabber like geese or ducks. Some sorta cacklin' language."

Thaddeus nodded. "You don't seem surprised to see a Black man. You've seen one before?"

Bitters looked surprised. "What?" he said. "Ya mean you? You're not black. Sorta brown. We call 'em darkies. Plenty o' them. They come over here wif us in the begginin' when we escaped the religious oppression." He wrinkled up his nose and grimaced. "Everybody was gettin' around to wor- shippin' some god was a man, back there in the old country where we come from. At least that's what they tell us. Ugly thought. But anyway, they was some darkies come over here with us, and we treat 'em as equals. Well," he amended, "sometimes. But me?" He patted his chest proudly. "Some of me best friends is dark-skinned."

Thaddeus and Raphael exchanged amused glances.

"All this talk about language," Raphael said, trying to keep him moving along, "all these 'thee's' and 'thou's.' How do you know when to say 'thou' and when to say 'you'? I would find it most confusing."

Bitters grinned. "Got it wrong there. Couldn't be simpler. 'Thou' is correct every time. A gentleman never says 'you.' It's ugly slang. All you have to do is to remember that and you'll talk like a king, you will."

Thaddeus shook his head. "But 'you' is becoming more popular, right?"

Bitters thought that one over, looking a little displeased. "Well," he said hesitantly, "only with the lower classes. Myself, I always say 'thee' or 'thou.' Surely you must have noticed—" He slapped himself loudly on the thigh. "There I've gone and made meself a mistake there. Must be from all this pressure and changin o' jobs."

A ways further down the road, after listening to Bitters's comparison of the various taverns of Sou Wiccingham and Nor Wiccingham, Raphael suggested, "You know, Bitters, if you're really good with that sword, maybe you can teach me a little. I'll teach you some hand-to-hand fighting in exchange."

Bitters smiled. "Thanks anyway, got me own hand-to-hand style. Tavern brawling, I calls it, and ain't nobody much wants to find out just how deadly it is. How come yer wearin' that fancy sword if ya can't use it?"

Raphael paused for a moment, as if thinking seriously about his answer. "I took it away from my enemies and killed four of them with it."

"Well, then, you must know how to use it. I mean, what's the main criterion that we're judgin' by here, I ask you, if it ain't killin'?"

"Actually," Thaddeus broke in, "my main man here just went crazy and beat them senseless with his bare hands. You know, broke their arms and such. Then it was easy to kill them with a sword."

Bitters nodded sagely. "Not a bad way to go about it. Makes a lotta sense when ya think it out. Then ya don't have to go through all that silly prancing around.

"Still, no hard feelin's and all, but you're a big un, and all you darkies are strong and quick. You bein so recently civilized an all. But your friend here, he isn't so big or tough lookin', and his skin's almost as white as me own. Oh, he's stout, all right, maybe even a wee bit more than me, but he's shorter 'n me. So I can't honestly say's I see him as much of a barroom brawler. Sure it weren't you doing the fighting? Be glad to teach either of you a few tricks with the sword, or"—he looked at Raphael a bit disdainfully— "even some o' my fist-fightin' tricks."

Raphael looked at Thaddeus and shook his head. "Time out," he said. "This will only take a minute." And then to Bitters, "Come on off the road here with me." He led Bitters off a short distance into some tall grass.

"Now, fight with everything you've got."

Bitters looked nervous. "I don't want to hurt you."

Raphael actually laughed. And Thaddeus encouraged Bitters with, "Believe me, you're not going to hurt anyone. Better go all out, or my man Rafe kick your butt so bad we won't be able to find it. Give it back to your mama to cherish."

"All right, you ast for it," Bitters growled, putting up his guard in a strange, old-fashioned-looking style with his fists turned inward. He began to prance.

As all practitioners of Brazilian jiujitsu are most likely to do, Raphael began to circle to Bitters's left, then almost immediately threw a sloppy, low kick which wasn't really intended to land. As Bitters tried to ward off the kick with his hands, Raphael charged in and clinched with him. A few seconds later and Bitters was down on his stomach with Raphael on top of him, applying a Brazilian choke hold.

"I can't believe it," Bitters complained when he was able to walk again. "Ya almost killed me wif 'at bloody choke. Never seen nothin' like it. But I'm willin' ta bet all my coins ya can't do it again now's I know about it."

A few seconds later and he was down on the ground again, this time on his back with his arm scissored between Raphael's legs—just one jerk away from being cleanly broken at the elbow.

"I still can't believe it," Bitters said, staggering up and putting up his guard again. "But since that was an arm lock, and not a choke hold, you're going ta have ta—"

So instantly Raphael swarmed him and threw him, mounted, and slapped him in the face until he turned over on his stomach to protect himself, and then elbowed him on the top of the head to daze and distract him, then slipped his arm underneath his chin and choked him out again.

"I can't believe it," Bitters said when he was back on his feet again. But this time his voice was only a hoarse whisper. "You must be the greatest fighter in the world." He began to cough, and Raphael patted him good-naturedly on the back.

Thaddeus took all this in with a wry expression. "Can't you do some kind of mystical jiujitsu healing on him and heal him up again?" he wondered.

Raphael smiled but shook his head. "I could put him out of his misery, though."

But here Bitters, ruefully holding his head, suggested, "How 'bout all that magic. I'm gettin' one hell of a headache comin' on here, what with all that poundin' with your elbow and slappin' across the face." He sighed in ecstasy as Raphael placed the palm of his hand on his forehead and directed the healing power of his stone through it. It only took a few seconds and Bitters was back to chattering their ears off with stories about his experiences in the pubs of Wiccingham.

And now, as they were continuing down the road again, when Thaddeus could get a word in, he confessed to Raphael: "You know, studly, you surprised the hell out of me. I'm the one took you to all those Brazilian jiujitsu classes, at least the first year or so. I'm the one suggested it in the first place, but you never seemed that good at it to me."

Raphael nodded, thinking about it. "I was, though. To start with, you got me one of the greatest martial arts teachers in the world, Rickson Gracie." (This was pronounced "Hickson," for some reason Thaddeus could never figure, instead of with an *r* sound.) "And I stuck with it and I learned it well. I had to. I wasn't big, strong, or quick."

He nodded as if he had just convinced himself. "I was slow learning it at first, but by the time I stopped going regularly, I was plenty good at it. But now, Thad, now I've thrown on maybe a hundred pounds of muscle, practically overnight. I'm like Superman. I don't think anyone could take me now. Know something?" He shook his head and smiled. "All those techniques that I knew so well, but that used to be so hard for me to apply? Everything is easy once you're strong enough."

"Spare me, Tarzan," Thaddeus retorted. "My gun is all the strength and skill I need."

"A lot of good that did you back at the jolly old Faire."

"Yeah, you got a point," Thaddeus admitted.

Bitters, looking quite dubious, said, "Gun—'at's the thing throws around little pellets, is it?"

Thaddeus shook his head. "Ah, Bitters," he remarked, "man don't believe nobody. We go out here in the grass and I put a cap in your butt. Convince you, right? Or you already beat up enough by Tarzan here? Maybe you can wait till tomorrow, when you're feelin' your oats again."

"Tomorrow," Bitters explained grimly, "I'm not about to be feelin' me oats—if I get yer meaning there. I'll be sore all over and all bruised and swollen up. Figure I'll get it all over with today. So what I means ta say is, all right, let's go out there and we'll see whether you can throw little pieces of metal outta that gun thing fast enough ta stop me."

Raphael laughed.

Thaddeus just shook his head. "Believe me, Jack," he said, "you be a lot happier not knowing. And no, you are not going to be sore, bruised up, or swollen. When we heal you, you be healed all the way."

Bitters shook his head in wonder, but still looked a little doubtful. "We'll see," he insisted.

They continued walking for a long time more in silence, while Bitters carefully monitored himself for any aches or pains, and Raphael and Thaddeus speculated on where the hell they were and where they were going.

At last, just when they were starting to get the sensation that the towns and castles Bitters had been describing were mere myth and they were just going to go on walking down this endless road to nowhere forever, they came around a curve, and there was aptly named Greenstone Castle, sitting pretty atop a low hill.

"There she is. We're almost there now. See off around that curve in the road up there? Well, ya can't see it, but there's a nice little inn there. The Dog and Cat, it calls itself, from the old days back when we had all those pit fights. Nice place it is, even if it be a bit rustic for me own taste. Nevertheless, it brews up a nice creamy brown ale." He looked at Raphael slyly. "Like a young maid, she is, w' her skirts gettin' tossed up a bit by the wind. Big teats," he added wistfully.

"Why, Bitters," Raphael responded, "you turn out to be a connoisseur. Who would have guessed? But the Dog and Cat—you're telling me they pitted dogs against cats in fighting pits? Did the, uh, cats ever win?"

After a short but thoughtful pause, Bitters answered, "No I don't suppose they did. But you know what it's like. It's a cruel world. But look on the bright side. Now we only pit dogs against dogs."

The white dog Blackjack perked up his already perked-up ears, looking interested.

Another silence. "And sometimes the dogs win," Bitters added. "Then again, sometimes they lose."

With that sobering thought in mind, they continued down the empty road toward the inn around the bend.

# 2

THE OLD MAN lived for a long, long time in ancient Greece. Some of it he liked and some of it he didn't. And that in itself struck him as suspicious. Hadn't it always been his nature to enjoy it all, regardless of how it affected him personally? Hadn't he always been somewhere outside himself? (In fact, hadn't he been his whole universe, watching himself and thinking stuff like, *Ha ha, look what happened to that old fool Corbo. Won't he ever learn?*)

He just couldn't remember anymore. Living in ancient Greece seemed to have somehow greatly diminished his ability to remember, and also his ability to reason. He supposed the lack of one was due to the lack of the other, but he couldn't say for sure. What, me worry?

Why living in ancient Greece should have any effect on one's memory or reasoning he had no idea, but there it was. Sometimes he forgot who he was or what he was supposed to be doing here—well, most of the time.

But all this did not stop him from doing his "fountain of wisdom" routine for the local yokels.

"No, no, no," he tried to explain. "How many times do I have to tell you, it's not 'Know thyself.' It's 'Be aware.' Just be aware."

Plato looked puzzled. "But be aware of thyself?"

The old man rolled his eyes to the heavens. What philosophical lightweights these ancients were.

"All right, all right, that's okay to start with, see? But after a while you've got to see that everything is yourself. I mean it's obvious, isn't it?"

Plato's expression said, *I don't think so.*

"Sure, look, it's you seeing it all, smelling it all. For you there's no universe except for your perceptions of it all. See—you're relating to stuff. Okay, but here's the funny part. Stick with it long enough and it becomes clear that even though you're everything, you don't really exist, see? You're an idea. Get it?"

Plato's expression said, *Never have, never will.*

"Sure, you just need the speed to catch it. It happens right at the start, and you've got to catch it then. At first there's only consciousness—and that includes all the objects it's perceiving. Then all of a sudden it tries to split itself into an observer who's separate from what he's observing. Get it? You have to be quick enough to get it right there, where the split is taking place. Adam and Eve getting thrown out of the garden. Putting on clothes. All that."

Plato looked especially puzzled. "Who are Adam and Eve? Barbarians. They must be. Those are not good Greek names. What can they matter, Socrates?"

"It's not 'Socrates,' it's 'Sock it to me's.' Get it? It's a joke."

"Then what do you do when you see this . . . very strange thing?"

"You stay there, watching it like a snake. Because—see, as long as you're watching it, it can't happen because you are seeing that it's an illusion that's trying to hypnotize you. So as long as you are watching it, you are your whole universe, but there is no you, see?"

"Still," Plato said slyly, "what's wrong with 'Know thyself'?"

The old man popped himself on the forehead with his hand and mumbled, *"Mama mia,"* then started in again.

"Okay, forget the 'thyself' part. Let's look at the 'know' part. Knowledge is always of the past, do you see? To know something means you go through it or someone tells you about it, and you memorize what happened and then you file it in your head so you can pull it out and say, Hey, I know that: 'Put your hand in the fire, it hurts.' Or: 'I used to live over on that side of town.' Get it? Knowledge is the past. But this is happening now, not in the past, not in the future. So if it becomes knowledge, you've already lost it, see?"

"I guess so." But Plato looked most doubtful.

"So it's not 'Know thyself.' It's just 'Wake up.' 'Ob-serve.' " He hissed this out as two separate words.

A few minutes later he heard Plato's voice outside the open window of his hut, saying, "Know thyself, Socrates hath proclaimed, and you will know everything."

Corbo cursed and doubled up his fists. He felt like running out there and punching Plato out. And that was another odd thing about ancient Greece: you got madder here.

When he left the hut for a stroll into town there was that beautiful blue sky with all those fluffy white clouds, and those picturesque whitewashed cottages, and all those fluffy white sheep.

"Baaa," one of them said to him, charmingly enough.

"Fuck you," he said back, and he ran over and booted it a good hard one, sending it flying up into that blue, blue sky, just soaring up and up like a cloud, until finally it looked so much like a cloud that it *was* a cloud.

"That's weird, too," the old man said to himself out loud. "Kick a sheep in ancient Greece hard enough and it flies up into the sky and turns into a cloud. It has a certain kind of logic, but what kind?"

He kicked a couple more, with the same results. Charming.

"Just wake up," he repeated for Plato's benefit, should he happen to be hiding here somewhere. And as he continued his little jaunt, every so often he would run maniacally out into the fields, launch one of the fluffy little mothers.

"At last," he muttered to himself, "man is aiming for the stars. Who knows, maybe I'll be the first man ever to put a sheep on the moon. A small step for mankind, but a big one for sheepdom."

He paused, then added, "A very small one for the moon, too." Shook his head sadly. "Not even that much for sheep, when you think about it."

After a while he arrived at his destination, which turned out to be back at his little country cottage, rather than town, which turned out to be something of a surprise, but what the hell, ancient Greece was *très* weird, and no one could argue with that.

Plato was inside, seated at the small wooden table in one of the small wooden chairs. The place was bare: white walls, white as the purest of clouds, and with some odd depth to them so that sometimes you felt you could look into them. White ceiling, little chairs and table, that was it. But that wasn't always it. Sometimes it would change; but what did that mean? Plato was always around, the perennial can't-quite-get-it student that Corbo was always cursed with.

"Can't I even get away from you in my dreams?" And there it was. Uh-oh, he was not in ancient Greece. He was only dreaming that he was in ancient Greece.

Plato smiled. "So that's it," he said calmly. "This is all a dream. A lovely dream, but just a dream?"

"Lovely for some," the old man groused. "But the question is, if I'm not here, then where am I?"

"Sit down. Relax," Plato suggested. "You are probably back lying down on that rocky ledge where Ketoko pretended to leave you. Sleeping. Completely at his mercy."

The old man smiled and said, "I may be asleep, but I'm a long ways away from being at anyone's mercy. Even Ketoko's. Naturally I've prepared for this situation, on the unlikely chance that it should ever occur."

Plato nodded wisely. "Somehow that doesn't surprise me."

"After all," Corbo shot back, "I'm only a minor in philosophy."

"I'd hate to ask you what you majored in."

"Don't worry," Corbo reassured him, "I wouldn't tell you."

"Then there's that other problem," Plato continued calmly. "If you're dreaming this—and I am willing to accept your premise about that—then why am I also dreaming it?"

The old man nodded as if he had known it from the start and said, "Yes, you're dreaming it, too. I'll go for that one. It seems to me as if I'm partly in my dream but also partly in someone else's."

He was pacing the floor as he spoke, causing Plato to suggest, "Won't you take a chair? All your pacing is making me nervous."

Corbo shook his head. "I hate chairs. Those ugly chairs must be your part of the dream." Still pacing, he continued, "How about this little scenario? Ketoko tells me I'm in ancient Greece, and I've got to figure it out, see? I'm not as alert as usual because I'm using all my concentration to find out if I'm really in ancient Greece, so he is able to hypnotize me, put me to sleep. But since ancient Greece is the last thing I'm thinking of as I go into my dream, I automatically call out to someone from ancient Greece for help. You. Since my original purpose was to reach Elena through a dream, I reached out to you in one of your dreams, and here we are."

Plato looked truly puzzled. "Why me?"

The old man walked over to where he was sitting and patted him on the shoulder. "Because you are famous. Known for your great mind. Big as a balloon."

Plato continued to look lost. "What's a balloon?"

Ignoring his question, Corbo continued. "But that's probably because of this dream in the first place. Marvelous. Now even I'm confused."

Plato began drumming his fingers nervously on the table. "So you need to wake yourself up."

Corbo pointed a finger at him accusingly. "No," he said sharply. "This is what I was aiming at. This is my chance. I'm already dreaming, so let that imp Ketoko fight it out with my body. It's go team, go. Straight to Elena. So help me out here. After all, this is what made you famous."

If Plato had looked puzzled before, he looked truly astounded now. "But how can that be?"

"Know anyone else named Socrates?"

Plato shook his head.

"Then this is it. God knows how much of this, or what distorted version of it, you'll remember when you wake up. But you will know this was not an ordinary dream."

Plato smiled ruefully at him, "That is one thing I know for certain."

"So you will try to remember as much of it as you possibly can. Write it down. From that experience you will derive your world-famous philosophy. So help me out a little here and we'll both get something from this weird dream-vision."

"So you are Socrates, and not Sock-it-to-me's? What is so funny?"

For the old man was having one of his fits of laughter.

"*Everything* is so funny," he said when he could speak again. "I guess I'm both. But also you should see what just happened to that moron Ketoko. But let's not digress here. Come on, O great philosopher. Do your stuff."

Plato smiled. "Well, there is one thing that you may or may not find useful, O man behind the great ones. You know how you pointed out to me that the table and chairs were from my dream?"

Corbo nodded.

"Those appalling nothing white walls are yours. Knowing you, I'm sure you have them here for a purpose."

"What would you have done, decorated them with flowers and bas-reliefs of the gods?"

Plato's smile broadened. "Naked men, actually. I say, is this thing finally, thank all the gods, going to end?"

The old man said, "Thanks for the hint. Your role in this is over. Wake up whenever you wish."

And, just like that, the platonic one blinked out and was gone.

"I've always hated Greek philosophy," the old man grumbled, moving over to the amorphous white walls, "only to find out that I practically invented it."

He moved to the far wall.

At first he saw only the same swirling motion of depth. But then he looked at it with the eye in the middle of his forehead and saw what it really was. Then he looked at it with the eye just below his belly button and went into it.

It was like a lake, but it was not. And it was like a mirror but it was not. But he chose mirror, and so now it *was* mirror.

"Elena, my little pigeon, where are you? Come to Papa in the hour of your need."

But then he saw that that was not the way. He took out his stone from inside his tunic and held it, still chained around his neck.

"Yawtlée calling Yawtlée," he said. "Come in, Yawtlée. Somewhere Elena is in trouble. Well, ha ha, that could be a lot of places. But you know when I'm talking about, little stone. For are you not alive? More than alive? Are you not caring? More than caring. Find yourself, zip through time, and give yourself a call."

And suddenly there was the face staring at him. Hypnotized. Those green eyes. He remembered them. But the rest of it.

"My God, Elena," he cackled, "you're even uglier than I remember." And, of course, broke into laughter.

# 3

---

K ETOKO HOWLED IN pain and confusion. Triple voice and all. It sounded like three elephants bellowing. He had seen the old fool go to sleep, dreaming of ancient Greece. And he had been so eager to get his hand on that stone that he had not been at all alert. But who would have thought—?

First had been a blast of totally devastating psychic pain, the world's worst headache, followed by—believe it or not—the old fool sitting up and, without even bothering to wake from his dream, jamming the first two fingers of his right hand into Ketoko's eyes, blinding him. Then had followed that overwhelming cloud of hideous stench, like a psychic skunk. How on earth—or off it—had Corbo learned to do that?

The old man had obediently mumbled the answer to his unasked question in his sleep, but Ketoko was in too much pain and confusion to catch it. Of course the eyes could easily be repaired. But in his agonized condition, he just couldn't focus enough to heal himself. And that smell!

"All right, you old fool, keep your stone for now!" he shouted, in all three voices. "I'll be back for it. As soon as I get rid of this nauseating stink and clear up this headache. Should only take a few million years," he added wistfully, his voice dwindling from its three-horned assault down to one rather pleasant one, speaking in English with the trace of an African accent. And then he, too, laughed and shook his head.

"Who would guess that this senile old clown would have conditioned himself to fight when he was unconscious? Not even the omniscient one they call Ketoko would have thought of it. Talk about paranoia!" He shook his head, which would have been terribly confusing had anyone been around to see it, because the excitement or the headache or whatever was already causing his features to swirl and shift at a dizzying pace.

"Anyway, see how you like it in jolly old Greece, because I'm going to leave you right here, and never ever will you be finding me again, so here you will stay."

He wrinkled up his nose (not that you could see it) and shuddered. "I've got to go somewhere where I can think and heal myself. Get rid of this most terrible stink."

As he disappeared, he heard the old man mumble from his dream, chuckling, "Have a nice trip."

THE PLAN WAS to stay the night at the Dog and Cat Inn, and in the morning see if they could purchase a couple of horses. From there the ride into town should only take a couple of hours.

"Suppose no one wants to sell their horse?"

Thaddeus smiled. "Oh, they will, though."

Bitters nodded. "Guess they would at that."

The sign over the door was a delightful rendition of a ferocious dog and cat, all squared off and ready to fight each other in the blink of an eye.

As evening apparently came on a little early here in the mountains, it was already quite dark, and the dining room was lit by candles and fireplace. The walls were decorated with primitive but colorful paintings of the hunt.

Several groups of people were seated around small, plain wooden tables, chatting, drinking, and eating what appeared mostly to be plain fare—large bowls of stew and thick chunks of dipping bread. There was a strong smell of garlic and something like beef, only a little stronger.

"Smells like venison stew again," Bitters complained. "It's almost all they ever have. This one's got carrots in it, though, judging from the smell of it."

One group of rough-looking men seated at a large table in the center of the room had a pair of very large dogs—again reminiscent of, but not actually, great Danes—tied to a chair, and those dogs rose up bristling at the sight of Blackjack, who wagged his tail merrily in response.

"Silence, Bruno. Silence, Striker," a tall, whip-thin man snapped. The big dogs settled down again. The man, who was at once dangerous looking and elegant in posture, pointed a turkey leg at Raphael and spoke in a haughty tone, as one would to a servant, "I'd keep a close eye on that little white mouse if I were thou. These large dogs of mine tend to be a trifle cantankerous at mealtime."

Raphael shook his head, "He just wants to play," he answered, and Blackjack hopped up and down excitedly and barked a couple of times as if to confirm Raphael's take on his feelings.

"Oh, shut up, Blackjack," Thaddeus said, looking around the place, carefully checking it all out.

As his gaze moved around the cheery scene, pausing here and there to focus in on some colorful-looking character, he found himself particularly intrigued by the slender figure seated all alone at a corner table. Since the candle was not lit, and he or she was dressed all in black and apparently wearing some kind of mask or veil, Thaddeus could not see enough of whoever it was to make any judgments, but he had the strong feeling that it was a woman or girl. But then again, something about the posture seemed to suggest otherwise. Even from across the room, in this light, he could make out a kind of devil-may-care jauntiness. Robin the Boy Wonder, maybe? Thaddeus shook his head.

Raphael meanwhile was also warming to the simple country charm of the place, but found himself wondering where all the people were coming from. This joint was really jumping.

"Main road outta town," Bitters explained around a giant mug of ale, "or into it. Some of 'em are land barons. Got a bit o' property out there. Like the one, I won't mention his name, used ta be me boss. They got ta come ta town all the time. Pick up supplies and such. Some of 'em is goin a-huntin', also like my used-ta-be boss. Also the only road—well, at least the main road—for that."

The people were friendly enough. "Take out thy sweet lute and play us a merry tune, won't thou?" one of them, a saucy wench, requested, and this time, to the delight of all, Thaddeus acquiesced.

"Be interesting to see what they make of this," he murmured in a low voice to Raphael as he took out his round-backed guitar from its case.

Cries of wonder greeted the emerald-green guitar with the flashy abalone fretwork.

"Learned this one from an old blind Black man called hisself Blind Bill. Always getting the blues fer London—he come from there—hearin' old Big Ben's chimes. He be so old and blind and all fucked up on whiskey he can't remember what he doin', though, so his blues sound a little bit like blues, but then he forget and it sound like jazz or something."

*Poking a little fun at me here,* Raphael was thinking. But the fact was,

Thaddeus was doing such a good job at this "ethnic" routine that you couldn't really be sure.

The folks in the audience, obviously aware that they were encountering something unique here, although not having a clue as to what Thaddeus was talking about, joined right in, nodding and uttering encouraging remarks.

He moved his chair out more toward the middle of the room and commandeered a wooden footstool from one of the wealthier-looking patrons, tuned up a little, and took up his position, which turned out to be, surprisingly, a fairly strict, classical one. He played without a plectrum, using all of his fingers on the strings except for the little one, which he braced on the pick guard. Sometimes, though not that often, he might even be using that little one on the strings, Raphael thought, but maybe not. It was hard to tell.

"He start like this, but then he forget where he goin' to. Just keep on goin' down. Sometimes I think he figure out where to stop, that be it. Whole song be over before it starts. Anyway, here it is: 'Big Ben Blues.' "

He began with a common descending blues turnaround started high on the neck. But he just kept on going down, past the turnaround point. From there he used harmonics to chime out the Big Ben theme, causing folks to utter little cries of astonishment at the sweet, bell-like tones of the steel-stringed guitar.

He went on to a standard though rather subdued blues riff, but, as if of its own accord, it shuffled into a sweet jazz chord and continued along those lines. After following through that same pattern once again, it ended up with the same descending turnaround—only this time when he hit the stopping point, he got off.

Raphael found it a lovely and touching, if odd, piece of music. Easily as sad as any blues, but a lot more wistful. He looked around the crowed, trying to interpret their expressions, but all he could find was amazement. They were sitting there with their mouths open, some of them with forks full of venison or some such hovering in the air. Clearly they had never encountered anything like this before. But as to whether they liked it or not—the place was dead silent.

Then it dawned on Raphael: there was something else going on with Thaddeus, something other than just "making music."

He himself would never have considered trying to use his mystic powers in this noisy, confusing milieu. One of the main problems with the "gift" of psychic power was figuring out exactly when to use it.

For instance, he had tried to *read* Bitters's thoughts back when they were struggling so laboriously to extract information out of him. Some short-cut. All Raphael had wound up with was a collage of mixed-up fragments of memories, twitches of unfocused anger or nervousness. A mental image of big tits—a cartoon, almost—a desire for a drink of ale, and other assorted static. It had almost short-circuited Raphael's own brain, and somehow even managed to give him a slight headache. Which of course was here and gone in a flash.

But in fact, unlike reading thoughts, when he simply turned his attention to the crowd, it was easy to sense what they were now feeling. It was the same for all of them—a sort of poignant, sweet sadness. Thaddeus immediately jumped right into the next number. "Just some be-bop," he said by way of introduction, "maybe even rebop."

He ran through a long complicated river of jazzy chord changes, which even Raphael found dazzling. The audience, by now, appeared simply dumbfounded, but several found their voices enough to shout out "More."

Thaddeus nodded. "I'll play another," he said. "This one when old Blind Bill find himself in Brazil. Jumpin' and jivin'. Do his samba. Call it 'Kato,' after someone's cat."

He began to play a sort of, but not quite, bossa nova. It moved along swiftly and smoothly as a dark river through the Brazilian jungle at night, and it obviously required a lot of chops to keep on top of it. But the thing that nagged at Raphael was the "not quite" part. Just as the other song had been not quite blues. Then suddenly he had it. It didn't sound like bossa nova really, but more like some Gypsy idea of it. Having himself spent some time listening to recordings of Django Reinhardt, and then to some other nameless Parisian Gypsy guitar players, the answer, mind-boggling as it was, came to Raphael in a flash: Thaddeus played the guitar a little like a Gypsy from France. Had he been to France? Lived in France? Raphael set that one aside to explore later.

As the playing went on, the psychic emotion that Thaddeus was deliberately projecting with the music grew steadily stronger, until suddenly it surged and fragmented into a quick succession of brief, delightful images, each of them involving an incredibly beautiful and mischievous lynx-pointed Siamese cat. There was no doubt in Raphael's mind whose cat Kato had been.

Raphael was as overwhelmed by this fairy-tale display of magic as anyone in the inn, perhaps more so because he was aware that Thaddeus was creating it. What the rest of them attributed the visions to, he hadn't the slightest idea. But there was no doubt that they were, each and every one of them, sharing this experience.

By all rights, all of these "primitive" medieval citizens should have been terrified by this display of magic, but in fact the patrons of the inn were all sharing a state of childlike ecstasy, murmuring out loud at the "pretty pictures," giggling blissfully, or sighing.

"Oh, look at that one," someone shouted ecstatically, as the cat stretched out impossibly, like a gray snake, twined down from the top of an entertainment center, and cheerfully swatted the cap off the head of an irate little man, who apparently was trying hard to concentrate on fixing the TV set.

Laid out this way for all of them to view, it was obvious that the cat's life had been a dance, as were all lives, the difference being that he had been aware of it and had danced it through to the end without ever hesitating. And he had died young and beautiful, and dancing. Raphael could see him leap up onto a bathroom sink and demand that it be filled with water. Then demand that the window be opened. Then he had followed Thaddeus back to bed, walked up onto his chest, licked his chin, and then snuggled up under his hand and . . . stopped. Oh, Jesus, it suddenly hit Raphael and everyone else in the room. What loss, and yet the joy remained. The song suddenly ended.

Everyone just sat there, not sure how they were feeling, just overwhelmed. Some were crying, some smiling, still seeing into that special place.

The white dog whined miserably, and pawed the floor. He seemed to have gone through the experience along with everyone else, and although he might not have been able to understand it, he had responded to the emotions.

Finally someone broke the silence. "What a funny cat," he said, "but so pretty." Then everybody was talking at once. Now a sprinkling of applause. Then a few began cheering and applauding wildly. Others joined in. Even the group of rowdies with the giant dogs were begging for more. Even the dogs were whining anxiously.

Thaddeus rose to his feet and, and holding out his guitar by the neck, bowed to his audience. As usual, his expression was impossible to read. While the patrons of the inn were still whistling, applauding, and crying out for more, he turned to Raphael and said sotto voce, "Keep them busy for a few minutes, will you?"

"What? How?"

Thaddeus looked annoyed. "I don't care how. Tell them a joke, a story. You play the guitar, right? Okay, play them a tune."

"I can't play your guitar," Raphael complained. "I hate steel strings. They're like wire."

Thaddeus stared at him in disbelief. "Mr. Muscle can't play with steel strings?"

Raphael looked positively terrified. "It's not that. It's the clunky sound. I don't play that way. I—"

"That was amazin'," Bitters cut in. "And now, ladies and gentlemen, me other partner, Raphael here, is goin' to perform. But he's in need o' a more delicate instrument to weave his special magic. Anybody here packing a lute?"

Surprisingly, several of the guests raised their hands eagerly and shouted affirmation. Then one of them, a tall, elegantly dressed man with a saturnine expression, stood up from his table and spoke in a deep voice that had the self-conscious beauty of the trained orator. "Many of us carry our lutes with us when we travel. And a sweet companion she can be at the day's end of a weary journey when we are seated around the campfire, far from home.

"But alas, these are usually mere travelers' lutes—not our best instruments, but our sturdiest. I, however, who was born the son of a luthier who was himself the son of a luthier, have always allowed myself the luxury of playing only the finest of my instruments. It would make me most happy if you would honor Mirabelle here by plucking her strings and allowing her to sing for you. Thee may find her voice to be as sweet as fresh honey."

He picked up a case with a rounded bottom, which apparently he had kept at the ready beside his chair, and, removing a lute from it, carried it over gingerly, as if indeed he were carrying his sweetheart, and presented it to Raphael. "Allow me to introduce Mirabelle,"

Raphael exclaimed: "Whoa, holy shit! Will you look at this, Thaddeus?"

The two astonished men examined the exquisite instrument, a large seven-string lute, embellished with gleaming gold tuners and engravings of unicorns. Raphael brushed his fingers across the strings. The tone was exceptionally bright, but well balanced, with a strong base. The extra string was at the high end of the lute, what Raphael would have normally thought of as a high A, but in this case who would know what it was tuned to, because the entire tuning was very peculiar, and neither Raphael nor Thaddeus had ever experimented with alternate tunings.

"All right if I tune, uh, Mirabelle?"

"But of course." The luthier gestured cavalierly. "Do what thou must to make thy sweetest song, I beg thee. Break it if thou must. It would be a small price to pay for what I have heard here today." He held his elegant hand out toward Thaddeus in a gesture of yearning, as though he wished he could wrest the music from Thaddeus's heart and press it to his own.

"It would be the only time anyone paid a small price for anything o' yourn," groused Bitters, who was well into his third mug of ale.

"You know each other?" Thaddeus said, in a manner that suggested he was confirming information rather than asking a question.

Bitters shrugged. "High-priced shopkeeper in Nor Wiccingham. They all are. Spend a little more energy in perfecting yer craft, and less in stealin' poor people's money, I always say."

The elegant luthier fairly snorted in derision. "Is that what you always say? I've always had trouble deciphering it."

But both men were wearing dazed smiles, so that even this bit of bickering gave the feeling of being largely habitual and without real rancor in it. Indeed, everyone in the place seemed to be floating along in a cloud of residual ecstasy. And it was obvious to Raphael that Thaddeus had put everyone in the tavern into some kind of pleasant altered state in which they were mentally receptive to his consciousness. He reminded himself, *We're at work here—this is no game!*

Without further ado, Raphael took an E from Thaddeus's guitar and tuned the lute. The tall, slender luthier watched curiously as he performed this function, and remarked dubiously, "The two of you tune your lutes to the same pitch? What an odd gesture of comradeship. You must be the dearest of friends."

Raphael looked at Thaddeus and smiled. "Hey, big guy, this one's for you."

"Perhaps when you are finished, I might . . . If only I could . . ." the luthier interrupted Raphael just as he was positioning himself to play, seated cross-legged on the table, curled around the lute.

"Could what?" Thaddeus asked.

"Play just a bit on your extraordinary lute. I've never in all my life"—he choked up, almost ready to cry—"seen such beauty as well as heard it, from any instrument. It veritably gleams."

Thaddeus grinned. "The miracle of glossy green paint on fiberglass and abalone shell," he said. "Know what abalone is? Thought not. Sure, you can play my Legend. But the strings are steel. Hurt your fingers till you get used to it. Then hurt them some more.

"But right now my main man here is dying to do his thing. Ladies and gentlemen—Raphael."

Raphael tuned up and sang his song, accompanying himself in a strangely unpolished and yet quite original and complex style. His singing voice was pure and straightforward, without any mannerisms. And the song itself was quite odd, haunting. Something about the loneliness of some comic-book character. Thaddeus, who was not really listening, caught the words "Do you know what love is, Dr. Strange?"

And as the song went on, Thaddeus was surprised to find himself admitting that this kid had some real talent. He hadn't forced himself to learn to play his guitar as Thaddeus had. He hadn't forced himself to practice. He obviously wasn't at all dedicated to music. In fact, this was probably just something he was doing because of Thaddeus's influence. But he was really gifted! And furthermore, he had charisma. He had a beautiful face, a beautiful body, and a beautiful, though not big, voice. Thaddeus knew instinctively that if they were to perform together, no matter how good he got, as long as he wasn't using magic, Raphael would wind up the star of the show.

And even though the kid wasn't using any mystical tricks, as Thaddeus had, and had started out hesitantly and from time to time made a mistake, the crowd was one hundred percent into his music. No one so much as muttered or signaled the barkeep for another ale.

So Raphael sang his song and Thaddeus did his work.

"A magician, is he, this Dr. Strange?" Bitters inquired when the song had ended and the applause had, at long last, died down. Raphael nodded. "A great one?" Nod. "The most powerful of all?"

Raphael smiled. "There are four greater. Myself and Thaddeus. A woman named Violet. And we don't know who the other one is."

"And Tippi," Thaddeus cut in. "You always forgetting Tippi. No one stronger than her."

"She has no stone," Raphael reminded him.

"Well," Thaddeus said, "if she ever gets her hands on one, look out."

This had obviously never occurred to Raphael, and his expression showed it.

Thaddeus smiled. "I doubt she give it back. And you know what? Violet letting her hang around like that. Dangling the stone in front of her like a carrot to a donkey. Sooner or later, my man. Sooner or later."

While the luthier, who introduced himself as Jeremy, familiarized himself with Thaddeus's instrument and its—to him—unorthodox tuning, Thaddeus explained to Raphael, as well as to Bitters and Blackjack, how his new musical technique worked.

"I'm not that good at giving psychic commands, as you may have noticed. Besides, you pretty much only affect one person at a time that way.

"So I figured, use me some sounds, ease on in. But you know what? Works much stronger than I ever figured. First off, it tunes me to the same sounds it's tuning them into. Everybody—all of us on the same wavelength.

Then we all start feeling the emotion behind what I'm playing. And when you feelin' emotion, you can't think—dig? And all that thought, most of it just nervous-reflex shit. All that static dissolves and they start gettin' all the images goin' on inside me. I goose it a little, but it's pretty automatic.

"Anyway, they all blissed out, their minds all open and ready, good idea, right then you or someone else play them a tune. Keep them floatin' along on that cloud while I go over them individually, see what they feeling, thinking."

Raphael looked interested. "You can read their thoughts? Mostly all I get is a lot of junk, memories and like static. I hardly ever get a solid chain of logic."

Thaddeus nodded agreement. "Lot easier when they in this mood, though. Their thoughts a lot slower, fewer, but stronger, more coherent. What I'm saying here, Rafe, is we in a strange place. You mama's in big trouble. We almost got ourselves killed already. We outnumbered. But we don't have to go it alone."

Raphael nodded. "Like we've pretty much always done, right? So, what did you come up with?"

Thaddeus frowned. "Not much, really. But this much. They all split up. All of them excited about some big-time thing coming up." Bitters raised his hand. "Some of them feelin' their oats, like this guitar maker, Jeremy. But some of them, most of them, feel angry. Humiliated. What you want, Bitters?"

"It's the Festival of Our Lady seven days from today, 'at's what yer seein. 'At's the big festival when we all get together an' Nor Wiccingham'll so kindly demonstrate its domination over all us poor folk from Sou Wiccingham. Make us all grovel a bit. 'At's because the old king up and ate too much o' that fancy partridge pie. Washed it down w' a big swig o' ale and toppled over right at the table. So Nor Wiccingham gets a new king. And 'at's when we got to go through this festival. It's the witches—make sure they rub our noses in it. Lots o folk gettin' tired of it. Tired enough maybe even ta fight."

His expression, although he was still under that cloud of bliss, was definitely tinged with bitterness. "Frankly, that would be about the same results I got from tryin' ta fight with you. Only they wouldn't stop chokin' when we gave it up. Me now, well, I care not a whit. I don't even know where I belong no more."

Raphael frowned. "A rebellion. Interesting."

"And I've got another piece of interesting news for you," Thaddeus started, then hushed up. The luthier had began to play on Thaddeus's in-

strument a tricky little number that definitely had a bit of Spanish influence
and was very brief. But it was burdened with the title "In the Gardens of the
Young Prince at Twilight."

The crowd greeted this performance with yet another round of deeply
enthusiastic applause.

"That shall have to be the whole of it on this most celestial of instruments, as it has already savaged my fingers. But if you like, I could probably be persuaded to coax a soft ballad from mine own sweet Mirabelle."

He gave Thaddeus back his instrument and took up his lovely lute, and
announced: "I shall sing for thee 'The Snow Queen,' alas a sad ballad drawn
from all too-personal experience."

"The warmth of her smile turns to cold as the first snow falls," he sang
out in a thin voice as he flamboyantly accompanied himself on his lute.

*Quintessential medieval,* Raphael thought as he followed the plaint of
unrequited love.

They were definitely somewhere back in time, he was convinced of
that, whether cut off from England by mountains or not, whether visited
from time to time by witches or not. Everything about this place exuded an
ambience medieval.

Jeremy finished his plaint to yet more feverish applause. One of the tavern's patrons stood up and proclaimed ecstatically, "In all my life I've never
seen nor heard such wondrous things as I have here in this humble, shabby
country inn. Even the glorious entertainments of cosmopolitan Nor Wiccingham pale beside what we have all heard here tonight. The thing we have
all shared here must not be tossed aside and forgot like so many other of our
experiences. I suggest that we all drink a toast and vow to remember. And
perhaps—I know I would be willing—perhaps we can tell each other where
we live, so that from time to time we can gather together and remind ourselves of this wonderful night."

Thaddeus grinned at Raphael and shrugged. "Power of sounds. Where
were we? Oh yeah, I promised you something else get your interest here.
Come on with me." He led Raphael across the room to the far corner, where,
at the dark table with the candle out, the slender hooded form wearing the
black veil sat. Looking down at the table, avoiding their eyes.

"Mind if we make ourselves at home here?" Thaddeus said as he pulled
over a chair from another table, sat down in it, reached over, and casually
snatched off the veil before he finished his sentence. "Mrs. Lim," he said.

To Raphael's astonishment, Violet's demure-looking but actually brazen
tai chi instructress smiled mischievously up at him and winked.

"Ah yes, you so right, it is me. You little guardian angel. Violet say to me that you go quickly on great adventure, and that, like she herself, the both of you very powerful wizards, but rash and foolish without her guidance. As you Anglos would put it, I fairly jumped at the bait. I followed through mystic doorway you created. Alas, I did not arrive in time to aid you in you battle, and you almost die because of that. But since then I have been guarding you backs, you two big strong handsome men." She winked again. "You probably be many times dead if I not have done this."

Raphael stared openmouthed in wonder. "You killed all those people?"

The slender, demure-looking Chinese woman shrugged. "They annoy me," she said happily, "so I slashed them all to bits, and now here I am, who knows where, and I loving it."

Thaddeus and Raphael exchanged glances.

"Uh-huh," Thaddeus said. "And how about Mr. Lim?"

Mrs. Lim smiled brightly. "That poor man is probably cry in his pillow," she said. Then, "No, only joking. Mr. Lim is swinger, like myself. Probably he go sex orgy, forget even that I am gone. If I live, it 'Oh boy, welcome home, you cute thing.' But if I should die here, it more like, 'Whatever happen to what's-her-name?' So here am I. Here you. What now?"

Thaddeus merely shook his head, like *So what?* But Raphael reeled from the overload. For a moment he looked actually dizzy, held out his hands as if to stop a fall or ward off . . .

"Mrs.—?" he said. "Uh, sorry, I can't stand any more weirdness right now. I'm going to find ye old outhouse, or whatever they call the men's room here. When I come back, we'll start over. I'll, uh, comprehend. Whatever."

He wheeled abruptly and walked away. And when he did not come back after quite some time, Thaddeus went to look for him.

He was in the men's room, all right, standing dazed before the mirror Right! A huge fucking mirror that practically covered one of the huge fucking walls in the huge fucking men's restroom at the Dog and Cat Inn. Between gleaming rows of porcelain urinals, he stood. Behind him, enclosed stalls with shiny white toilets hidden therein.

"Shit," Thaddeus mumbled, taking it all in in one nauseating gulp. "Medieval, my ass. Sorry—too scatological for the men's room."

Then, after a long pause: "Uh, what's up, blade? Enjoying the mirror?"

No answer.

So what do you do? Thaddeus moseyed over and looked into the mirror where Raphael stood transfixed by his own image.

Only—and here was the hardest part of all—only it wasn't his own image looking back at him, it was a funky-looking old man complete with beard and fluffy, fine-spun, white, white hair. Looked like he was about a million years old, but could still kick your ass.

Had to be Corbo, Thaddeus figured, with grave misgivings. And, as usual, Thaddeus was right as rain, but was sure that he probably would have been happier had he not been.

# 5

MEANWHILE, BACK AT the ranch, having sent the fearless and expertly trained (as only the Chinese seem to have the patience to train) Mrs. Lim to look after her reckless boys, Violet decided it was about time to do some work on her own.

"Let's see, should I use money, power, bring in our professional detectives and such, or just grab a sword and charge right in there like the boys?" Joke, of course. "What do you think, Tippi?"

Tippi, at the other end of the enormous room, was eagerly applying paint to a large canvas, and, naturally enough, did not hear her. As far as Violet could tell, she was studying something most intently, staring at it through the big glass doors, but, as Violet had made a note of earlier, painting something else entirely—typical Tippi.

Now she paused. Put down the brush and walked barefoot, as usual—she almost never wore shoes—across the wood floor over to where Violet was halfheartedly practicing her tai chi. She was working somewhat lackadaisically on a move that she couldn't seem to get right. She knew, of course, that what she should have done was gone outside to the shaded platform which had been constructed for that purpose, and buckled down and worked through the entire form. Try to get it holistically instead of one piece at a time.

Before going off on her "big adventure," Mrs. Lim had given Violet this new form to get the feel of. Even left her a videotape should she forget some part or other. The intrepid mistress of tai chi had spent all morning demonstrating the form and would not leave until Violet got the order of the moves down pat. This one was a combination made up of equal parts of the four major styles as practiced in China. Mostly it was an advanced form designed

primarily for competition, and not one practiced by the common people for
health. It was therefore very difficult, and knowing the order of the moves
was a long way from doing them correctly. But at least it gave Violet something to work on until Mrs. Lim returned.

"You no practice, I quit," the enigmatic Mrs. Lim had told her. And she
had looked like she meant it. Like "There will be a quiz."

Tippi, Violet now noted as she approached, had been mostly painting
herself. As usual, she even had paint on her feet.

"About what?" Tippi asked innocently. "I'm not a mind reader."

"Yeah, I bet," Violet answered, thinking to herself, *My God, I've got to
the point where I'm consulting the Tipster. Great!* "Shall we get to work, see
if we can save the boys? Hire some private dicks?"

Tippi grinned. "Hey, I'm always in favor of private dicks."

But was she? She never went out with men, or boys, or even girls, for
that matter. But then, neither did Violet. That thought sobered her.

She studied her watch. It was a slender, elegant Cartier, the very one,
in fact, that Thaddeus had recently thrown away.

"Well, as it turns out, I've already got our boys on it. Got a meeting with
one of them in just a few minutes."

Tippi looked curious. "Something up already?"

Violet frowned. "Apparently. He's got something to say, but he didn't
want to say it over the phone."

Tippi sobered instantly. "Shit, that sounds bad to me. When did he
call?"

"Just a few minutes ago. He's on his way. I want you to be there
with me."

Tippi looked amazed. "What? I don't believe this. Do you mean to tell
me that at last my sage advice is being sought?"

Violet frowned. "Don't flatter yourself. You're not exactly a guru, but
you've been in these situations before. Anyone's advice might be helpful."

Tippi kept staring at her with her big eyes, waiting.

"Besides, if something should happen to one of us, you have the—You
know how to use the stones."

Tippi looked a little disappointed. "I'm an apprentice? Like Mickey
Mouse in *Fantasia?*"

"You're"—Violet hesitated—"you're family," she said, having trouble
getting it out.

Tippi shook her head. "I don't believe this. You're—what? Forgiving me?"

"It's not a matter of forgiving, it's just that this is a crisis—maybe." She held out her right hand to show crossed fingers. "And we may need help. Even yours. Besides which"—Violet smiled—"whoever forgives their family for anything? I thought that was the whole point of family, holding grudges but hanging in there anyway. But then again, I would hardly be the one to know."

Suddenly, Tippi of the big bright eyes grew furious, and yes Violet could see it in her eyes.

"Damn you, Violet, you always have to have everything—even all the pity. You had your brother until you were grown up, and you had Elena and Raphael. That's three more than I ever had.

"I killed my brother when I was eight. I hated my mother, I left home when I was sixteen, and I've never been back since. I only had one real friend, and I never appreciated him until he was . . . gone. You think I wouldn't settle for what you've got? Can't you just back the fuck off in that area and let me have a little of the pity for a change, without trying to steal a piece for yourself?"

Violet nodded, trying to appear calm in the middle of what she saw as a storm of meaningless anger. "Hey," she said, "take it all. Uh . . . you, uh, killed your brother?"

"I don't want to talk about it."

Violet nodded and said carefully, "That's probably a good policy." Checking out her watch again. "Shall we?"

The two women received the investigative agent in what Violet liked to allude to as the library. As in, "We shall receive him in the library, Mary," causing Tippi to wrinkle her nose in distaste. Having been born and raised in and around Los Angeles, she found Violet's small-town pretensions somewhat tacky.

There were many books in the library, but nobody ever read them. They were mostly fancy-edition sets which had obviously been bought mainly for ambience.

James Fenimore Cooper? The complete works of? Had anyone ever read the complete works of James Fenimore Cooper, or Sir Walter Scott, or Henry James? Tippi had once started to read *The Europeans* by Henry James. It had taken her what seemed like forever just to get through the first chapter. In fact, it had taken Tippi forever just to get through the first paragraph. You could get lost in one of his paragraphs. You could start to read one of his sentences and by the time you reached the end forget how it had started. In fact, after she had given up on the book, she had rented a tape of the movie version, but could not force herself to sit through that either. Perhaps if she had been comfortably seated in a big movie theater, eating an enormous box of really good popcorn. Yeah, strapped in her chair maybe.

And Thomas Hardy was worse. But Proust was the worst of all. She had practically passed out trying to decipher a sentence or two of *Remembrance of Things Past*. What a title! What else did one remember?

"I don't see a copy of *Remembrance of Stuff That Hasn't Happened Yet* in the library. Surely you must obtain one," she remarked out of nowhere.

Violet ignored her childish outburst. Especially since Tippi's childishness was, quite possibly, going to last damn near forever.

Just then had come the knock on the door, and Mary Red Boots's solemn (almost truculent), "Announcing Chief Investigator Daniel Reed."

Chief Investigator Daniel Reed was a showstopper. He had a noticeable paralyzing effect on both Violet and Tippi, the former overemphasizing her cool and unconcerned look, the latter busy discovering that there was a lot of bright red paint on her bare legs and feet.

This guy was so good-looking that he caused a reaction in Tippi even though he did not appeal to her. He was too even-featured, reminding her of a store mannequin. It didn't help that he wore a charcoal-gray Brooks Brothers suit and a conservative wine-red tie. He looked rather like one of those smaller, slightly less grandiose imitations of Rock Hudson that you came across in movies from the fifties. Unlike Violet, she really did not like that kind of guy, but . . .

Another factor here which Tippi seemed to suffer, perhaps just by mere proximity, but perhaps not, was that when you became a Guardian and received that gift of healing energy from one of the four mystic stones, it put an end to your participation in that great human pageant of procreation. (Was it a beauty pageant?) After all, if you lived forever, what would be the point of your cells trying to escape and start up in another body? But what of the ritual of sex? For the men, that most all-encompassing of urges seemed simply to cease, then and there. But for the women it was not so cut and dried.

For the men, sex was pretty much just sex. Scratching an itch. If there was no itch, they weren't about to scratch it.

But for the women there was the *ritual* of sex. And, as had been the case with Drusilla, it was sometimes a sacred ritual.

For the men, romance was something which sprang up mischievously from time to time, in the vicinity of sex. For the women, sex was more often only a physical gesture to enhance the romance.

These things were so inextricably woven together into such a mysterious web that Violet would have not been able to tell you whether the strong feelings elicited by the elegant investigator were due to sex, romance, just the excitement of meeting someone new who was young and attractive, or some kind of archetypal response that would always plague her, for no particular reason. It was sort of like *Dress for Success:* it wasn't that you really wanted to react to the clothes people wore; you simply had no choice—in fact, you weren't even aware it was happening.

What had brought *Dress for Success* to mind was that the ancient, battered yellow paperback was one of the few mementos Violet had left of her parents. It had been her suave father's book, and she had read it when she was quite young—not only read it, but had become a sort of living illustration of it. Or so she sometimes thought. Yet if she was consciously dressed to take advantage of the hidden urges we all have, then why did guys always pay so much attention to Tippi, who was so obviously dressed for failure? As seemed to be happening now, as this great example of how to project a successful image so confidently introduced himself to Violet, but couldn't keep from unmistakably eyeing Tippi.

"Just Daniel," he said to Violet, shaking her hand briskly. "Saves time and energy."

"Tippi," Violet acknowledged reluctantly, waving her hand in that direction. "I'm Violet. Let's get right to it, shall we? I'm a little worried about our boys."

Daniel nodded solemnly. "I would be, too. We've lost track of them, and there are dead bodies all over the place. Four, to be exact."

Tippi said simply, "Shit," causing the handsome young investigator to grimace.

Violet frowned. "I don't get it. How could you have lost them? Where is Mrs. Lim?"

He shrugged helplessly. "Uh . . . we lost her, too."

"At the Renaissance Faire?" Tippi and Violet exchanged puzzled glances.

"To be honest with you, I don't get it either. She was following them. My men were on her. They went into a big tent and she waited outside. We, uh, we heard shots. Handgun. She pulled out a, uh, a sword. Japanese-style, what they call a *katana.* We, uh, went in, and surprise, no boys, no Mrs. Lim. But dead bodies. Really dead, hacked-up ones. It was as if they, uh, disappeared off the face of the earth. I know it's my fault but—"

Violet and Tippi exchanged glances again and this time Tippi nodded. "Relax," she said. "It's not your fault at all. Where they went, you couldn't have followed."

It was dashing Dan's turn to look puzzled.

"But it sounds like bad news, just the same," she finished.

"Let me ask you this," he said, touching his right index finger to his wine-red tie as if it were a talisman. "How was Mrs. Lim able to find him in the first place? I mean, even if she knew he was going to be at the Faire?"

"Raphael had a—how do you say?—a bug in his wristwatch, and Mrs. Lim had the tracking device," Violet answered.

Now it was Tippi's turn to look astonished. "You mean the watch you gave him for his birthday?"

"Look," Violet said angrily, "can we just not waste any more time on this, okay?

"So where were we? They disappeared. Then what? I assume you're telling me we have nothing to go on?"

He cleared his throat, looking a little more confident. "Actually, we do have a little something here." He handed Violet a typed report.

She looked at it and blinked. "Rudy's Cute Seats?"

Less sure again. "They're, uh, toilet seats," he said, "but cute ones. You know, with hearts on them or risqué slogans. Let me explain how I came up with this info. All this is happening just as the Faire is closing. Someone is watching the place out front, turning people away. Then shots. First just one. She's pacing back and forth like she doesn't know what to do. I deduced that she has been told to stay out there. Another shot. She can't stand it, but first she gets a key, unlocks a case, takes out a big sword, holds it up over her head like a Kurosawa movie, only it's a Celtic sword."

"You could see this?"

He shrugged. "I had binoculars, really good ones. You know, night vision, all that. Anyway, I'm pretty sure that's what I saw. Bill, he was watching Mrs. Lim, which was getting a little tricky as it was getting dark, and she was all dressed up for the Faire as a ninja or whatever a Chinese version of a ninja is. Anyway, Bill signals me she's moving in.

"We wait a couple minutes, but it's quiet now. So we start down the hill where we're doing the surveillance, but by the time we get there, some other guy has shown up and he's keeping the crowd off. When I ask him what's going on, he tells me mind my own business. Just somebody shooting off a gun where they shouldn't.

"Here I had to make a decision." He looked as if he weren't too sure he'd made the right one. "I could either back off, which would have been prudent, I guess, and do surveillance on him—"

"I hope you weren't that prudent, Dan, after hearing the shots and all," Tippi suggested.

He shrugged. "Exactly. So we, uh, put him out, and I checked inside, and then we dragged him out and tossed him in the van, and then we woke him up, and interrogated him, uh, rather harshly, and got this info." He pointed at the sheet he'd just handed her.

"Of course they had to do a clean-up sooner or later, and we left some guys around to do some surveillance on their clean up crew when they finally showed. A few more names and license plates to run down." He shrugged again. "We expect to get a lot more out of Curry—that's the, uh, suspect's name—once he wakes up again and we have another go at him."

Tippi and Violet exchanged glances. "How the hell did you knock him out and get him through that circus?" Violet asked.

Dan smiled. "It wasn't really that hard. Bill's pretty big, and he held him while I gave him a sedative. Needle gun. We carry fake FBI cards. Most people back off when they see them. Hard part was waking him up again.

"Anyway, according to him, he's part of some gang or religious cult run by women. He's small potatoes. The leader's name is Diana, but she's using an alias here in LA 'Brenda Lake,' no less. According to Curry, who really seemed to want to stay alive, she's here in LA on some kind of religious mission. But while she's here, she's taking care of some of the cult's financial business. They've just taken over some of of one of their new member's businesses, and that's where she is right now, at Rudy's Cute Seats, checking the operation out, going over the books, hiring and firing. Tomorrow and the next day she's got a few more of the late Rudy's enterprises to check out, then she's planning to join the rest of them. So, what now?"

"She's there right now?"

He checked his watch, a no-nonsense Huer chronometer. "At least till six. That's when the place closes. But Curry tells us that she'll probably stay as late as it takes. She's running short on time and this Rudy was apparently quite the entrepreneur. I've got some people outside the place already, just waiting to hear the word."

"All right," Violet said casually, "let's go. What kind of car do you have?"

Daniel looked astonished, "You're coming? Really, I don't know if that's such a good idea. You know, we're paid to take the risks and you—"

His voice died out as Violet merely stood there and silently glared in answer.

"Uh, I have a new Lexus. It's a company car."

"Fine, we'll take your car to the airport. Tippi, tell Jimmy to have our jet ready pronto. You better throw on something else. It's cold in LA."

Tippi smiled. "Yeah, freezing."

"You might even want to wear shoes," Violet suggested, checking her watch. "I'll be back in ten." With that she left the room.

"You're coming, too?" Dan said to Tippi. His tone seemed one of disbelief.

Tippi smiled. "You bet. Back in ten."

"Is there something I should—"

"Read a book," Tippi suggested, and she, too, was out of there.

Chief Investigator Daniel Reed put his hand to his head. This was all getting too weird for him. But when the company car was a Lexus . . .

He studied the rows of books. It was the sort of library he had always wanted to have for himself. All the great books were there. And one day, when he was older, he intended to read them. But for now he had the Lexus. He took down one of them and browsed. Natty Bumpo. The Deerslayer's name was Natty Bumppo? He shook his head and put the book back.

# 6

THE FACE FLOATED there in the mirror for only a moment; then, like the chimera it was, it disappeared. It was only Raphael looking at Raphael once more. In the modern twentieth-century rest room of a medieval English inn. But one other anomaly to the ordinariness of it all was that he appeared to be in a trance. Thaddeus shrugged, went over to one of the urinals, and relieved himself. It seemed to him that he had a lot to get rid of, and people in trances came out of them sooner or later. He obviously hadn't been keeping track of Elena for the last several years, but luckily, in this instance he was right.

After sighing, zipping up, watching the urinals automatically flush in unison, he turned to see Raphael coming out of it.

As in "Holy shit! What the—"

"So . . ." Thaddeus strolled back over to where Raphael still lingered at the washbasin before the mirror. "What just happened here, dude?"

Raphael shook his head. "I don't know. Maybe it was just shock. I was so dazed by the, uh, modern plumbing. You know, I just wandered in here and started to wander over to one of the urinals and I'm thinking like, 'Oh boy, it's good to get to a public rest room.' Then all of a sudden it hits me. I'm so stunned by it all, I go over to one of the sinks and splash some cold water on my face. Then I look into the mirror. I don't know, maybe I passed out or something, but I have this dream, or hallucination—whatever." He shook his head as if still trying to clear out the cobwebs.

"It wasn't a dream or hallucination," Thaddeus informed him. "I saw it, too. It was Corbo, right?"

Raphael actually rapped on his head with the knuckles of his right hand as if to say, "Hello-o, anyone there?" and said, "Yeah, I know, it wasn't a dream, and yeah, it was Corbo. "He was searching for Elena, like us. Only from somewhere else. Far away."

Thaddeus nodded. "Yeah, death is about as far away as you can get, I guess."

"Anyway," Raphael continued, "he looks at me with this eerie look and he says, 'Beware the ides of March.' Just joking."

Thaddeus rolled his eyes. "I do think flippant humor is out of place here. Just joking. But what the fuck *did* he say?"

" 'Find Elena, get the stone in her hands. Get her in front of a mirror.' I ask him, 'What time? What place?' And he starts laughing like a madman. Till he has to wipe the tears out of his eyes. Then he gives me this serious look and says, 'You let me worry about time and space, and you just worry about getting Yawtlée into Elena's hands. That should be enough of an in-tellectual puzzle for any son of Elena's, right?' Then he goes into another laughing fit. Till he chokes on it. Then he gives me another serious look and says, 'This is no laughing matter. Your friend is here.' He says something snotty about you, and disappears."

Thaddeus looked dumbfounded. " 'Yawtlée,' " he said. "Your stone has a name, and it's Yawtlée?"

Raphael shrugged.

"And just what was it he said about me?"

Obviously working hard to suppress a smile, Raphael informed him. "He said, 'Your friend's here. Perhaps he can help you figure things out. After all, a man with an eternity to live and unfathomable power at his fingertips, whose only ambition is to become a jazz musician, sounds like he would make a good advisor for Elena and her offspring, don't you think?' Then he blinked out."

Thaddeus looked stunned. It had never occurred to him that anyone would consider jazz trivial.

Music and art, what were they, really? Had they started out as a failed attempt at magic and evolved into mere entertainment? Momentary plea-sures, to escape the confines of your own mind? Did enlightened people have any need for that? Was there really such a thing as enlightened people? The face of the old man in the mirror loomed large. There had been some-thing special there, but whatever it was, it was not sweet and gentle. It was as sharp and nasty as a razor, and as impersonal as the plague.

He shuddered. "Don't tell me any more. I got all I can deal with right now." He gestured at the stalls of urinals.

Raphael nodded. "Me, too. Let's just take some time here and catch up."

Just then the door opened and Bitters entered.

"Beggin' your pardon, gents, but, uh, you been in here long enough to dump a month of rations, if ya get what I mean. And somethin' ugly seems to be startin' up in yer absence. It seems Lord Broadbent, or at least he calls himself Lord, has had a bit to drink and loosed one o' his doggies on Blackjack, and chased him outta the inn, and his pals and him, they're all having a good laugh over it, and sayin' a lotta things about how men who play musical instruments—"

"I get it, I get it," Raphael said between gritted teeth, and shook his head. "I think I'm starting to understand why the old man laughs all the time," he said to Thaddeus as they headed back out the door.

"It be either that or cry," Thaddeus agreed.

"There they are, fellows, those fine sensitive makers of song. Alas, I fear in the coming times we may be more in need of the fine art of swordsmanship than that of crooning love ditties."

It was the tall man dressed all in russet brown, the one who had thrown a few jibes toward Raphael about Blackjack earlier.

"Funny thing," Thaddeus informed Raphael, who was heading right for the man, "is they all stirred up by the music. But they aiming it the wrong way."

"Sorry about your little white doggie. But he turned out to be a coward, as befits a . . ."

Raphael looked at Thaddeus, sighed, and then slapped Lord Broadbent crisply across the face. Since it was Raphael, the man went clear out of his chair, and, grabbing the tablecloth for support, took a lot of food and ale with him to the floor, where he sat in it, blinking and seeing stars. Or at least little white flecks of nothing. One of the lord's enormous dogs, the one tied to his chair, reacted by surging for Raphael, pulling the chair behind him as if it were made of cork.

But dogs are easy to control, and Thaddeus dropped him in his tracks with a mental command reinforced by the power of his stone.

"Play dead, Fido," he said, and the dog whipped around and lay down on the floor, where he stayed, whimpering pitifully.

The men around the table jumped up and all made suitable exclamations, but it was clear that they were waiting for their leader to react.

Staring furiously at Raphael, he rose up, mustering what dignity he could out of the situation, and said, "Very well, then, you leave me no choice. If indeed you are on an equal social level to mine, I demand from you the satisfaction of a trial by arms. A gentlemen's duel."

Thaddeus took one of his handguns out of its shoulder holster and offered it to Raphael. "Shoot the mo'fucker," he suggested.

Raphael smiled and shook his head wearily. "I'm so tired and confused. If I weren't immune to disease, I'd say I'm getting a headache. Where were we? Oh yeah, a duel. Yes, we're equals. I'm, uh, Lord Raphael, and my friend here is Lord Thaddeus. This is our man-at-arms, Lord Bitters, and actually the white dog you just chased out of here is Lord Blackjack. So a duel is fine."

Lord Broadbent looked seriously perplexed. "A gentleman doesn't joke about such things," he said, rubbing his jaw. "And so I doubt you really are a lord. Yet I will only be satisfied in this matter when you are dead. Let us immediately go outside and get this affair over with."

He brought his hand up from his chin to tenderly caress the top of his head. "I, too," he said lugubriously, "am getting a headache."

Outside, they found Blackjack waiting for them on the porch, wagging his tail end furiously, and even crouching down and springing into the air a couple of times in his ecstasy to see them. If he was a coward, he was a shameless one.

"Guess I might as well take care this right now," Thaddeus said as he laid down his guitar case and opened it, took the chain choke collar off Blackjack, and replaced it with the spiked one.

"Hold your horses," Raphael remarked to the impatient nobleman and his rowdy followers. "Be with you in a minute."

The dog, apparently thrilled with his new image, jumped for joy, almost knocking Thaddeus over again.

"You look great, Blackjack," Raphael said. "Someone sics their dog on you again, let them eat spikes. Okay, let's get it over with. I'm tired and I want to get to bed early."

Everyone in the inn cheerfully followed them down off the porch and into the road, ladies along with their men, children with their mothers, obviously delighted that an evening's musical entertainment was to be followed by a bloody fight to the death. Although the moon was full, some of them had brought torches, and they formed a circle around the two men as they moved into the middle of the dirt road and squared off, facing each other.

"Yours is the choice of weapons," Lord Broadbent announced, drawing his sword: apparently you had a choice here, but you always chose swords.

Raphael held up his hands for everyone to see. "These," he said softly.

This was answered by a loud murmur from the crowd.

Broadbent frowned. "You wish to fight to the death with your hands?"

"They are deadly weapons," Raphael answered.

Thaddeus chuckled. "What this, a king fu movie?" But he still held his pistol in his right hand.

"Could you tell your friend to put that away?" Lord Broadbent asked Raphael. "For some reason it maketh me nervous."

Raphael smiled. "You have good instincts," he said, "but the answer is no. It's insurance that your friends won't join in."

"He thinks to hold them back with that?"

"He'll kill every one of them."

Lord Broadbent, who was obviously sobering up quickly, said, "Very well, but you can reassure him that no matter what happens, my friends won't interfere. You know, perhaps I was wrong to malign your small white doggie, I can see that now. I was stirred up. We are heading into hard times. A few of us feel the answer is . . . revolution." He swallowed, as if trying to take back the word. "I'm willing to forget and forgive, if you want to call it . . ." A moan from the crowd drowned him out.

When they were silent again, Raphael said, "Don't try to weasel out of it. That's my dog. Anyone cruel to my dog is going to pay for it through the teeth."

Lord Broadbent nodded. He was looking sadder by the moment.

"Of course," he said, taking off his fancy jacket and tossing it to one of his men. "Well, anyway," he said, holding up his fists, "I am bigger than you."

Another murmur from the crowd as they could see Raphael smiling in the torchlight. He began to circle.

A few seconds later Lord Broadbent was facedown in the dirt, squirming helplessly, while Raphael, who had his hooks in, as the Brazilians like to put it, rode him effortlessly, taking his time about getting the choke hold in just right, before the final touch of barring the left arm across the back of the neck and clamping down.

"Who bigger now, dude?" Thaddeus trash-talked from the crowd.

Raphael clamped down, grinding the lord's face into the dirt, then let up. "Want to live or die?" he said.

But Broadbent could only answer by choking and coughing.

"Think about it. Here's another taste."

The crowd howled as he clamped down again.

"What? I couldn't hear it."

"Live." It was a choked whisper.

"Sure you do," Raphael agreed. "You've probably got plenty to live for, right? A lot of good deeds left to do. And I want you to do them, too. I don't want to kill you, but . . ." And once again he clamped down, and let up.

Broadbent lay there choking and wheezing like a dying asthmatic.

"But," Raphael continued, "I would like to avoid any further meaningless conflicts like this one by making it clear what happens to lords who fuck with my dog. Do you get it?"

"Kill me?" the poor man choked.

"Not necessarily, but it's got to be clear, see. Now I'm going to let you back up, and you have a choice. You can stand up and brush yourself off and say, loud enough for everyone to hear you—" Raphael paused, composing. "Let's see, how about, 'I am no gentleman, but alas, a lowborn lackey, and the white dog is my master.' Or you can figure it was a fluke and come at me again. This time I'll break your right arm. If that doesn't work, I'll have to kill you."

He let go of Broadbent and back-somersaulted away from him and back onto his feet again.

Broadbent got up slowly and mumbled, "You can do it that easily?"

Raphael smiled. "Brazilian jiujitsu rules," he said by way of explanation.

Lord Broadbent sighed. "Oh, very well," he said. "If it has to be." Then he continued haltingly. "Let's see. I am no gentleman, but alas—there was an 'alas' there, no?—alas, a lackey . . ."

"Lowborn," Raphael reminded him.

"Ods bodkins, man, all lackeys are lowborn, by definition. Oh, all right, I am a lowborn lackey, and the white dog—ugly as he is—is my master. Oh, all right, all right. I'm a lowborn, dirty lackey and—what?—a religious fanatic. And the white dog is my god. And I grovel before him in the dirt."

The crowd roared laughter.

"And to kiss his white ass would be like another man kissing his fairest maiden's lips. What's more . . ." The man was grinning like an idiot. The crowd—even Raphael—was laughing.

"Enough, you fool." Raphael shook his head and turned wearily back to the inn.

It was quite chilly out, and all at once, as the excitement wore off, everybody was becoming aware of it.

"Not only a lowborn lackey, but a freezing one. And like thyself, with a headache. A big one."

Raphael smiled ruefully and said, "Funny, mine's gone already."

Later, when he was seated back at his table, drinking the ale, which would only affect him momentarily, the beat-up lord came over and held his big hands out in a peace gesture.

"I know, I know," he said. "I've been a fool, but I can learn. All that has to be done is choke the ignorance out of me." He was an ugly man in a way, gaunt high cheekbones, big nose bent at the bridge ("broad bent"?), small blue eyes, stringy blond hair, big mouth, big teeth, but his smile was quick and sweet.

Raphael motioned to a chair, and Broadbent sighed and sat down in it.

"What I'm trying to say is you caught me at just the wrong time. I'm not like that. I don't care who's a lord and who's not. I know that in our hearts, we all have the same—" He paused and closed his eyes, seeking the right word. "The same everything."

"Renounce your title," Thaddeus suggested.

He looked amazed. "Can you do that?"

"Sure. Why not?" Thaddeus stood up and announced, "Ladies and gentlemen. Kiddies, too. Let it hereby be known that I, Thaddeus, do renounce my, uh, lordship, and barony and such. And from now on will only be, uh, treated in the manner with which you would treat the lowest of those among you." He bowed. The announcement was greeted with a lot of muttering, and sparse applause—the latter mostly from the children.

But Lord Broadbent was stunned. Tears brimmed up in his eyes. "By God's bodkin." They spilled over and rolled down over his knifelike ridge of cheekbones and down his hollow cheeks. He reached across the table and clasped Thaddeus's hands. "You are what we have all been waiting for. What we have been here balancing on the edge looking for, which way to jump. You are the sign. The word."

He jumped to his feet and passionately renounced his titles. And after a pause, one of the men in his group followed suit. An hour later and everyone in the place was an ecstatic, newborn peasant.

It was only as they were finally heading up the stairs to their beds that Raphael remembered to question Bitters about the rest-room plumbing.

"Oh, it's the witches," he said. "You know, when you got a world run by women, the plumbing is going to be first class."

# 7

Floating in the luxurious cabin of the Lexus to the airport, then the jet to LA, where a brand-new Mercedes awaited them. The Mercedes, the latest top-of-the-line model, was to impress upon Daniel Reed, chief investigator, and his ilk, that while the company Lexus was a status perk the Guardians bestowed upon their firms of lawyers and private investigators, there were levels beyond that. Not that the Mercedes was any better than the Lexus. In fact, it was probably not as good, but in Violet's dress-for-success world, it scarcely mattered which was the better product. It was all a matter of the power of symbols. And she was right this time, as she was most of the time. Daniel was impressed.

"Great car," he mumbled as Violet asked him if he would mind driving. Only Tippi was so out of it as to not care a whit what she was chauffeured around in. Usually she fought to drive.

But today she had a headache. Of course the proximity of Violet's stone meant that she did not have a headache for long. But she felt funny. Apprehensive. Ridiculously jumpy.

LA was supposed to be home, but Tippi had been gone for a while. And LA, of all the cities in the world, was the city of absolute, irrevocable change. You almost got the feeling that if you closed your eyes, everything, both sentient and inanimate, would be spinning like pieces of junk in a kaleidoscope. Problem was, it only got uglier and uglier. It was moving more quickly than any eye could follow, yet it was crawling along wounded and battered. LA had the policy of not quite ever recovering from any injury. It bore hideous scars from every riot, every earthquake, every injustice (and there were, as you might imagine, quite a few of those). Every grudge was nurtured—revered, even. The Blacks especially were encouraged to take everything out on whomever they wished, and were currently going all-out to do to the Jews and Koreans everything that had been done to them at an earlier time. LA had started out a sadist, but when you've dealt out all the pain you can and it's still not enough, there's only one thing left to hurt. So, like all sadists, it was turning into more and more of a masochist as it went along its merry way.

Its astral structure was woven of broken dreams and hideously ruthless ambitions, jazzed up here and there with vivid flashes of bizarre, unfulfillable surges of flipped-out, erotically obsessed maniacs. The astral soundtrack was all the time, every hour of the day and night, millions of hoarse, damaged voices singing "me, me, me." At the top of their tortured lungs. It had started out bad but only gotten worse. And like all truly sensitive people, it hurt Tippi just to be there.

It was she who had insisted that they get off the freeway and drive up the surface streets. Since she was the one who "knew LA," it was either that or dig out maps.

But driving up Pico for a ways, and later switching over to Olympic Boulevard in order to avoid (ha) traffic, had bewildered and depressed her immeasurably.

It was not so much like driving through a foreign country as it was like driving through several all shoved in together against their wills. Only just the slums. Nothing charming or picturesque need apply.

They passed Pat's Bar, all done up in Irish green, and upstairs, Schmucker and Schmucker's Law Offices. Followed by Happy Breakfast—a small Korean breakfast joint? Tippi envisioned a scene where Pat, furiously polishing a glass, says to Mike, "Did ya notice, Mike me boy, all of that turrible turrible racket those Jew lawyers are makin' upstairs just now?"

"But, Pat," Mike says, "I don't hear a single solitary thing."

"Exactly," Pat shoots back. "Wonder what those sneaky little devils are up ta?"

Just then a procession of colorfully dressed Koreans enters the bar, carrying a steaming platter of quail eggs. "Happy breakfast to you," they sing charmingly, "happy breakfast to you, happy breakfast, dear Pat," etc., etc. "Today is your five-millionth breakfast, so happy breakfast to you, Pat."

Tippi blinked.

"What's the matter?" Violet said, obviously exasperated. "It was you who wanted to get off the freeway. I just hope we're not too late."

"We've got plenty of time," Daniel said from up front. "This woman's all business. She's probably going to hang out there till midnight."

"How would you—?"

"Hey, surveillance team out there, right?" he said. "We're listening in, taping phone calls, taking photos, checking out everyone we can identify in the police files. If anything at all happens, they'll call me on the car phone here."

Tippi looked skeptical. "The LAPD cooperates with you?"

Daniel nodded. "Sure. We bribe them. We bribe everybody. Everyone cooperates with us."

Violet looked pleased. *See,* she was obviously thinking, *told you so.* Causing Tippi's frown to deepen.

"I've got a headache is all," Tippi said, almost wishing for a real one to help her block out the terrifying vision of LA. "I hate this place," she continued. "Only bad things will happen to us here. We should have just let them handle it for us."

"That would be my advice," Daniel offered from behind the wheel.

"In the first place," Violet said, ignoring Daniel, "as you should certainly be the one to know, there are all kinds of things we can do that these people can't. If the boys are really in trouble we need to get all the necessary information immediately. We can hardly afford to wait around for them to follow their 'procedures.' " She said the word with obvious disdain, causing a puzzled expression on Daniel's face.

"In the second place, don't tell me you have a headache, because you can't have a headache. The stone won't let you have a headache."

"I can have a headache if I want to," Tippi snapped angrily. Then, "No, you're right, of course. I can't even have a fucking headache, because your fucking stone won't let me. But this place makes me sick—somehow."

"Look, dream child," Violet snapped back, "wake up. You forced us to the streets and now you don't like it. Okay. But not liking something is not related to being sick. Why don't you turn over a new leaf and start describing the real world in realistic terms. You know," she added cruelly, "as if you were one of the sane."

"My, my, that would be a goal," Tippi replied. Then, "But I thought that insanity was an illness. And didn't you just tell me that your little stone won't allow me to be ill? So how can that be, O wise one?"

"The illness part of it is euphemism," Violet informed her. "The mental part is real enough. And there are no little germies sneaking around spreading it."

"But it spreads." Tippi pointed out the window. "Maybe LA causes it, do you think?"

"There you go again," Violet groused, then shut up.

After a while, Daniel, knowing he shouldn't but unable to resist, remarked, "You have a stone that cures, uh, cures headaches?"

"Cures everything," Violet corrected. "Want to sample?"

"But I don't have a headache," he said, obviously thinking, *These two women are really shooting a few blanks here.*

"No problem," Violet answered.

The car swerved. "Oh, Jesus," Daniel moaned. "Shit. Stop it. Stop it."

"What the fuck are you doing?" Tippi yelled at Violet. "Trying to get us in an accident? That will be a real big help to the 'boys,' as you like to call them, won't it?"

"You're right, of course," Violet agreed.

Daniel gave a loud sigh of relief from the driver's seat and said, "Oh, thank you, thank you, thank you."

And for a while they rode along in silence, each thinking their own radically different thoughts, but keeping them all inside.

Next they drove through a shabbier area, where mariachi music blasted through the open doors of shops and the dirty sidewalks were decorated with mannequins modeling many varieties of clothes. Here the streets were full of people, and studying them, Tippi could not judge whether their expressions were happy or sad or angry.

This could not be America, Tippi thought. We must be in the slums of Guadalajara. Someplace like that.

"Does look foreign," Violet commented, "but so what?"

Nobody answered. But it was then that they took a wrong turn and wound up in hell. And hell was definitely American. Demented beggars all dressed in rags, with expressions like zombies, drifted up and down the sidewalk. Everything was shades of gray, but covered with grime. A sign on a generic building read proudly, RAGFINDERS OF AMERICA, causing even Violet to shudder.

It was not far from here that they found what they were looking for.

"I don't get it," Violet said, staring at the ugly building. "I thought Rudy was rich."

"This is how he got rich," Daniel pointed out. "He didn't just put out toilet seats. He opened a couple other shops in LA, mostly wholesale clothing, but this is the main one. He also had some in Florida, couple in Texas. He used illegal aliens, mainly Mexicans, here and in Texas. Florida he shopped around, mixed it up a little. Cheap labor, cheap rent. One of his workers tried to make a break for it, he turned him or her in. Now the whole setup's got the woman, once was his secretary in Florida, to worry about.

Didn't I tell you? Weirder and weirder. His widow signed virtually all of his enterprises over to a corporation called—get this—Artemis Enterprises. Turns out that's his secretary, Brenda. Former secretary," he amended. "Pretty suspect, don't you think?"

"It reeks," Violet agreed.

"Anyway, there we are." He pointed to a dirty white van parked down the street, drove on past it, made a U-turn, and parked behind it.

A tall slender fit-looking black woman opened the back door of the van, stepped out, closed it behind her, and said, "Danny boy, a Mercedes. I always knew you'd make it big someday. Going in?"

"Violet, Tippi, this is one of my crew, Shawnee. Good with computers, guns, hand-to-hand. You name it, she's good at it Shawnee, this is—these are—our bosses. Big bosses, that is, as in 'Thy will be done.' "

Shawnee nodded. "Men," she said. "I'm not that good with men. I'll trade the hand-to-hand talent for the man thing." She grinned.

"That's not what I heard," Daniel retorted. "Who's in there with you?"

"Willie and Benton. Norm should be here"—she checked her Seiko— "any minute. He went to get a cup of joe."

Daniel frowned. "He should be here now. Damn it, Shawnee, you know that."

She glared right back at him. "What the fuck am I supposed to do, tackle him and put the cuffs on? He was hungry. He left."

Daniel said, through gritted teeth, "We'll talk about this later. And believe me, talk we will. You're either in charge or you're not. Meanwhile, back at the ranch: yes, we're going in. The three of us. You keep awake. I'm not expecting trouble, but . . ." He rolled his eyes. "You know me, trouble is my business."

Shawnee grinned. "That evokes an ugly picture, but me and old Betsy will be hanging out here waiting for your call." She patted the short barreled colt she wore in a shoulder holster.

"Seriously," he said, "I don't anticipate anything dangerous here, but . . ." He shrugged. "Ladies," he said.

Violet looked ready, but Tippi was staring at the building, expression filled with what was obviously, at the very least, apprehension.

"I don't like it," she said. "You got a gun, Vi?"

Violet said, "Oh, come on, Tippi. Get real. You're not going to need a gat, partner. We'll just mosey on down and have a few words with the late great Rudy's former secretary, and then we can get out of this hellhole they call the City of Angels."

Tippi shook her head. "I'm not going in there without a gun," she said.

She had her arms wrapped around her shoulders as if it were a cold night, which it was not.

"Oh, for—"

"Here, take one of mine," Shawnee said, and put one foot up on the van's bumper, pushed up one leg of her loose-fitting slacks, and revealed a small automatic in an ankle holster.

"Here, okay? It's a thirty-two. I carry"—she shrugged—"more than one, so you take this baby."

Daniel, who did not believe in very small handguns, grimaced and rolled his eyes, but said nothing.

"Here's the safety. You push it off with your thumb. Hold it in both hands like in the movies. And once you start firing, keep firing. Don't stop till the gun stops, okay?"

Tippi shook her head. "I don't like guns," she muttered.

"Oh, for God's sake," Violet moaned. "Give me the gun. I'll carry it in with me and protect the little lady with my life. How's that, Tip?"

Still looking unhappy, Tippi nodded and said, "Let's do it."

Violet put the gun in the small black-velvet purse she was carrying; and they crossed the street, walked up the block, and knocked at the door.

Daniel took out his weapon, a considerably larger handgun, but Violet said, "You won't need that," so he shrugged and put it back under his coat.

It was a while before the door was opened by a weary-looking, skinny young Hispanic woman dressed in jeans and a generic white blouse.

"*No hablo inglés,*" she said, "but is *mucho* closed *ahora.*" She tried to shut the door.

Violet answered, "Close this, why don't you?"

The woman grabbed her head and howled, "Aiee!" Then just stood there in the doorway, eyes shut tight in pain, muttering a steady stream of swear words in Spanish. But she made no move to stop them as they squeezed by her and entered.

"Upstairs. Aiee, *mamá!*" she muttered in answer to their question as to where they would find Brenda.

"There, there, it's all gone now," Violet said as they headed for the door marked STAIRS, but the woman's only response was to make the sign of the cross with her index fingers, point it at Violet, and hiss the word "*Brujas.*"

Tippi smiled. "She says we're witches. But what about all these cutesie toilet seats? Aren't they a certain kind of magic?"

"Focus, Tippi," Violet snapped. There were a few of the "cute seats" scattered on a big table, and many more of them stacked in the rows of bins in the back of the big room they were moving through.

Tippi picked one up, bright red. THE HOT SEAT, it said. Another was labeled USED BUTTS. Yet another with cartoons of pigeons said, IT'S YOUR BIG CHANCE TO GET EVEN—THIS TOILET'S FULL OF PIGEONS. One had red hearts and pink, chubby, winged cupids on a white plastic surface.

"That one's nice," Tippi remarked, causing Violet to wince and suggest again, "Focus, Tippi."

But the last one she saw as they went through the door and started up the stairs was a plain wooden one labeled, YOUR ASS IS MINE. Causing Tippi to shiver involuntarily.

Daniel led the way, Violet followed on his heels, and Tippi tagged along after them.

"You know," Tippi said, "you're getting to where you can dish out the headaches as well as I ever could, and it was my specialty. Sometimes I feel like we're melting together, into one being. Despite the fact that I—"

"Will you shut the fuck up and focus! This is a real-life, adventure, Tippi. Tighten up or get out of here."

Violet had actually stopped and turned around on the stairway.

"Sure," Tippi said. "Why not? Fuck you." And she started back down the stairs. But went only a couple of steps before she sat down and, bracing her elbows on her thighs, held her head in her hands and sighed. "Wait a minute," she said. "Wait up, will you?"

Near the top of the stairs, Violet and Daniel paused to exchange exasperated glances. As this assignment wore on, Tippi was fast losing her allure for Daniel, while Violet, on the other hand, was looking better and better. Cool under pressure, strong-willed—a survivor like himself. And really a lot better-looking than you thought when first you saw her. Strong bone structure, elegant posture. She grew on you. Perhaps underneath that cold facade . . . ? But then again, perhaps not. When you were as young, successful, and good-looking as Daniel Reed, chief investigator, the world was an ocean of eternity brimming with eligible, attractive young fish. Thing to do was hook them. You could always throw them back.

But as Tippi caught them at the top of the stairs, he had to admit to himself that, nutcase or not, Tippi was hot!

"Look, I'm sorry," Tippi panted, "but something is really wrong here. I can feel it."

Without a word, Violet proceeded through the door and down the hall to another door labeled OFFICE.

Again Violet and Daniel exchanged glances. Daniel unbuttoned his jacket and took his nine-millimeter out of the little fast-draw holster. Checked it out. Put it back and, leaving the coat unbuttoned, nodded.

Violet tried the door and, finding it unlocked, opened it and went in first. It was a large and surprisingly well-furnished office, clashing with the spareness of rest of the factory. There were a lot of filing cabinets and thick beige carpet. There were paintings on the wall and a few books in a small bookcase. There was even a small refrigerator in one corner.

Apparently this had been Rudy's West Coast headquarters, when he was in LA. Either that or Rudy had just plain taken good care of Rudy.

A tall, rawboned, strong but attractive-looking woman in a simple brown business suit sat behind the big desk that faced the door, writing in a spiral notebook. She did not look up from the littered desk until she had finished what she was working on. Then she put down her pen and looked up, frowning at Violet.

At one side of the desk, sprawled out comfortably in a plush leather chair, was a very large, tough-looking woman with crew-cut short hair and a perpetual scowl, who jumped up immediately and hovered, staring at the woman behind the desk. Waiting for the word.

"Brenda, I presume," Violet said to the one behind the desk.

The woman's frown disappeared. She actually looked amused. She held out her hand, apparently signaling her bodyguard to calm down, and said, "What on earth do you think you're doing? This is private property and I'm quite busy. I'm sure you don't have an appointment, so—"

She gestured to her bodyguard, who thrust out her lower lip and advanced toward them, muttering "Outta here," in a low, gravelly voice.

Tippi, who had followed them in the door, leaned back against the wall and took in the whole scene. A surge of grief overwhelmed her, causing her to almost collapse and slide down the wall like jelly. But somehow she kept her feet.

Suddenly she was in the world of auras, and in this room, murky browns and grays all mixed up with a swirling black cloud predominated. Somehow the mixture made her ill. Queasy. But immediately, she felt Violet's stone soothing her, curing her. "It's you I really love," it whispered.

As always in this world, time disappeared, and her little brother Toby was there with them.

"Hi, I'm dead," he said, causing Tippi to moan.

Violet's head turned and she flashed an angry glance at Tippi. But only for a moment.

"Actually," Violet said, "as charming as this place is, we aren't planning on hanging around for tea. Just as soon as you tell us everything we want to know, we'll be out of here."

"Dead," Tippi's little lost brother repeated. Could nobody see him but her? "But then so are some grown-ups in this room. See that thing on the corner of her desk? Football hat, helmet? Who wants ta play wif me?"

Tippi moaned again. What *was* that thing on the woman's desk, which did look something like a football helmet?

"Bad news, Tippi," he answered. Then he laughed.

"Go away," Tippi said—unfortunately, aloud. "You're not really here and you're bothering . . ."

Everyone was staring at her, of course. She was losing it. Her fat little brother Toby grinned and shrugged. He was not going away. Like always, he was hanging around just when you hoped he would get lost.

"Well, well," Brenda said jovially, "how charming. An old-fashioned nutcase. I suggest you rush her to the emergency shrink. And also, get out of here right now or I call the police."

"I don't think so," Daniel said, "not with all those dead bodies you left lying around at the Faire. I don't know where you put them, but I'm sure that with a little nudging the police can dig them up."

Brenda looked amused. "Well, you're wrong there," she said. "But still, you obviously know too much for your own good. How thoughtful of you to come traipsing in here and notify me. The amateurs in the van outside, right?"

Violet blinked, and Daniel said, sounding genuinely offended, "What van?"

Brenda pressed a button on her intercom and said, "Jenny, have your crew take out the van. Now. Oh, and send a couple of shooters in here, will you? Thanks." Click. "Glad to hear it's not your van, though. Jodine"—she motioned to the big woman who was obviously her muscle—"take him out. We'll keep her and the twinkie till we figure this one out."

The twinkie? Tippi snapped out of her fugue state, for the moment, and zeroed in on the now. Jodine and Daniel, facing each other off, looked like something out of an old western. Violet thrust out her hand at Jodine and said, "Hold it, Jodine. I don't think you'll be taking anyone out tonight."

"But she's wrong," whispered Tippi's dead little brother as he dropped back in.

Jodine, meanwhile, put both hands to her head and moaned. Staggered and fell back in the chair. "She's Wicca," she muttered.

It was Brenda's turn to look astonished. "That's not possible," she was saying, when Tippi managed to block out her little brother again and throw some punishment Brenda's way.

In contrast to Jodine, Brenda, despite the pain, got up out of her chair, staggered around her desk, and, gritting her teeth, took a few steps toward her tormentors.

"Let up, please. I'll tell you whatever you want to know."

Meanwhile, Daniel made use of their advantage by locking the door from the inside; and just in time, too, because now someone was trying to get in, pounding on the door.

"Brenda, you okay?"

"Tell them to go away," Violet suggested.

"Sure. Go away. I'm fine, okay?"

"Now you're going to tell us what this is all about. What you're doing with Elena, Rafe, and Thaddeus."

"Elena?" Brenda looked genuinely puzzled. "Actually, I don't know what you're talking about. Listen, babe, you've got a lot of power. The both of you. Why fight with us? Join us. Make sense?"

"Oh, yeah," Violet said, "lot of sense. Now don't say anything more until I ask you something. And if you're thinking of throwing that funky-looking bicycle helmet at me, forget it."

Brenda had backed up and come to rest with her back against her desk and her right hand on the odd-looking helmet.

"What, throw this? It's a fashion statement."

Violet and Tippi watched in amazement as Brenda coyly put it on and winked. "Pretty *Vogue,* huh?"

Then too many things happened too fast for Tippi to ever put them in order and make sense out of them. She yelled at Violet, "Something's wrong! She's blocking us off!"

Both Tippi and Violet strained to break through the barrier protecting Brenda from their psychic assault, leaving Brenda's bodyguard, Jodine, who was now coming up out of her chair, free to act.

Daniel quick-drew his gun, fell into his two-handed shooter's stance, aiming at Brenda but hesitating to shoot. Big Jodine came free of her chair, piece already in hand, and shot Daniel, who swiveled around and shot her back. Both of them, looking surprised, but still on their feet, took aim and fired again. Both of them went down.

Brenda, meanwhile, had opened up her suit coat and come out with a small automatic, reminding Tippi of the one in Violet's purse.

"You cannot pull the trigger," Violet said in amazement as the bullet plowed into her chest, knocking her down. Her purse went flying. Tippi kicked it, skidding across the hardwood floor toward the big desk, took a few low fast steps, and threw herself down, scrambling around behind the desk.

Brenda, making sure she'd hit Violet, turned too late and got off a shot but missed Tippi, who had by now scurried around the desk on all fours and crawled into the space underneath, and on up to the front. There was room enough for her to reach out and pull—yes, it was right there—the purse through. Frantically she opened it and tossed the contents on the floor, huddled there underneath the desk, and snatched up the gun. Safety? Was it this latch? Had to be. She pushed it off with her thumb.

"Brenda, Brenda, let us in!" someone was shouting.

"Shut up!" Brenda shouted back. "I'm okay, but I need to concentrate here."

Brenda's gun went off again, and again. She was finishing them off, Tippi realized, rising to a new level of horror.

"Nice piece," Brenda mumbled to herself as she picked up Daniel's Glock nine. One thing she envied about men, though not the only, was that, the way they dressed, they could conceal bigger weapons.

"Okay, nutso, come on out here where I can see you and we'll keep you alive. Come on. I'm armed big-time now, so don't make me mad." She fired off a shot into the desk, but deliberately high up, indicating that while she didn't want to kill Tippi, it would be a mistake she could live with. Bullet, of course, went clear through.

Shit! Tippi looked at the little .32. Should she stand up and fire over the top? If she hit her, would it stop her, or once the maniac in the helmet knew she had a gun wouldn't she just blast the desk full of holes with her nine-millimeter?

Tippi started to scoot back out to where she could stand up. If Brenda turned her back to unlock the door, she would stand up and try to nail her then.

"Brenda, Brenda!" they were yelling again. Tippi readied herself.

"I said shut the fuck up!" Brenda shouted back. She was zeroed in on the desk, waiting for some part or another of Tippi to show.

"I said stand up." Another bullet through the desk. Tippi scooted back under again, and as far forward as she could get.

"I can't," she said softly, trying to sound weak. "You, you already hit me."

The back wall of the desk went down practically to the floor, but not all the way. Just as Tippi had been able to pull the purse in through it, she was now able to lie flat and press her cheek to the wood floor and peek out through the crack. What she saw was astonishing. Apparently Brenda had kicked off her high-heeled shoes and was sneaking up on the desk, because what Tippi saw here was two bare feet with the neatly trimmed and manicured toenails painted a bright red, quite close. Doubtlessly Brenda was holding the gun in both hands, covering the top of the desk.

"I said stand up! Shot or not, babe. Get your ass up where I can . . ."

The feet were so close now she could almost bite them. Instead, Tippi placed the flat little automatic on the floor, thrust it up to the edge of the desk, and, trying to see around it as best she could, fired it. Twice.

There was a scream of pain and fury. One of the toes disappeared in a blur of blood, and now the feet disappeared, and there was a thud on the desk. For a moment or two Tippi didn't get it. Then she realized Brenda had thrown herself on top of the desk to get her feet out of the line of fire.

Would the little .32 have the power to get through the desk? No time to figure it out. Tippi rolled over onto her back and began shooting up into the desktop.

Had it gotten through? It made clean holes, but still had to go through another layer.

But then she heard a strange rasping sound which had to be somebody trying hard to suck air, and something wet began to drip through one of the holes, splashing onto her chest. Something red.

So she shot up into the desk again and again until the little gun was empty, which was a surprisingly long time.

Then, shaking so badly she could hardly hold the gun, she scooted back out and got the courage to stand up, half expecting to find Brenda waiting for her, aiming the big nine. Surprise!

But Brenda was dead and the room was full of the dead, including her little brother, who was laughing and hopping up and down on his chubby little legs and singing, "Told ya, told ya." Whoever was pounding on the door was dead. He just didn't know it yet.

"Brenda," the person at the door was yelling. Then, "Whoever you are, you'd better let us in right now. We took out all your people in the van. They're dead as doornails, and you will be too, you don't open up this door."

Ignoring this, Tippi picked up the Glock nine that had once belonged to a handsome youth named Daniel, and went over and kneeled beside Violet's body and reached down inside her blouse and fished out the stone, where it hung in an amulet against her bloodstained pale clear skin, and held it in her hand, felt the surge of power.

"No, it's you who are dead!" she shouted at the voice behind the door. "Now move over and press your body up against the door just to the right of the doorknob." She sent the mental command along with the spoken one. "Knock when you're ready," she suggested.

After a moment's hesitation, there came a knock. Tippi fired off two shots into the door, holding the gun two-handed as she had overheard Jimmy Running Deer instructing Violet, back at the ranch.

And even though she was already dazed and her ears were ringing, the loud crash of the gun going off in her hands shocked her and the recoil threw her arms straight up, so that she had to bring them down and aim again to get the second shot off.

"Ohh, I'm hit." And then other voices, muddled, excited, shocked.

"That's how I'm going to open the fucking door," Tippi shouted. She was crying now. Violet was not dead, but Violet was hit hard, and was as close to dead as you could get and still be alive. The stone had wonderful healing powers, but she didn't look all that much as if she was going to make it here.

Tippi laid down the gun next to her within easy reach, and covered the stone with her hands where it lay on Violet's chest. Tried to direct the healing current to Violet's wounds. Would this make any difference? There were no rules here. But she felt instinctively that her own psychic abilities were greater than Violet's.

"I promise you, I won't let you die," she said, choking on the words. "You are not going to die, Violet."

"Oh, yes she is." It was her little brother Toby again. "Will too, will too, will too," he chanted.

Trying to heal Violet, not expecting it at all, let alone willing it, she felt the healing power of the stone pour back into her hands and rush up into her brain, radiating her with the power to see more clearly than she had ever seen before.

A series of visions flashed before her in a moment, and she had the power to identify them, to label them, and then file them away in her memory. Order them. And she had the power to see herself, almost as if she were someone else looking in, to see that all of that crippling guilt, all of the problems that plagued her, were based on one simple misunderstanding. She had never clearly realized that the past was dead and gone. Totally, irrevocably gone. A myth.

Only the now was real, and it was totally unrelated to the past. It was a living, moving, rushing, opening . . . Careful, you cannot name it. For a *name* is the past.

"Am I healing you or are you healing me?" she asked Violet. Toby, her fat, goofy little brother, was gone, of course, only not really, because he had never been here. It had just been her guilt that had haunted her, not Toby. *Me, haunting me,* she thought to herself. *As if there were two of us.*

More pounding on the door. She ignored it.

"Listen up in there. It's okay. Daniel, it's Norman Meyers from the van. We got 'em, okay? I'm coming in, so don't panic."

Bodies kept pounding into the door. Cursing. *Guess they just don't fly open like in the movies when the big he-man rams his shoulder into them.*

The pounding stopped. Though Tippi couldn't see it, she could sense someone opening it with a credit card.

First man through was about five-six, heavy build, plump even. He held his hands out, empty. "Christ, don't shoot me. I told you, I'm Norman from the van. Oh shit, Danny, too. He never wanted anyone to call him Danny," he said, sounding surprised.

Tippi put down the gun and put both hands over the stone again. "Don't die," she whispered. Then to Norm, "Ambulance."

Norm, who at this moment was down on his knees, examining Daniel, got up, went over, and kneeled beside Tippi.

"Ambulance may not be such a hot idea right now. We've got our own people. We can handle these things, see, but you call in an ambulance, and I don't know if we can keep the police out of it."

Tippi looked up at him with those big eyes, magnified by tears, and said, "Call a fucking ambulance right fucking now, okay?"

He got up and said something to one of the other men, then he began to examine the bodies in the room. All pretty dead. Tippi forgot about him, focused only on Violet. "You saved me. Now it's my turn, so you just hang in there."

"Ambulance on the way," somebody said.

Tippi nodded. The plump agent concluded his examination of the room and went back over to Tippi. He fastidiously pulled up the legs of his trousers and kneeled down next to her; he did not look at home there, but willing to endure.

"Look, I'm Norm. I told you, right? Norman Meyers. I was in the van. I was down the corner, getting something to eat. I came back and it was locked up and nobody answered. I got it unlocked and . . ." He choked. "And they must have used some kind of poison gas bomb, thrown it in, and closed the door or something. I phoned in for backup, and here we are."

"You have them all?"

He nodded. "Pretty sure."

"Let the poor wetbacks go. They're just cheap labor. LA slaves. Give them a couple of hundred bucks each, okay? In fact, give them more, say a grand each, take them back over the border, and tell them to apply for legal entrance, otherwise stay in Mexico."

Norm's expression told her that something was wrong.

"Yeah, what?"

"It—it disturbs me to hear you call them 'wetbacks.' "

Tippi buried her face in her hands and grumbled something he couldn't hear. When she looked back at him, her eyes were, he thought, enormous and fierce. He actually flinched.

"For God's sake, Norm, what do you want me to call them?"

"I think 'illegal aliens' would be appropriate," he said, holding his ground, though he looked as though he would have liked to back up.

"Okay, then take the illegal aliens, the ones who sneaked over the Rio Grande, back to Mexico, but don't take any of the illegal aliens from Iran to Mexico, get it?"

Norm winced. "I get what you mean. I guess they are all from Mexico."

"Gee, that's my guess, too, Norm. And the others—"

"The others?"

"The ones who aren't illegal aliens from Mexico. I want to know everything they know, and I mean everything. I don't care how you get it. Torture wouldn't upset me right now. But keep them alive."

Tears were streaming down her cheeks but she hung in there.

"I've got to stay with her. Until she's okay. But if you haven't gotten it out of them by then, I assure you I will."

"Is she gonna live?" Norm seemed doubtful.

"I personally guarantee it. Violet, you are going to live."

But Violet said nothing. Not dead, she looked nonetheless closer to communing with Daniel than with Tippi. Norm had his doubts.

No longer able to endure the kneeling position, he rose back up to his feet.

"Shit, they're all dead," he said. "If I hadn't gone for that fucking hot dog . . ." For a moment he looked as if he were struggling to control himself. "Fucking pig," he mumbled.

"Listen to me," Tippi said. "Hey, up there. Listen to me. Everybody did what everybody did, and that's over. Nothing can change it. We've got work to do."

Norm nodded. "You're right, of course. It's just that . . ." he stammered. "Everything went so wrong."

Tippi could already hear, from a great distance, the wail of a siren. Suddenly she felt an overwhelming rush of weariness. Jet lag, she thought, and almost laughed.

She was seated cross-legged on the floor now, with Violet's head in her lap.

Keep me awake, little stone, she said to herself.

And to Violet, over and over again like a prayer: Live. Live. Live.

# 8

T HADDEUS AWOKE IN the middle of the night. The mattress was too soft, a fat pocket stuffed with . . . ? His guess was rags or some such. Yet it was a very good job of it and would have been quite comfortable for someone who liked to sink, out of sight, in a mountain of cotton balls and sleep thus. The comforter was too thick, too soft, and too warm. He thought of Bitters's wry jest, "You know, when you got a world run by women, the plumbing is going to be first class," and smiled.

But it was not a happy smile. What had he been dreaming? He just could not catch it, but it lingered at the edge of his consciousness, playing hide-and-seek with him. And it was responsible for this terrible sad feeling he had, which was a difficult one for him to define. Something like: *So many possibilities, too many, out of control. One wrong step, and you fall out of sight. Forever.*

But it was only a dream, wasn't it? Or was it?

On the mattress next to him, Raphael moaned and mumbled, "Oh no, oh no," and suddenly sat up. "They crushed it," he said.

Thaddeus could barely see him in the dark, but knew that he was drenched in sweat.

"They crushed what?" Thaddeus asked him.

There was a long silence, and then Raphael answered.

"I can't describe it. It was pretty. Maybe like a flower. It was trying to grow, but it kept growing back into itself. And then, just when I thought maybe it was going to find a way out, they, someone, stepped on it. It was only a dream. Everything's too soft here. I can't sleep." And he lay back down and was instantly asleep again.

. . . *but too hard there,* Thaddeus completed the thought, himself drifting back to the labyrinth of shattered knowledge that awaited him, underneath his conscious mind.

# 9

THE OLD MAN, on the other hand, didn't care if life was too soft, too hard, if flowers got crushed. He knew that the choice to move out of the original stillness was the choice to struggle, forever, *period*. That the choice to identify oneself as an individual was to eventually be crushed, for each and every one of us, back to where we came from. It was only a matter of time. But to identify with the struggle—ah, there was no possibility of defeat there, but no rest either. Sometimes he asked himself, *Why the fuck did we make this choice?* And, of course, with the question arose the answer: *It was the only choice.* This caused him to laugh and laugh as he encountered this same joke over and over again in every facet of existence. We were fools—yet there was no other choice. If that wouldn't make you laugh . . .

Here he was, stranded in ancient Greece, waging a losing battle, not even sure of what he was trying to accomplish, let alone how.

For a brief moment or so he allowed himself the luxury of the blues. "Or should I say, maybe, the 'wine darks'?"

This caused him to howl with laughter. "What kind of idiot would describe the blue of the ocean as resembling wine?" He shook his head.

The old man did not much respect the ancient Greeks, whom he thought of as very creative and imaginative children. About five years old. (Oh, did one of the gods come out of the sky and talk to you today, darling? That's nice!)

He saw the Romans as mostly rather dull adolescents. But that golden age just before Rome fell—hey, no wars (the longest period of world peace ever), the children of slaves were born citizens—that had almost been a mature society. Till the barbarians got it, that is. After that takeover, the Greeks had looked wise. The Dark Ages was a world run by brutes forever stuck in their tantrum-throwing terrible-twos. It had taken them hundreds of years to mature enough in order to usher in what would later be lovingly christened the Renaissance. And now, everyone was behaving like creative, imaginative seven-year-olds.

From there, gradually they had marched onward through the late Middle Ages into stalwart ten-year-old consciousness. But not without having lost their spark of creativity.

America was more of a mixture—everybody who couldn't make it in their own country or was just plain thrown out, or fools with get-rich-quick schemes. But in spite of that, or maybe even because of it, they had that spark of creativity that seemed to have disappeared in the Middle Ages. Yet how could you give high marks to a nation of people who, in a presidential campaign, could be unerringly counted upon to elect the tallest man? To whom it had never occurred to select their leader on the basis of intelligence, let alone spirituality?

He felt that, in the entire history of mankind, there had been maybe ten mature men. He didn't count himself—when you have a couple thousand years to learn your lessons, you're a special case.

The crux of the matter was that things got better, worse; better, worse; but each time they got better again, they were slightly better than the time before.

And here he was facing all the same shit he had endured before, only from an even worse starting point. And how long would he live, anyway? He had not the slightest idea, but it seemed a safe bet that he'd never make it to as good a place as he'd already been. Imagine the gloom of having to live through the Dark Ages—twice! And all for Elena?

"Hey, fuck you, Elena," he said out loud. "I take it all back."

Then, "Maybe if I click my heels together three times and—shit, they stole my little red slippers."

He sat down on the dry earth, cross-legged, and added pensively, "I've kicked a lot of ass for a lot less than that."

At last, he opened up the paper bag that was, yes, still clutched in his left hand and said to himself, "At least I've still got my little pineapple, even though it's still not ready to use yet." Folded up the bag and just sat there, looking a little sad.

But Corbo was not one to indulge himself long with the blues, and unlike the others, before him and after, who had worn the mystic amulets, he had long ago adopted tactics and strategies for situations such as this, which were as automatic to him as brushing his teeth. So after a while, he got up, dusted himself off, and walked along the road.

Soon he encountered a few people, touched their consciousness, but passed them by. Then he found the one he was looking for: a plump merchant who was followed by two heavily burdened donkeys and a dour-looking slave.

"Oh, look at those funny clothes," the fellow shouted. "What fools strangers are."

"You will come with me," Corbo said aloud, in English, mainly to himself. The mental command that accompanied this statement was automatic and irrevocable.

"Bar, bar, bar," the merchant retorted, making fun of "barbarian" speech. But he followed him, as did his slave, who was leading the two donkeys.

It was rough, hilly terrain, and it took a few minutes for Corbo to find a suitable gully where they would be out of sight to the passersby on the road.

"Lie down here."

"Bar, bar, bar." The pudgy comic continued to find delight in comparing the language of strangers to dogs barking. But then added, "This is not very comfortable. There are stickers here."

Corbo knelt beside the two men and put his hands on the merchant's head. He was not particularly quick at gleaning information in this manner, but he could do it. And, as he had done so many times in the past, he forced the man to repeat certain key sentences over and over again, while he mapped the merchant's active neural pathways and opened ones in his own brain to match. Drusilla had been the best at this, then probably came that wheeler-dealer Popillius, but Corbo had always been a jack-of-all-trades, and as usual, he got the job done.

"Since you like my clothes so well, you can put them on, and give me that sheet of yours. Don't forget the coin purse."

Then he stood up, moved around, and knelt by the slave. Touched his head. Waited for the poor man's life to unfold. He was not even sure what language he was learning here. A northerner, from a colder clime. Kidnapped as a child by . . . ? The man wasn't sure. Sold to the Greeks.

Whatever the language was, Corbo learned it and whatever bits of information he could glean from the flow that he felt might prove useful.

Satisfied, he stood up and sighed. He was in ancient Athens, all right. And this time for real. Probably. (No wonder he had been dreaming about ancient Greece.)

The first thing he had done here was to write a paragraph in the dust. Close his eyes, then open them and read it. Then close his eyes, open them, and read it again. It was the same. This was a test Corbo had devised to be certain he wasn't dreaming. If he had been in a dream, the paragraph would not have read the same twice.

Another test was to take inventory of your surroundings, then close your eyes and count to ten. Then open them again. If nothing had changed . . . Where Ketoko was concerned, you couldn't be too careful.

Before sending the duo on their merry way, Corbo had them unload the heavy burdens of the two donkeys. Then he ordered the slave to pack as much of it as possible on the naked merchant. "Pity you are too fat to wear my shorts," he remarked casually.

Then he spoke briefly to the slave. "Cheer up. You are a slave, but you are fundamentally a human being. The fact that you wound up a slave is not really important. It is strictly a matter of luck. But being a human being is wonderful. When fully realized, it is greater than being a god. Everything you can see, everything you can imagine, is yourself. But only a part of yourself."

He saw he was getting carried away, and shook his head.

"But we all have our little enclosed roles to play out. We have no choice but to imagine our restrictions and"—he shook his head again—"act them out. But today's different, you see, because you encountered me. You may wish to think of me as the god of humor, or drunkenness, or some such. Maybe Hermes—he was a prankster, no?

"Anyhow, I want you take your little whip, only instead of the donkeys, you get to whip your master's fat ass and keep him moving down that road. That will be something for you to remember, to tell your grandchildren about, no? Hermes made me do it?"

But the slave's eyes filled with tears. "I don't want to hurt my master," he said. "He is kind to me. Sometimes," he added wistfully. Then, "Well, once or twice, when he'd had too much to drink, he was okay But he is my master. Please don't make me do it."

The old man shrugged. "As you wish. Help him carry some of this junk, then. The donkeys are going free."

He whispered something to each of the donkeys. One of them brayed and took off, running up the gully. "That one's like me," the old man commented.

The other donkey docilely followed the slave and his naked master as they made their way back to the road.

By that evening the old man was situated in a ritzy inn on the outskirts of Athens. Of course a ritzy inn in ancient Greece meant bare feet and earthen floors, barley mint porridge and bread for dinner. But at least there was entertainment.

The meal over, the men had drawn lots to see who would be the wine master. The winner, a sad-looking little old man who limped, was awarded the honor of choosing what proportion of water would be added to the wine they were about to drink.

"I feel my oats tonight," he proclaimed. "Half and half it shall be. And may we all drink ourselves into a reverie."

Indeed, most of them had, and were still drinking.

All the men, including Corbo, were reclining on couches (a position that Corbo detested), watching the main act, which consisted of a young slave girl playing a morose tune on a wooden flute while another danced and juggled a pair of hoops—if you call throwing a hoop up in the air every once in a while and catching it juggling.

But the crowd loved it. "How would you like to take her to your couch and make her dance to your own tune?" one of the men commented.

Probably one reason for the excitement was the total absence of women in everyday life. At least in Sparta the girls got to exercise a little. These Athenian women stayed in their parents' home until they were old enough to barter off. Then, without any say in the matter, they were married off to whomever their parents chose. Strictly business. Then they lived out the rest of their miserable existence in their husband's house, scarcely ever venturing outdoors, until the day they died.

*What a waste of half of humanity's resources,* the old man thought bitterly. It would be at least two hundred years before women were allowed to be interesting, he reckoned gloomily.

Inevitably, the men sang drinking songs and Corbo was forced to throw in a verse or two glorifying the wine. This was not real singing, simply chanting poetry while a young entertainer played the lute. But the spirit was the same. Corbo had the presence of mind to compliment the Greek talent for metaphor in the mythological pairing of the god of drunkenness, Dionysus, with the origin of music, even as he composed his greeting-card-quality verse. He despised music, and had no doubt that it sprang from maudlin, drunken sentiment.

"The wine is sweet," he sang. No lie there. The Greeks had the abysmal habit of mixing their wine with honey until it was a thick, nauseating syrup. Then they diluted it with water.

> "The moon is bright. (Could be.)
> But none can beat
> Our host tonight."

Everyone applauded this, none more enthusiastically than the owner of the inn.

The singing over with, one of the men suggested in a serious tone, "Now that the wine has given wings to our words, let us discuss the nature of truth, and is truth different from beauty? And if so, how?"

The men began to argue earnestly about the nature of truth and beauty, causing Corbo to smile. They were, after all, ancient Greeks, and that label did imply something special, a virginal curiosity about the nature of life that was to jump-start Western civilization.

"And you, sir, I believe you gave your name as Corbo. Have you nothing to say in this matter? Are we perhaps boring you?"

Corbo scrutinized the man speaking. There was something about the manner in which he said it. Mocking, almost. He had described himself as a wine merchant. Lysippius the wine merchant. A tall, gaunt man with a fierce, curly black beard and hair, but a quizzical, alert expression. Whatever it was Corbo was searching for in his face, he did not find.

"Forgive me if I seem preoccupied," Corbo said, "but I have a problem that's been going around in my mind for some time now that I've been unable to solve. Would you like to hear it?"

The men applauded as if he were an entertainer, and Lysippius announced, "Bravo. This calls for another round of my fine honey-sweet wine. I am now certain that our friend Corbo here will provide the spice."

There was a brief silence as Corbo gathered his thoughts. Then he suggested, "Instead of focusing our attention on the philosophical concerns of the human race, shall we examine, for a change, one of the problems of the gods?"

There was an astonished silence. Then one of the men, a Sicilian called Dolius, wondered, "What practical knowledge could we possibly glean from that?"

"Who knows?" Corbo admitted. "But let's see."

He sat up on his couch, cross-legged, surprising everyone. And closed his eyes, visualizing what he was about to say.

"To start with, let me tell you a story."

Murmurs of enthusiasm from the bright-eyed, childlike drinking clique.

"There is a stone which conveys upon its bearer great powers."

Even more enthusiastic oohs and aahs.

"Where does it come from?" Dolius inquired.

"According to your legend," Corbo continued, "it was forged by Hephaestus and given to the human most favored by the gods."

"You don't believe this legend?" Dolius the Sicilian sounded amazed.
"I have no beliefs," Corbo answered casually.

Now, not just oohs and aahs, but shouts and protests from everywhere.
"What kind of fellow are you?" Lysippius demanded.

"Let me get on with this story," Corbo said, ignoring all the uproar.
He'd heard it before. "We don't need to know how the stone got here. I have
my theories, but I don't give them much weight. Or even any, for that matter. But I know that the stone exists. The first man—"

"The one the gods gave it to?" Lysippius insisted, in the guise of a
question.

Corbo smiled and shook his head. "All right. Yes, the one the gods
gave it to. This man kept the stone for hundreds of years."

More excited outbursts, which Corbo ignored.

"Yes, he lived for a long time. Then he was killed, and the stone, which
was quite large, was broken up into four equal parts by a very skillful gem
cutter and given to four humans who were chosen to guard the world. In
those days the world was thought of as flat, and the four Guardians were supposed to guard the four corners."

"But," Lysippius sputtered, "the world is flat."

Corbo nodded. "That's because it's still those days."

"And I will bet that the skilled gem smith actually was Hephaestus in
disguise," Lysippius insisted.

"Oh, who else?" Corbo snapped. "Anyway, one of these new Guardians
goes back in time."

Shouts of excitement and encouragement such as, "Has anyone ever
told such a story? Cheers for Corbo." All of which Corbo ignored.

"He is forced to go back, you understand? He doesn't really want to."

"But by whom?" Lysippius interjected. "Who in the world—?"

"By one of the other Guardians," Dolius answered. "They want to steal
his stone."

"Exactly," Corbo approved. "Now then, here he is, against his will, in
the other magician's domain. So then, naturally, the first thing he does is to
use his magic powers to see if he can locate this other man, the one who had
the stone first, when it was whole. He should be able to sense this . . . other
talisman. You see?"

"Go on, go on," Lysippius gestured impatiently, "lest you leave us as
lost and confused as the man in your story. So he uses his magic to locate the
other magician. What follows then? A magical war?"

"No, no," Corbo said, "it's not like that. He doesn't want to fight or steal
the magician's magic. He needs the fellow to help him get back to where he

came from. But here's the thing. He can't find any sign of the other magician or his talisman, or feel any of the effects of its magic. It's as if the man isn't there. But he *is* there. Now, what does this mean? And what should this man do?"

Conversation buzzed as the revelers at the inn consulted with each other. Several suggestions were shouted. Then Lysippius raised his cup and called for order.

"We must speak in turn. Since I have suggested it and supplied the wine necessary to loosen our minds . . ."

One of the others raised his cup and shouted, "Looser would be better."

"Very well, one more round of wine, on me."

Everyone cheered.

"But I demand the privilege of going first."

Young boys poured out the wine. The revelers drank, and praised the wine merchant and his product.

"Now," Lysippius continued, "we must have a name. What shall we call this . . . not-quite-human, not-quite-god of yours, who is one of the four Guardians?"

"Bozo," Corbo suggested.

"And the other one, with the more powerful talisman?"

"Theseus."

"Ah, Theseus, that sneaky devil. The man was always getting advice from Hermes. That explains it. Surely he must be deliberately hiding himself and his magic because he plans to steal Bozo's talisman."

Shouts of approval from the revelers.

"It seems to me," Corbo suggested, "that if Theseus is already hiding from Bozo, then he obviously must be aware that Bozo is there. True?"

"But of course," Lysippius agreed.

"Probably monitoring his every move. Correct?"

"Surely that must be the case," one of the others agreed.

"In other words, if Bozo can't find Theseus, it must be because Theseus has already found Bozo."

"Yes, yes," Lysippius agreed, "that's it."

"Now, then, what can Bozo do to save himself?"

"Why, one thing only. Pray to the gods. And hope they are listening."

The revelers laughed loud and long at this.

"And if he does not believe in the gods?"

"Then pray to Theseus for mercy. And hope he is in one of his rare moods to grant it."

More laughter.

"Very well, then. This is Bozo. I give up, Theseus. Assuming you are in this room—which seems likely to me, at the moment—show me some mercy here, will you?"

More laughter from the revelers, and shouts of "Excellent!" "Most witty!"

"And now, Corbo—or should I say Bozo?—have you any other problems of such a wonderfully strange nature for us to contemplate here tonight?"

"Too many of them to count," Corbo groused.

"But give us one more," Lysippius pleaded, "and I will supply the drink."

"Oh, for the sake of all the gods, go to sleep, Lysippius, will you?" Dolius said. "And the rest of you, too."

Hammered goblets fell from limp hands, and instant snoring and wheezing issued from bodies of men fast asleep on their couches. The fat Sicilian stretched, climbed down off his couch, and looked down upon the serving boys fast asleep on the cold dirt floor. Twitching and snorting in the excitement of their youthful dreams. One of them was already purring and pawing at the empty air like a kitten.

Dolius smiled sweetly down on them.

"Not you kids—first cover the guests so that they may sleep warm and comfortable through the night. Then you may curl up where you wish and go back to sleep again."

The wine servers yawned, got up from the earthen floor where they had collapsed, and went from couch to couch, covering up the guests.

As the small, plump, self-described playwright from Sicily moved across the room toward Corbo, his shape shifted, elongated, and his features dissolved, reminding Corbo somewhat of Ketoko.

Corbo studied him as he drew near. "Theseus," he said, with a great deal of uncertainty. The man he was looking at was now tall and slender, but, at the same time, powerfully built. He moved in the fluid, graceful, even cocky manner of the natural athlete who is proudly aware of his physicality.

"What's the matter, don't recognize me?" he said, amused. "Why would you expect to? The years can change a man, or haven't you noticed?"

"Not that much," Corbo noted.

"Well, I like to change my appearance a bit from time to time. A little indulgence I allow myself. It hardly seemed appropriate to offer myself up to my killer like this—too robust." He patted himself on the chest. "But here we are, speaking about the future as if it were the past."

"For me it *is* the past," Corbo said, "but for you . . ."

"Well, for me," Theseus pointed out, "the past and the future are not really so very different. I remember them both. It only takes a small push of will, either direction, for me to make the trip."

"You're not even Greek," Corbo realized.

"Not any more than I was Mesopotamian when they first trudged out of the muck, or Egyptian when I watched them build the first pyramid. Even nudged them a little."

Corbo was no historian, but the implication struck him immediately. The passage of time between ancient Mesopotamia and whatever period this was in early Greece would make this man many times older than Corbo, yet he appeared to be somewhere in his midtwenties.

"Oh, get that fearful look off your face, Corbo. You are so paranoid. No, I'm not planning to steal your little trinket. Why would I? I gave it to you, or rather, will give it to you, in the first place. Or in my case I guess it would be in the last place.

"And I am not hiding my 'light' from you, of course, but from Ketoko. And others like him."

"Others like Ketoko?"

Theseus laughed. "Well, not really like him, but there are astral beings with bad intentions. Still, the truth is that I enjoy my anonymity too much to let anyone have an unnecessary glimpse of it. You should understand that."

"I do. I do."

"And oh, those owl eyes—wheeling and dealing, are we? Relax, *you're* the one who kills *me*. Is that not the very nature of paranoia? You are thinking of killing someone, so then you imagine he might want to kill you, and get yourself all fired up."

Corbo vaulted from his couch and landed on the earthen floor, facing Theseus. Even though his beard and hair were like white, finely spun cotton candy, and he was small, he moved with such a graceful mixture of precision and flexibility that it clearly rivaled even the physicality of Theseus.

They stood face to face. Theseus smiling, handsome, like a lion with its awesome musculature relaxed. Corbo's posture was more alert. Aggressive, even. Not threatening, but completely unafraid, and ready for anything. If Theseus was a lion, the old man was more of a poisonous snake on the alert and ready to strike.

Corbo was smiling at him. "Do I look like I'm afraid?"

"You look like you're ready for a fight. Followed by another. Then another, over and over again. That's a form of fear, if you ask me. But seriously, I wasn't hiding from you. After all, I'm here."

Corbo nodded. "You're here," he agreed. "The question is, Why?"

"We will get to that. All in good time. Ah, time. Let's discuss all this in more pleasant surroundings, shall we? This way." He gestured toward a corner of the room, and walked over to it.

"A moment," Corbo said, and, sorting through some of the leftovers from his dinner tray, took a thick chunk of bread and put it in his paper bag, which was on his couch, rolled it up, and followed Theseus. "Lunch," he explained.

Theseus smiled and shook his head. "There will be food where we are going," he assured Corbo. "I have an entrance to my island here. Pretty much everywhere, I guess. But right here in the corner. Like a mouse hole. True?"

Indeed, what started as a small black dot and instantly dilated into a large, round, black hole in the rear wall looked for all the world like a giant mouse hole. The two men stepped through it.

Warm breezes and butterflies. Bright round moon. They walked barefoot through tall grass.

"My island," Theseus said lovingly.

They walked through an orchard of fruit trees. Surprisingly, a covey of three nubile young women, joking and smiling, dressed in tunics, waved and giggled as they passed. Most unlike the women of Greece Corbo had seen, who would have had downcast eyes from which issued only furtive, frightened glances.

They walked along the seashore, which was oddly abrupt. "Well," Corbo said, "your island you have here is like a boat."

"It is a boat," Theseus agreed. "But it is also an island."

"Which is it, an island or a boat?" said Corbo, who was never much for metaphors.

"Well, it started out as an island. Then I had to move it. Then I had to move it again. Then I thought, why not just keep it moving on? And on?"

The first delicate glow of light began to separate the darkness of the horizon into sea and sky, and by the time they finally walked across a wide lawn toward what looked for all the world like a big southern American plantation house, the rich molten sun was just beginning to thrust itself out of the sea.

"Tara?" Corbo wondered.

"Not exactly," Theseus admitted, and when the front door was opened by a beautiful Black girl in a harem outfit, Corbo was forced to agree with him.

"Beautiful girls . . ." someone warbled, like a bird. Could it be?

"Tiny Tim," Corbo mumbled—truly, and maybe for the first time in hundreds of years, astonished.

"My favorite song," Theseus admitted. "It goes on automatically whenever I enter this place. It's a weakness of mine."

"I take it back about Tara," Corbo said. "More like the Playboy mansion."

"Well, I've always felt comfortable in the company of beautiful women."

"Scantily clothed," Corbo added. "Don't you find it distracting?"

Theseus thought about it for a moment. "From what?"

Corbo nodded. "You've got a point."

"And if you find something you like to look at, why cover it up with clothes?"

"Don't ask me," Corbo answered.

As if in response, a young woman wearing a bright red flower in her black hair and nothing else padded in on bare feet from what must have been the kitchen, or a hall leading to it, bearing a tray of assorted fruit.

"It's clothing-optional," Theseus explained, taking a bunch of black grapes from the tray.

Corbo waved the fruit away, but the nude beauty winked at him.

"You look very spry for an old man," she said in a husky, seductive voice.

"And you, for a young woman," Corbo shot back, "but I don't mate."

The beauty shrugged, providing some delightful breast movement, and said, "Nobody around here ever does." Then turned and padded back toward the kitchen.

"They're always complaining about that," Theseus admitted. "Sex, sex, sex—it's all they ever think about."

"Somehow I can easily imagine that," Corbo said. "Are you the only man on the island?"

Theseus shrugged. "Maybe I should bring in a couple."

"They wouldn't last long," Corbo pointed out.

"Yes, I guess that's true," Theseus said, "but they would die happy."

"Delirious, anyway," Corbo corrected.

"The, uh, ladies get vacation," Theseus said defensively. "Expenses paid. Six weeks a year."

"Where on earth do they go?" Corbo said, finding himself truly baffled by all this.

"They tell me exactly what kind of place they want to go to, and what they want to do when they get there, and I try to arrange it."

"That must make for some interesting listening." Corbo shook his head.

"Follow me, and we'll unwind. I'm sure, after all you've been through, you could use a bit of relaxation." Theseus led Corbo across the big main room and down a long hall into an enormous bathroom. He continued without pause across the colored tiles, throwing off his tunic and walking down the steps into what could have been either an immense bath or an indoor swimming pool. Corbo followed.

"Ah, warm as soup," Theseus commented as he waded in and sat down.

Lovely naked women paddled and sported playfully in the pool, or lay drying on its tiled shores.

"Where do you get them?"

"Oh, everywhere. A lot of them from ancient Egypt or Crete. One of two from Mesopotamia, but . . ." He grimaced and shrugged, as if to say, "You know those Mesopotamians."

"You extend their life spans?"

"No, they reach a certain age and I retire them. Then I have to go shopping for a new one."

Corbo looked interested. "You can time-travel."

Theseus shook his head, but said, "To a degree. Nothing like Ketoko. But just a few places. Places I have already been. Can't you get back to wherever you came from?" He looked truly puzzled.

Corbo laughed. "No, I can only go forward, a little at a time like everyone else. Of course I can't go back, you buffoon."

Both men were sitting in the shallow end in very warm water, Corbo up to his neck and Theseus barely to his muscular chest. He frowned. "You sure are a tough guy," he said. "Always the fearless aggressor. and you are certainly right about the only-going-forward part. But why not stop once in a while to think? When you knifed—or will knife, or however we describe it—that poor, frail little old Greek man, Theseus, did you never stop to think about how you were so easily able to defeat someone who was the wielder of such incredible powers? Powers that went beyond your wildest dreams?"

Corbo shook his head. "No," he said simply.

The four had captured Theseus, and tortured him. Corbo had never liked torture, but the others had felt it necessary. When Corbo had knifed the old Greek, it had been an act of mercy.

"I wanted to put you out of your misery," he said. "And luckily for you, I did. After that I had other things to think about."

Theseus was incredulous, "But you never wondered how it was that you were able to capture and torture me? Take away the stone? You never once thought about it?"

"What would have been the point?" Corbo said. "But speaking of idle speculation, I notice that the stone you wear around your neck is no bigger than mine. Can it be . . . ?"

"Of course," Theseus laughed. "Child's play. I made it big enough so that idea of dividing it four ways would enter your mind. Just as I made myself old and frail."

Two of the nude beauties near them grappled and fell with a huge splash, one atop the other.

"Hey," Theseus complained.

"Sorry," one of them replied, but still keeping her hold. The two thrashed and rolled about.

Theseus shook his head. "Obviously I'm too lenient."

"Self-indulgent," Corbo corrected dryly.

"Self-indulgent?" Theseus repeated, as if he couldn't get himself to believe it.

"We're sitting naked up to our necks in hot water, surrounded by beautiful young nude women, and you wonder if you're really a bit self-indulgent?"

"Hey, I'm practically immortal. I've lived for thousands of years and I've still got a few hundred to go. I'm the most powerful man who ever lived, and I can do anything I want. This is it. Furthermore," he added with finality, "I am and always have been the happiest man I've ever known."

"Wonderful," Corbo retorted. "The rest of us are all so happy for you."

"I've done more than my share. Do you think all those thousands of years in dull old Mesopotamia protecting those stuffy, portly little forerunners of future businessmen was my idea of a vacation? Egypt now, well, you could have some fun in jolly old Egypt. But even so. Do you think I have to answer to you? Why, I could crush you like a flea."

Corbo, typically, expressed himself by laughter. "So what?" he said. "I'm not afraid to be crushed like a flea, so go ahead."

Even Theseus had to smile at this.

"And," Corbo continued, "if I were the happiest man on earth, I sure as shit wouldn't be able to tell you, because I don't go around monitoring myself. And frankly, I don't even care if I'm happy or miserable. I've got better things to worry about."

"Elena?"

Corbo shook his head in disgust. "You self-indulgent lech, how typical. No, I don't care about Elena. I only do what I exist in order to do. Like a bird sings."

"Which is?" Theseus was getting interested here.

"And Elena is only a reason for me to perform my art. And when I am through performing, if I am relentless enough and more than just a little lucky as well, Elena will carry on my art beyond my death, only she will transform it to the next level. And in doing so, we will be separate in life, but one in art; and furthermore, Elena will find someone to follow her. And this stone of mine, which is only a quarter of yours, is the force that drives this art and all of us pawns who practice it."

He was silent. After a while, Theseus said, "And what is your art?"

Corbo smiled. "It doesn't have a name, but it's listed under 'Martial' in the phone book of life."

If Theseus needed to know what a phone book was, he gave no sign of it.

"Well, congratulations to you, I guess." But he shook his head sadly. "What a dismal picture."

The old man smiled. "I enjoy it."

"But," Theseus pointed out, "you wouldn't care if you didn't, have I got it right?"

"That's it." Corbo laughed, one of his long, crazy, loopy ones.

"Come to think of it," Theseus mused, "maybe you're the happiest man I've ever met. Anyhow, we've got business to attend to. Ladies, out of here," he shouted, and clapped his hands. The girls froze in the middle of their frolicking and laughter, then scurried out of the pool and hurried through the far door.

"How about that?" Theseus proclaimed proudly.

"You nudged them," Corbo answered.

"How could you tell? I am impressed. I thought I had developed the art of disguising my mental machinations to perfection."

"I deduced it, of course. Why would they have responded any differently than they did before? Could it have something to do with the fact that you have unparalleled psychic powers? Gosh, I wonder. You know, Theseus, you may be the most powerful man who ever lived, but you should really make an effort to sharpen your wits. They're only half there. And all this world needs is a superpowered cretin at the helm."

For a long time the two men just sat there staring at each other, Theseus with his mouth open, resembling for all the world the simpleton the old man had just labeled him.

"Oh, close your mouth," Corbo said. "The world situation probably didn't end up the worst-case scenario it might have been."

Theseus shook his head sadly. "Well, as it turns out, that may no longer be the case. Uh, a new twist has just been added and—well, that's really why you're here."

Now it was the old man's turn to stare in openmouthed astonishment. "You nudged me? You reached all the way up into the twentieth century and pushed me into executing that half-baked plan of mine that landed me in all this trouble?"

Theseus shrugged, causing the water to slosh all around him. "You might have done it anyway," he said. "The idea was there, sloshing around in the back of your brain. I just blew it up a little."

"Might have, my ass," Corbo growled. "It was obviously just one of those ridiculous ideas that pop up when you're trying to examine every last possibility. Normally, I would have probably looked at it and then dropped it like a rock."

"Well, maybe we can make it work yet."

"We had better," Corbo threatened. "And would you please tell me what we're doing sitting here up to our necks in lukewarm water? We're probably starting to rot."

Once again Theseus looked amazed. "You don't like it?"

"I hate it," Corbo answered.

"Oh, come now, tell me you haven't taken a bath before."

"Only when it rains," Corbo answered. "I do hope we're in here for a purpose."

Theseus explained: "Water is the doorway through time. It only needs someone with the key to open it. You've noticed, I assume, that Ketoko lives in a pond?"

"Why would one notice something as commonplace as that? Of course I noticed, you buffoon. Get on with it."

"I sensed you searching for Elena through time. You were dreaming, you connected with someone through a mirror, but it wasn't Elena. Was it the stone?"

"Of course," Corbo said. "It was her stone, but someone else had it. He was staring into a mirror."

"Same way I reached you," Theseus pointed out. "You were standing in front of a mirror, playing with a tooth. My stone was drawn to your stone, but the mirror was the doorway. You were thinking about forcing Ketoko to take you back to Constantinople, or something like that. I needed you, so I nudged you, and, when the time was right, I nudged the demon, and so here you are."

"All right, so what is the problem?"

"The problem is that you're not the only one who's harnessing Ketoko's ability to travel against the time stream. There's"—he paused for effect—"Germanicus."

"Shit," Corbo answered.

"Exactly. What could be worse?" Theseus agreed. "He learned the trick, of course, by spying on you. You really ought to be more careful."

"You know," Corbo said, "I feel like a child, sitting here in all this water."

"You never learned the art of the segue," Theseus pointed out.

"I know," Corbo said. "It was deliberate." He shook his head. The water swished around. "Where were we? Oh, yeah—I should be more careful, because Germanicus was watching me. Brilliant deduction, Watson."

"And you never learned to suffer fools," Theseus added. He had the habit of pointing at you often while he was talking to you, and he was doing it now, albeit underwater.

"I know," Corbo agreed again. "And it's too bad, too, because we're all of us fools. But once again, deliberate. You know," he continued, "it seems strange your sitting here and talking to me like you've known me forever, when you haven't ever met me before."

Now it was Theseus who laughed. "Do you think I would choose you to be my executioner without some knowledge of what you would become? I have watched you throughout the ages. In fact, I even know how you're going to die. Want me to . . . ?"

The old man held up his hand. With his white hair and beard all plastered down with water, he looked strangely different. Comical. Rather like a soaked squirrel.

"Spare me," he said. "I'm a simple man. So you and Germanicus have both been spying on me, and somehow he managed to get some kind of control over Ketoko. Just how did that happen, I wonder?"

Theseus shrugged. "We'll probably never know."

"And so?" Corbo coaxed him.

"Well, this is the bad part. You are familiar with the Red King of England? William Rufus?"

Once again the old man looked astonished. "You're all boned up on the history of England?"

Theseus shrugged—slosh. "You know, Corbo, in a way, although I've lived through Mesopotamia and several dynasties in Egypt, at heart I am something of a Greek. The freedom idea was mine; it just didn't catch on in Babylon or Egypt. But the Greeks were ready for it. They will pass it on to Rome, but where it will truly blossom is in your England. You helped me out without knowing it. Or rather, we were working together, although I was the only one aware of it."

Corbo nodded, but his expression was skeptical. "So?"

"So, Rufus was about the worst king that England will ever have to endure."

"But only briefly," Corbo added. "He died of food poisoning."

"Ah, that's the problem," Theseus said. "Germanicus goes back there, heals Rufus up. He doesn't even know he was sick. Germanicus moves in, using Rufus as a puppet, rules England for twenty more years."

"I still don't get it. What would he want with England?"

"Look at it this way. The old Germanicus is running Germany. The future Germanicus goes back and gets behind the most tyrannical Norman ever to rule England. The Saxons in England have had it with the Normans. The Saxons in Germany offer a helping hand to their oppressed brothers."

"Ah, I get it," Corbo said. "And Germanicus probably gets along so well with himself, too. Lucky thing."

"Lucky for him," Theseus agreed. "But as for England, not so lucky. Or should I call it New Saxony, instead of England?"

"Germany, Part Two," Corbo agreed. "All right, so what is it you want me to do here?"

"The hard part, as usual, I'm afraid. I'm not really a fighter, you know. More of a lover, I guess."

Corbo, once again amazed, said, "The stone allows you to . . . ?"

Theseus raised his hand out of the water and waved the question aside. "The stone gives me the power to do anything I want," he said. "The same is probably true for you. But since it didn't seem right to force it, I let all those physical urges waft away like smoke. Was it like that with you?"

Corbo snorted. "It was like jumping out of a fetid swamp. I can't remember when I've ever been quite so happy to see something go."

Theseus grimaced at the description. "Very colorful. Anyway, the sex is gone, but strangely enough, the love remains. The fascination. Women," he said dreamily.

The old man, looking disgusted, shook his head. "I would think that when the stone cured you of the disease of sex, you would at least have been cleansed of all that meaningless romanticism."

"Some things never change," Theseus said, causing Corbo once again to snort in protest. "Let's put it this way. First we address your problem. Then I send you back. You stop off in England. Solve the William Rufus problem for me, as well as for yourself and England. Then you return to your own time."

Corbo looked skeptical. "You can do that?"

Theseus shrugged—slosh. "What can I say? I've got the whole stone, not just a fourth of it. If Ketoko can do it . . ."

"Then let's get going," Corbo said. "I'm already getting bored with this island of yours. How do we start?"

Theseus nodded slowly. "All right, then, it's a bargain. I'll show you how to use the water. Together we should be powerful enough to reach anyone through it. Let's ignore the mirrors for now, see if we can find your Elena somewhere near the place in time you were searching. Only it would be best if she were submerged in water. Mirrors are only effective because they are a convenient symbol for water, but the real thing . . . Ah, you will see."

"If not?" Corbo said.

"If not, we go back and this time we catch her through a mirror." Theseus pointed underwater again. "So, shall we start?"

Corbo was staring down now into the bath, through it. His eyes were bright, yet distant. "I've already started," he said.

Both men looked down, and as Corbo's mind opened up, Theseus silently led him through the dimensional gate that leads through water into the web of time. But while both men worked their magic, something happened that only one of them was aware of. The other would never know.

# 10

———✦———

THADDEUS WOKE LATE. Once again he was engulfed in a strange bed that was as soft as a sponge. But he was getting used to it. This time it was a room in the Laughing Ghost Inn, overlooking the river that separated South and North Wiccingham. He could hear the sounds of pseudo battle from the courtyard below, Raphael training the eager would-be troops.

He couldn't shake the feeling that something had gone terribly wrong back home. That events were tumbling over rocks, like a river sweeping the two of them along the wrong way here. It was only too clear to him, now that it was possibly too late to rectify, what a foolish thing it had been for the Guardians to split up, men and women, instead of working together. And not just on this trip, either. But from the start. Men here, women there. What was the point of it? But somehow it just happened, when you weren't looking.

He wasn't obvious to the meaning behind the reign of terror perpetrated by those brutal cowboys who had taken over that little podunk town in Montana that the Guardians had visited just before this trip: the horror story of the rule of the macho male.

But here he was in a world ruled by women, and was it any better? He didn't think so, really. It was a more subtle evil, but evil just the same. Death by stagnation mostly, instead of open annihilation. By suffocation instead of the knife. The common man was murdered by never being allowed to grow up. They were all mama's little boys here for all of their adult life. And they were stuck in a medieval stage of development, forever. They would never be allowed to develop a modern technology, become part of the modern world, because mama wanted them to stay just the way they were. They could only accept the gifts the ruling caste of women brought them—such as modern plumbing—disguised as magic. The all-powerful Wicca, the self-

professed owners of wisdom, were looking after their children. On top of
that, Thaddeus had already seen how easily they could turn to all-out violence if they were opposed. He was reminded of the viciousness of the Kali
worshipping Thuggees in India.

*Why can't men and women simply work together?* he wondered. For instance, what the fuck was the meaning of the president of the United States?
Would a zoo represent a species of animal with only the male? Why couldn't
we elect a husband-and-wife team—both with equal power—to work problems out together? Thaddeus couldn't prove it, but he was willing to bet humanity would suffer a lot less that way.

And he had also been deeply disturbed by Corbo's sarcastic remark
about him, delivered by mirror. It had made him question music, the only
thing in his existence that he had accepted wholeheartedly. Now it was hard
for him to play without being painfully aware of the hypnotic effect it was
having on the audience. For there was no doubt about it, the building revolution was being fueled by music. As had been the case in most revolutions
before it.

Word had spread. People had followed them from the Dog and Cat Inn
here to the Laughing Ghost. Other citizens of all classes and occupations
were pouring in from all over South Wiccingham, and even a few from the
north town. Each night after the songs were sung and the guitar pieces
played, the stoked-up crowd would want to talk freedom, freedom, nothing
but freedom. Following Thaddeus's comic example, there would be a flurry
of ingenuous lords and even a few ladies passionately renouncing their titles.
Swearing to share the lot of the common man.

At first Raphael had fought against the whole idea. "Who are we to
cause a revolution?"

But Thaddeus had pointed out, "With us or without us, dude, there's
going to be a revolution. It's only a matter of when. Only with us, they could
win. I think that's best for us and best for them."

"But what if you're wrong? Who gave us the right to make that decision?"

"That's easy," Thaddeus had answered him. "Stones gave us the power
to make it."

"And might makes right?"

"If you have the power to do something you think right, that be one decision. If you don't use that power, that still be a decision. You be responsible that way, too, dig?"

And Raphael had dug. After a brief period of comically serious, eyes-closed thought, he said suddenly, "Okay, let's win it, then," shocking Thaddeus as usual with his naive open-mindedness.

The first night's performance at the Laughing Ghost turned out to be a mind-boggling success. People were standing outside packed shoulder to shoulder, filling up the huge courtyard, listening at all the doors and windows.

"What did I tell you?" Jeremy had exulted. The slender, saturnine luthier had accompanied them here from the Dog and Cat Inn, and coerced the owner into canceling his current, quite successful show (singing twins who specialized in ribald versc) and allowing the dynamic twentieth-century duo to perform in their place. They played forty-minute sets. The owner, an overjoyed, plump man named Gimble, for the first time ever was forced to clear the room between sets and usher in a new crowd.

Lots of these people were rowdy peasants. No doubt it appealed to the benevolent Wicca to have masses of uneducated "followers" to look up to the higher castes for guidance. And of course the Wicca were the highest of the high.

But apparently the charm of this situation was lost on the peasants themselves, because their minds were seething with lust for violence. Most of them could not afford the price to get into the inn, but Thaddeus had stated just before the show, "You let the niggas in, or you let me out."

The pudgy little landlord had fidgeted back and forth, rubbing his hands and whining, "But who are niggas? They can't pay. But if you refuse to play they'll burn the place down. But . . . but . . . but . . ."

In the end he had given in, of course, and soon the renounced nobles were experiencing a new and unexpected form of ecstasy. They were not only no longer lords and ladies—they were bonding with serfs. Make that ex-oorfs.

Bitters had led the way. After the first set was over, and several of the lords and ladies had renounced their titles, Bitters had stood up and with his empty copper mug had pounded on a table for attention.

"Seems as how these lords and ladies have seen fit ta renounce they fancy titles and all, I feel it's the least meself can do to renounce the lack o' one. I hereby, with all o' you as me witnesses, renounce me serfdom and all the jolly shit 'at goes wif it."

He sat down to silence. Then a sudden roar of approval from both the titled gentry and the lowest of the low. From then on, when lords and ladies renounced, serfs renounced.

So Bitters, charming rogue that he was, became one of the instant leaders of the revolution. Plus it took the lascivious Mrs. Lim only one night at the Laughing Ghost to wind up in bed with him. Moved in, samurai sword and all.

"So ashame myself," she said slyly, "but he so handsome, so strong. You should see . . ."

"Spare me," Thaddeus had begged, holding out his hand.

"You pretty big handsome, too," Mrs. Lim admitted, causing him to back up a step.

"I wonder," Raphael said evenly, "what Mr. Lim would think if he saw this?"

Mrs. Lim smiled. "Are you kid?" she said. "Mr. Lim give his gold tooth to see, but sometime I too modest." She smiled a bewitching smile. "Not very often," she admitted.

The mixed crowd, drunk with revolutionary ecstasy, responded with amazing zeal to Thaddeus's subtlest of telepathic suggestions. It became a ragtime revolution. Mostly Raphael played ragtime pieces, some of which were edging toward a drunken cowboy's favorite honky-tonk number. (In fact, he had reworked Cal's earthquake song into this style, and it had proved to be a real crowd-pleaser.) But a lot of Raphael's music, even to Thaddeus's ears, seemed to be quite Black by nature. The blues were in there underneath the rag.

And while it was true that there were very few Blacks in the crowd, the ones there were were never lords or ladies. Thaddeus had expected that, of course, and it did not offend him that much.

He had grown up Black, and as such had learned to hate Jews and Orientals. But he had—as do all very intelligent people—grown out of that stage when he was an adolescent. He had seen it for what it was—fear of strangers, mixed with the compulsion to find a scapegoat. And while the plight of the Black man struck him as a sad tragedy of life, he suffered no illusion that life would be any better if Blacks were the dominant race. They would, he knew without the shadow of a doubt, be just as quick to persecute to the max.

The real secret, the one that turned it all around for Thaddeus, was that we are all the same. All that bullshit about differences was just culture. And culture if it came from Africa was bound to differ from culture if it came from Korea. Let alone the culture developed by the wandering Jews, who had learned from virtually all of the greatest cultures of history—Egypt, Babylon, Rome, you name it.

When he was in high school, Thaddeus had been deeply attracted to a Jewish girl, and had gotten as far as visiting her house before the culture clash had broken them up. All the many bookshelves in the small apartment overflowed with books. Classical music played on the record player. When they had taken the record off, a cloud of silence had overwhelmed him.

Later that afternoon, when he had gone home, rhythm and blues was blaring from the big speakers which were his pop's pride and joy. Some of his little sister's friends were there, as usual, and at the moment they had formed a sort of conga line and were all practicing the latest dance steps— as usual.

His pop and Grover B. from next door were arguing about basketball, trying to be heard over the R&B—fat chance. "Turn that shit down, or put on some sounds," Pop had yelled. There was not a book in sight, and now some young bloods from the neighborhood had followed Thaddeus in. They were getting up a game of dice.

You could bet your ass, Thaddeus realized, that someone raised in that house was going to be slower to learn at school than someone raised in Becky Goldstein's. There was no doubt about it. Just as there was no doubt that kids who grew up in an environment where basketball skill was touted as the most important achievement in the world were going to play better than most white boys by the time they were sixteen. But this was only culture. And culture was not what we were. It was only the surface. Underneath the surface, we all got hungry, needed love, needed close to eight hours' sleep, and so on. That's what we really were: the sameness, not the differences.

We all really, deep down inside, wanted to be the good guy. But culture was separating us. Culture, unless it could be shared, was the killer, the torturer. When you taught your kid to be a Jew or a proud African-American, you were sowing the seeds of violence, racism, and oppression. That was the bad fruit. It was the parts of culture that had transcended race and become universal that were benign. You didn't have to be Italian to enjoy a painting by da Vinci, or a Black to dig Bird or Coltrane. And in fact, that was what had drawn Thaddeus to jazz. It had started Black but, unlike R&B, it had almost immediately spread to include everybody.

So in short, Thaddeus did not believe in the salad bowl theory—it had better be a fucking soup. Which was what you were going to have happen when the fucking salad heated up past the melting point, which was just about now. Both here and back where he came from.

He went to the window and looked out. Down below he could make out Bitters, who was pretty good with his sword, but not as good as he thought, training Raphael, under the supervision of Mrs. Lim. He smiled, remembering Mrs. Lim's clear superiority with blade that had been so obvious to everyone at the first training session. What had that been, a couple of days ago?

She had made a fool out of Bitters in their first encounter, besting him at every turn of swordplay.

He had merely shrugged, and confided to Thaddeus when they were alone, "She's very skillful, she is. But skill's only one part of a fight. What do you think would happen if she went and got in a fight with, say, our boy Rafe? All he's got to do is block her blade once, rush in and grab her and take her down, or just even bang into her and shove with his left hand. She'd go down like a rag doll.

"Oh, she's good, mind you. Really good. I love to watch her. And that movin' real slow is somethin' I never thoughta. But real battle . . ." He shook his head.

Thaddeus wasn't so sure. After all, it was Mrs. Lim who had killed all those sword-toting dudes trailing them.

"Oh, don't get me wrong," Bitters had assured him, "she's more 'n just good. She's very, very good. Too good for some bums wi' no talent fer the blade. She'd 'av an easier time wi' them than I would. But when you get up there with the best, the muscle counts a lot. Take me old boss, arrogant fool 'at he is. Same thing. Take my word for it. Best in the world at practice, but a real fight—I'd break 'im in half. 'Ope I gets the chance."

He grinned from ear to ear, forcing Thaddeus to grin with him. Any way you looked at it, Bitters was a lovable rogue, and Thaddeus hoped, for all their sakes, he was right. With all these hardworking peasants, they were packing a lot of muscle mass and very few fencing lessons.

And there was a point to it. He had never been that interested in basketball, but his pop had made a life's study in philosophy out of it.

"See that cute little white dude with that beautiful jumper? One of the best shooters I've ever seen. Look at that fallaway. Dude gets up, too. Got some pretty D, too. Great hands. Never make it in the pros."

He had been looking at Thaddeus with that strange, intense expression that he came to use more and more, before the stroke had changed his expression for keeps.

"Why, because he white?" This delivered with some sarcasm.

Pop shook his head and looked suddenly sad. "You calling me a racist, boy?"

"Are you a racist?"

Still shaking his head, Pop said, "I don't know. How you like that answer? Fucked up? *Po-lit-i-cal-ly incorrect?* Yeah, the truth ain't no fun, and don't nobody ever like it. But that the truth for sure. Don't hardly nobody know."

Thaddeus had snickered at that.

"You know?"

Thaddeus had nodded.

Then Pop had cut him short with, "That because you believe your own lies. But to get back to wherever we were headed, no, not because he white. Not because he don't got his chops. Because he just plain ain't strong enough. Studs in the NBA tear his ass up bad. The real game of hoops is war. No matter how good you are, you just got to have the muscle." So his pop would have agreed with Bitters.

And his pop had been right about what's-his-name, the guy with the jumper—Thaddeus had already forgotten his name. That sweet shooter had never gone pro. Well, who knows? Maybe the dude had taken a job as a nuclear physicist instead, or some other low-paying work like that.

Thaddeus walked over to where the emerald-green guitar stood up against the wall, but picked up the beautiful, elaborately decorated lute next to it instead. Carried it over to the simple wooden chair, sat down, and began to play.

The lute felt sweetly at home to his long delicate fingers now that it was strung with nylon. God knows what they had strung it with before. Neither he nor Raphael had wanted to ask.

"Uh, you haven't got some nylon strings in that case of yours, have you?" Raphael had asked hopefully.

"Got everything a man could want in this case." Thaddeus had rummaged through the compartment under the neck, and yeah, just on the off chance that he might want to string a Custom Legend with nylon strings, there they were. Three sets of Savarez.

"I find that suspicious," Raphael had quipped.

And Thaddeus figured that Raphael might have had a point there, because recently he found himself playing the lovely handmade instrument more and more. While Raphael, just to keep up, had taken to playing his Ovation. Funny thing was how natural the shift felt to the both of them.

Now Thaddeus settled in and felt the silence in the room, then began to play. The song was a lonely one that seemed to be just trickling in out of the silence. Bits and pieces, so delicate that it almost wasn't there. He had no name for it. It floated in and out of focus. Like a ghost whispering, maybe laughing like the name of the inn, only it was a sad laugh. Or something you almost saw in the rain. But not quite.

He finished playing, aware that Raphael had entered the room.

"Fooling around," he murmured absently, the song still trickling through his head.

"She's at Ironwall," he said without preamble.

Thaddeus blinked. "Elena, at the big castle?"

"Right. I'm outta here." Raphael was stuffing his old duds into his backpack. His new ones he wore, looking quite suitable in his green medieval jerkin and earth-colored tights. The only thing he was wearing from LA was his track shoes.

"Uh, maybe we should talk this over, blood. We just about in the middle of a revolution, case you never noticed."

Raphael shook his head, "No, man, you stay here. I'll get in the castle, see if I can get her out. If not . . ." He grinned. "Start the revolution without me."

"How the fuck you goin' to pull that one off, studly?"

Raphael's expression became serious. "Got to be done, man. You stay here and get things going. Once I get to Mom, nobody reaches her again except through me."

To Thaddeus's surprise, Raphael seemed to be on the verge of tears. "Tell you what, blood, you better take one of these." Thaddeus went over to his guitar case, opened it, and took out one of his handguns.

Raphael shook his head. "Got my blade," he said. "You better keep the guns. And, Thaddeus, you were right, of course, I should sure as shit have taken one of those babies along, but I didn't. And you did. You keep it. I've got a feeling you're going to need both of yours."

Thaddeus nodded. "First, stop packing for a minute and tell me where you got all this info."

"It was Jeremy, of course." The luthier had turned out to be the two towns' main font not only of musical knowledge but also of just plain gossip.

"Here's the story I got from him, as best as I could understand it. There is some kind of festival coming up. Big deal, happens once with each king. I think he said twenty-fifth birthday, something like that. Anyway, the holy people choose a queen."

Thaddeus frowned. "Who the fuck the holy people?"

Raphael said "Right. I don't know. I think they mean witches."

"Who the fuck the witches?"

Raphael grinned despite himself. "Right," he said. "I think they mean Drusilla's followers."

This was news. "You mean Drusilla of the stone? All of a sudden I'm starting to get it."

"Explains a lot," Raphael admitted. "Anyway, way Jeremy tells it, these people were from England. Worshiped the Mother Goddess, but in the form of the Goddess of Love and Beauty."

"Yeah, that sound like Drusilla from what I heard."

"But they were being persecuted by the evil Christians."

Thaddeus's grin widened. "Somehow I don't have any difficulty picturing that one."

For a moment Raphael thought about what it must have been like for Thaddeus growing up in the Deep South, under the watchful eye of all those good-old-boy Christians. Every once in a while you had to remind yourself of that kind of thing if you wanted to really be his friend, Raphael figured.

"Anyway," he went on, "she led them here. The promised land. No more wars. And the crops shall flourish as long as you shall worship me. And you shall have your own king to rule over you, subject only to my law, which shall be interpreted by my servants, the Wicca." He rolled his green eyes.

"So we come to the main part here. The Wicca choose some poor fool like my mom, and she becomes queen for a day, or a week—whatever. Then they have this ceremony. She represents Sou Wiccingham and the king represents the north. They have some kind of royal scepter. Jeremy calls it a royal wand. Must have some kind of minor power like those fake stones you guys were using back before we got together."

Thaddeus frowned. Those were not, for either him or Tippi, good times to remember. The point was that the laboratory where the two of them had been resident psychics had discovered that ordinary black volcanic quartz would take a charge from one of the four major stones of power. This could give a user who already had psychic powers a tremendous boost. But of course it paled to insignificance beside the power of the true stones. They had learned that the hard way. Maybe this royal scepter was something along those lines.

"Anyway," Raphael went on, "they both hold this scepter thing, and some kind of power goes through it, and the one who's left standing rules over both north and south towns. But it's always the north who wins."

Thaddeus looked interested. "Wonder if it was always a setup?"

"Jeremy really doesn't know, but he thinks things have changed since 'the Goddess,' as he puts it, stopped coming around. Apparently Drusilla hasn't been here in quite some time."

"Ah. That may be because she dead, Rafe."

"I know that, but he says it's been three hundred years, more like four, since anybody's seen her. I get the feeling that once she set this place up, she put her people in charge of it. As long as her people brought her whatever it was she wanted from this place, she just let them have control of it."

"You figure there's something here she wanted?"

Raphael shrugged. "We're talking about Drusilla here. I'm sure she enjoyed setting up a place that worshiped her, but from what I've heard of her, she was practical. There's got to be more of a reason for all this."

"Okay," Thaddeus said after a pause. "You probably right, blood, but you be careful. Try to get in there and get out before the real trouble starts, you dig? I'll try to slow all this rampaging revolutionary spirit down, but—"

"Thaddeus," Raphael said softly, "I know I'm a fool."

Thaddeus shook his head. "You're a man, Raphael, and you're doing what you have to do."

Raphael grinned. "You mean the duke was right?"

" 'Bout everything but smoking cigarettes," Thaddeus said. "You taking your lute?"

"How 'bout this," Raphael answered after a moment's pause. "I'll trade you. This grisly green Ovation of yours is more of a travel guitar. After all, it's made out of fiberglass. You couldn't break it by throwing it out the window. While that delicate baby you got there . . . No, you keep the lute here. It seems to be turning into some kind of important symbol for the crowd that comes to see you play."

"Us," Thaddeus corrected. "Comes to see us play."

Raphael shook his head, finished jamming the rest of his clothes into his pack, and slung it on. He got up and went over and put his hand on Thaddeus's shoulder.

Thaddeus was still sitting in the wooden chair, cradling the beautiful hand-carved lute.

"They come to see you, Thad. You're the main course, man. I'm just dessert. Anyway, just tell them I've worked my way into Ironwall, right? When the revolution starts, I'll be their inside man."

"Yeah, that would be wise," Thaddeus groused. "Seriously, blood, keep your mouth shut about this shit, you dig?"

He got up from the chair and leaned the lute up against the wall. Then he began to empty an enormous amount of junk, starting with the twin handguns, out of his guitar case and into the empty wooden case which had once contained the lute.

"Meanwhile, with a little luck, I can drag this out until you get your mama out of there. But you get caught—"

Raphael reached over his shoulder and fished something out of his pack. It was the goofy-looking dunce cap the fool he had met on the road had given him. He put it on.

"I'm in disguise," he said.

"Look the same to me," Thaddeus replied. Then, "Okay, go. Get yourself an early start. Here, take all my money. I'll get plenty more tonight. Serious, blade, get in, get out. Talk to you later."

Raphael picked up the guitar case with the Ovation in it, smiled, and said, "Where you going to keep the lute?"

Thaddeus sighed. "Don't know. No room for it in here. Just throw it up against the wall, I guess." Raphael grimaced at the thought of this.

Suddenly there came a brisk, powerful barking from the side door.

"Blackjack?" Raphael said. The white dog was usually silent. But he was barking furiously now.

"Take him with you," Thaddeus suggested. "He guard you from those big mean bandoggies all the macho dudes around here own."

Raphael grinned. "Wouldn't go without him. Looks like you were right and he's psychic. He sure seems to know I'm leaving. What do you think, the stones?"

Thaddeus took up the lute, went over, and sat back down again. "Don't neither of us know diddly about those things, you dig? Remember what the old fart in the mirror said?"

Raphael shook his head. "I don't remember much about it."

"First he say something really weird like 'Yawtlée calling Yawtlée.' From there it progressed to 'Yawtlée says this,' or 'Yawtlée wants that.' For instance, 'Yawtlée wants to *visit* your mama.' "

Raphael chuckled. "He's just whacked out."

"Is he? I don't think so. I think he may be the least whacked out of all of us."

"Oh, come on," Raphael said. "Please don't tell me you believe the stones are alive. I don't know if I could handle that."

"What I believe," Thaddeus said slowly, in a measured way, "is that if Corbo believes something, maybe we ought to consider it."

"Well, I've got to run, so you consider my share for me, will you? I really wouldn't waste a lot of energy on it, though. *Hasta la vista.*"

"At last," Thaddeus replied, "the Mexican comes out in him. *Vaya con Dios, amigo.*"

But Raphael was already out the door.

Thaddeus leaned forward and carefully laid the lute on the floor at his feet, then took the amulet off from around his neck. Staring at it gave him a strange feeling he couldn't quite place. Had he never really just sat there and looked at it for a while? He couldn't remember ever having done so.

"Well, hi there," he said after a bit. "If you're alive, say something."

But the stone said nothing.

"You got a name, too? Like your brother Yawtlée?"

He put the stone back around his neck and then dropped it inside the loose, floppy shirt he wore.

"Kid's right," he said out loud. "Got more important things to worry about here."

Once again the stone said nothing, which, as Thaddeus saw it, was just how it should be.

He got up and looked out the window, but Raphael was already gone. It was starting to warm up now, and the courtyard was empty. A bird sang from the tree in the center. Just what kind of bird or what kind of tree, Thaddeus didn't know. But the bird was alive, and the tree was alive, right? Why not the stone he wore around his neck? He shook his head.

"Get yourself back down to earth where you belong," he told himself, since Raphael wasn't there to tell him. *And good luck to you, Rafe,* he said silently, *because I've got a feeling you're going to need it. That we're both going to need it. Now that we're splitting up.*

For the first time it dawned on him that they were no longer working together.

*Why the fuck are we always splitting up when we're so strong together? Me from Rafe. Me and Rafe from Tippi and Violet. Come to think of it, why in the hell is everybody always splitting up? Men and women. Blacks and whites. Peasants and aristocrats. Can you answer that one for me, little stone?*

The stone, perhaps wisely, said nothing.

# *11*

—◆—

$K$ ING WILLIAM HAD just finished showing Elena his gardens, which were
quite famous for their beauty. In fact, they had been the inspiration
for the lute piece which Jeremy had played that fateful night at the Dog and
Cat Inn.

If Elena had even the slightest interest in the profusion of brightly colored, odoriferous flowers, she had not shown it.

Nonetheless, for whatever reason—Elspeth could but guess—the king
had carried on exactly as if conducting a tour for a group of intensely interested students of horticulture.

Now he was continuing with a similar tone in the main room of the castle. Pointing out and dating all the relics and various royal bric-a-brac.

Elena, allowing herself to be guided along by Elspeth's light touch on
her arm, never once uttered a word of encouragement or discouragement to
the king such as, "Oh my, what a lovely throne you have there. Is that really
the royal vase the great witch Drusilla presented to your great-great-great-
grandfather for distinguished service? Heard so much about it."

Only the mercurial Elspeth showed any response, and that was of
rolling her dark eyes upwards in aggravation whenever he wasn't looking.

"I d-d-do so hope you enjoy your stay here," he told Elena, stuttering
as usual, as he finally led them to her room. "B-b-brief, alas, as it inevitably
will b-b-be," he added gloomily. "Ca-cannot she talk at all?" he asked Elspeth. "Not even a wh-whit?"

"Nay, my lord, not even a fucking whit," Elspeth shot back. "Assuming I've got it right what a 'whit' is."

"As usual, Elspeth, you amaze me. It's a wonder you haven't b-b-been
be-be-beheaded by now."

Elspeth nodded. "It's always been a bother to me. I probably wouldn't miss it all that much, Your Majesty."

"Oh, d-d-do not call me 'Your Ma-Majesty.' You make me sound too much like a real k-king instead of some w-witch's lackey."

Now it was Elspeth's eyes which widened in surprise; they had been wide enough before. She looked as if she were going to say something in answer, but had no chance as he continued:

"You know, when I was a ca-ca-ca-callow youth, my father, r-r-reeling under the first assa-assa-assault of old age, informed me, 'You know, Will, you have got to be k-k-king one day. Get thyself ready. It is an awesome responsibility.' He p-p-puffed himself up like one of those little puffer fish, with a crown on it—alas, a red one. And—I remember it so cl-cl-clearly— odd, that—and I said—I was at that age, you know?—I said, 'Wh-wh-what's an awesome responsibility? To do what Diana tells you?' "

William laughed at the memory. He had a funny, low laugh, like someone trying to hold it in, but out it came anyway, "bruff, bruff, bruff," almost like coughing. And in fact he held his hand over his mouth exactly as if stifling a cough, and looked a little embarrassed.

He was a good-looking man, and if slightly plump and unathletic, he was at least tall and regal. He wore an elegant royal gown, gold, trimmed in purple, but the oversized sleeves kept slipping down around his elbows whenever he raised his arm. As now.

"Damn these ridiculous accou-accou-accoutrements of the royal c-c-court," he swore. "One day I shall strip them off and go na-na-na-naked. I swear I shall."

He looked at Elena with obvious concern. "Oh d-dear, I hope I have not offended her in there. Wherever she-she is."

Elspeth shook her head. "Nay, thy royal fool, how couldst thou have offended this mindless wretch? Forsooth, why dost thou go on and on with thy dim-witted courtesies? Thou couldst fart in her face for all she cares."

King William, as he was wont to do whenever he was ruffled, stammered even more. "I-I-I f-f-f-feel sorry for the p-p-poor wo-woman. D-d-dost thou never feel anything like remorse? And thou, the m-m-most evil of witches."

He got control of himself, and slowed his rapid breathing. The slight flush drained from his face, and suddenly he was quite pale, having gotten it all out.

"Well, not that evil, perhaps," he amended kindly.

"Like yourself, Your Highness, I simply do what I'm told. I cherish the joys of the flesh, 'tis true, but surely thou dost not consider sex evil. Surely the Goddess wouldst not have blessed us with genitals if—"

He waved her silent. An imperious gesture, save for the flapping of the enormous regal sleeve.

"I suppose you are correct," he said. Now he seemed to have calmed himself way down, and for the moment, anyway, there was not a trace of a stutter in his speech. "A witch, but a lackey of other witches higher up. No better and no worse off than myself. But I wonder what course of action we would choose were we free to do so?"

*Thou might well find out, great fool,* Elspeth thought, but did not say aloud.

"So allow me to make these few suggestions," the king went on. "We have certain areas where we can be free in our actions. Alas, they are too few, but they are there. This, then, is how we must judge ourselves. This poor woman is our sacrificial victim. She represents the commoner. The impoverished peasant. She is their queen, and must be treated as such. When Diana hands us the royal scepter, this poor woman's royal qualities, including the love of her subjects, will pass from her over to me."

"Or yours to her, should the scepter choose her," Elspeth reminded him.

"Yes, well, since that has never happened . . . Would she like to sit down?"

Elspeth rolled her eyes. "I don't know."

"Where was I?"

Elspeth mimed holding something which was obviously causing her to twitch and shake.

"Ah yes, the scepter. Well, it is hardly a real contest, since I have been living with the scepter since the good king William, my father, died. Practicing holding it every day for an hour. Did you know that?"

Elspeth stifled a yawn.

"One grows accustomed to enduring that awful power, during that sacred ritual. You know, it's rather like ale. The more you drink . . . or so I've been told. So she must sacrifice herself to the power in order to transfer her sovereignty to me. Then everybody will be happy, united again. All this talk about rebellion will be quelled once the transformation takes place. And I, a king in name only, will . . ." He paused, searching for the words, waving his hand and sleeve dramatically. ". . . emerge from my cocoon as the man of the people, as well as the representative of the lords and ladies of the court."

"So what?" Elspeth asked, truly puzzled.

"So what? So she is important. She is tragic. She is going to save us all.

Restore order to our kingdom. The least we can do is treat her with respect and kindness. Can you not see that?"

Actually, it made sense, and Elspeth wasn't really cruel, mostly just self-indulgent and thoughtless.

She sighed. "Your Majesty is right. I shall try to behave suitably."

He strolled to the window and looked out. The light was fading from the flower garden below, and birds were singing excitedly in anticipation of the coming night. Everything seemed so lovely to King William II, and yet so fleeting. So momentary. Like this poor, nameless, beautiful, mindless sacrificial victim.

He turned from the window and walked back over and stared into her green eyes. But there was no response, of course. Just cool emptiness.

"Would that there were some other way. Hath she not a name?"

*Dumbella* popped into Elspeth's mind, and she almost said it, but caught herself in time and instead remarked, "Call her what thou wishest, and I will see to it that she comes."

The king shook his head sadly. "I shall call her . . . the fair Marguerite, queen of the poor people of this land."

"Then she shall answer to it," Elspeth assured him.

"Thou wilt be nice to her, wilt thou not?" the king inquired nervously. Then, not waiting for an answer, he continued, "Very well, then. Let her feast early on whatever foods she desires, and then take to her bed, for tonight is the night—"

"Of the ladies and the lake," Elspeth interjected. "The sacred ceremony upon which no man may cast his eyes and live."

The king nodded wearily. "And tomorrow she will leave for Greenstone Castle, where she will take the throne. Let us get this over with as soon as we can. Before those fools start a war over nothing, and tear the kingdom in half. And then, one wonders, do what with it? Make all the serfs lords and the lords serfs, I suppose. Ah, well. Good night, Lady Elspeth. Good night, fair Marguerite, my poor sweet queen."

Elspeth had to resist the urge to grasp Elena by the neck and manipulate her like a hand puppet, throw her voice like a ventriloquist and force the imbecile to spout, "Good night, Kingie. Thank thee for the royal tour. Loved the flowers."

But having no such talent, she merely said, "Good night," as his large soft form glided as graceful as a ghost or a shadow, from the room.

# 12

———◈———

OICES IN THE dark. The soft voices of young ladies. Whispering.
Chanting.

"Tonight the past shall be washed from thy body and thou shalt be a fresh young doe from the forest," Elspeth whispered in the dark.

Candles were lit, faces glowed.

Elena recorded the sounds and sights, but no one was there to interpret them.

The ladies were dressed in simple white silk shifts and sandals, with their hair all loose and combed out.

"Come, it is not far, and we must be there while the gleaming Goddess watches over us from the night sky."

The ladies in white moved single-file through the dark castle, down the winding stairs, and out the door, where indeed the fat moon shone down upon them.

They moved silently through the forest behind the castle, and up the forbidden path. The lake was over the first hill, nestled in a nearby glen, silently drawing them to its dark surface and within.

They disrobed on the shore and, guiding Elena, turned their backs on the water.

"O Goddess above," Elspeth chanted to the moon, "guide us backward through the door to our youth."

And now, with happy giggling and chatter, the women entered the water, walking backwards.

Soon they were splashing and sporting like the young girls they were becoming, for the mystic waters affected not only the body but the mind and spirit as well. It was a giddy high, filled with wild delight, this "water of youth." And it was, as well, the secret ingredient in Diana's ointment, which she and Elspeth used to recruit the new witches.

But using the ointment had nowhere near the effect of being fully submerged in the waters, and the weary battering of time was being visibly drained from these ladies' flesh.

Wrinkles dissolved, skin grew milky and taut, sexual urges stirred and whispered. The weariness of passing years poured away into the night sky like smoke from fire. All of this merely subtexts of a great, overwhelming, spine-tingling bliss. All of the ladies except Elena were laughing, and their laughter was the tune of young, carefree voices.

For Melissa it was the first time in the lake, and if the witches' balm had been enough to recruit her, this ecstatic bath was enough to convert her forever to the religion of the Wicca.

For her, the revelation was that the wisdom Wicca was describing was not something new to be added on, but something that had been there all along, within her, waiting for her to tune into it. Something that the power and energy of youth pouring back into her had given her the strength and quickness to see, but which was far more important than the mere reversal of aging. That something was her real self!

Giggling and girlish, yet filled with ageless bliss, Elspeth put her hands on Elena's shoulders. It was her blessing to love the flesh.

"Ah, sweet one," she giggled. "Poor thingie. Is nobody there?"

And indeed, if all these ladies were lovely in the rush of their oncoming youth, Elena was the most beautiful of them all. Rising from the lake in the moonlight, she was, with her soft reddish-blond hair, her great green eyes and pale, perfect flesh, vacant expression and all, Botticelli's Venus reborn.

So it happened just then, as the young ladies sported naked and reborn in the sacred lake by moonlight. At the peak of their ecstasy. As Elspeth touched Elena on her shoulders with her hands. As the stone Elspeth wore in the ring on the fourth finger of her left hand—as if it were a wedding ring to the Goddess—began to pulse from the little bit of residual power left in it . . .

Two men in another then, in another place, sitting in what reminded Corbo of a giant kiddie pool for adults, were using the spiritual qualities of the water as an entranceway for their consciousness, which, like the water they were sitting in, was steadily moving, flowing—changing its content but remaining the same—into that cosmic ocean which exists outside of time and space, but connects to everything, composes everything. The old man called Corbo allowed the older but younger-appearing demigod, possesser of all four stones in one, to lead him. But Corbo was a fast learner. It was his consciousness which burst through time and space, drawn by the meager power in Elspeth's ring, by the ecstatic, psychedelically augmented consciousness of the girls in the lake, and by the mystic force of the lake itself, and entered the body of Elena.

Elspeth wasn't sure what she was feeling, but she sure felt something. She let out a little cry and fell away from Elena backward, and submerged in the water. Came up again, blowing out water like a naiad, hair streaming and glinting moonlight. The ring on her finger was close to exploding with power, and Elena . . . had changed.

"Theseus, are you within reach?" Elena said in the hoarse but clear voice of the old man.

The ladies cried out, then, even in their ecstasy, were silent, watching in wonder. Clearly, they thought, it was a miracle of Our Lady of the Lake. And in a way it was. But as with most truly magical events that open mankind's eyes to its own limitless potential, this miracle was the result of more than one force at work, for it was also caused by the indomitable will of two male seers from another time and dimension, a veritable wedding of yin and yang. Or perhaps, as old man Corbo might have seen it, it was simply the will of the stones.

"I've got you," was Theseus's answer, though none of the fair ladies of the lake could hear it.

"Then hold me here," Elena said aloud.

Still sitting submerged to her neck in the lake, looking up at Elena, Elspeth could not be certain if the woman with the old man's voice was talking to her, but decided even she was not rash enough to jump up and grab the momentary queen of the people. She just sat and watched.

"O Goddess, let thy mysteries unfold," she mumbled to herself. "But don't hurt thy humble servant," she could not help adding.

"Amen," the young woman closest to her whispered back.

"What I can't find here," the old man's voice said, "is Elena. Everything else is fine, but she's gone. Destroyed. But then," he added, "she always was destroyed." Wild cackling laughter that verged on the insane emanated from the classically beautiful nude bather, causing the lovely mouths of many a young lady to open in astonishment. And many hackles to rise on many swanlike necks.

"Her body is in the ecstasy of rejuvenation here, but no will, not even the old confused one. It's not as if she was catatonic—there's just nothing here."

"Consciousness is a form of energy," came the silent answer from wher-

ever. "And energy cannot be destroyed, only transformed. Surely they must
have discovered that in your time—even the Greeks were close to understanding that."

"I wouldn't know," the old man said through Elena. "I was hardly a science major. But if you say so . . ."

"Oh, I guarantee it," Theseus assured him. "The body can be broken,
but consciousness cannot be touched."

"Then what happens when you die?" Corbo had never been even remotely curious about this—one of the differences in being a Roman prag-
matist (or if you prefer, a man of action, Zen or otherwise) rather than a
Greek idea-man. He was merely bringing it up because of Elena.

One of the ladies in the pool, uncertain to whom the question was addressed, answered meekly, "The Mother Goddess takes thee up to live with
her in the heavens."

"Hush," Elspeth warned.

"What the fuck would she want with a dead woman, you idiot?" the old
man could not resist pointing out.

At the same time, Theseus was answering, "The memory banks, of
course, are chemical and go bad right away. Are hers still working? The
body is like a generator that focuses the consciousness down into a certain
time, place, and dimension. When the body is broken, the consciousness
implodes back into the cosmic ocean whence it came. It's everywhere and
nowhere, but no focus, you see?"

"Well, the memory banks are still here. Working fine. But there's no one
to call them up or organize them. She's like a robot. If her consciousness is
still around, can't you cause it to refocus, with me guiding you from here?
You know, man," Corbo reminded him slyly, "you're the one with the biggest
stone."

"It's not really bigger," Theseus reminded him. "It's just more complete.
But very well. Of course I can do it, or I wouldn't have attempted it in the
first place, would I? You see, it's not like I have to separate out her particular consciousness. Any of it will do. The individuality part is only in the
memory banks. As I said before, the consciousness itself is pure, undiffer-
entiated energy. Here goes."

A burst of oohs and aahs came from the fair ladies of the lake as Elena,
looking more like Botticelli's Venus than ever, raised up one pale-skinned
arm, pointed at the heavens, and said in her old man's voice, "Into the lips
and over the gums. Look out stomach, here it comes."

At the same moment that he was sucked out and woke up sitting back
in the wading pool on Theseus's island, pure consciousness was focused

into a stream and experienced dimension through the form of Elena of the lake.

First came the sensation of ecstasy of physical rejuvenation, brought on by the mystic powers of the lake. The body sighed; then the happy consciousness played with the memory banks, instantaneously organizing them. Then the seer viewed, through the hazy movie of past experiences, the evanescent loveliness of the dimension of now. Tuned in fully. And once again for a moment the memory banks faded and the consciousness was pure. And that moment was an eternity with no relationship whatever to time.

Then the Venus of the lake said in the voice of a mature but young woman, "I am Elena, did you know that?"

And once again there were cries and gasps of sheer amazement.

Finally Elspeth gathered together enough composure to speak. "No," she said, "we did not know your name."

Later, when all the ladies had returned to the castle and to their beds, when the first rays of the sun were rising over Nor Wiccingham, while the cooks still lay abed dreaming of erotic aromas and rich unimaginable tastes and textures, or lakes of stew and jungles of salad, Elspeth spoke with Morgan, the morose commander-at-arms of the Wicca, seated alone at a large table in the royal kitchen at Ironwall Castle.

Morgan said in his emotionless rasp of a voice, "I'm puzzled."

"Of course thou art puzzled, thou great fool. Who would not be puzzled? Too much is clearly happening too fast. The imbecile we chose for the sacrifice has regained her memory. The revolution we originally instigated has gone out of control, and looks as if it might break out any minute. The sacrifice of the queen is only a handful of days away, and Diana has disappeared. No one has heard from the old witch since she returned to the City of Angels."

"But," Morgan protested, "I thought we wanted to overthrow Diana and her boss Dame B. That's why we stirred up everyone in the first place, isn't it?"

Elspeth shook her weary head and took another sip from her cup.

"Oh, great oaf," she said, "canst thou not see that we cannot overthrow Diana if we do not even know where she is or what she is up to? And we did not wish for a revolution, merely the threat of one. Our hope was that, with the help of my wonderful mystic ring, bestowed upon my great-grandmother by the Goddess Drusilla herself, our fair imbecile would be able to survive the onslaught of power from the royal scepter and, along with the threat of

South Wiccingham's unrest, put pressure on the system to usher in a new balance of power. The Wicca might then be persuaded to replace Dame Beatrice with another, younger witch, more worthy of leadership—and with Diana out of the way, whom would they choose?"

Alas, Morgan, looking even more confused, did not answer. Elspeth waited, then gave up, cleared her throat, and tapped herself on her lovely bosom, which was spilling out of her low, red blouse. "Namely me," she reminded him. (*And particularly if she meets with an accident, delivered by her own dull-witted master of arms,* she thought but did not say.)

"Then I would get to invade LA." He had a taste of his coffee. It was delicious, and like all good things, it was a restricted luxury item imported by the Wicca direct from the City of Angels. He picked up the little can and examined it. How exquisitely it was designed and decorated. And it was "naturally decaffeinated," whatever that meant.

"I love the white chocolate," he muttered.

Elspeth shook her head. Did this great oaf, as she liked to call him, actually believe that it was possible to invade Los Angeles? His stupidity amazed her. On the other hand, you could conquer Woodland Hills, for example, and the people living in Van Nuys would not even notice it. They didn't even speak the same language. In fact, hardly anyone in LA spoke the same language as anyone else. It was almost as if languages were being invented just to destroy the system. On top of that, bizarrely diverse Angelenos were all slowly suffocating in the smog, waiting to be destroyed in the next "big one"—tsunami, earthquake, mad atom-bomber, or whatever.

Maybe Morgan would be successful and some tiny portion of that immense, hideous, maniac-infested, smoking electronic swamp would break off and call itself Englishville. But so what?

She shook her head, but said, "But certainly then thou shalt have Los Angeles for thy very own, and all the sweet decaf that goes with it. But only if thou listen closely to what I ask of thee. And understand. So listen well.

"These things can come to pass only if the imbecile endures the test and becomes joint ruler. But alas, she is no longer an imbecile, and thus no longer under my control, so that even should she survive the ordeal of the royal scepter and achieve joint rulership, I can no longer guarantee that she will settle the souls of those poor unfortunate subjects of hers that we have stirred up by appointing her dear interpreter head lady of the Wicca, should Dame B. and her lackey Diana meet with an accident.

"Furthermore, the last thing we want is an actual revolution, but by the Goddess, somehow we are almost there. Dost thou not get it?"

Morgan nodded. "Oh, how I hate thee," he muttered into his decaf. "Yet thou art right again."

Then he looked up into her narrow, slanty, mysterious dark eyes, which he found not a whit attractive, and said, "All right, you go find Diana. I wish we could but slay the bitch now, but I will have to settle for later. In the meantime, I will make good and certain to slow down the revolution for the time being. We can always stir it up again later. My spies, poor fellows, have told me stories about some tavern where the fools all go to get drunk on wine and song to the point where they all stagger outside and share the mysteries of swordsmanship with each other. Somehow that's the source, and I'll keep an eye on it. It's somewhere in South Wiccingham. So this very day I'll escort the people's queen back to her city and then search out this meeting place of fools, and, if it seemeth necessary, put a stop to these fools' futile fantasy of freedom."

Elspeth's eyes widened; the way he was hissing she practically expected him to turn into a snake.

"I would go slow in this matter were I thou," Elspeth advised him, "else thou might drive them over the edge."

Morgan rolled his eyes, "Surely thy counsel in matters of war is not something which generals travel from afar to seek out. But this once I will heed thee and hold back. But I will keep the fools under surveillance, and I will keep a special force of trained soldiers at the ready. Should the need arise . . ."

Elspeth nodded, wisely keeping her mouth shut here.

"Meanwhile," he continued, "thou must find Diana and then either assassinate her there or get the two of thee back here so we can put things quickly back in order."

He rose and turned to leave, so that he did not see Elspeth stick out her long, pretty tongue. But then he paused and turned back again.

"And get me some more of this white chocolate decaf from the City of Angels, wouldst thou?"

*One day I won't have to ask,* he said to himself as he left. *I'll have it all.*

So it was that later that same day a royal carriage left the great castle, headed south. The king, now dressed, oddly enough, as a peasant, charmingly stammered his good-bye, and Elena smiled and answered, *"Hasta luego."*

"Why, why, thou canst speak," King William stammered. "But thou couldst not before."

Elena must have been feeling some residual effect from the old man's possession of her body, because, quite uncharacteristically, she said, "Thus has it always been, and thus shall it always be."

"Well, I suppose so," he agreed reluctantly. "H-have a f-felicitous journey."

And As the carriage moved across the drawbridge there was one joyful moment when Elena looked out into the swarm of peddlers and merchants pouring into the city to sell their daily wares: her glance was irresistibly drawn to a young man, as strong and proud as a lion, striding boldly—indeed, one might even say fearlessly—along, with one of those funny white bull terriers prancing at his side. Pack on his back, exuberant, innocent expression. *The Fool,* she thought, remembering the image of the tarot card.

But such a handsome Fool—openhearted and ready for anything. Any journey. Something about the sight of him, and it was only a glimpse, touched her deeply.

*And I'll never even know who he was,* she thought, quite correctly, as she and the young hero went their separate ways.

# 13

---

Tippi had insisted on riding in the ambulance with Violet, but had to settle instead for riding in the police car with Duke and Martin. Norm had merely shrugged as they packed her in the back of the black-and-white. He was having his own problems.

"Whatever you do, do not, under any circumstances, take that necklace off of her. Do you understand? I'll fucking kill you if you do!" she had shouted as the cops dragged her away.

"Okay, okay, no big deal. We understand," they had answered.

"You tell the doctors, too. You be sure to—"

"Okay, already," the paramedic who was humoring her said. "I'll make sure everyone gets the message." Quickly and with almost supernatural efficiency, they popped an oxygen mask on Violet and packed her in the white van and took off, tires squealing, sirens blaring away, then fainter, farther away, then gone.

"Anything you say can and will be used against you," the big cop Duke had informed her.

"A giraffe," Tippi had answered.

He had written it down. If it struck him as odd, he did not remark on it.

"How are you going to use 'a giraffe' against me, I wonder?"

He wrote that down, too, and if he allowed himself a smile, it was only a little one at the corners of his mouth.

"Writing a thriller?"

Again, not much of a smile. "Just procedure, ma'am."

And then jail. And not just jail, but jail in LA.

"When the fuck am I getting outta here?" Tippi had yelled at her jailer, a big, very muscular-looking woman, who had ignored her.

"When the earthquake hits, we all go free," one of her cellmates volunteered.

"But then they just catch you looting and drag you back here again," the other cellmate threw in.

"Yeah, but then you got you a TV for your cell," the tall, skinny Black woman with the wry expression shot back. "My name be Sondra. Don't ya'll be confusin' me wif Sandra, ya hear? It be Sondra wif an *o.*"

"B.O.," the other cellmate, a short, heavyset, jolly-looking redhead, replied. "My name's Heddy."

"Don't you be talkin' about B.O., woman, you gots B.O. so bad it be all over yo ugly self."

Tippi started to say something but Heddy held up her hand to stop her, obviously concentrating hard here, with eyes shut. Then she opened them up again. "You got B.O. so bad that yo mama . . ." She paused again, obviously not satisfied with her insult.

"Oh, for God's sake," Tippi snapped, "the both of you stink so much that it's a wonder LA didn't just dump you into the bay with all the rest of the shit instead of put you in jail. All right? Enough?"

Sondra looked at Heddy, then back at Tippi, and nodded. "That be pretty fly," she admitted. "You get you phone call?"

Tippi nodded.

"They tell you when you arraignment is?"

Tippi nodded. "They said sometime early tomorrow morning."

"Then you might as well get some sleep, honey."

Heddy leered and cut in with, "Unless you want to . . ." etc., etc.

Tippi listened to her list of obscene suggestions, obviously annoyed, but it was clearly a lesser source of aggravation for her at this moment.

Sondra shook her head and frowned. "Ugly bitch'd fuck a snake justa see it squirm," was her comment.

"What's the matter, baby?" Heddy leered. "Got a headache?"

"No, you've got a headache," Tippi answered, and was a little surprised to find out that she still had enough residual power left over to give one cellmate a very vicious burst of pain. It was gratifying to see the heavyset, aggressive redhead grab both sides of her head, moan, and sink down to her knees.

"Ain't that somefin'," Sondra said happily. "Bitch be curse herself all over wif her bad mouf. Now I gots to be send her some pretty flowers. Maybe some candy make yo fat ass happy, woman."

"Oh, shut the fuck up," Heddy moaned.

"What you in here fo', girl?"

"What about you?"

Sondra looked around the cell furtively. "Ah allegedly hit my boyfriend Dontell upside the head wif a vase whilst he were playin' poker."

"In front of about thirty witnesses," Heddy groaned, still holding her head.

"They all niggas," Sondra replied. "This do be LA. Don't nobody listen to no niggas. How 'bout you, honey?"

"Shot some bitch full of holes."

"Kill her?"

"You bet."

"The bitch aks for it?"

"You bet."

"Well, good for you, honey. You be gettin' real serious wif her ass. Only wish I'd used me a piece instead of that fucking lamp."

"The gun is mightier than the lamp, or the pen," Heddy added, obviously coming out of it. "Did you leave prints on the gun?"

"Of course I left prints on the gun," Tippi snapped. "I had to use my fucking fingers to hold it."

Sondra nodded sagely. "Be the same fuckin' way wif my lamp."

"If there's anything left of it," Heddy threw in.

"They be pickin' it outta Dontell's big ugly head."

"And what's your scene, Heddy?" Tippi was almost afraid to ask.

"Uh, drug-related," Heddy replied.

Tippi had gone to sleep. And then to her arraignment, and then back to her cell again. Days went by. The only thing Tippi had to look forward to was Friday, when she was being transferred to the charming Sybil Brand Women's Facility.

Sondra's comment had been, "Oh, baby, please don' go. You ever hear that song? Believe it. They aks fo' a lotta money fo' you bail, honey?"

Tippi nodded.

"You rich?"

Tippi nodded again. "I think so."

"Uh-huh, honey, but you not sure?"

"That's right."

Tippi had reached Mary Red Boots with her phone call, given her orders, but no one had shown up to bail her out. She had been aware, over the phone, that people weren't snapping to, the way they would have had Violet been dishing it out.

"How's Violet doing?"

Click, phone dead. Had that been an accident, or . . . . ?

It was only a few hours later when she was informed by the morose jailer, Miss Baker, "Must be your lucky day. Visitor to see you. A real fox," she added wistfully. "Wish she was visitin' me."

Tippi hadn't caught Sondra's answer to that one, but it must have been a good one, judging by Heddy's raucous bout of laughter.

And sure enough, the visitor was a fox. A tallish, slender, but excellently stacked limber fox with long, silky black hair and wicked, slanty, darkest-of-dark eyes. Dressed all in black. And strangest yet—it was someone Tippi had never laid eyes on before.

"I pray thee, tell me what has happened to Diana," she said right off. "Or perhaps thou dost know her as Brenda. The authorities refused to tell me anything of use, except that there was some sort of altercation a few days ago, and that thou hast been put in the dungeon. Well."

Tippi shook her head. *Great! Somebody crazier than me.*

"Ah, I didst shoot her full of holes with my little gun," Tippi replied with a straight face, "and her spirit didst fly off to heaven to be with God."

"Thou meanst, with the Goddess," Elspeth corrected. "Is she dead?"

"Boy, I sure hope so. I just pulled the trigger until I ran out of bullets, but it would just about be my typical luck if somehow that evil bitch lived and Violet—" She choked up for a moment. "You know anything about Violet?"

"Nay, save that it is a lovely name. So thou hast slain the Lady Diana. So many things are happening here that I must take pause and try to figure what this doth imply."

"Let me help you here." Tippi leaned toward the partition which separated the two of them. "You need help," she continued in a soothing voice, "and so do I. We're going to help each other, but there is no time to waste. You're going to get me out of here, now. And then we're going to solve my problem first and then we're going to solve yours. Do you see?"

Elspeth was clearly puzzled. She had never had the experience of having someone turn the powers of her own ring on her. She was psychically sensitive enough to realize something strange was happening here, but she just couldn't seem to put her finger on it.

"Go on, just do it," Tippi insisted. "There's no time to think about it. Get thee moving, right?"

Elspeth nodded, looking unconvinced, but turned to leave.

"A oh, while you're at it, see if you can bail out my friend Sondra"— she spelled it—"and hell, Heddy, too, while you're at it."

Elspeth turned and muttered, "Thou hast made a point. We maids must needs stand together," sounding unconvinced.

"Sure, it's a fem lib thing," Tippi said. "But hop to it, okay? I mean, hurry thyself about thy merry way."

Elspeth turned without another word, and left.

Tippi was not sure if her psychic push had worked. But the chances were good. She felt she was more strongly psychically gifted than any of the Guardians, even Violet—with the possible exception of Thaddeus, whose powers were of a totally different nature from hers. And when she had realized that her visitor was wearing a stone in her ring which was storing a charge of psychic power, she had decided to go for it.

There was no way to glean the results by scrutinizing her weird visitor for telltale body signs—she might as well have been from Mars. So there was nothing to do but wait and see.

Sure enough, though, a few hours later and she was given back the meager contents of her purse and ushered out of the jail onto the broad front steps, where Elspeth awaited her.

The amazing Elspeth was now all decked out in an ultralow black halter top and short-shorts. She wore blazing red high heels and lipstick. She looked, Tippi thought, rather like an ingenuous whore out to score a trick on the front steps of one of LA's myriad jails.

" 'Ods blood, but it cost a fortune to bail thee out of here. Goddess only knows why I did it. Alas, I shall have to go back for more money to bail out thy friends."

"What better way to spend a few bucks?" Tippi said. She was feeling her oats now, but she was still in a hurry to get out of sight of the "dungeon." They might well, she felt, decide to take it back.

"Come on with me. We'll worry about Sondra and Heddy later. Hurry. Do you have a car?"

Elspeth shook her head. "Of course not. How would I know how to navigate one of those ugly metal beasts?"

Tippi said, "Driver training? What, then, you took a cab?"

Looking uncertain, Elspeth nodded.

"Then where is it?"

"It drove away as soon as I got out of it and paid the servant in the coin of your realm."

"I'll bet," Tippi said. "Let's find us a pay phone—uh, not here—and summon another, uh, servant. We can talk on the way to the airport."

Elspeth looked even more uncertain. "I know not what to do. Pray tell me the fate of Diana. I must know for certain. I can't go on an airplane with thee," she said, "because of both my fear of going up in the sky and my fear of Diana. Is she really quite dead, or perhaps only hurt?"

Tippi patted her on the back and said, "Well, let me put it this way. If you are afraid of her, that's one worry you can forget about. But yes, you are to come with me in the airplane. Diana checked out without giving me the information I was looking for. First stop, Arizona. I've got some unfinished business there. Come on, keep up."

Tippi was moving fast, and Elspeth clattered along behind her in her heels. "Art thou certain about this, uh, trip through the sky? About Diana? Her temper can be quite terrifying."

"She's dead, all right," Tippi assured her. "As I keep on telling you, I killed her myself."

Elspeth chortled in joyful relief, and even clapped her hands together enthusiastically. "Why, good for thee! Perhaps we can help each other, then. Somehow I feel strongly that will be the case, but I don't know why I feel that way."

"Trust your heart," Tippi suggested. It was hard to keep a straight face while using this odd, witchy woman's own ring against her.

In the cab and on through the airplane flight, once Elspeth got settled in, they continued to exchange information, taking turns astonishing each other—as well as everyone within earshot.

"Thou hast the original talismans, like the Goddess Drusilla had? Why, that was how my grandmother got this magic ring. The great lady would from time to time invigorate lesser stones with her magic and give them as rewards to her most faithful followers. Oh, pray thee, do take it out and show it to me."

"Well, I don't actually have it," Tippi confessed, "but Violet has one. If it's done its work, she should be ready to go by now. But something's happened, or she would have bailed me out. In fact, I sure as shit should have been bailed out anyway."

It was early evening by the time they got off the plane in Phoenix and drove the little rental to Blackstone Ranch. Jimmy Running Deer met them out front before they could get halfway to the door.

"You're out?" he said, looking and sounding furious. His copper skin was flushed darker than usual, and his posture was tense and threatening.

"Why didn't you bail me out, Jimmy?"

"Get this straight," he growled. "I don't take orders from you. You're not one of the Guardians. You're just some nutcase Violet picked up that she couldn't get rid of. I've already done everything I intend to for you. I had to pull a lot of strings just to see to it that you were eligible for bail. Believe me, there's no way else they would have let you loose for the next fifty years or so. And I was waiting to hear from one of the Guardians what to do with you. Whether to bail you out or let you rot. My vote would be to let you rot."

"But you don't have a vote, Jimmy," Tippi said calmly. "Because this isn't a democracy here, you see. Now where's Violet?"

"You ought to know where Violet is," Jimmy said in a voice that shook with rage. "She's right where you left her. She's dead."

Tippi moaned and took a step backward and buried her face in her hands. "I told them not to take off her necklace, not to touch it."

"Well, they figured you for the lunatic you are, I guess, and took it off, so she's dead. And where the fuck did you get the money to bail yourself out, anyway? We'd all be better off if you'd just stayed back in jail where you belong, till the others get back."

Suddenly Elspeth, whom Jimmy had hardly noticed, took Tippi by the shoulders, shook her until her head whipped back and forth, and snapped, "For shame, stop thy weeping. This is no time to mourn."

Tippi blinked. "You're right," she said. Then to Jimmy, "So they took the stone off her, did they, and now what? You have it? Is that what's going on here, Jimmy? You think you might just nominate yourself to take her place?"

"Not at all," he sneered. "Unlike you, I'm leaving everything up to the others. I've got it locked up in the house."

Now Tippi took a step toward him, and though tears were still streaming down her cheeks and her eyes were bright and wet, she was smiling an eerie smile.

"No you don't, Jimmy. You've got it on you. And that's one big fucking mistake. What did you think, you were going to try to use it on me?"

"You just stay away from the ranch till the others return. Then you can complain to them." But he took a step back.

Tippi shook her head. "You don't get it, do you, Jimmy? I was born to be a Guardian, and the others know it. And Violet knew it, and I know it. And even the damn stone knows it. I can feel it calling to me. It wants to cook, Jimmy. So take it out of your pocket right now, and give it to me."

He started to shake his head, then he howled like a dog. And fell to his knees. "Oh, you fuckin' bitch," he groaned. "Oh, my head."

The door swung open and Mary Red Boots came rushing out. She was getting very old and very fat, Tippi noticed, suddenly aware that that was not going to happen to her for a long, long time to come.

"What are you doing to my boy, you bitch?"

Tippi smiled. "Better tell him to give me the stone, Mary. It's mine now."

Mary kneeled down and put her hands on her son's cheeks. He was moaning and groaning, eyes clamped shut. Face scrunched up in pain.

"Says who?" she grumbled.

"Says me. I'll kill him, Mary. I want that fuckin' stone right now, and it wants me."

"Oh, Jesus Christ," Jimmy screeched, and he wasn't even a Christian.

His mother fished it out of the pocket of his T-shirt and tossed it to Tippi. You better believe she caught it.

For a moment she just stood there, holding it. Her eyes were closed. *This is it,* she thought.

Jimmy, whose eyes were now open a slit, simply stared at her. As did his mother.

Then Tippi opened her eyes and looked back at them.

"Listen up," she said. "Jimmy, you head to LA right this fucking minute. Use one of our private planes. I want about thirty shooters with shotguns and a lot of heavy ammo ready to leave when Elspeth and me arrive tomorrow.

"Oh, and first thing in the morning you go to . . ." She turned to Elspeth. "I don't even know where the fuck I was in jail."

Elspeth gave her the address.

"And you bail out Sondra Wilkins and Heddy—what was her last name? Just get Sondra and her roommate out. Tell them if they want a job shooting, the pay's good. You guys meet us at the Samo Airport around three P.M. tomorrow. Get moving."

He got up and, without another word, started walking slowly, stumbling a little toward the Ford pickup in the big circular driveway. Mary Red Boots got up, but just stood there.

Tippi put the necklace on. *At last,* she thought. "And oh, yes," she said.

Jimmy stopped but did not turn.

"You ever fuck me over like that again, I'll crush the both of you like insects."

Without a word, Mary turned and went into the house, and Jimmy got into the truck and drove off.

Elspeth, who hadn't said a word for a long time, suddenly smiled and said, "An excellent handling of servants. I congratulate you."

"They're not really servants," Tippi said a little uncertainly.

"They are now," Elspeth pointed out cheerfully. "And what do we do, O mistress, while the lackeys toil?"

"We dine and then sleep," Tippi said. "I think we've got a busy day ahead of us tomorrow."

# 14

R APHAEL'S JOURNEY WAS not really such a long one. The Laughing Ghost
 Inn was situated in the middle of Sou Wiccingham, overlooking the
river. It was only a few strides to the main bridge across into Nor Wiccingham, and from there, easy walking distance to the castle on the hill. For although the city stretched for many miles east and west along the river, its
north end was nestled into the foothills of a range of high mountains, and
there the city ended abruptly. Further to east and west, beyond the two cities,
lay the inevitable farmland necessary to sustain this small enclave, but, as
Raphael had learned from Bitters, farm products were not really the main-
stay of the Wicca community. There was gold in them thar hills. Plenty of it.
Even a little silver thrown in for good measure.

Over the years, the mountains had been judiciously mined, and the
product carefully infiltrated into the outside world, diversified into banks in
several countries, and then used to supply much-needed commodities to
North and South Wiccingham. (Mostly to the north, it became apparent to
Raphael as he began his walk into Nor Wiccingham.) The mines themselves
were also in the north—maybe that was why the north had become the chosen land. It wouldn't be the first place that access to riches had made "holy."

Raphael figured that gold had been the factor that had originally persuaded Drusilla to form a settlement here. But he was wrong about that. He
did not know about the sacred lake.

This place was beautiful, boasted a temperate climate, and had enough
arable land to sustain it, and, most importantly, the lake which kept Drusilla
even younger than the other Guardians.

The gold was a discovery made hundreds of years later, just at the beginning of the California rush, when Drusilla had blindfolded and brought

in a few mining engineers to check out the mountain range above the lake. She had not expected a rich strike, but in light of what had been recently happening in California, it had seemed the obvious step to take.

Of course they had not found anywhere near as much gold in the Wiccan mountains as they had in California, but much less was needed to keep Wiccingham posh and pad Drusilla's organization's already flush financial kingdom. So she had begun to modernize the kingdom, mostly the north part, where she stayed to be near the lake. But this modernization had been approached very conservatively.

The journey took him less than two hours from the river to the big castle on the hill. Nevertheless, it was a trip that led from one world into another.

Low tech to high tech; drab to colorful; dirty to squeaky clean. If Sou Wiccingham was medieval with a few high-tech surprises thrown in, the north part of the city was pure Disney Bavarian. The quaint cobblestone (not dirt) streets looked as if they were swept clean by elves every night, but Raphael figured that it was more likely by peasant laborers from Sou Wiccingham. Even the clothes were different here, far less medieval and much more colorful. Apparently these more modern garments cost a great deal more money, and there was a plethora of fancy little shoppes selling them, as well as everything else the more wealthy might covet. There were actually espresso shops—had Raphael visited here first, there would have been no chance of his mistaking it for "real" medieval England. Even so, he had to admit that he had been a fool to argue with Thaddeus about it. Thaddeus was smarter than he was, and he knew it well.

Back when he had been a kid for real, he had allowed Thaddeus to guide him without question, as in choosing Brazilian jiu-jitsu as the basis of his training in self-defense. But of course, as he entered his teen years, he had rebelled. Problem was that he had not yet come out of that stage. Perhaps the same power that kept his body young also operated on his emotions. (What Thaddeus would have been able to point out here was that body and emotions were not separate.)

Anyway, let's face it, if you were smart, you did not argue with Thaddeus, except occasionally to give him something new to think about. He was by far the most intelligent of all the Guardians Raphael had known, and he figured that probably included all the rest of them as well. In fact, Raphael wondered, could it be that Thaddeus's intelligence was what had caused him to develop his psychic powers in such a yin direction? For there was no doubt that of them all, Thaddeus had control over the most passive abilities. He was the best psychic locater (the best at every form of psychometry), the best receiver.

On the other hand, strangely enough, Tippi and Violet seemed to have the most yang talents. Whereas he was more in the middle. Their powers were so different that he would have been hard put to guess which of them was psychic top dog. But one thing he was certain of: he was the least gifted of them all. Had he pointed this out to Thaddeus, he would have been surprised at the answer he would have got thrown back at him.

More and more, as he walked along these clean-enough-to-eat-on cobblestone streets, he perceived a current of anger crackling through the air, jumping from one person to the next.

"Go back south, beggar," he was told by one irate-looking aristocratic man, "unless thou hast some business here to attend to. We do not want lowborns wandering the streets, looking to steal something."

Raphael smiled and nodded, but he mischievously used his power to push the irate fellow, who was accompanied by his wife and daughter, into taking out his purse and throwing it to Raphael.

"Here, I've just thought of a solution," the poor fellow said. "If I give thee all of my coin, thou shalt have no need to steal. Why didn't I think o' that before?"

He looked genuinely puzzled, as did his daughter, but his wife suddenly turned quite pale and looked ready to faint.

"Many thanks," Raphael said, catching the purse and tying it on his belt alongside his own. "Remember to work hard so you may continue in this way to deter crime."

The last he saw of the man, his robust wife, whose face was rapidly turning red, was now swatting him with a heavy-looking parasol she carried.

By the time Raphael arrived at the big castle, the sun was in the middle of the sky, and he was convinced that revolution was inevitable.

There was a vast grassy field, a gigantic lawn actually, with a redbrick path cutting across to a moat—not really much of one, but a moat nonetheless, complete with drawbridge. The drawbridge was down.

He wandered across it along with a mass of sullen, silent peasants who were either returning to the castle after a lunch break in the village or just coming on for the night shift.

A carriage was crossing the other way, and Raphael suddenly became aware that the peasants around him had, to a man or woman, taken off their hats and bonnets and were standing motionless and staring at it.

Someone important, he thought, but he was too excited by the prospect of finally seeing his mother after all these years to pay any attention. Smiling, he strode on boldly toward the castle, the white dog bouncing along beside him.

At the entrance he took out the pointy hat the jester had given him and said to Blackjack, "Time has come for me to play the Fool," and put the hat on.

The dog barked excitedly, as if to say "Me, too," and this was odd, because this dog hardly ever barked at all.

"I do not recognize thee." The gatekeeper pointed at him. "What business hast thou in Ironwall Castle? What art thou smiling at, Fool?"

"By my Fool's cap," Raphael swore, getting in the spirit of things, "canst thou not see my lute and my cap? I come to make music, and to make merry. My business is to make a fool of myself, and of you. The first one will be an easy enough task, the second has already been accomplished. Thus do I smile, for only a fool would not smile under these circumstances. Thus am I a fool or am I not a fool?"

Amazingly, Blackjack barked once more.

"Correct," Raphael commented. "At least the white dog has brains enough to answer." He looked around him nervously. He wasn't sure if he'd got the hang of this thing or not. Nobody was laughing, but a few people had paused to watch, and a couple of these were smiling. He plunged ahead.

"I demand to be the king. Did I say I demand to be the king? Excuse me, I meant I demand to see the king. But then if I could be him, I wouldn't have to see him, would I? So-o-o . . . maybe I was right the first time."

Actually a couple of laughs.

One man, a handsome, gentle-looking fellow, if a bit plump, actually applauded. "I s-s-say," he stammered, "one w-w-wonders wh-what would b-b-be the first thing you would do if you were made king."

Raphael, who had no idea of the rules of the game, at that moment made the decision that, regardless of the tradition of jesters, he would never make fun of someone who stuttered.

Besides, there was something about the guy; even Blackjack perked up and turned his head to make little-piggie-eye contact with Raphael, as if to say "May I?" and then rushed over to greet the man. In an explosion of joy, he took to the air, head first into the fellow's chest, and, of course, down the man went.

"Your Majesty!" the guardian of the castle gate exclaimed.

Raphael ran over and pulled Blackjack, who was writhing and whining, off the man and helped him up.

"I s-s-say," he said. "Wh-what a muscular little dog. Th-that is, he looks little, but he f-f-feels quite large."

"His name is Blackjack. He looks little, but he eats and shits like a giant. Blackjack, meet"—he gestured—"the king who dresses like a peasant."

To his surprise, Blackjack barked once, crisply, as if to announce himself. It was right then that Raphael became certain that the psychic powers of his stone were affecting Blackjack.

"Wh-wh-why not?" the king said. "I represent your people as well as the aristocracy, do I not? So sometimes I dress like them, walk among them. Well," he added wistfully, "at least as far as the drawbridge. But then, I asked you a question, which you have yet to answer."

He had suddenly stopped stammering. His expression was so earnest. Raphael looked into his eyes, which were big and blue and rather sad, and decided impulsively, as was his way, *Hell, I like this guy.*

"Your eyes remind me of someone," the king said, "but you have yet to answer."

"I would eat when I was hungry," Raphael tried, "and sleep when I was sleepy, only now it would be the king eating, and the king sleeping."

The man applauded again. His hands, which were soft but strong-looking, seemed to move about more than necessary, as if they had a life of their own.

"Yes," he said enthusiastically, "how right you are. We are all of us, from peasant to king, the same in every way that really counts. I agree with you. Did you notice how I say 'you' instead of 'thou'? When I dress as a peasant, I try to speak as a peasant."

"You should stick with it," Raphael suggested. "It's the way people will all talk in the future."

"Is it really?" The king looked doubtful. "You claim to know the future?"

"I am the future."

"And he?" The king pointed at the squirming white dog.

"He, too."

"So everything is in the process of becoming short and muscular. What do you call the process? Does it have a name?"

"Evolution," Raphael said.

"And no one says 'thou.' "

"Right."

"Well, go on then, jester. What else would you do first as king?"

"I would make the rich poor and the poor rich."

"Why not simply make everyone equally rich? Tell me that one, if you pl-pl-please." He had suddenly started in stammering again.

"No, no, won't do. The poor have earned the right to be rich, but it wouldn't be the same if the rich were rich, too. Besides, the rich have also earned the right to be poor. It's a natural law."

The king nodded, looking very serious. "And wh-wh-what is this l-l-law called?"

"Revolution," Raphael said casually.

The small but noisy crowd that had gathered around them hushed so fast that you could hear the hiss of air intake.

The king stared silently into Raphael's eyes. Only the index finger and thumb on his right hand moved, rubbing each other in a light circular movement.

"I s-s-say, thou hast . . . I m-mean, you have your n-n-nerve."

"Nobody else wants it."

The king looked sober for a moment, then smiled. He had a beautiful, relaxed smile that showed a lot of gleaming teeth.

"Of course," he said. "Who would?"

Then he turned to the crowd that was now gathering around them in earnest.

"Do you know who I am?"

A few of them nodded.

"Then bl-bl-bless you. Go away, please."

Grumbling, the crowd broke up.

The king, who was taller than Raphael, put his arm around his shoulders and said, "By G-G-Goddess, what a sturdy frame thou hast. N-n-never have two b-beings so small carried such a . . . how shall I put it?"

"Wallop," Raphael suggested.

"Oh, what a magnificent word," the king said, once again losing his stutter. "I love it. 'Wallop.' It's one of those rarest of words that means what it sounds like—" He blushed, only able to conjure up the unmentionable one, and, guiding Raphael with his arm still draped around his shoulder, began walking inside the castle, murmuring to himself, "Wallop, wallop."

The king led Raphael through a long entranceway and out into the castle courtyard.

Raphael blinked and restrained himself from mumbling, "What the fuck?" This place was more like a posh shopping mall than a castle. He could not help but smile at the image which popped into his head—outraged peasants breaking into "Hats R Us" or the frozen yogurt parlor, fancy hats on their heads and yogurt cones in their hands, shouting "It's all ours!"

The sunny courtyard was lined with fancy shops and fast-food stands, while the courtyard itself was a carefully manicured garden with several cobbled pathways leading through it and a waterfall in the center which cascaded from a man-made hill into a pond with—he couldn't tell from here; surely it would have goldfish?

He must have unconsciously shaken his head, because the king said, "Y-y-you d-do not like it?"

"I'm just surprised," Raphael answered, forgetting that he was out of character here for a jester.

"Surely you must have seen it before. Everyone c-comes to see it. Y-you must b-be from one of the outlying farms, b-but . . ."

"No, I've never seen it."

"Then th-that is why you did not understand you have to h-have a p-permit to enter the grounds, you see."

"But all those people pouring in?"

"Workmen. The g-guard recognizes them. If I h-had not been there—"

"Well, I'm lucky that you were."

"—seeing the queen off, and recognized y-your hat—"

Raphael froze. "The queen off? To where?"

"To Greenstone, where else? It's S-Sou Wiccingham she represents. She is to st-stay there until the ceremony next week. Y-y-you're wearing my jester Rono's h-hat. I h-hope it br-brings you better luck than it did him."

"Where is he, by the way?"

The king blinked. "He is dead, did you not know? Hunting accident. Dr-drunken b-bums." He shook his head. "Wh-what a foolish tragedy. I detest w-w-wine. D-d-don't tell anyone. It will reflect on my manhood, I'm sure."

Raphael, still trying to pull himself back together after the bad news about Elena, barely heard the king as he chattered on.

"Over there is the Chapel of Our Lady. It is quite famous, you know. And th-th-that leads to the main hall, where you will join us for dinner tonight. Perhaps you can entertain us? I assume you play and sing? I will have you paged. But you must first bathe and rest up from your journey. There are a few apartments over the shops off the west end path. I will have you set up there. It is a short walk, but the apartments are very nice. That is where Rono always stayed. I will see to it that you get his room. To be frank, you do not seem all that f-f-funny, but if Rono liked you well enough to give you his hat, you deserve a try at it. I liked him, you know. He had a wicked tongue, but I—liked him."

"Me, too," Raphael said. The goofy looking little mystic-clown with the lugubrious philosophy. Here and gone, so fast. "And I hardly knew him."

"Well, he must have liked you, too, to have given you his hat. Wh-what would he have done without it?" He stopped and put his soft but strong hand on Raphael's shoulder and looked into his eyes. "Do you suppose," he said, "that he knew he was going to die?"

Raphael thought about it. He didn't like it, but couldn't deny it. "Yeah," he said, "he sure seemed to."

Later, alone in his swank castle apartment, waiting to be summoned, he

couldn't get the sad jester out of his mind. *Your death or mine? Or both?
Or . . . ?* For some reason, he could hardly stand to think it, but must: Or more?

Later, in the royal dining room, he sat with everyone, yet alone, eating
in silence while everyone at the banquet chatted and laughed and watched
him expectantly. No doubt he was supposed to joke and do weird things
with his food.

But he couldn't shake the shadow.

Suddenly he was aware that people were shouting at him.

"A jest, a jest! Make merry, Fool!"

"A man goes into a tavern with a parrot on his shoulder . . ." Then he
had to explain what a parrot was. The description of its plumage brought
enough oohs and aahs itself to qualify the joke as a showstopper, but when
he got to the part about the bird talking, the crowd went wild.

"So the bartender says, 'How much did he cost you?' And the parrot answers, 'He was inexpensive, but he eats too much.' "

Stunned silence.

Suddenly the king began to laugh. "D-d-do you not see?" he stammered. "The man is the b-bird's pet."

Then everybody began to laugh. Whether it was because they were at
court or because of the copious amounts of wine downed, or just because
of their king's endorsement, their laughter seemed overblown to the point
that it verged on hysteria. But no doubt about it, Raffo the clown was an instant hit.

"Since I am a Fool, I shall sing you the Fool's song."

More oohs and aahs as he unveiled the gleaming, emerald-green Ovation guitar.

But as he positioned himself a ways back from the table and took up the
classical guitar position, with his left foot on the footstool they had brought
him, and began to sing, he found himself looking at a familiar face. One he
had seen often back at the Laughing Ghost. The man only nodded and
winked, reminding Raphael that these were dangerous times.

> " 'All the time that you've wasted
> Counting petals
> On your roses
> Watching rainbows from your windows,' he cried.
> 'I will spend them in the garden
> With your daughter with her clothes off,
> She just wants to have me inside.'
> Fa la la, tiyi yippie yippie yay . . .''

Which turned out to be another big winner. But did not really suit his mood. He next performed "Raffo the Clown," which was a little funny, but probably a little more sad. And yet, even a bit defiant, definitely a jester's song:

"So if you catch the act
And don't know what to say
Just remember, the laughs are my lines in the play
And if you're looking deeper
And you feel let down
What more can you ask
'Cause I'm only a lonely clown

Faster and faster
Around goes the merry-go-round
Faster and faster
Around goes the merry-go-round
Faster and faster
Then some fool comes tumbling down
Now who in the world could that silly fool be?

Raindrops are falling
And he's outside getting wet
Raindrops are falling
And he's outside getting wet
I keep on calling
But he's just a silhouette
Oh, who in the world could that silly fool be?
It's me."

Here again was a big silence, and here again it was the king who applauded first. Raphael was surprised to see that the man's huge, sad eyes were brimming with tears. For what? The song? Or did he share Raphael's mood? Tuned in to the late great Rono?

Did he feel death hovering here, waiting to lash out left and right? Over what? How could this sad, thoughtful man, who obviously meant so well, possibly be the enemy?

It wasn't until he was back in his oversize bed trying to fall asleep that the many subtle ironies of the situation began to strike him.

Should he go back to where he came from and try to gain entrance to that castle or wait here for his mother to come back? He tried to imagine what Thaddeus would have advised. *No, better stick with it, wait it out until she returns.* He had through a stroke of luck worked his way in here. She probably wouldn't even recognize him after all this time. She had actually been riding in that carriage he had passed on the drawbridge.

Was he a fool or a warrior? Was there any real difference? Was all this oncoming flood of bloodshed a tragedy or a joke? Or both?

He slept, and dreamed that he was climbing, moving up and up. But whenever he looked up he could not see the top of the mountain. Just more and more to climb. But he did not dream of quitting and he did not dream of falling. He was Elena's son. He just climbed on and on.

# *15*

---

WITH RAPHAEL AND Blackjack gone, Thaddeus found himself obligated to shoulder almost the entire burden of being revolutionary hero to the burgeoning crowds at the Laughing Ghost Inn. But luckily for him, Bitters, along with Jeremy, the luthier, and "just plain Bill" Broadbent, the swashbuckler whom Raphael had forced to buckle, were eager to take on a larger share.

Bitters was still, as he always had been, the main trainer of the would-be knights in the area of swordplay. But now, being Raphael's one and only student in jiu-jitsu, he also took on the hand-to-hand instruction. Broadbent was his assistant in both these enterprises, and from time to time Mrs. Lim stepped in and took over, making it clear that she was the ultimate authority in these matters. The two men either accepted her dominance or merely tolerated it; Thaddeus couldn't tell which.

Jeremy, it turned out, was not only an extremely skilled luthier, but a fine archer as well. The courtyard now had several targets set up around the edges, with bales of hay to break the flight of the arrows. Things seemed to be moving along fine, but suddenly Thaddeus realized that this enormous fight they were all headed for was actually going to happen any day now, and then of course he realized that nothing was moving along fast enough after all.

"Is there any point at all in the hand-to-hand training? It's a complete waste of time. They're going to fight with weapons, right?"

Bitters nodded. "There's some truth to that, there is. But fact is, most o' these poor farmers are going to end up fighting with sticks, pitchforks, hoes. They're pretty likely to lose those, and then what? They ain't going to have that much choice, ya see. Besides, you get someone wif all that heavy metal-plate stuff off his feet, and he might as well be a turtle. He won't never get up again."

As Thaddeus attended more practices in the courtyard, the pattern became clearer to him. Everybody wanted to be a swordsman. But there were not that many swords and fewer yet, people who could use them well enough to make it worth the bother to train them.

Bows and arrows, on the other hand, were made of wood. He had a consultation with Jeremy.

"We can't hope to match them as far as swords and armor goes, so let's concentrate on archers."

Jeremy was ecstatic. "A bow, like a lute, is a work of art, and those who use them, artists." But he wrinkled his nose at the prospect of mass production.

"No carving, no decorations, just good strong bows and lots of arrows—a couple or three quivers per," Thaddeus insisted.

"I will need several assistants," Jeremy said.

"You pick them," Thaddeus replied. "However many you need. We want an army of well-armed, well-trained archers, as fast as possible, and everyone who's not an expert swordsman had better be in it."

"It would be most helpful if thou wouldst have a few words with them. They all quite naturally want to be knights, in shining armor."

"Do we have shining armor?"

Jeremy smiled. "What little we have does not shine."

"Then let's see to it that the small group of swordsmen we have get all the armor they need, and as for the archers, more arrows. Let a good offense be their defense."

"Let a good offense be their defense," Jeremy echoed. "I like that phrase. May I use it?"

"Be my guest," Thaddeus replied.

The third night after Raphael had left, after Thaddeus and Jeremy finished performing their nightly stint at the tavern, Thaddeus gave a short speech to the archers gathered outside in the courtyard.

"You are mostly farmers, which is to say that you are used to hard work. War is the hardest kind of work. You guys are the heart of this revolution. We're going to win or lose because of your arrows.

"The men you are going to be facing will have superior arms and superior armor, but they are aristocrats and they hate to work. They think that war is an art, but let me guarantee you, they are wrong."

A frown here from silent but suffering Jeremy.

"And if they don't win right away, in all that heavy armor, they are going to get tired. They are not used to getting tired like you are, so they are going to start to wonder just how long they can go on. But you know how long you can go on. Hour after hour, day after day, year after year, you just grit your teeth and go on.

"So they are going to get tired and doubt themselves, and you are going to get tired but you are not going to doubt yourselves. And when they get tired and doubt themselves, they are going to go down."

He waited for the cheering to fade.

"All I ask is that you shoot each arrow just as Jeremy shows you. One right after another, but each one carefully. Exactly. If you do that, we will win."

"But what about the horses?" one of them asked nervously, after the applause had finally died down. "They've got such a lot of them."

"I've got plans for the horses," Thaddeus assured the man. "If the arrows don't take care of them. Any more questions?"

There were none.

"Very well, then, we've got only one more worry. That's getting enough arrows made in time. I want all of you to ask Jeremy what you can do to help. He'll put you to work. So just work and be patient. That's what farmers have always done best. Your day is coming."

The next night he gave a different sermon to the small group of swordsmen.

"From what I hear, you guys are tough and you know what you're doing. Well, you had better be tough, because there's damn few of you, and you're going to have to do all of the infighting, and you're going to be outnumbered, outarmed, outweighed, and you're going to have to take the brunt of their charge and hold it. Turn it back."

"I don't understand," a big guy who wore a patch over his left eye said. "Why ain't there more o' us?"

Thaddeus shrugged. "Everyone who can't fight is going to be shooting arrows. You're the only ones we've got that can fight."

"Arrows can be a nuisance," the guy with the patch argued. "They take a few fellows out, cause some minor wounds. They can make you mad, but they can't win a battle. It's the blade got to do that for ya."

The other fighters muttered agreement with this philosophy.

"We'll, we're changing that in this coming battle," Thaddeus argued. "We're just going to keep on pumping arrows into them until they become more than just a nuisance. But you guys are going to have to hold the line, and you're going to have to do the finishing."

The men grumbled. "Never heard o' nothin' like that before," one of them said. "Can't see how that'll work."

"Have any of you ever been in an actual war?" Thaddeus asked.

Silence.

"Has there ever been anything resembling a war around here?"

Silence.

Then one of the men offered, "There were a peasants' uprising about sixty year ago. Me Grandpa died in it."

"Then you're better off listening to me. We can win this one, but not with swords. So arrows is all we've got. All you have to do is drag it out while the arrows do their job. But it's going to be a lot of hard, dirty work."

There were still some doubtful stares, and frankly, Thaddeus wished (not for the first time) that Raphael were here. He knew deep inside his gut that they would all rather follow the heroic-looking, easygoing, green-eyed blond warrior than they ever would him. And he understood, without bitterness, that part of it was because he was Black. There were few Blacks here, and naturally people would rather follow someone who looked like them, only better.

"Look," he said in a conciliatory tone, "I don't want this to be spread around, outside of the group. Loose lips sink ships." (Puzzled looks here, and a few guffaws.) "But I'm from someplace a long ways away from here. Both in time and space. We've lived through all of this. Wars are more and more going to be fought from a distance. Arrows are the way to go. The only way."

After a brief silence, one of the men, a short but very stout fellow with a bushy black beard, said, "From where the Wicca come and go sometime, maybe?"

Thaddeus nodded.

"Aye, that's forbidden," the fellow added, nodding his head. "Good for you. Personally, I like the idea. It's fresh."

Thaddeus smiled. "Fresh" was an expression Black kids would have used where he came from. Lately he had kept a careful watch on his language, stripping it of any slang, not only to avoid misunderstanding but also so these citizens of medieval Wiccingham would feel at home around him. Accuracy had now become, for him, the most important factor in his speech. Where before his slang had worked more like poetry or music, the language of war had to be exact.

"The only question I have left," the stout, bearded would-be soldier continued, "is what are we waiting for?"

Thaddeus nodded, thinking how to put it.

"When the time is right," he said, "we'll know it. Meanwhile, we've got to continue to make arrows, and to practice. We've got nothing to lose, and everything to gain, by waiting." *And hopefully Raphael will get his mom out of that castle before it begins,* he thought but did not mention. "One more thing," he said. "Any of you seen one of these?"

He had taken to wearing one of his pistols in a shoulder holster under a loose tunic. He now took one out and held it up for everyone to have a look at.

The answer was no.

"Well, that's some good news, anyway," he said. And when they asked him what that metal thing was, he repeated, "When the time is right, you'll know."

Meanwhile, in big Ironwall Castle, Raphael had settled into his role as a clown-minstrel, and was waiting anxiously for his mother's return. He was as much an instant success here as he had been at the Dog and Cat Inn. Although his jokes and patter were not the wittiest, they had a bizarre other-worldliness about them that the royal court found intriguing. But the main attraction was his singing and playing on the flashy, bright green guitar, for nobody at court had ever heard anything remotely like blues, swing, boogie-woogie, or ragtime.

Another factor was the popularity of the white dog. In working with the beast in order to teach it a few tricks, Raphael had immediately verified his earlier hunch: the power of his mystic stone had been affecting the bull terrier.

Blackjack, who now when entertaining wore a little red hat tied onto his broad, fighter's head, and a matching red vest, would almost instantly pick up any trick his master tried to teach him. Would bark whenever Raphael gave him the psychic nudge. (Such as, "Don't bark at this man—unless, that is, his wife happens to be cheating on him." "Woof!" Or, "Don't do it twice unless she is cheating with two of his friends at once." Blackjack looks puzzled, then suddenly barks five times.)

King William and Raphael had swiftly become friends. One evening after dinner, the king drew him aside and pointed to a tall, muscular but slender man, and said, "D-d-didst thou n-notice that man, the one who n-never smiles at thy j-jests?"

"Couldn't hardly have missed him." Raphael had wondered who the big, mean-looking dude dressed all in black was.

"W-well, he's the m-man-at-arms for the Wicca. A quite ruthless warrior, proficient with any weapon. Th-thou knowest, my fr-fr-friend, there are fellows with a lot of muscle and a little knowledge of swordplay, probably thyself among them, I w-would g-guess. There are also fighters with a great mountain of knowledge and no muscle. Th-th-this fellow—whose name is Morgan, by the way—has too much of both. Just as he is b-both my b-bodyguard and m-m-my jailer. Wh-what I am trying to say is, d-d-do not g-g-get to thinking that m-mayhap with all thy muscle th-th-thou can best him."

Raphael tried to look genuinely surprised. "Why would I think that, anyway?"

The king shrugged. There was a sad expression on his face. "I d-d-do not know, but I've s-s-seen the w-way thou look at him. And he at thee."

Raphael shrugged back, still trying to look indifferent. "I don't know what you mean," he said. "Why would I ever mix it up with him?"

"These are trying times," King William continued, speaking slowly and without a stutter. "There is going to be trouble. He doth guard the castle, and me. He watcheth over the drawbridge. Thou didst appear out of nowhere. I don't know what any of that means, but it means something. So I am warning thee. Be careful, my friend."

A few days later, and Raphael learned that his mother had arrived early that morning back at Ironwall Castle. What he did not know was that the ceremony to unite the kingdom under his new friend, King William, had been moved ahead to the very next day. Or that Morgan, saddled down with the responsibility of protecting the new queen both before and during the coming ceremony, and having received no contact from Elspeth or any word of Diana, had decided to send out his squad of well-armed horsemen to arrest the small group of malcontents who had taken to hanging out at the Laughing Ghost Inn.

# *16*

———■———

THADDEUS SAT ALONE in his room at the inn, cradling the lute but not playing anything, just listening to the rain hit the roof. After a while he got up, put the lute back in its case, and sat down again.

Earlier in the week he had learned about Elena's shift to the local castle, and he had inwardly congratulated Raphael for not showing up back on his doorstep. Obviously the kid was maturing, and had decided to wait it out where he was, which was the only logical decision to come to. A couple more days and, hopefully, he would have his mother out of there. And then the North and South Wiccinghams could conduct their civil war to their hearts' content.

And yet he could not shake the feeling that something was right now going very wrong. Couldn't even play the lute. Which was weird.

Day before yesterday, as if the sky was somehow related to the growing discontent, Thaddeus had looked out the window to see the horizon pregnant with dark, grumbling clouds. Little nervous flashes in the distance. Soon, everything grew dark and gloomy. Spring rain. Even for the mountains, that seemed unlikely.

It had been raining hard ever since. But that did not in any way seem to hamper the oncoming revolution. People's raging spirits were at the point where everything seemed to fuel the flames.

Thaddeus had watched them down below, training in the courtyard, freezing, shaking, clutching their icy swords or shooting arrows into the rain. The dark.

In fact they were making a lot of noise, he realized, right this minute, down below his window, rain and all. He blinked, and came out of his reverie. Too much noise. He blinked again. Way too much noise. And the tone of the voices—!

He rushed to the window, muttered "Shit!" Ran back to an open chest in a corner of the room where he now kept everything he owned, and came out with a shooting vest and his guns. He slung on the vest, which was weighted down by several nine-millimeter clips in the pockets, then the holsters, one a shoulder holster, the other one clipped to his belt. Then he drew the handgun from the shoulder holster. Switched off the safety, ran back over and aimed out the window, but you don't shoot a handgun into a crowd, from a second-story window, unless you don't care whom you hit.

So he rushed downstairs and outside, keeping his cool. It was what he was best at.

Outside, training was over and they were fighting for real in the courtyard. Several archers were down, but so was one of the attacking knights.

There were only four of Thaddeus's swordsmen in the group, and none of them were mounted. Two more archers and one of the swordsmen went down. It was clear they were losing fast here, and Thaddeus saw no signs that any mercy was going to be shown.

"Shit," he said again, and then, because there was nothing else to do, he drew a careful bead on a man wearing a silver helmet, whom he assumed was their leader. Shot him twice, knocking him off his horse. Even in this turmoil, the irony of the situation did not escape him, that while the helmets protected the most important people from all forms of psychic attack, they also marked whom to shoot first.

Everything stopped, and there was one of those strange moments of eerie silence, except that one of the horses whinnied. Taking it as a sign, Thaddeus took careful aim and shot that horse. One of his swordsmen, the short heavy one with the beard, came to life and made quick work of the soldier as he lay stunned, partially pinned under his dead mount.

Thaddeus shot another horse, and it reared, throwing off its rider. Now the archers, gathering their wits in this respite, nocked arrows, aimed, and loosed. There was a dry whistling sound, followed by the scream of a man as well as the scream of another horse.

Flash of lightning. Close. Everything seemed to freeze, waiting for the clap of thunder to catch up.

Out of the corner of his eye Thaddeus caught sight of a shadow rushing out of the inn behind him and into the downpour. It was Mrs. Lim, moving past him so fast he barely had time to shout, "Block off the courtyard! Don't let any of them out!" before she was beyond him and swallowed up in the fray. Thunder crashed.

The courtyard was almost entirely surrounded by the sprawling inn. Only one narrow passage gave access to it. And now, just when Thaddeus thought he'd lost sight of her, the shadow warrior appeared at this entrance. Even from here he could see the distinct shape of her Japanese-style sword. "Japanese make the best swords, and automobiles," she had admitted to him once, grudgingly.

"Come on, boys, it only me," Mrs. Lim shouted, and then stood there waiting.

Three of the knights panicked, whipped their mounts around, and rushed her, spurring their horses, but she moved back into the narrow entranceway, where there was room for only one at a time.

Out of the corner of his eye, Thaddeus saw the slender figure with the wicked *katana* blade raised over her head, calmly waiting for the charging stallion to reach her.

For one breathtaking moment almost everyone paused fighting and froze wherever they were to watch.

Suddenly the blade flashed out and the huge stallion crumpled and crashed down, as limp as a clod of mud, its thick skull cleaved in half. But momentum carried it onward, knocking the slender figure head over heels. Miraculously, she back-somersaulted onto her feet, and just as the second horse leaped up over the body of the first one, the blade flashed out again. This horse, a big bay gelding, reared up, throwing its rider, twisted sideways, and toppled back on top of him.

Thaddeus could feel the bones break from where he was, across the courtyard, could hear the shout of pain. The third horse whinnied, shied, and broke away, avoiding the other two and ignoring the spurs digging into its flanks.

The slender black figure darted forward, and the blade slashed twice as, like a farmer slaughtering geese, she finished off the two stunned riders. Then she stood on top of the carcass of the second horse, the big bay, and shouted, "Come on, boys. I still here. You no want me?"

Now, finally, Bitters came sprinting out of the inn, into the pounding rain, wearing only a pair of sloppy trousers and cursing.

"Damn it all, someone's going to pay for waking me up, is all I says," he shouted, waving a sword. And pay they did, as he charged into the fray and, being unable to reach the nearest knight from behind, hamstrung the man's horse, and then went after the man. The poor creature screamed like a human, but Bitters, who was normally as kind to animals as anyone could be, had no illusions about the nature of war: it was hell for everyone in it, but it was worse for the loser.

Now the tide of the battle had turned. The archers were gaining some self-control, learning what it was like to have the disposition and skills of the long-distance killer. It was with a lot more calm and a lot more accuracy that they loosed the next flight of arrows, and Thaddeus realized that it was no longer necessary to use any more of his precious bullets.

To Bitters, who was still within hearing range, he shouted, just making sure, "Kill every one of them! No prisoners!"

To which Bitters answered, "Oh, don't worry about that. It were me very intention from the start."

Soon the battle was over. For a moment Thaddeus just stood there with his face in his hands, murmuring something unintelligible even to himself.

Then he shook his head and opened his eyes and looked around him.

"Okay, this is it," he said. "The war has come to us, and there's no backing off. Jeremy?"

The blood-streaked archer-luthier blinked and seemed momentarily unaware of anything except the awful carnage. The terrible odors. The blood drained from his face and he swayed.

"Jeremy," Thaddeus repeated. "You're the leader of the archers. Pull yourself together. See that very dead guy in the silver helmet? He won't be needing it anymore, so you take it and put it on. Don't take it off until the fighting is over. Understand?"

Jeremy, though still looking grim, nodded.

Thaddeus turned to the small figure in black splashed with clouds of still-bright blood.

"Mrs. Lim," he said, shaking his head in awe, for once at a loss for words. "Mrs. Lim, my goodness," was all he could manage, followed with the wry, "Where were you when I needed you?"

"I might suggest you stop you fooling around," she did indeed suggest. "War serious, maybe everybody here dead soon."

"Yeah, you're right." Thaddeus nodded. "Of course you're right. What else would you be?"

She frowned.

"Look here, Mrs. Lim," he continued, before she could interrupt, "why don't you take a few archers and whatever swordsmen are here, except for Bitters, and get across the main bridge. Right now. Defend the bridge at all costs. We'll need to get some of our men across to help you hold it as soon as we can.

"Bitters, get upstairs to my room and pick up all my clips of ammo from the chest. Get the other silver helmet—it's wrapped up in a blanket—and put it on. Then get back down here. Then you and me will head for the bridge. Help out your little woman.

"The rest of you, spread out and notify everyone. Commandeer horses any way you have to, and ride like hell. I want you to get everyone that's willing and able to fight across that bridge by tonight. So don't spare the horses. Do you understand?"

Murmurs, mostly unintelligible, rose from the survivors.

"Gentlemen," Thaddeus said solemnly, "we are now at war."

# 17

━━━ ◈ ━━━

I T WAS NOW early evening, and Thaddeus and his invading army were gathered just across the central bridge, which was on fire. Thaddeus was waiting to see it collapse before he moved his army out. He wanted to be certain they *all* got the message.

The first move he had made was to send small groups to take over and knock out the auxiliary bridges; he wanted every individual joining their army to march across the main bridge. He wanted to shake hands with each one individually. To each one, he wanted to make the same statement:

"Welcome to war. Anyone who is not willing to die, turn back across the bridge now."

But to his astonishment, there were just too many of them, and too little time. Soon all the newly promoted generals—Jeremy, Bitters, the arrogant Lord Broadbent (now simply "Bill"), and of course Mrs. Lim—were shaking hands and spouting off his lines. Surprisingly, only three people turned around and retreated across the bridge. Everyone else joined. They were an unskilled army, but a big and eager one.

"We've got the numbers. What do you think?" Bitters had asked him.

Thaddeus shook his head. "One thing we can count on, we're going to fight like hell." But as to win or lose, how could anyone know?

By nightfall only a few scraggly farmers were coming across the bridge, mostly in groups of two or three, without arms or training. Fewer and fewer, as time wore on. Finally Thaddeus had judged there would not be enough straglers to make it worth sacrificing the element of surprise.

"Fire the bridge," he said. And solemnly, as if it were a sacred rite, they had.

And now, quite suddenly, it stopped raining, and at last the bridge collapsed and crashed into the rain-swollen, swiftly moving river. Most of them shuddered as the significance struck home.

"Finders keepers," Thaddeus announced, waving about him to take up the entire landscape and everything in it. "Losers weepers."

Then he turned and led them off into the swiftly gathering bank of fog.

Fog—a curse or a blessing? It could get you where you were going without attracting attention. But when the time to fight came, Thaddeus knew that the most important element necessary to win a battle with archers was clarity and depth of vision. This looked bad! Whether it was better or worse than driving rain he did not know.

Furthermore, the dense clots of fallen cloud made the fancy town with all its elegant little medievalesque shoppes appear frightening and other-worldly to the enormous army of mostly farmers moving through it.

It was hard to tell who knew what. Many shops were open, many shut. Whether this was normal for this time of night or not, none could really say. From brightly lit rooms that glowed eerily in the fog, clerks with wary expressions watched from behind their counters. A few shoppers froze and stared out the windows at them as they passed.

An army of shabby farmers, each one carrying exceptionally long, unstrung bows and one long wooden stake, pointed on both ends. Each man bristling with several quivers of arrows slung over his shoulder. These preceded by a small group of swashbuckling knights, clanking along in armor (if you can call someone a knight who doesn't ride a horse).

One man, a skinny little fellow, watching from the window of Ye Olde Café Latte Shoppe, crossed to the door and opened it.

"Mind if I join you?" he asked casually.

"You're not armed," Thaddeus pointed out.

But he held up a butcher knife. "I'll pick something up off of someone."

"You don't have armor."

"I'm pretty tough," the little guy insisted.

Thaddeus smiled. "Sure," he said. "Glad to have you. Can you shoot a bow?"

He thought about it and shook his head. "Never tried it."

Thaddeus figured that. These bows were mostly longer than ordinary bows and were designed by Jeremy and Thaddeus to take advantage of the long, lanky build that seemed so common among the farmers. There were only a few smaller bows made for the men who were too small to handle the longer ones, and these were the size of the traditional bows the enemy would be using.

But these were few and far between. Mostly, if you were too small to use one of Jeremy's specials and you had no training with blades, you had a long, crude, wooden spear. It was one of these that was dug up for the feisty little shop owner.

"What makes you want to join, just like that?" Thaddeus asked him.

He looked puzzled and said, "Why, you're right. That's all."

But this was the only incident as they moved like ghosts through the fog.

After what seemed like forever, they stood outside the town on the edge of a wide field of tall green grass which swiftly disappeared into what was now an impenetrable fog bank.

"Castle's up there," Bill Broadbent informed Thaddeus. "Looks flat, but it's a slight uphill grade. Just a big field, then the moat, drawbridge."

The men inched forward, led now by Jeremy and Broadbent, the goal being to stop just short of longbow range.

But it was tricky business. Finally Jeremy called a halt.

"I can't go any farther and be sure," he said. "We'd better send out a scout."

Thaddeus agreed, and sent out a volunteer.

They waited in silence. Then they heard galloping hoofbeats. A rider pulled up in front of them and threw something that whipped through the air and landed in the grass, rolling.

Suddenly Jeremy lurched and a few men cried out. It was the head of their scout.

The rider whipped his horse around but . . . went nowhere. Just sat motionless while Thaddeus motioned to go get him.

"That was you that caused him to freeze up like that?" Broadbent asked in awe. "You never told us you're a wizard."

"I'm modest," Thaddeus said, motioning them to bring the man to him. "They should have put one of those silver helmets on him."

"There are only a few of those," Jeremy cut in, getting his composure back. "The Wicca ration them out very sparingly. What will we do with him?" Sounding nervous.

Thaddeus frowned. They had to all get it through their heads that this was no game.

"I'm just a messenger," the poor fellow pleaded as they dragged him up to Thaddeus.

"Now you the message," Thaddeus said, still frowning. "Broadbent, you a good rider, right?"

"The very best."

"Ride back there. They'll think it's him. In a way, it will be. Toss them his head, then turn and get back here fast."

Even in the moonlight, Broadbent paled a little.

"This is the real thing, you dig?" Thaddeus said, suddenly aware that under the pressure he was slipping back into the pattern of his colloquial speech again. *Stop that,* he said to himself. *It is essential to be exact here. To not be misunderstood. But is that not always essential?* he wondered briefly, but did not ponder.

"You, too, Jeremy," he said. "Wake up. You're going to see a lot more blood and guts before this is over."

Broadbent took out his sword, but hesitated as the men shoved the weeping messenger toward him.

But a figure dressed in black darted at the unfortunate prisoner from one side and twisted. There was a chunking sound, and the head popped off the body.

"Come on, boys," Mrs. Lim complained. "Let us all now be fierce. Why your women no fight? Shame on you!"

Thaddeus nodded. He knew where she was coming from, but there was a world of difference between medieval China and medieval Europe. There were no British lady knights in armor and there were no lady archers. Just mothers, daughters, and a few damsels in distress, for inspirational purposes only. Several of the armored swordsmen sported colorful silk scarves as tokens. When Thaddeus pointed out to Mrs. Lim what this represented, she snorted in disgust.

"Maybe I carry with me Mr. Lim's stinky socks," she groused, not really getting it.

Thaddeus silently agreed, but said nothing. After a few minutes, he said, "He's coming back now. Nobody's following."

Jeremy eyed him warily. "You can tell that?"

Thaddeus nodded. "At first I guess I was too excited to try, but I've got them located now." He closed his eyes and continued, "The horsemen are lined up in rows four deep in front of the moat. They've got small groups of archers on each side. But they're kind of an afterthought. I'd say they're too far out on the wings to get much range. They're shooting from too much of an angle, and if Jeremy's right, they've got shorter bows, with less pull."

Suddenly Thaddeus opened his eyes and smiled. "Okay," he said. "We cookin' now."

Mrs. Lim and Jeremy looked at each other and shrugged. Bitters, who had been quiet up till now, said, "The boss is right. Here he comes."

And when Broadbent raced in and, in a flashy move, dismounted while the horse was still moving, Bitters added, "Nice touch with the head and all. Liked that one, I did."

Broadbent was one of the few men who had chosen to wear light chain-mail armor, probably to showcase his athletic fencing style. But even so, he clanged, rattled, and practically crashed when he landed. Thaddeus frowned. He felt light armor was a foolish choice, but could hardly disallow his general's freedom of choice.

Startled, the horse reared and whinnied. Still, Broadbent managed to hold on to the reins.

"What do we do with the horse?"

Thaddeus thought about it. "Tie the body on and send it back to them." They swiftly did so. Then Thaddeus declared, "All right, let's move out."

They were now marching in a formation similar to their enemy's, except that there was only one small group of swordsmen in the center, while the lines of archers on the wings were much longer.

Finally Thaddeus ordered a halt.

"I think we're in range," he explained to Jeremy, "but I'm not positive. But probably close enough. Let's set up. We want them to come to us. Not hang out there in front of the moat so's they can retreat and then pull up the drawbridge and defend the castle if they start to lose. Meanwhile, we want to wait for dawn. Pray to all the gods and goddesses that the fog lifts, so our archers can see who they're shootin' at."

The rebel army settled in to wait out the night. The archers pounded stakes into the earth behind them at a forty-five-degree angle, with the points facing out about the height of a man's chest. As they were instructed, they left room enough between them to move in and out from behind them easily.

Next they struck most of the arrows point first into the ground behind the stakes, with a few special arrows grouped separately. Then each man moved out in front of his stake, wearing a quiver with just a few arrows in it. A burning torch was stuck into the ground between each two stakes.

Now the swordsmen simply stood around and waited out the night, weighed down with heavy armor.

Thaddeus also wore armor: a heavy metal chestplate and chain-mail sleeves. He wore the shooting vest and shoulder holster over it. He also had a helmet—not one of the silver ones—but he had not put it on yet.

It was a long night.

"How long are we going to wait?" Broadbent asked as his nerves wore thin.

"I'm willing to wait forever," was Thaddeus's answer. "I don't want to fight them where they are now. So let's see if we can get them to come to us."

People were actually drifting off to sleep on their feet.

After what seemed an eternity, the fog began to glow a little, and then, so suddenly that it seemed miraculous, it simply receded, evaporating in the light of a new day. It moved back and back, and suddenly the walls of the castle emerged as if it were a huge boat moving toward them. And then, down below, shadowy figures, which then solidified into an army of knights on horseback.

Thaddeus nodded to something he was thinking, and said, "Wait a minute, let's try a little distraction. Who knows, maybe I'll get lucky."

Those near him watched, puzzled, as he closed his eyes for a few minutes. When he opened them again, he was smiling. "Best I can do," he said. Then, "Okay, range?" he yelled at Jeremy.

"Not quite."

"Then move them into range and let's get it on."

Jeremy looked a little confused, but nodded and moved one of the wings forward. The other wing, under command of one of the luthier's close friends, imitated them.

The swordsmen stayed where they were.

The archers moved only a short distance before they stopped.

"This is it," Jeremy shouted back at Thaddeus.

"Then let's do it," Thaddeus shouted back.

"Now?" Jeremy sounded uncertain. There were a lot of heavily armed knights out there.

"Yeah, now," Thaddeus shouted back.

"Gentlemen," Jeremy announced, "draw your bows. Ignore their archers. Aim high, at the top of the castle wall. Gentlemen, release arrows!"

At the other end of the field, in front of his soldiers lined up along the castle moat, safely out of bowshot, Morgan waited. Waiting was the obvious thing to do. The pressure was on the peasants. Soon they would grow hungry and tired, and then they would charge. The arrows would hit them first; then Morgan would give the order to countercharge, break through the middle of their line, crush them. It would be easy. Things like this were always easy when you were mapping them out in your head. But in real battle, weird things happened.

Suddenly one of his own men aimed a bow and shot an arrow at him. It missed, but what the—? As soon as the poor fellow was struck down, one of the men on horseback tried to get at him.

"Wait, don't kill him!" he yelled, too late. "They've got a wizard with them out there. Damn it."

"I told you that," his arrogant general, Hugh Marshal, shouted out indignantly. "There are two of them. But don't kill them. Take them alive. They are both mine."

Morgan seemed to remember some drunken blather from Marshal about how he'd been set upon and humiliated by wizards on a recent hunting trip. But it was hard to take the aristocratic oaf seriously; the lout had been so drunk that for a moment he had taken the court jester for one of them. Morgan still remembered the saucy fool with his muscular white dog, winking at him and shaking his head sadly.

"Shut up, Hugh, I'm trying to think." He stared across the field. *Come on,* he urged them silently. *Come on, charge.*

"The archers are shooting!" someone yelled.

Morgan was puzzled. They were well out of range. He could barely make them out, but yes, they were shooting.

There was a strange whistling noise, followed by a sound much like trees rattling their branches in a severe burst of wind.

Then for one brief moment it was raining arrows. Something made a *pong*ing noise off his helmet, did no damage. But a horse whinnied and went down. A couple of men cursed, shouted, fell off their horses. All of the horses pranced and shied.

Not only were these peasant archers in range, but somehow they were close enough so they could arch the arrows up and allow them to fall down over Morgan's knights' shields and breastplates, seeking out the areas of their shoulders, arms, and legs protected only by chain mail.

His first reaction was to charge and destroy them now. But he quickly had second thoughts, and it was clear to him that the prudent thing to do was simply to take his men back inside the castle and raise the drawbridge. Let them fire away at old Ironwall.

After a nice lunch, when he'd had the chance to reevaluate the alarming change that had occurred in the range of their arrows, he and his army could always drop the bridge and charge out over it, moving fast enough to make themselves more difficult targets, and crush them then. Or, if they wanted to, they could just lie back and let the peasants stew outside the gates for a couple of days. Morgan would be willing to bet a lot of them would simply disappear after a night or two of having to scrounge up dinner and sleep on the ground.

After all, these were farmers, and fences needed to be mended, cows milked, that sort of thing. He did not know that the bridges had been burned. But he was probably right that retreating into the castle was the prudent course of action here.

Only, to his astonishment, as he turned and looked toward the glorious Ironwall, he was greeted by the sight of the drawbridge unmistakably shuddering and beginning to rise.

The second hail of arrows fell (not only was the peasant army's range greater than he had considered possible, but these guys were fast), and this time they seemed to have corrected for distance, because there were a lot more arrows hitting, and a lot more shouts and curses and groans of pain, and this time three horses went down, and . . .

He shouted to Hugh, who was, after all, his second in command, "Charge the archers! Break them up! I'll get the drawbridge back down. Then get everyone back inside the castle."

Sir Hugh looked puzzled. "The drawbridge? What . . . ?"

Morgan wheeled his horse and, hearing behind him the command to charge but unable to watch it acted out, galloped to the bridge. It was already raised so high that he had to stop his horse, stand up on his saddle, and jump.

This was no mean trick, but he managed it. And then his armor almost dragged him down. But he was very strong. Somehow he scrambled up onto the bridge and ran partway across before the angle got steep enough to trip him and cause him to roll the rest of the way down, all doubled up in a metal ball, and finally bowl over several onlookers who for one reason or another were exempt from the fighting and had gathered to watch what little could be seen from the castle gates.

For a moment Morgan just lay there stunned, along with two old men and one woman. Then he shouted in rage, "Who gave the order to raise the drawbridge?"

"Why, we don't know," someone from the crowd said. "We want to watch the fight. We thought it were you."

Morgan moaned and put his hand to his head, but was unable to soothe his helmet. *I cannot allow myself to get a headache now,* he thought, and ordered himself to stop. He stopped!

A loud barking assailed his already tormented ears, and he turned to where his two favorite dogs of war were chained to a long wooden tether-rail that ran the length of one of the walls. At the last moment he had chained them there, out of fear (correctly, as it turned out) that they would simply be shot down by the peasant archers before they could cover the distance between armies. 'Ods blood, had that turned out to be an accurate assessment. So he had saved their sorry asses. And this was how they thanked him?

"So you do not care if you give your kind master a headache? And I beat you so sparingly, particularly thee, Nighthawk. I do warn thee, when this is over—"

The big black dog, hearing his name, emitted an excited fusillade of much louder barks.

Morgan closed his eyes and moaned. "There," he said in a disarmingly soft voice, "that does it. Bark all you want, O hounds of hell. When I have finished crushing the peasant army, as well as a few of my so-called allies and drinking cohorts who have dredged up from Goddess knows where the courage to defy me, I shall return and crush you as well. But not now. No time. No time."

He turned and stalked off down the entrance hall, heading for the draw-bridge control room, muttering to himself like a madman.

"We can just pile 'em all up under the bridge," one of the shrewd observers in the crowd pointed out in his wake. "And he can fall on 'em in all 'at bloody armor."

# 18

![ornament]

THE NIGHT BEFORE had been a strange one for Raphael as well as all the guests at Ironwall Castle. Something was obviously wrong. Almost nobody seemed to know what, and those who did know weren't talking.

Later in the day, Raphael had taken a walk with Blackjack out onto the drawbridge, which despite the storm that had settled in was loaded with citizens staring out into the darkening sky, trying to see something. But all they were able to see was the barest outline of knights and their mounts just the other side of the moat, glistening in the rain. Blackjack had whined unhappily, as if he knew what was out there, and it was not good news.

That night at dinner, the king made an announcement. Looking very serious and stuttering worse than ever, he rose from the table (when the king rose, everyone rose), and said:

"P-p-please forgive me for h-h-having to ma—g-give you folks this p-painful and s-sad inf-inf-information." He proceeded slowly and reluctantly to inform them that there had been a petty rebellion and the Wiccan chief General Morgan had sent a small group of soldiers to quell it. But they had not returned, and now the worst was expected.

He explained that there was nothing for them to worry about. There was no way the rebel army, composed of peasant farmers and thieves, could breach Ironwall Castle. And the Wiccan army was positioned out front primarily as a show of force. When the fog lifted and the army of peasants (if indeed there was one) saw them in all their armored might, that in itself would be enough to cause them to panic and break ranks.

The queen had made the decision to keep to her quarters under these conditions, and would not dine with them tonight, after all. Groans of disappointment from many of the guests at court, who were hoping to meet her.

Under these circumstances the date for the sacrificial ceremony (or Festival of Renewal, as the king euphemistically labeled it) would be moved up, and once that was over, he suspected that things would swiftly return to normal.

"Meanwhile, since none of us may leave the castle, let us enjoy ourselves. Make merry, Fool."

Raphael nodded, but replied, "Alas, but these are serious times. I wouldn't be able to tell you jokes under these circumstances, feeling that many innocents may soon die. It's just too sad."

This statement drew another round of surprised exclamations from the court. Apparently one did not meet the king's requests in such a manner. But the king held up his hand, silencing them.

"My good friend Raphael is perfectly right," he agreed, "as usual. Perhaps, though, if he feels up to it, we could have a sweet song or two to soothe us. To calm us. Certainly there can be nothing wrong with calm at a time like this."

Raphael sang a sad, haunting song:

"There are days, of course,
When one wants to climb down, to climb down, to climb down
For a cup of warm tea, warm tea
In our dreamy past

But then we are caught up
In the whistling of our one-way trip, our one-way trip, our one-way trip
To tomorrow, to tomorrow, to tomorrow, to tomorrow, to tomorrow

Then alas, oh alas
We are all victims of a life gone by too fast
Too fast . . ."

Here the song paused, and out of nowhere came the triumphant explosion that finished the thought:

"Only our love can last forever, last forever, last forever
Only our love can last forever, last forever, last forever
Only our love can last forever, last forever, last forever, last forever, last
   forever
Last . . ."

This final part was sung the way a bird warbles its refrain, over and over—a call to mate or a declaration of war, or maybe just something inside that has to get out. Who knows? Everyone was quite silent, no one applauding or remarking. Maybe this was a version of immortality they had never considered before.

Raphael himself did not really understand it. But he knew that somehow it was true. Maybe someone smarter than he would one day hear it and explain it to him. But he knew that someone would not be Thaddeus. This was a different kind of wisdom than what came from Thaddeus's supply, and Raphael did not know anyone who had it.

He was surprised to find tears in the king's eyes when he turned to look at him.

"By the tears of the Goddess," he said, without stuttering, "I do not know what to say. And just when many of us are on the verge of killing each other over nothing. Thou art right. Thy song is right. Ladies and gentlemen of the court, I am tired."

For a moment King William choked up and could not speak.

"And I am going to bed. Good night. May the Goddess bless each of you. May you each escape the harmful, hateful violence I have been unable to prevent. Good night, good night."

The king left the room, walking as if he were carrying a great burden.

"Me, too," Raphael agreed. "Good night."

But when he left the royal dining room, he found the king waiting outside in the hall.

William put his plump, soft hand on Raphael's shoulder and squeezed, and Raphael could feel the glint of steel through the softness.

"Promise me that thou wilt stay out of this, my friend, for believe me, this formless flow of anger and greed and possessiveness is going to turn into a snake that strikes down everyone it touches. At least you can survive it. Do me a favor and survive it for me. Stay out."

He turned and walked away.

Raphael went outside, across the courtyard, looking up into the sky, expecting to see rain, or if it had let up then the stars, the moon. But there was no sky, no stars, no moon; they had all been swallowed up by fog. The white dog slunk along beside him, obviously sharing his mood.

On the other side, he entered the castle again and went straight up to his room, where he lay on the bed, looking up at the ceiling. How often had he lain in bed alone, looking up at the ceiling, and finding nothing there? A vast sense of uprootedness engulfed him. Swallowed him up, the way the fog had swallowed up the night sky.

What was he? He was supposed to be half Mexican, but he did not look it. Did not feel it. Had bothered to learn the language, but did not speak it. Or want to. His mother had not looked Mexican, with her pale skin, reddish-blond hair, big green eyes.

His mother. It was hard to recognize her as his mother. That had been so long ago, and she had seemed—almost generic. Everybody's mother, anybody's mother. Certainly she had been William's and Violet's mother as much as his, as if blood didn't count.

And his father. Dead before he was born, but—and here was the good part—a fucking ghost merged with one of the most destructive creatures in the universe. Dear old dad. Happily, Raphael had never seen him thus, but it was true. Mother had told him so, and Mother did not lie. There was nothing for him in that bizarre story.

And yet, his grandfather had been a great folksinger, a razzle-dazzle hitchhiking songwriter and guitarist. And his dad *had* played the guitar. His uncle supposedly had been a martial artist of legendary skill. Had these traits somehow been swept along in genes through those rivers of blood into his body and his life? Would he have looked at his uncle, or father, or grandfather, and seen something of himself there?

He did not think so. Thaddeus was the only father—older brother, whatever—that he had. Violet his only sister, even though not by blood. Every bit as much, if not more so, than Elena was his mother. "You're my only dog," he said aloud, causing Blackjack, who was conked out on the floor, to writhe and whine affectionately.

"Come on up here. You deserve it." Raphael patted the bed. Blackjack was overjoyed. He had never been allowed up there before. He sprang up on the bed and, shivering with delight, curled up touching Raphael's feet, and immediately dropped off to sleep again.

Raphael also nodded off. When he awoke once more, it was clear to him. They were out there in the fog. Thaddeus, the army from the tavern of the Laughing Ghost. It was about to happen. Too soon.

He sat up, put his shoes back on, track shoes this time and, calling Blackjack to him, left the room.

Outside, he made his way to the drawbridge.

"I wouldn't go out there," one of the small group hanging out suggested. "The armies are all lined up. They're going to start fighting any minute now."

Raphael could make out the backs of a few horses and armored knights.

"I don't get it," he said. "Why is the drawbridge down?"

"That's easy," the old man informed him. "They win, it don't matter. They lose, they just come in here and close it."

Raphael nodded, turned, and started back inside. Soon the sun would come up, and things would happen fast then.

He started for his mother's room. But halfway there he turned around and started back again. She would be heavily guarded. And if he got past the guards and got her out, where would he take her? Through two armies facing each other off, waiting for the fog to lift?

He went instead to the drawbridge control room. Knocked on the door, and shouted "A fool arriveth."

"No entrance. Be gone, Fool."

"The king has sent me to entertain you," Raphael argued. The argument, of course, was absolutely ridiculous. But that was one of the advantages of wielding one of the stones. As he spoke, Raphael tried to visualize a warm scene with himself singing and playing guitar while a group of jolly guards sat around and listened.

After a moment, the door opened a notch.

"Are you sure it was the king?" A puzzled-looking man peeked out at him.

"Why, surely you know who I am? Me and my white bull terrier. The king's jester. Who else but the king would send me?"

"Well, then . . ." He pushed the door open, and Raphael and Blackjack entered.

There were four guards in the room, but these were not really fighting men; all of those were outside, lined up along the moat. These were men too old to fight, and one young fellow who was too pale and thin. Raphael probably could have taken the four of them. But there were better ways to accomplish things, and he had not the slightest desire to hurt people when it was unnecessary.

"What did you come here for, fool?" the young man said. His voice was a wheeze. Maybe he was an asthmatic.

"I've just come to sing you a song, cheer you up. Bolster the troops. The king personally insisted. You have such an important job."

"Well, as long as the king says so."

Raphael went over to a wooden stool, tossed the cushion off on the floor, unslung the guitar and cradled it on his lap. He began to sing a lullaby, but it was a weird one. Had his mother really sung this macabre song to him when he was a child, or was he making it up? But he seemed to remember being terrified by it and yet put to sleep at the same time. And Salsa at that. Only Elena, he figured as he sang:

"Go to sleep, we're all just some bubbles in a lake
Too soon we pop, before we ever really wake"

But once again, the song seemed to be working its weird charm on the guards. They looked both disturbed and mesmerized at the same time, as he had been as a child.

Clearly the music had a magic of its own. He had simply to focus on the floating dreaminess of the tune, the bitter-sweetness of it. It was almost automatic to project this as he sang.

When he finished, everyone was remarkably relaxed. Blinking their eyes a little. One of them, the young one, even nodded off for a moment, then jerked awake with a "Huh?"

Now Raphael played a slower tune, a waltz. This time he spoke to them as he played.

"You know it would be so nice to go to sleep," he suggested. "And not to wake up until all this ugliness is over with. Because there is going to be a lot of violence. A lot of bloodshed. But how can that reach you when you are asleep? That's why sleep is so wonderful. So refreshing.

"And when you wake up, the war will be over. All the ugliness will be over, and we can all celebrate then. We will all feel so good then, and so rested."

He went on and on like this, reinforcing the notion that no matter what happened, they would not wake up till the fighting was over. They were clearly beginning to be convinced, nodding, yawning, and mumbling sleepy agreement. The thing that made it so easy was that Raphael had no trouble convincing himself: the best place for these guys was sweet, sweet sleep.

# 19

H E HAD STOPPED playing the guitar a while ago. Now it was silent in the room, save for two of the men: the younger one, who made a wheezing noise, and one of the others, who rhythmically gurgled.

Quiet in here, but out there, the killing had begun. Raphael couldn't see it or hear it, but he could track it with some indescribable sense which, Thaddeus would have explained to him, all of us have to some degree or another, but learn to ignore, to never trust. You couldn't ignore it as strong as it was in Raphael, however: the pain, the fear, the death, were all silent screams that he heard effortlessly.

He studied the drawbridge controls and was relieved to discover that the complicated wheel-and-pulley systems that he had expected from movies he had seen had been replaced by a control board with a few neatly labeled switches and buttons. Next he went over and questioned one of the sleepers to make sure. The answer was simple enough:

"Main switch down—drawbridge down. Switch up—drawbridge up. Nobody's sure how it works, 'cept the Wicca. It's the craft."

Raphael rose, went back and flipped the switch, then picked up his guitar. But here he paused. What now?

They probably had a few more of the old-timers up on top of the front wall. Shooters. He could put them to sleep, or take them with him. Then go for his mother. But what then?

He was still standing there holding the garish green guitar when someone tried to open the door. Luckily Raphael had kept his composure enough to remember to bolt it. Soon, though, whoever was out there began to pound on it and shout. Even under these intense circumstances Raphael could not help but smile. It was that loudmouthed bully, Morgan. He recognized that voice—who wouldn't? It was like a knife blade of ice, cruel and uncaring. Savage, but under a kind of nasty self-control. You could only hope its owner would go over the edge and suffer a homemade stroke or heart attack. But of course you knew better. The motherfucker would probably live to a ripe old age. If you didn't stop him.

The thought occurred to Raphael that it would probably be a job for which he was well qualified. But no, obviously the only prudent thing to do here was stall and hide. So he simply waited and listened in a state of amusement as Morgan described the tortures he was going to apply to all the guards in the room as soon as he got the door open.

Finally he went away, but he would surely be back. How soon? Raphael looked around him, then up. It was one of those quaint-looking rooms, as were many in the castle, which got a large dose of its charm from having its rafters out in the open. Raphael wondered if he could jump that high. Surely a professional basketball player could get up there, and after all, jumping was primarily a matter of strength, and he was stronger than any professional ball player.

He was astonished at how easy it turned out to be. He would be able, he realized, to dunk with the greatest of ease, if he lived to try it. And it was even easier to pull himself up to where he could twist around and sit on one of the rafters, a stunt he had seen done by the swashbuckling stars of old restored *Three Musketeers* movies he had watched on digitalized videodisc as a kid. He seemed to remember that the old song-and-dance man, Gene Kelly, had surprised him by doing such a dazzling job of this sort of thing. *Maybe I should take up tap dancing,* he thought.

Morgan was back already; Raphael could hear him admonishing some poor gofer to "get that key into that lock, open it, throw open the door, and swing swiftly out of the way, because I am determined to kill whoever is in that room, and anyone who gets in my way shall earn the right to share their fate."

Raphael had to smile yet again, for while it was true that the door had a modern locking mechanism, they had neglected to remove the old-fashioned wooden drop bolt—probably figured the more locks the better. And he had dropped that bolt.

Next he heard, "Don't jump out of the way if the door won't open, you idiot. Do you think I'm going to leap through a closed door?"

Now it was actual laughter that Raphael was struggling to stifle, even though he knew it shouldn't be funny to hear the poor servant howl in pain. *Sitting in the rafters is making me high,* he thought giddily.

"Who is that? I hear you in there. I swear to you, when I get into that room I'll—" Morgan imaginatively described several terrible forms of torture he was planning to practice on Raphael. Then silence. Then he said in a controlled voice, "Very well, then. I shall be back. Do not go away."

It turned out to be a fair wait. When they finally arrived, whatever it was that they were trying to use as a battering ram evidently proved too fragile. He could hear the wood breaking and Morgan's cursing, followed by the threat, "Very well, I go again, but I will get in there with you, and when I do, I will do everything I threatened to do to you before, and I will do it twice."

Fourth time proved to be the charm for Morgan. The door finally smashed off its hinges, apparently struck by something quite sturdy, a table perhaps—Raphael could not see it from his perch in the rafters—and after a brief pause, Morgan leaped into the room brandishing a sword.

Seeing no one there to slash at, he looked down. "Well, taking a little nap, are we? That's nice, isn't it? Wake up, my little ones, Uncle Morgan's come to visit you. And he's brought you a lovely gift. See?" He brandished his long, sharp sword. No answer.

"Hope you don't cut yourself on it. But what am I doing? Time is of the essence here." Morgan ran over and tripped the switch back down. The small group of men who had followed him into the room just stood around and watched. Probably afraid to breathe.

"What the hell is this? The jester's dog came to entertain the guards, but put them to sleep instead?"

He had spotted Blackjack, who was sitting quietly in the corner, as Raphael had instructed him to do. But when the joyful creature realized he was being addressed, he stood up and wagged, as was his habit, not just his tail, but his whole body. Raphael tensed up and got ready to do something drastic, but to his amazement Morgan merely gave the dog a prolonged scrutiny.

"Nice dog," he said to himself aloud, "but too small to do much fighting. Still, bigger than he looks. Wait a minute, what have we here?" He had spotted the guitar. "So your master's been here. Yes, I've suspected him from the start."

One of the onlookers forgot himself enough to mutter, quite audibly, "What did he think, dog come on his own?"

Morgan darted across the distance that separated them, sword raised overhead, and before anyone could move, brought the flat of it expertly down on the unfortunate fellow's head. The man went down like a stone.

"Why not join your friends in their nap? Sweet dreams. Any of the rest of you have any questions? Or better yet, answers? Very well, then." Mission accomplished, he turned and led them out the door. "Keep an eye out for the king's Fool. Wherever his guitar and his dog are, he will not be far away."

The last thing Raphael heard as they left was one of the men asking innocently, "What was it you suspected him of?"

And the answer: "Making me suspicious is enough."

After a while, Raphael dropped down out of the rafters, to the delight of Blackjack, and went back over to the control panel. "Let's give him a few more minutes to get wherever he's going."

After allowing a few minutes to go by, he absently flipped the switch, walked over and jumped back up into the rafters. Only this time he thought to take one of the sleeping guards' swords along with him, scabbard and all.

# 20

OUTSIDE, THE BATTLE was being waged hot and heavy. Morgan could not tell who was winning or losing. Standing just across the drawbridge, and deciding to take the prudent course, he shouted for someone to bring him an elk's horn. Then stood there motioning impatiently as whoever it was ran across the bridge carrying one to him. He blew on it, making a loud but ugly wailing sound, causing his head to pulsate. Then he observed nature's musical instrument, frowning. "What an awful horn," he remarked. Absolutely nothing was going his way.

But at least it was loud enough, for now he saw his men were in full retreat. He sighed in relief. *Get my knights back into the castle right now,* he was thinking, *then we can go from there*—when he heard something, he wasn't sure what, that prompted him to turn and look behind him.

*Probably it was just the drawbridge creaking a little bit,* he thought. *No excuse for that. First thing I'll do when this is over is get somebody to oil*— Then it hit him: the bridge was heading back up!

He ran. He dived. He conquered. *But this is wearing me out,* he silently complained. *What a way to fight a war.* Up and over, and what else? Falling and rolling into the crowd gathered at the base, naturally. Would they never learn? Bridge goes up, man decked out in heavy armor comes rolling down, knocks you over?

"How many times must I do this before you learn to get out of my way?"

"I dunno," one of them ventured. "How many?"

Others just lay there groaning and complaining, possibly of broken bones.

"I swear to the Goddess, if you get under my feet one more time . . . Ah, what's the use?"

A fierce, excited barking caused him to look over to where his fighting dogs were chained.

"Ah, Nighthawk, you persist in your folly," he said, pointing at the huge black creature and by doing so, of course, causing more excitement. He clapped both his hands to his head, forgetting his helmet, which naturally made a loud percussive noise. "Oh," he sighed, as he closed his eyes and swayed.

When he opened them, he remarked, "Very well, we shall settle all this later. I shall need a new dog, but what the hell? Meanwhile, we have work to do that has need of the two of us. So I warn thee, settle thy ugly self down now."

He turned back to the crowd and singled out one of the peasants he had just bowled over. "Go fetch me my fierce black bandoggie," he ordered. "But be careful, he bites."

The peasant just stood there wide-eyed, frozen to the spot, afraid to say anything, afraid to move.

"Oh, for the sake of Our Lady," Morgan swore, "can't anyone do anything except me?" He stalked over and slipped the chain off the rail and took the giant black dog with him.

"Heel!" he shouted. Immediately the dog surged, or tried to, but Morgan was a very strong man, and he jerked it back. "Now," he threatened vaguely, drawing out the word.

Everyone gasped and jumped back, banging into one another and knocking another old man down as Morgan's sword fairly sprang from its scabbard, and he started off, dog in one hand, sword in the other.

"I would love to kill you all," he shouted back as he rushed toward the control room. "But I just haven't got time, damn it."

# 21

S ITTING IN THE rafters was beginning to have an odd effect on Raphael. He was starting to feel strangely invulnerable, like: *Who can reach me here! Most unrealistic,* he reminded himself. In fact, the door was open, smashed off the hinges, and if Morgan had any sense, he would send in a group of soldiers to search for him, and there was sure to be an archer or two among them.

But no, the tall, stringy but muscular form of Morgan the Dark fairly flew into the room, dragged along by his snarling dog. The arrogant buffoon was alone.

"Let us see if this ugly little white doggie wants to play with mine. Wait a minute." He looked up. Raphael could almost see the lightbulb light up over his head inside a thought bubble, as if in a cartoon.

"You would have thought," the furious warrior snarled, "that climbing the drawbridge twice would have told me where to look. Fool in the rafters, Like a bird. Won't you come down? Oh, don't worry. I will not attack you while you're off balance. I want you prepared to the best of your ability, whatever that is. I plan to torture you."

"I won't be off balance," Raphael tossed back as he dropped from his perch and landed lightly on the balls of his feet, sword in hand. The fact that an almost magical amount of strength would be required to perform this feat did not escape Morgan. But it did not bother him much either. "Well, well," he remarked, "a herculean fool, but a fool all the same. Good. It will take you longer to die."

The dog at his side surged at the leash, clashing its teeth and growling horribly, while Blackjack whined and looked expectantly at Raphael. His expression was so intent that he seemed almost human in his concern.

"And as for thine ugly white doggie, alas, I cannot hold mine back and fight at the same time." He smiled as he said this. Then, still without taking his eyes off Raphael, he said, "Kill his dog, Nighthawk," and dropped the chain.

"Fight, Blackjack!" Raphael shouted with all the urgency he could muster. Then he amended it to, "Kill, Blackjack," as it sank home that mere scrapping wouldn't be enough here.

By the time the words were out, the dogs had crashed together in the center of the floor, the bigger one, of course, overwhelming the smaller, knocking him over backwards but unable to get a grip because the white dog was so fast and scrambling for his life.

They surged clear across the room, the big one pushing the little one over a couple of the sleeping guards, until they crashed into the far wall, where each secured a grip, the mastiff around the back of Blackjack's thick muscular neck, but being forced by the studded collar to go too far back and get some shoulder in the bargain, while Blackjack took hold of one of the big dog's front legs. Both dogs clamped down.

Morgan remarked, "The Fool longeth in his foolish heart to be a knight. So be it. But know thee this, there is not a man alive who can best me with blades."

"Boy, am I sick of hearing that kind of shit," Raphael shot back, holding the sword the way Bitters had taught him and beginning to circle.

Without hesitation, Morgan moved in after him with very quick little shuffling steps, cutting off the circle. Almost immediately the blades clashed together once, and almost twice, except that Morgan's twisted around underneath Raphael's swing and nearly gutted him.

Raphael, who was trying to close behind his blade, had only his incredibly quick reflexes to thank for his momentary survival as he twisted sideways and managed to whip his blade around and engage Morgan's once again. But as Morgan drew back he slid his own blade across his opponent's ribs. And just like that, he had drawn first blood.

"So the Fool is strong—a veritable Hercules among jesters—but he will learn today that there is more to blades than mere power. There is art."

Raphael was silently inclined to agree with him. The man was as skilled as Bitters had been, but much quicker and much stronger. Which meant more skilled. Bad news.

The dogs were still snarling behind him. *At least Blackjack's putting up a fight,* he thought. Then he said, "If you're such a hot fighter, Morgan, take off that helmet. Meet me fair and square. Like a man."

Morgan smiled. "Fair and square," he mused. "Why not round and sound, eh? And like a man? Like what else, Fool? No, I think I will keep the helmet on. If a Fool can be a knight, why not a witch as well?"

And once again, Raphael started to circle in the big room, and Morgan charged straight at him. Moving fast. Very, very fast.

# 22

---◈---

OLD MAN CORBO was once again flashing through the psychedelic liquid of time—fast forward. Under the guidance of Theseus.

He was experiencing no metaphors to make it easier on himself. It wasn't really like anything else. But it *was* movement. Not some kind of movement to or from something, but the very essence of movement, slippery and squirmy, like penetrating waves of Jell-O. Uh-oh, there came the metaphors creeping in again, disguising it, labeling it. *Stop that,* he told himself, and did.

"Now!" Theseus shouted to him mentally. "Get off now."

A doorway opened up. Corbo ignored it and the movement continued, pushing him on further into the future.

"What? Stop. What are you . . . Why can't I stop myself from pushing you on?"

Corbo ignored him, kept on moving. What would be the point of explaining to Theseus that he had found the moment of weakness back there in the wading pool, when they were both going under, and planted his suggestion where it could not be ignored. Comfort and warmth + performing a familiar act which involved relaxation = vulnerability to Corbo. It was the kind of math that Corbo was so good at.

Soon he opened his own doorway and got off. What—thirty, forty, a hundred years later? Who knew? But one thing he did know, there would be no traps set for him here.

Cobblestone street; he had just appeared in it out of nowhere. But it was dark. Nobody about but two drunks. They were walking along arm in arm, singing a ditty in some language he was sort of familiar with, but after all those years—hundreds?

At first he thought it was only ye very olde English, but then he got it. It was ye very olde German.

He couldn't translate the song right off, but he got the general idea. Something about, "If you want to live free, live in New Saxony."

And it didn't help that all the time Theseus kept yammering away in his brain, nonsense like, "What? How dare you? Go back to where I want you to be. What are you . . . ?"

"Shut up," he said to Theseus. Fool was probably bubbling up his enormous bathtub with farts of anguish. This image made the old man smile.

Then he wondered, Why weren't these two fellows frightened? Hadn't he just appeared out of nowhere?

They sauntered casually over and one of them, the fat red-bearded one, said something he couldn't quite catch.

He reached out, put his hand on the man's forehead, and closed his eyes. Fed his brain the info, freshened up the neural pathways. Then he had it. The drunk was asking him, "Are you an angel of Our Lord, sent to deliver his message to one of the chosen race?"

Corbo smiled. "Indeed I am," he answered. "He wants to bestow upon you the honor of giving all your money to me. Now. Hurry, it's a great honor."

Stumbling drunkenly, the men fished their coin purses from their belts and gave them up.

The old man calmly opened his brown paper bag and fed it the purses. Rolled it up.

"Now you must tell me where I would go to get one of these." He tapped the man's helmet, an ugly gray affair with a spike in the middle and a black swastika painted on it.

The two men conferred. Then the red-bearded one answered, "First you must get off the streets until morning. There are thieves about."

"But I'm an angel of the Lord," Corbo reminded him.

For a moment both drunks looked puzzled. Corbo managed to block off Theseus's incoherent pleading long enough to reinforce the notion.

"Oh, we forgot. There is an old smithy who has a shop over by the Green Lady Tavern—"

Here the other broke in and they argued for a moment. It appeared that each had his own favorite forger of armor.

"Which is closest?" the old man asked patiently. They finally directed him to one, then wheeled off down the street, still singing. The language was now quite familiar to Corbo. The song, unfortunately, also kept insinuating itself into his thought stream. How he detested music. All forms of hypnotism, for that matter—which reminded him . . .

He paused in the middle of the dirt street, closed his eyes, and dealt with Theseus. As soon as he lifted the barrier, in poured a lot of static, the main gist of which was, "How dare you?"

"Gosh, I don't know," he answered. "Where would I get the courage to cross some all-powerful baby who spends eternity in a wading pool surrounded by naked women? Now, you listen to me. It looks like what you've told me is true. If it is, we'll deal with it my way. I'm not about to step off this time river or whatever into some trap set up for me by Germanicus."

"Trap?" Theseus somehow was managing to shout inside his head. "By Germanicus? You accuse me of collaborating with that brute? You don't trust me?"

"Why wouldn't I trust some idiot who sits around naked in a—"

The old man stopped himself. What was the point? No matter how many times he said it, Theseus would never get it.

"No, I have no reason to trust you," Corbo amended. "But if what you were telling me has any truth in it at all, you can stay in touch and help me out as I go along. I'll do it my own way."

"And I," the voice in his head shouted, "am reduced to helper!"

"Actually," the old man pointed out, "you were promoted." (*From wading pool toddler to Boy Scout,* he thought, but shielded from his brand-new helper.)

Before morning, he arrived at the shop, pounded on the door, and informed the owner, "You will get to work on this now. Use your savings to purchase the silver."

The old smithy answered this with an expression of absolute astonishment.

"Don't have that much money? Oh, all right, then, I'll get up in the morning and make us some money. Big money. You like that one, huh?"

The fellow was beaming.

"Meanwhile, I'm sleepy. Where's your bed—upstairs? Good. You stay up and start working with whatever you got, huh?"

The poor fellow looked thoroughly befuddled. "Ain't I sleepy?"

Corbo smiled tolerantly. "No, you feel full of energy and ready to work all night long. Even though you don't look it," he added truthfully. "Oh, and have you got some beans? No? Go out and get me some beans for breakfast. Bread and beans, okay? Good night."

Without another word, the old man went upstairs and woke up the man's plump, surly-looking wife.

"Huh, who are you? Why am I not screaming for help?"

"You have a spare bed here?"

The drowsy woman shook her head. "Shouldn't I be screaming?"

Corbo shook his head back at her. "You can scream after I'm gone," he said. "For now, just go outside into the hall and curl up there on the floor, and sleep till morning."

She frowned. "But it's a hard wood floor and it's cold there."

Corbo handed her a wool blanket and a pillow and pulled off his T-shirt. His body was slender, but covered with ropy muscles which writhed like snakes whenever he moved.

She seemed determined to hang around. "You've got a lot of muscle for an old man. You sure you don't want me to stay? After all, it's my bed."

Corbo held out his hand palm out toward her—ward off!—and said, "Go out and sleep in the hall. And oh, don't go downstairs until morning."

Sighing, he dropped his shorts on the floor and crawled into the smithy's bed, snuggled up to the brown paper bag he carried, and went to sleep.

Downstairs, the smithy got out his wife's fancy silver candlesticks, and prepared to melt them down.

"Told her it were a foolish expense," he grumbled to himself as he went to work.

# 23

───◈───

ALL OF RAPHAEL'S knowledge about sword fighting was turning out to be bogus, and he was learning this in the most painful way imaginable. In truth, he was not so much involved in a duel as he was being tortured to death—played with the way a cat would toy with a mouse.

Deep down inside, Morgan, who at first had been so focused on lowering the drawbridge as quickly as humanly possible, was simply too cruel not to slow down and enjoy his opponent's death, once the fight started. He was too much of a swordsman to deny the Fool a lesson or two before he finished him.

The first balloon to pop was the notion of circling. Raphael went wherever his tormenter drove him. Morgan, who was an expert at footwork as well as all other aspects of swordsmanship, shuffled, hopped, and occasionally even pranced and stamped, cutting him off in every attempt to change direction, and then driving him steadily backward with a dazzling, almost magical flurry of swordplay. At the end of each combination attack, he would place an exclamation point, say a little slice across Raphael's forearm or shoulder, a jab at his thigh, perhaps just a tear in his loose-fitting blouse, and once even batting Raphael comically on the top of his head with the flat of the blade, causing him to reel dizzily for a moment. But pain quickly brought him back.

Morgan had soon established the path they were to take: around and around along the walls of the room, with Raphael moving backwards and Morgan driving him. At one point, there was a body to get over. The first time around Raphael had fallen over it and Morgan had calmly waited for him to get up again.

"Watch your step, Fool," Morgan said, smiling most cruelly. "You'll have to avoid the dogs in yon corner. I must say, that mutt of thine is putting up a far better fight than thou."

The second balloon to pop was the idea that Raphael's superior strength would make any difference at all. It had with Mrs. Lim, it had with Bitters and with everyone else he had paired off with, but Morgan actually turned it against him, punishing him every time he tried to use it by giving way and then snapping back.

These were no fencing foils, but heavy combat weapons. Everyone Raphael had trained with had been forced to use the full strength of their arm to *swing* the blade. But for Morgan, the arm, wrist, even the fingers played an equal role. The blade whipped, twisted, curled around, weaved, snaked in, around and under his parries, as spontaneously as if it were a living creature.

The times Raphael tried to take the fight to close quarters and use his superior strength he was met with either the butt of the handle in the middle of his forehead or a feeling of resistance, causing him to surge, and then— nobody there. He had actually fallen down twice, just when he thought he had caught up with Morgan.

"Got on your dancing shoes, Fool?" the Wicca's master at arms had playfully asked him.

To his credit, Raphael *was* extremely quick, and strong as a gorilla, and the fight was fast and furious enough to have astonished many a skilled swordsman. All this in only a very few minutes— the dogs were still snarling and rolling in the corner—but all of it belonged to Morgan. He orchestrated it and carried it out with such exquisite control that Raphael felt for the first time that he had at last fully established himself in the role of court jester.

He knew Morgan would have to finish him off soon, and there was nothing to gain by waiting but more wounds, so he tried one last desperate ploy. At last he managed to engage Morgan's blade long enough to surge to close quarters, where in a surprise attack he dropped the sword, hurled himself at Morgan, and tried to rip off the swordsman's silver helmet.

To his amazement and exultation, his strength and speed triumphed and he found himself standing there holding the prize in his hands. Now all he had to do was use the powers of his mystic stone.

But then he became aware of Morgan's expression. The man whose left hand had momentarily disappeared behind his back as Raphael charged was smiling.

"Don't you think it's a fair trade?" he remarked caustically. "You get my helmet and my dagger and I get to live."

And this was what popped the Fool's last and biggest balloon. The hero's dream that somehow, even when you were getting beaten at all the

little things, you could come up with something big and wonderful and turn
it all around. And with the popping of this balloon came an echo, a smaller
but no less scary realization: *Bitters can't fight for shit!*

For as he looked down, he saw the blade of a dagger protruding from
his chest, and he realized that he had stopped breathing because something
terrible was sweeping through his body, and though it hadn't reached his
brain yet, it was traveling fast.

He closed his eyes and tried to fall, but couldn't. Opened them up again,
to see that Morgan was holding him up by having grabbed hold of the helmet with one hand and, already having sheathed his sword in one spectacular swashbuckling display, had got the handle of the dagger in the other.

"Come to think of it," he said, "you won't be in need of these."

And with one swift wrench he took them both back. Raphael crashed
to the floor.

A moment later something white, with red splashed all over, shot across
the room and crouched in front of Raphael's inert form, snarling.

"Thine ugly little white doggie won?" Morgan was amazed. Yet, when
he took a closer look, the thing, like its master, was a veritable mound of
muscle, with broad head and square jaws.

He looked over to the corner, where Nighthawk lay sprawled out, obviously dead, one of his forelegs horribly mangled, throat torn out.

"By the Goddess, what a fight that must have been. And I never even
noticed." He was suddenly overwhelmed with a strong feeling, admiration
for the brave little dog—who really wasn't as little as he thought, possibly
four, even five stones. All muscle, tenacity, courage. But perhaps, he realized,
some of that feeling was for the dog's master, who had displayed similar
traits.

"Not dead yet," he said to no one in particular. "Well, you soon will
be." But one odd thing he noticed. The Fool wasn't bleeding as much as he
should be.

Morgan went over and tripped the switch. "Drawbridge down," he said
aloud. Then, "Sorry."

He unsheathed his sword and started toward Raphael, but the dog
snarled and crouched, obviously determined to defend his master with his
life.

"Damn," Morgan said. Suddenly his vision was blurry and he wiped his
eyes with his hand. Tears?

"I can kill thee easily enough, Fool," he said, "though I admire thy
spunk. But what a shame to kill thy doggie. What a loss. He could be bred . . ."

Visions of white fighting doggies danced in his head. He turned and left the room.

"Don't let anybody in or out of the control room!" he shouted at one of the old lackeys outside. "And quickly, bring me a horn."

Someone handed him a horn of some sort.

He crossed the drawbridge, carrying the horn, and stared off across the field. Yes, the knights looked out of line, in disarray. Shouts and screams came to him all the way from there. Some of them, he could see, still had their mounts, but not too many.

"I could not bring myself to kill thee, Fool, perhaps because of thy doggie. But once I bring my army back here to regroup, and drive the enemy back with a few arrows from the parapet, then we will ride out again. And this time I guarantee you, I will kill and kill, and I will spare none of thy cohorts. Not a one."

He blew furiously on the horn, a loud bellowing cry, and sure enough, they must have seen that the drawbridge was down and understood what he was signaling, for they were now in full retreat. The horsemen in the lead, the others following.

He was, he realized, for no reason that he could pinpoint, carrying on an argument with the jester, who surely was dead by now. Wasn't he? So what was he doing?

Then he witnessed a very strange thing, which confused him even further. A small white ball of muscle came from behind him, moving with great speed and energy, and started across the field at full tilt. Were his wits deceiving him, or was it now wearing jewelry around its thick neck? Did that make any kind of sense? No. No. No. It did not.

And then he must have felt what was happening behind him, because for no reason at all, he turned—and yes, unbelievably, that damned drawbridge was going back up.

He dropped the horn. Hardly needed it, because the howling noise issuing from his lips was very loud. Sprinted to the bridge, jumped, and, armor and all, hauled his ass up over it and yes, tumbled all the long way down again, bowling over a couple of idiots standing around in the crowd.

Out came his sword, hissing free of its scabbard, and once again people were knocking each other over to get out of his way.

"This time I vow to make so certain of thy death that I shall put thine arms in two corners of the room, one leg each in the others, and thy head in the exact center. Thy body I shall most eagerly eat."

Parting the crowd like the Red Sea, he ran back toward the control

room, expertly smiting the guard, who was saluting him, with the flat of his
blade, and knocking the poor old volunteer unconscious as a reward for
following his orders. Probably destroying the fellow's last illusions of a
glorious career in the Wiccan army, if that hadn't already happened a long
time ago.

# 24

---

R APHAEL WAS NOT dead yet, but close. Too close. For a while he swam in
a sea of pain, but didn't recognize it as pain, merely sensation. He woke
briefly; Blackjack was anxiously licking his face and whining. He said, "I'm
dying," or rather, tried to say it but couldn't get anything out except an ugly,
rattling wheeze. Then he passed out again, then he woke up again. He was
aware that had the healing powers of the stone not been working fully, he
would not be conscious.

"Knife in the heart," he whispered to Blackjack, who nodded his broad
white head eagerly, trying to understand. Could even the power of one of the
stones heal a torn heart?

*I don't know if I can move,* he thought, and at first he couldn't; it hurt
too much to try.

Then he managed to somehow move his hand up to his neck and for just
a moment, painful as it was, lift his head up enough to get the necklace with
the amulet off. And then, coaxing Blackjack nearer, he draped it around the
dog's thick, muscular neck and twined it through his collar and back around
and through itself again. It was sort of tied on, but it was still too long, so he
twined it around the collar once more. Then he groaned and let his arm fall
back on the floor. *Have to do,* he said to himself.

Uh-oh, his eyes were closed again. "Not yet," he hissed. "Blackjack?"

He was deeply aware of the ecstatic state the dog was in. *Like it, do
you?* he would have said if he could have.

Something he had sensed when he was passed out. The battle outside,
the pain, the dying, what else? It was why he had forced himself to wake up
again. But damn if he could remember.

He was about to give up when it came back to him. It was Tippi. "Blackjack," he whispered. "Tippi." He closed his eyes and visualized her. Blackjack barked to say he'd picked up her psychic scent.

*Go to Tippi and lead her to Thaddeus.* He was no longer speaking out loud; he was sure the dog was getting it.

"Go on," he rasped. "Find Tippi."

The dog came over to him—he could hear its feet padding on the cold floor—and licked his face, and whined. *Good-bye.*

Then he heard Blackjack's nails scrabbling on the floor as he took off, running fast, through the open doorway and past the startled guard who was just now waking up. He sensed that Blackjack . . . that the stone was gone.

But some of its residual power was left behind. He moaned, trying to badger himself into staying conscious just a little while longer. The way Blackjack was running, he was probably at the drawbridge already, so . . .

He closed his eyes and visualized the control switch. He fought against dissolving into that sea of pain, forcing the vision to come clearer and clearer until he could no longer tell whether he was seeing it with closed eyes or it was actually there. Then, in his mind and simultaneously in the world he threw the switch down. He smiled as he heard it click. Happy birthday, Morgan!

At last he tried to think if there was anything he really needed to do before he sank into the dark. If there was any part of his life he had left tangled up. And he thought of only one.

*I don't even know you,* he thought as he drifted off. *I never asked about you or tried to know you. I don't even know what you looked like, do I?* But hadn't there been a photo? He seemed to remember seeing one when he was a kid. He focused in on it. *Forgive me, Father. It's too late. Good-bye.*

Then he fell back into that soothing pool of endless dark.

# 25

A T FIRST THERE was only a sense of waking up, of more energy. Of every sensation steadily becoming more and more intense. The edges of his body, for instance, had never been so defined, so alive, so ecstatic.

And this effect just kept snowballing. Outside the castle, crashing through the grass toward the distant group of clumsy, fighting humans, he was cognizant that he was running faster than he had ever run before, and that instead of making him tired, the running seemed to call forth more energy. As he ran on, and adjusted to some degree to the overwhelming increase in information flooding his expanding senses, he became aware of an increase in intelligence. It was not so much in the area of organization as it was simply the possession of so much more information to deal with.

And there was something else, an intensely magnified sense of purpose, of devotion to the master, of duty, even. It had always been there; that was the strong point of fighting dogs the world over—they would, and often did, die for you—but never before had this unswerving desire to perform the good work been paired with this increase in clarity. No longer simply a white dog, Blackjack was now the white Guardian, and he knew it.

His sense of smell, always beyond human comprehension, was now heightened to the point where he could track the terrain and pinpoint any living creature within miles—far beyond that of any bloodhound's. His sense of hearing was also expanding.

It was easy for him to be aware of the men in battle, even his beloved Thaddeus, and beyond them the city, the people hiding in their shops, reeking of fear. And beyond them, the river and the small group on the far bank, just now approaching it; and among that group, the small female that his master had pointed out with his mind. It had been clear to Blackjack at once what she would look like, smell like, be like. And as soon as he had become what he was now, he had known where she was, what she was feeling. And her name.

A minute or two later, a battle-weary, slightly delirious Thaddeus was amazed to see the white Guardian break through the fighting men and just keep going, without so much as a bark hello. He didn't have time to mull it over, though, as he ejected an empty clip, holstered the gun, took out the second gun, and kept on firing.

It had turned out that having a handgun had proved far less of an advantage than he had originally imagined, what with the heavy armor and the general difficulty of hitting anything much with a pistol.

Even while he was firing, he acted on impulse and yelled to Mrs. Lim, who was slightly forward of him, bunched up in a group of hacking, grunting, exhausted men: "Mrs. Lim, go follow that white dog!"

If she thought this order peculiar, she gave no sign of it, but simply backed out of the line of fighting men, singled out one of the riderless horses wandering about, and made for it.

"Take an extra horse!" Thaddeus yelled between shots.

Moving behind the fighting men, his tactic was to pick someone on the other side who was fighting well and looked particularly strong and shoot him, then move sideways looking for another target.

He allowed himself a momentary sense of relief, but not much. Mrs. Lim, the great swordswoman, had not fared so well, packed in with the other fighting men like a sardine in a tin. Here swordplay was mostly heavily armored men hammering at a wall of other heavily armored men. Footwork consisted of trying not to trip over bodies or slip in blood. She had already gone down twice, and was battered and dazed. Only her fantastic agility and endurance had kept her alive this long. *At least there's a chance that I've saved her,* Thaddeus thought. *But who knows?* Who knew anything? One minute they were winning, then losing.

And Thaddeus also had sensed Tippi's presence. Through her stone, though he had not noticed it till he took a moment to concentrate on the dog—who was also wearing, amazingly, a stone. Luckily he didn't have time to think about what this meant for Raphael. All the planning, evaluating, wheeling and dealing had finally been swallowed up in the chaos of war.

# 26

HE LOOKS DEAD, Morgan thought upon entering, yet once more, the control room. *"Oh, please, please, please, don't be dead,"* he begged. *"Let me do it."*

His sword was out and thirsty, and he was thinking, *First an arm and I'll throw it against the wall; then a leg, and then I'll* . . . when he saw it.

Whatever it was, it stopped him cold, sword frozen out in front of him. That it was some incredibly powerful creature of a magical nature, some sort of ghost, he had no doubt. And he was right about that.

That it was a study in indescribable anguish, he also had no doubt. And he was right about that.

"It's going to kill me," he whispered to himself, without even being aware he had said it. And he was right about that, too.

Somewhere in that swirling, sickly yellow cloud, from moment to moment, Morgan could make out a face. It would almost come clear, and then submerge underneath the fog again. It was the face of a youngish man, and it was heartrendingly tormented. But right now, too much of Morgan was invested in staying alive to allow any empathy. Not that empathy had ever been his strong point.

The thing had been hovering over Raphael's body—feeding off him? This thought caused even Morgan to shudder and back off, but not off enough.

It came billowing at him like smoke blown in a high wind. The world's greatest swordsman slashed about wildly, as if there were something to cut, and then he was engulfed.

His fancy footwork became a spasmodic dance of death, and he tried to, but could not, scream. Then nothing was left of he who would be king of Los Angeles but a husk, instantly discarded by the hungry ghost, which floated back and settled onto the inert form of Raphael.

# 27

———◈———

A FTER A MERE twenty wretched years of additional rule under William Rufus, merry olde England had become, Corbo swiftly discovered, slightly more Nazi than German Saxony. Of course this had probably required some help from the man's only friends: that other and primary Germanicus (his earlier, definitely not wiser, self) and the latest of his long line of Frankish puppet rulers. Whether this was one of Charlemagne's sons, Otto the this or that, or maybe by now Henry II, Corbo couldn't remember and didn't much care; they were pretty much all the same with Germanicus guiding them. If this was what England, that most individualistic of countries, had become, to what hellish level had the rest of Europe devolved?

There were swastikas everywhere: on the doors of shops, stores, inns; on goblets, plates, dishes. There was even one on the silver helmet Corbo was carrying, not that he had asked for it—hardly. But the smithy had thought it a charming touch and thrown it in for free.

The Normans had been sent packing back to France (where they belonged, as the Saxons enjoyed pointing out) by the local Saxons, with a little help from their brothers from Germany. (Germanicus was always happy to give Germanicus a helping hand.) So Theseus had at least been telling the truth about this mess. As to what it boded for the future, Corbo did not even bother to think about it, though he did shudder for just a moment as the thought flashed through his mind's eye, in one ear as he booted it out the other.

The reason he was carrying the helmet instead of wearing it was that that most bizarre of all demons, Ketoko, was walking along beside him, and even though it was late at night and the streets were mostly deserted (naturally in Naziville there would be a curfew), the old man did not want any-

one he bumped into freaking out and blowing on one of those panic horns
they carried around with them here. There was actually an old Saxon law, recently put back into effect, that one was required to blow a horn to warn
whomever one was angry at before attacking him with a sword!

It had been easy enough to enlist Ketoko for this mission. In fact, Corbo
could even have forced him, now being back within the time period when he
exercised control over the demon. But he felt that it would be too much to
try to deal with Germanicus and worry about Ketoko at the same time. So he
had made the demon an offer.

"Why should I help you?" Ketoko had trumpeted in his most awesome
triple voice. "I despise you."

"And I you," the old man replied in his crackly dry one. "But surely you
want to be free of that pig Germanicus? I'll help you do so."

"But you don't understand . . ."

"Don't I?" Corbo said, smiling. "Let me take a guess."

And then he had revealed his deductions to Ketoko.

"Forgive this foolish one for ever daring to suggest that there was something somewhere that you wouldn't understand."

"I even amaze myself," Corbo had replied and laughed.

"Spare me the hideous cackling, and we will work out a deal of some
sort. If we can find some way to assure me that you will keep it."

"You don't trust me?" More cackling.

Ketoko did not bother to answer.

In the end, Ketoko had allowed the old man to implant the suggestion
that should Corbo fail to fulfill his part of the bargain, Ketoko would then be
free from his previous conditioning, which had put him under Corbo's control to start with. From there things moved fast, as always seemed to be the
case when Corbo was involved.

Now, already, the two of them were inside the castle and questioning
one of the guards, whom the old man had put into a deep trance.

"King is a little weasel," the big, tough-looking guard confided, "though
he has a good Old Saxon name. The godlike one you describe resides in the
big room at the very end of that hall, though he is not called Germanicus, but
Saxonius."

The old man shook his head. It was impossible to tell if Ketoko shook his.

"Saxonius, huh? How subtle. Anyhow, go back to guarding your post.
Don't let anyone in. Good man!"

"Except you, of course," the poor fellow clarified.

"Yes, except me. And I almost forgot, you've never seen him at all."
Corbo gestured at Ketoko.

The guard grimaced. "Thank God," he answered.

"Well, he knows we're here, anyway," the old man remarked to Ketoko as, halfway down the corridor, another guard charged them, shouting and waving a sword.

"That way," Corbo suggested to the guard, pointing back the way they had come. "There's two of them, and they look just like us. Call the other guards to you. You know, blow on that poor creature's horn"—he winced—"and protect this corridor from them. Don't be afraid, even though one of them looks like him." He pointed at Ketoko.

The guard grimaced, staring at the demon's rapidly shifting and blurring features. "At least I'm prepared," he said, and rushed off down the corridor.

Soon they heard the sounding of the horn.

"Sounds like a great fart," the old man remarked as they pulled up in front of a large door with—surprise—a swastika crowning it.

"Oh, purest of Aryans, let us in!" Corbo shouted. "We're just a couple of poor old wandering Jews looking for a little hospitality."

"I'm not Jewish," Ketoko complained in his stentorian triple voice.

"You're not anything," Corbo agreed. "It was a joke."

But the door swung open.

"So you are a Jew?" Germanicus said in a surprisingly high voice. "Zo, why does that not astonish me, I wonder?"

Corbo laughed. "I might well be a Jew, at that. They were using a lot of them as gladiators in those days in Rome. They made good ones. But Corbo is a Greek name." He entered the room and frowned at the enormous man behind the enormous wooden desk. "I think," he added.

"Don't you even know?" Germanicus complained.

The old man shook his head and widened his eyes, treating Germanicus to the owl look. "To remember my parents, my childhood, my race, would require effort," he explained patiently, as if to a child. "Since it's useless information, why would I bother?"

"For Got's sake, it is so little effort. These are the very memories which shaped my whole life, my very raison d'être."

"Which is why we are here." Corbo gestured to Ketoko. "I believe you are acquainted with the changing one. So let us get down to business." He put on the silver helmet.

"Oh, for Got's sake, didn't I just let you in?"

"I would have huffed and puffed and blown your house down."

"All right, all right, what do you want from me? I'm willing to bargain. Why should we waste our energy in fighting, no? Since you seem to hate so much to waste the stuff. And why are you wearing that handsome Saxon helmet, and why are you carrying und old paper bag; und what is he, or should I say *it,* doing here?" He pointed at Ketoko.

The old man shook his head. "Such a lot of questions. Talk about wasting energy. But I'll make an exception and answer them all. In reverse order."

He held up his index finger. "One, Ketoko is here because, once we settle our petty differences and make up, we might decide to go on another nice little trip back to the good old days."

Germanicus, big red face scrunched up in a comical frown, was shaking his head no steadily in answer.

"Two"—the old man peeled up the next finger—"this paper bag had my lunch in it, but now all it has left is one little pineapple." He opened the bag and looked in it. Then he crossed the room and set it down on Germanicus's desk. "It's not quite ready yet, so I have to carry it around with me."

"Oh, but of course," Germanicus said, still shaking his head.

"Three"—Corbo peeled off the third finger—"the helmet. You know the last three are all really the same question: the helmet, what do I want from you, and why waste energy with fighting. So let me treat them as one thing, which they are. Boy, that's all five of my fingers. The way you ask questions, I'll have to be using my toes soon."

Germanicus's grimace became even more exaggerated, if that was possible. "At least spare me that, won't you?" he commented.

"Sure," the old man agreed. "I've always been known for being merciful, right?"

At this point both Ketoko and Germanicus made perhaps involuntary noises of protest. Particularly Ketoko's, which was delivered *triple voz.* But the old man ignored them.

"I'll make it easy on you. Spare you all the unimportant details and get to what you will or won't do here.

"First, the helmet is based on information I've just gathered on this unpleasant little trip you've sent me on. I eased the info out of some young man's mind while he was occupied staring at his handsome face in the mirror. It will stop you from using your psychic powers on me as well as me using mine on you."

"But . . . but why? And why should I believe it?"

The old man shook his head. "Two more questions." He grimaced. "We'll be here until daylight at this rate. But okay: To start with, what you believe is irrelevant, so don't bother.

"Second, to simplify matters, nullify both our psychic attacks so that when I attack you physically, you will only be able to fight back physically."

Germanicus shouted something unintelligible and leaped out of his chair, smashing into his desk, so the desk skidded forward and the chair went over backwards. He whipped a sword out in a pretty impressive fast draw.

The old man took his out in a more leisurely manner. Or at least it looked casual, but the fact was that it came out pretty quickly, too.

As usual, he was smiling.

"Good," he said, "let's not waste any time. You are either going to come with Ketoko and me and do exactly what I tell you to do, or I am going to kill you right now."

"You idiot!" Germanicus shouted. "Haven't you got brains enough to see that you are a helpless old man and I am a strong young one? Besides which I am naturally bigger and stronger anyway."

Corbo smiled. "You know what? Killing you would be like swatting a fly to me, except that I don't like to kill flies. I feel sorry for the poor little fellows, you know? But killing you—what a pleasure that would be. But it won't happen. Do you know why?"

Germanicus said nothing, just glared.

The old man frowned. "Come on, give me some help here. Even when I ask all the questions I have to give all the answers. All right, then.

"You won't fight because, to start with, you know I may appear an old man but this is no old man's body. The stone doesn't allow it to develop arthritis or suffer ill effects from some old injury. It doesn't allow stiff joints or unlimber muscles, or even slowing down, for that matter. It's ready to go. All I have to do is give it the word.

"And I think that deep down inside you know I could always take you, no matter how big you are or how much you bluster. But you also know that I'm willing to die. Couldn't care less. In fact, I've been up all night and I'm a little sleepy here, so for me it's simple: either I take a nap or I die, you see? A little nap, or a big nap. It's all the same to me.

"And because even if I'm wrong and you do believe all of your own ridiculous posturing"—he smiled—"you've been in enough real-life battles to know that there's a chance you could lose, things could go wrong, and then that wonderful gigantic ego of yours would be unable to go on and on, fighting to dominate whatever it perceived as separate from itself. Falsely perceived, I might add."

Germanicus now looked not so much furious as just plain astounded.

"Falsely perceived?" he protested.

"No more question-and-answer. Possibly, for you, ever again. Either put your sword down on that desk and agree, or I'm going to come at you and one of us is going to die. I'll silently count to ten. Take your choice."

There were a few moments of silence. Germanicus towered over the desk, glowering down at Corbo and Ketoko, saying nothing.

"Time's up," Corbo announced cheerfully, moving toward the desk in a semilow but still casual fencing posture.

Germanicus's sword clattered onto the desk.

# 28

TIPPI WAS FRUSTRATED enough to cry. She felt as if everything around her had been on a downhill spiral, starting with her inability to convince Violet to avoid that fatal confrontation with Diana.

Now, finally, she and her small army were here—wherever "here" was—but found themselves on the wrong side of a raging, storm-swollen river. She could feel the vicious battle going on, could tune in to Thaddeus's stone, feel his emotional turmoil, but could not get there from here.

They had brought along typical minimal commando gear, so they had an inflatable rubber raft. But, as Norm had pointed out to her, the river was moving much too fast for them to use it.

They had nylon rope and had tried shooting it across with one of the locals' "borrowed" bow and arrows. But the wind was blowing the wrong way; the river was too wide.

They had wasted a lot of time on this, and now they had nowhere left to go.

"This is a river, isn't it? Got to be boats. Like rowboats, canoes. Where the hell are they?"

Elspeth, to whom the question had been directed, simply shrugged and looked perplexed, as if to say, *I never go boating.*

Again it was good old soothing Norm who supplied the answer. "Uh, whoever burned the bridges wouldn't have left the boats. What good would that have done?"

"Right, right, of course. Forget I asked," Tippi grumbled. "But just the same, send one guy upriver and one down. They must have missed one somewhere, right? Maybe they just burned the bridges and took the boats within reach."

"Sure." Norm didn't sound too enthusiastic. "But you know, it all takes time, and I don't know if we . . ." He trailed off.

He was right. After all, they had already sent people to look for other bridges, and the news they brought back had not been good. Still, those people were not searching for boats.

"Methinks the frugal peasant would hide well his quaint little canoe thingie," Elspeth tossed in, looking suitably bewitching in her black commando suit, "for it is his only means of livelihood."

Tippi shook her head. "Thanks," she said. "Heddy, you want to head downriver, find us a boat?"

Surprising Tippi, as life usually did, her cellmate Sondra had disappeared as soon as Norm had bailed her out of jail, and it had been the caustic Heddy who had decided to fill the storm-trooper opening.

"Sure," she said agreeably. "I find one, I can either ride further downriver in it or maybe just put it in my purse and carry it back."

"Oh, shit." Tippi, naturally enough, hadn't thought of that. "Well, just go a couple of miles. If you spot one, we'll send some guys to fetch it or we'll go to it, okay?"

Heddy was finally returning from that task when Tippi, watching her, suddenly caught sight of movement on the far side of the river and looked over just in time to see a small white animal of some kind, moving so fast that she couldn't think what it was, race to the bank and keep on going until it was instantly swept away downstream and lost to sight.

"What the fuck was that? A dog? Well, no matter, it's sure as hell gone now."

Norm, who hadn't seen it, frowned in obvious disbelief. Tippi thought it remarkably easy to read his expressions. She felt he was comically ingenuous for a tough detective. "No, for real, some white animal jumped in the river, moving so fast . . . Hey, didn't you say the guys bought a white dog of some kind at the Faire, when you had them under surveillance?"

He nodded enthusiastically. "Yeah, that's right. Talk about weird. It was a bull terrier. You know?"

"Bull terrier?" Tippi looked puzzled.

"Whatever," Norm said. "If it jumped in that river. It's gone."

"Could it be," Elspeth interjected, "that same white doggie who appeareth as a sign of the coming of the possession of the body of the queen by the spirit of an old man?"

"Uh, I don't think so," Tippi answered. "Probably another white doggie." She rolled her eyes at Norm.

But by the time Heddy reached them, something white and wet sped across the grass heading straight for Tippi and simply bowled over poor Norm, who got in its way trying to protect her.

"Ah, same doggie," Elspeth said, unnoticed.

Insane with joy, it sprang stiff-legged straight up in the air in front of her, so high that it was looking into her eyes, then down again, then up. It did not escape her what the dog wore around his neck.

"Oh, shit," she said, stunned. *Was it Thaddeus or Raphael?* Silently the dog gave her the answer. Projected the image instantly into her consciousness as soon as she thought the question. Damn, she could read the dog's mind, feel the dog's emotions clearer than she had been able to with Thaddeus or Raphael. Violet, even.

The dog, for instance, was oblivious to her sorrow, because he had completed the mission Raphael had sent him on. In his consciousness Raphael was still alive as he had left him, and the work was done. Good dog!

But what would keep the golden boy alive after the stone was gone? Tippi tried to feel for his consciousness out there somewhere, but could not manage it. The dog's consciousness, however, was another matter. She was just plain sucked in.

The joys of feeding at the teat, and the warmth and beauty of mother. And she *was* beautiful, Tippi could see that: the strength, the loyalty, the muscularity, and the purity of her female instincts. She would clearly have fought a tiger to protect her pups.

Then feeding, sleeping, playing, and feeding again in a sweet, unmeasurable haze, until taken away to the new house. Kittens. "No, you must be careful, Blackjack, you'll hurt the kittens. You don't know your own strength." Sarah, the little girl, had told him that over and over. And he had understood and he had not hurt the kittens. He had loved Sarah and then he had loved the kittens, and in fact he still did. And that love had expanded until it included practically everything on earth.

But Sarah had gotten sick, and the unimaginable had happened. She had died, and death was one thing which Blackjack understood as fully and completely as any human. It meant "gone into the unknown forever."

Broken with grief, and unable to bear the sight of Sarah's dog, her parents had given him away to that drunken, broken little Elmer Ratger. Somehow appropriate—broken man seeks broken dog, to fight!

Then came the hideousness of the dogfights, on top of the rest of it. The drunk had made it clear to Blackjack that he wanted the dog to hate everything. Fight. Kill. Be macho, tough. Not like him—Blackjack could read that part, too—but an example of what Elmer most fervently wanted to be, had to be, but never would be: feared, respected.

But Blackjack would always be true to what he had learned from Sarah, from the kittens. He would not hate. And he would not fight.

At least that had been the case until he had sensed that his latest master, the kind one, was in danger. Then it all rose up out of someplace deep within. The strength that could come only from generations of warrior bred to warrior. It was something as natural to him as sleeping or eating, and really, the big dog he had killed had not been much of a fighter. The size had only made the inevitable take longer. Morgan's favorite bandoggie, Nighthawk, had wasted all his energy trying to break through the barrier of Blackjack's massive neck muscles—fat chance—while Blackjack had instantly crushed the creature's front leg in his vicelike jaws. Then it was simply a matter of struggling till finally the bigger dog was too tired to hold on, and bowling him over, and . . .

"Whoa—dogsville," Tippi said, pulling herself out of it.

"It is the same doggie," Elspeth repeated.

"Yeah, I'm sure," Tippi answered.

She was now staring across the turbulent river at—was it Mrs. Lim in armor? Hauling a spare horse? On the wrong side? What else could possibly go wrong? A drop of rain hit her nose, another the top of her head: it was starting to rain again.

Norm had already got some light-gauge but very tough plastic rope and brought it over to where Blackjack was still prancing around Tippi.

"Can the dog make it back across again?" And then, answering his own question, "I don't see how any living creature could get across that mother. Oh, I see"—noticing the amulet—"he's developed a taste for Indian jewelry. Wonder what happened to his high heels?"

But the rope had a carabiner on one end, and he had already clipped it onto Blackjack's collar, as if it were a leash.

"Sorry. Give it all you've got, stud. I'll say a prayer or two."

The dog barked once, as if to say "Got you," and took off, launched into the air, hit the icy churning water, and instantly was swept away.

"Give him all the slack you can," Tippi said.

"Of course," Norm shot back. The rope was on a big reel and he was letting it unwind as if he had a big fish on the other end.

The line went slack. It was raining hard now and the sky was growing darker fast; it was hard to see anything.

"I think I lost him," Norm said. "Damn, what a dog."

"You don't know the half of it," Tippi answered, considering the possibility of losing the stone as well as the dog.

"I think he may be a great wizard's familiar," Elspeth suggested, "in which case he cannot drown. Indeed it may prove necessary to crush him with rocks." She shrugged as Tippi and Norm glared at her.

The line tightened up. "No, he's still kicking," Norm, who could feel him thrashing like a fish, informed Tippi.

After a few minutes, they saw something small and white racing across the green toward the woman on the far bank.

She dismounted, and Tippi could see that she was doing something with the rope, but what? Apparently she had attached it to her saddle, because she next got back on her horse and, with the spare horse following, walked it around and around one of the ruined bridge's uprights. Then she waved the go-ahead.

The rubber boat was now inflated and more short length of the nylon rope looped around the other rope and clipped back onto fasteners on the boat. Then they secured the rope to the remaining pilings on their side, in a manner similar to the method Mrs. Lim had used.

Their commando outfits had metal loops attached to the belts, and they secured themselves to the main rope, donned life jackets, and loaded three of the shotguns into the rubber raft; and Norm, Tippi, and one of the others, a shooter of some repute everyone called Smitty, started to cross the raging river.

But they were interrupted by Elspeth before they began. "Ah, thou mayest call me old-fashioned if thou wishes, but much as I fear drowning, it must be obvious to everyone that I am the most essential person here. And not just because of my great beauty . . . Joking," she was forced to explain as the other three glared at her.

"I saw only two horses over there, and someone is riding one of them. I would imagine that two ladies or gentlemen per horse is the limit. Do I have to point out to thee that I am the only one amongst thee who knows her way around, not only the city but the castle as well? And obviously this witch, Tippi, with her magical amulet, must also come along. After all, she's in charge. So the only real question is, which of these two men is going to ride with us?"

Tippi and Norm looked at each other and Tippi said, "She's right. She's got to come."

Norm turned to the taller man and said, "Sorry, Smitty, but it looks like you stay behind. See if you can get all the others across, and then follow us on foot."

Smitty shook his head. "I don't think so," he said.

"What?" Norm barked. Mutiny?

The taller, whip-thin dude smiled at him, but it was a mean-looking

smile. "Sorry, Norm, but I'm the shooter. And I can ride a horse. You're the
organizer. You stay here and organize everybody. See they get there. This
ain't a game," he added, seeing Norm's expression.

"What?" was all Norm could seem to come up with.

But Tippi took a good look at Smitty and nodded. "He's right, Norm.
He's the shooter, and we're probably going to need him. You stay."

So in the end, Norm stood watching on the bank as the three of them set
out, the two women in the boat, Smitty launching it into the angry river and
then jumping in. Hauling himself aboard, an astonishing feat which he just
managed with the help of the two women.

Almost immediately, the raft capsized, without any weight to hold it
back, was shot off along the rope. The guns were gone, and the three were
left struggling in the icy water.

It was paralyzingly cold, and had she not been secured to the main
rope, Tippi would have frozen and gone down with the guns. She figured
their only chance was for one of them to work his way along the line and
fetch the boat back. But the boat was whipping back and forth so violently
that either the securing ropes or the fasteners broke—they would never know
which—and the rubber raft leaped into the air like a hooked marlin and then
tumbled and flew downstream and out of sight.

Tippi felt someone grab hold of her with a very strong grip and force
her own right hand up onto the rope. It was Smitty. He shouted something
in her ear, but she couldn't hear it. He shouted again, and then she got the gist
of it.

"Drag yourself across, dammit, or at least die trying."

If it had not been for the recuperative powers of the stone, she would
never have made it. This was the first time she had experienced that phe-
nomenon, and it was a convincing if agonizing way to learn about it.

Drag herself a little way against the raging current, until she couldn't
force herself to tough out another inch. Then just hang there for a few minutes feeling the force in her body stimulated by the stone she wore around
her neck. Wash away the lactic acid all at once. Fresh start.

Elspeth simply could not make it, and halfway across gave out and just
let go, and they left her there bobbing up and down like a cork, semiconscious. But after Tippi made it to the other side, much to the obvious joy of
the white Guardian, Smitty went back for her.

To add to Tippi's amazement, the stringy but muscular commando had
managed to hold on to a shotgun, which he now handed her. "Hang on to this
one fer me," he said in some kind of hillbilly accent. "Reckon I better go

back and fetch the bossy witch, or she won't be able ta tell me whut ta do next, and I might fuck up a mite. Pardon my French, ma'am."

Tippi, still lying on her back exhausted in the wet grass, rain pounding down on her, a shotgun in her outstretched hand, looking up into his pale blue eyes, realized that he was smiling. And that he was just a kid, no more than twenty-one or twenty-two. Then he was gone into that maelstrom again, pulling himself along the rope with a grip like steel.

Eyes closed, rain washing her face, and something else. But she had known even before the creature began licking her cheek. She opened her eyes and blinked, he looked so tough. "What can I say?" she said, feeling foolish. "Thanks, good dog."

Blackjack barked back in answer, then turned and stiffened and pointed with his whole muscular body, like a hunting dog scenting game. He whined anxiously and looked back at Tippi.

"Okay, what is it?" Tippi sat up and looked back toward the river.

"He have her now," said Mrs. Lim, who had apparently satisfactorily secured the rope and ridden over to greet Tippi. "He pull her out like fish. But where my Violet, what I want to know?"

"We will talk about it when this is over. But I don't want to talk about it now," Tippi said. "Looks like he's going to make it with Elspeth."

"Better we talk now," Mrs. Lim insisted.

Tippi fished the amulet out from her shirt and showed it to Mrs. Lim. "That's all you need to know," she said.

Staring down at her from the horse, Mrs. Lim nodded solemnly and said, "Silly me. You the boss."

Both of them watched silently as Smitty emerged triumphantly from the river and walked over to them, carrying the semiconscious raving beauty Elspeth carelessly slung over his shoulder like a sack of potatoes. Without waiting for the poor witch to recover, Smitty simply piled her onto the back of Mrs. Lim's horse.

"My, you are soft pretty woman," Mrs. Lim cruelly observed. "Maybe good for sex, but not so good for fighting or riding horse. Better you get tough quickly."

"Oh, I shall, I shall," Elspeth wheezed in agreement.

Smitty mounted the other horse in one smooth movement, and pulled up up behind him.

"You hang on to the shotgun, grab me around the belly, and balance the gun across the saddle, like this. Get her right 'bout in the middle, and don't let go fer nothin'."

Mrs. Lim took off at a gallop, Elspeth holding frantically to her waist.

Smitty turned around and gave Tippi his stingy grin. "Well, it's back in the saddle again," he said. "Hang on."

She clamped down on the shotgun and held on, looking ahead at the horizon. What horizon? She realized what had been nagging at her but she had not taken time to pin down: it had stopped raining, a heavy afternoon fog was settling in fast, and already you couldn't see that far. As they took off, the white dog shot past, leading them fearlessly and joyfully into the unknown.

# 29

THADDEUS HAD SPENT enough time, many years ago, in an Oriental jungle shooting at cunning little men he could never see, to have some grasp of the vagaries of war. You would have thought that he would have been able to accept the fact that more often than not, all the plans you've so carefully concocted will start out working fine, then swiftly fall apart. But he was human, and like all humans was shocked out of his shoes to see how quickly order was eaten up by chaos on the battlefield. It reminded him of that glib, banal quote, he had forgotten by whom, that people loved to assail him with—something like, "If you don't study history you will be doomed to repeat it."

"Yeah," he had once answered, "that's why we don't have wars anymore." The unfortunate fact of human nature was that the more you studied wars, the more you had them, and they surprised you every time.

Take a simple thing like the weather. Fog—bad. Then no fog—good. But the early rain had soaked the ground, making it easy for the archers to plant their stakes—good. But blood and mud mixed together made for terrible footing when you were trying to hold ground against heavily armed opponents—bad. And finally, fog again—archers rendered useless.

So the war had started out according to his plans. Jeremy's archers had moved into range and fired, confusing and provoking the enemy. The archers had then moved back, each man behind the stake he had planted, and continued firing, only now they were using arrows dipped in tar and set aflame by the torches they had also stuck into the ground.

Infuriated and confused by the barrage of arrows, most of the knights ignored or forgot orders and charged at full gallop, shouting oaths and swinging their deadly swords—gone berserk!

Then the horses hit the stakes. Thaddeus would never forget the screaming of the horses. He would never be able to classify it as neighing or whinnying; it was screams of agony and terror. Now the flaming arrows accelerated the chaos. Stampede: horses were rearing, riders flying off, and then Thaddeus's small but well-trained group of foot soldiers, led by Bitters and Broadbent, was rushing in to finish off the fallen.

Then, as suddenly as it began, the charge was over. Thaddeus's men cheered as the Wiccan knights wheeled their horses around and raced off in retreat. Heading for . . .

Thaddeus's spirits fell as he realized where they were heading. They were simply going to ride into the castle, pull the drawbridge up, and plan a new attack.

For some strange reason this obvious course of action had never occurred to him, and he cursed himself for not having considered it. But there were so many complications to keep track of that something obvious always escaped you. It was these mistakes that usually cost you the battle.

Then, when he was beginning to despair, to his amazement, just as the mounted soldiers were about to reach the castle, up went the drawbridge. Could that be? He blinked. Even at this distance there was no mistaking it. Drawbridge up.

"Jeremy," he shouted, "start shooting!"

The surviving archers, which were most of them, ran out from behind their stakes, some of them slipping in blood or tripping over the bodies of men and horses, moved forward until they had the enemy in range again, and on Jeremy's orders started firing.

The knights, having adapted to this attack, now held their shields up over their heads, and escaped major damage this way. But this was tiring, and some of the horses were hit. There was only one thing to do, and they did it. Once again, they charged.

Only this time the charge was much more successful. The first wave smashed between the wings of archers, directly into Thaddeus's group of swordsmen in the middle. The wave that followed soon after was a smaller group of unhorsed knights, now fighting on foot.

The fighting was vicious and both sides sustained heavy losses. Thaddeus's swordsmen held, but just barely. And more horses went down. But now instead of retreating, the Wiccan swordsmen pushed sideways into both wings of archers, which had collapsed as the shooters tried to help out Thaddeus's swordsmen by joining the attack with stakes, hammers, and miscellaneous farm tools converted into weapons.

The heavily armored Wiccan knights wreaked havoc among the poor untrained, unarmored archers, killing them almost at will. The only thing hampering them was Bitters's and Broadbent's small crew of swordsmen at their backs now. But had the fight gone on here, the Wiccan army would surely have been able to win.

Thaddeus now realized that just as he had underrated the defensive value of the heavy plate armor, he had also underrated the skill and size of the enemy, who now were fighting better on foot than they had on their horses. And he was having difficulty penetrating their armor with his pistols, let alone arrows.

He had wasted several bullets trying to take out one of their leaders. He thought he recognized the arrogant fool who had quarreled with Raphael and him when they had first entered this world. What was his name—Hugh Marshal? Bitters's old boss. But he could not be sure, because the man wore one of those protective helmets and was moving around very fast. Thaddeus had tried to use his psychic powers on the man, but to no avail. However it worked, the helmet was doing its job. Watching one bullet ricochet off the helmet and another off the knight's chestplate (at least that was what he deduced from the pinging sound and where he had aimed) was enough to convince Thaddeus to go back to taking potshots at whoever was closest.

And then, just when he was starting to panic, someone signaled for retreat. All of them had heard the distant sound of the horn. And Thaddeus could see the drawbridge was down again. Several men yelled, "Retreat!" And they ran away.

At this point, one of Thaddeus's own archers took a shot at him—great way to waste arrows. It was turned aside by his armor. And the man was struck down. Thaddeus closed his eyes and searched. This was his specialty. And sure enough, there she was: back at the drawbridge, some old biddy about a thousand years old, with a minor talent and a minor talisman that gave her just enough ability to control a peasant with a bow and arrow.

Thaddeus reached across the distance and grabbed her brain. Squeezed it. He could feel her squirming to escape his grip, and then go unconscious.

He relinquished his hold on the old witch, and opened his eyes again to check the scenario. Drawbridge going up again!

Even though this was good news, something about it caused Thaddeus to feel a fluttering throughout his body that could easily stampede into full panic. The war was being dictated by the random lowering and raising of the drawbridge?

And make no mistake, these well-conditioned knights were being beaten down more by lugging all that heavy armor back and forth than by Thaddeus's army.

Again he could see them all up there milling around in front of the drawbridge, without a clue what to do next.

Suddenly he came out of his reverie. "Why aren't we shooting? Now's the time. Where's Jeremy? Jeremy, get your men shooting!"

But Bitters suddenly was at his side, saying something to him, something he did not want to hear.

"Jeremy's dead. Me old boss, Sir Hugh, got 'im, the bastard. Seen the helmet and took the head. Got it tied to 'is horse. God, let me have him, I'm prayin' to ya."

So this was war. A fine sensitive man, an artist, a musician, a luthier, and a fine teacher and citizen. A good friend. And his head was now decorating some fop's saddle.

There was no time to mourn, but there was no way to avoid the queasy, dead sensation that came over Thaddeus. Perhaps it was a necessary deadening of the senses to prepare him for what horrors would surely follow. But the effect was of being half-dead already.

He spotted the spunky little shopkeeper who had so recently joined them.

"The helmet—did he get it, too?"

"No, it came off," Bitters said in a dry voice. "I got it here." He tossed it to Thaddeus, who ran over and handed it to the little shopkeeper.

"Here, you're in charge now. Get them shooting." The little man nodded matter-of-factly and put on the silver helmet.

"What happens when we run out of arrows?"

"Stop shooting," Thaddeus answered.

And so they got off a few more arrows before the third and final charge. This time, no more lines of archers, rows of swordsmen. This time, chaos.

The Wiccan horsemen (there were so few on horses now) walked their mounts, wearily holding shields overhead to ward off the intermittent showers of arrows, not wanting to arrive without support, their foot soldiers marching behind.

It was only when they were quite close that they dragged themselves into their saddles and broke into a gallop, and that the army of exhausted farmers ran yelling to meet them.

This time the Wiccan knights broke through the middle of the swordsmen, and some of the archers, out of arrows, attacked. Some fled.

Everyone merged into one confused, thrashing, many-armed beast. No one was any longer sure who was friend, who was enemy, where they were supposed to be, or whom they were fighting with. But somehow they fought on with more intensity than before. Dead tired, terrified, lost, the men on both sides gritted their teeth and swung whatever weapon they had, drawing from some kind of immeasurable last-ditch energy.

For Thaddeus, it was as if he were looking through a funnel, fighting with little men who appeared there and then charged him, swinging their swords and growing larger till the bullet hit them and they went down. He felt as though he were stoned and shooting in a gallery in the arcade. Everything was distant, confused. His ears were ringing. Head aching.

Men were dying all around him. Going down, all chopped to bits. He could no longer tell whether they were his or theirs. No longer seemed to matter, really.

On top of the screams, swords, arrows, the air was full of all kinds of UFOs: farm tools, daggers, rocks, even large chunks of stone from the field. It was one of these that struck him. And he went down.

When he came to, he was aware of energy pouring into him. Bringing him back. He seemed to recall hearing claps of thunder. Was it raining again?

"Wake up, Thad. We haven't got all day." He recognized the voice. Opened his eyes too suddenly, which brought pain.

It was Tippi.

"Who won?"

Another voice that he recognized answered that one.

"Everyone go crazy. Break up, run around. Fight everywhere. Back in village, on field. Nobody win. Everybody lose. Everything go out of control."

Thaddeus sat up, bringing more pain to his head. A very dense bank of fog had settled in. He could hear the clash of weapon on armor. Moans of anguish and shouts of rage floating out of it. But he couldn't see more than a few feet. Some tall, lean, mean-looking guy, looked like a cracker, was standing behind Tippi in a shooter's stance with a short-barreled shotgun. There were bodies everywhere, and Thaddeus would have bet that this man had accounted for his fair share of them. That shotgun must have been the thunder he had heard when he was out.

"Where's Violet?"

Tippi said, "She's . . . uh . . . she's dead, so I . . ." She put her hand to her chest, where she wore the stone that had been Violet's.

For a moment Thaddeus was too stunned to speak. Then he said, "Of course, Tippi. Who else would wear her stone?"

But right then he heard joyful barking and he saw Blackjack, and it registered on him what he had sensed but been too involved in the battle to reg-

ister. The dog was wearing one of the four stones. Which meant that. . . . He
now noticed the woman, a stunner, on the horse behind Mrs. Lim. Tippi had
another horse by the reins, which shivered nervously.

"Rafe," he said, getting up too fast. Swaying. "He may still be alive. Get
the stone off the dog, and let's get moving."

Tippi shook her head. "I don't think so," she said. "Raphael gave him
the stone for a reason. I can communicate with him. He's sensitive, more than
you even, Thad. And he can see and hear things that we can't even imagine.
I think we let him keep it, follow him to Raphael."

"Already giving orders," Thaddeus groused. "Here, give me the shotgun, dude."

Without a word or a change of expression, Smitty handed the gun over.

"You going to stay here and wait for the others. I assume there be
others."

Smitty nodded. "Should be here, if'n they can get across thet river.
Some fool burned the bridges."

Thaddeus nodded noncommittally. "You'll need this," he said, unhol-
stering one of his handguns.

Smitty shook his head. "I'll be fine. Pick up one of these dead guys'
swords and do it the old-fashioned way. You take care of the ladies, hear?"

Tippi climbed back up on the horse and helped Thaddeus mount behind her.

"There's a castle straight ahead," Thaddeus informed Smitty. "Can't
make it out in all this fog, but it's there. That's where we're headed. See you
there."

Without another word, they took off at a slow canter, with the white dog
leading the way and the other horse following. It was too foggy to go even
that fast, but Tippi, who was tuned in to the dog's superior senses, was nav-
igating.

"Wouldn't it be better we slow down a little?" Thaddeus asked. If Tippi
was no equestrian, at least she had gone horseback riding a few times in her
youth, while the closest Thaddeus had ever gotten to a horse was tooling
around on a motorcycle. And that was about as close as he cared to be. Besides, it would be of no help to Raphael if they fell off the horse.

But Tippi merely shook her head in answer. And now Thaddeus, too,
had attained psychic rapport with the dog. The bull terrier was like a vastly
improved form of radar that was tuned in to all the little life-and-death battles going on all around them in the fog.

Suddenly, Thaddeus sighed and told Tippi, "Take a left." He pointed
into the formless murk.

"We haven't got time for—"

"Just be a minute," he insisted. "Be necessary."

A small group of men were finishing off one last farmer. One of them was on a horse. Thaddeus was relieved that the fog would not allow him to see clearly what was tied to the saddle horn.

"Well, well, fortune smiles on me today," Hugh Marshal said. "That is you, isn't it? The darkie who mocked me in the road, back when Bitters was still working for me instead of ornamenting my saddle."

Mrs. Lim wailed, realizing what it was she saw bobbing from the saddle of his horse.

"Oh, yes," he said, "I'm collecting them. Only my favorites. The luthier who thought he was an archer, the lackey who thought he was a great swordsman. Well, he *was,* among lackeys. But I, I'm proud to say, gave him a taste of humility for his betters, before I took his head. And now for thee, the darkie comedian. Be of good cheer. Thou wilt ride along in company with thy good friends up here on my saddle.

"But where is thine arrogant friend? The one with all the muscle and the nasty tongue? Never mind, I prefer to torture it out of you. So what wilt thou do now, I wonder? Run? Run to thy heart's content. My horse, Dazzle, is the fastest of all the horses in the kingdom. Is he not a splendid beast?

"But I digress. Feel free to run; I will catch thee. Dost fancy thyself a swordsman, as Bitters did? Here's thy chance to prove it."

Thaddeus got down off the horse.

"Oh, by the way, bad news, no more fancy Wiccan tricks." Sir Hugh tapped his helmet. "In case you haven't heard, this little helmet puts an end to that, so it's just thou and I—man to man." He leaped gracefully from his horse and stood, sword in hand, waiting. "What is that, anyway?" he said, sounding for the first time a trifle anxious. "One of those tubes that throw pellets? It will not do thee any good. I am wearing the finest armor, and I intend to be moving fast when thou triest to use it."

"That your pride and joy?" Thaddeus said, pointing the gun at Hugh's magnificent stallion, Dazzle. "I don't like him. He's got heads on his saddle." He pulled the trigger and the horse screamed, reared, and crashed down.

"You . . . you villain!" Hugh shouted, not only devastated by the loss of his great horse but shocked by his first glimpse of what a shotgun loaded with buckshot could do. The three men with him simply ran away.

Mrs. Lim vaulted from her horse and drew her sword. "Let me—" she started to say.

But Thaddeus shouted, "No, you stay out of it. That's an order. You think he worth takin' a chance on?"

He took aim, and Hugh started dancing back and forth in an obvious effort at evasion, so Thaddeus shot low.

"Didn't have all that great armor on your legs, I guess," he remarked.

Hugh lay in the bloody field, stunned, but still hanging on to his sword. He raised himself on one elbow and looked down his body. A small cry like that of a bird escaped him, and then he said through clenched teeth, "You coward."

"No, I'm not a coward," Thaddeus said. "You macho dudes just don't ever get it. You, you're the coward. Jeremy had no chance against you. Neither did Bitters. You had all the time and money in the world to study swordsmanship. You even learned what Bitters could teach you, then went on to somebody else. You just used your time and money to buy knowledge they couldn't acquire, you dig? Then you killed them with that knowledge.

"Well, see, that's what I'm doing. This here's a twelve-gauge pump automatic with a special short combat barrel. Carrying some kind of special combat load. That's my knowledge, see? Same deal." He took careful aim and finished the ugly job.

"You didn't have to kill the horse," Tippi complained.

"Yeah, I did, though. This is war, Tippi. Everything about it sucks."

Finally they reached the castle, where to nobody's surprise, they found chaos in command. And the drawbridge up.

# 30

I AM TELLING you," Germanicus fairly whined with fear, "it's some sort of science-fiction thing. Haven't you ever heard of it? If I should run into myself during time travel, I shall disappear or blow up, or some such thing. Surely you've heard of it?"

Corbo shook his head in disgust. "Don't be silly," he advised. "How could you run into yourself? You're not even the same person you were a moment ago, let alone a few years ago. Everything about you is different—the contents of your mind, the cells of your body. Everything except your colossal ego has changed."

"But that's the part I'm worried about."

Corbo walked on in silence. There was surely no point in trying to explain to this unenlightened oaf that the ego he thought of as his self was only an illusion of continuity, and not real in any way.

"Well, you've got my guarantee," Corbo assured him.

"Oh, how excellent!" he replied sarcastically.

"Corbo is right, you know," Ketoko threw in. "Everything is change."

"Well, of course everything is change for *you,*" Germanicus complained. "Look at your face, for God's sake. The way it keeps shifting around is driving me crazy."

Corbo laughed wildly. "That's a short drive," he choked. And now Ketoko laughed a phony, stentorian "Ho, ho, ho," in his enormous triple voice, sounding like a super Santa Claus.

"Most fine remarkable joke," he said. "I know one myself. Very humorous." He paused, obviously expecting an invitation; but receiving none, he plunged in anyway. "Why does the fireman wear red suspenders?"

Corbo and Germanicus looked at each other and grimaced. Ketoko waited.

Corbo said nothing, refused to answer, but Ketoko waited patiently.

"Oh, all right, then," Germanicus groaned. "Let me see. Obviously it's because he's a communist."

Corbo snorted.

"No," Ketoko roared. "It's to keep his pants up. Ho, ho, ho."

Once again Corbo and Germanicus looked at each other and grimaced.

"You're kidding me," Germanicus groused.

"Yes, it is a jest. Don't you get it?"

The three were striding down the same corridor that Corbo and Ketoko had traversed earlier that night, but now it was thirty-some years in the past, and things were quite different. Fewer guards, less decoration, no swastikas over the doors, save one. A guard stood to one side of that door, looking at them and blinking.

"Head start." Corbo pointed at the Nazi symbol.

Germanicus shrugged. "You see how I improved things, don't you? Everything is now—ach, I mean then—everything is then so spick-and-span. Guards at attention. You could eat off the floor. While here, before I got started—"

"Yes, yes," Corbo agreed wearily, "you should have been an interior decorator. Okay, open the door."

The guard, looking back and forth between them nervously, said to Germanicus, "Oh, it's you, sir."

"Yes, of course it's me, you fool. Now go guard the, uh, great hall."

Looking puzzled, the guard said, "I thought you were inside this room."

"Yes, of course I am in there," Germanicus said impatiently, "but so what? Are you questioning me?"

"No, sir." He clicked his heels. "The king," he said, and marched off down the corridor stiffly, as if he were on parade.

Corbo shook his head, looking sour.

"He is not supposed to think," Germanicus said defensively. "Now come on, won't you? I really don't want to see myself. I just feel that you may be wrong and the paradox would destroy me."

"Sure," Corbo agreed. "It's such an orderly world, surely it couldn't stand a paradox or two. Now get that door open. Maybe you won't even have to see yourself. I just need a moment."

Ketoko had once again transported them through time, this time back to within a few days of Germanicus's first arrival, which was as close as Corbo cared to venture to what he was sure was a trap. All the way with Germanicus complaining about the damage it might do if he were to encounter himself.

"I just don't see why you forced us to come here in the first place. I can answer any question you might have for my earlier self."

"Take my word for it. Open the door."

"How can I open the door? It's closed. Locked. There's a bolt in it. I always drop the bolt when I'm in there. I don't understand why I must be here with you."

"Something I want you to see," Corbo answered him. "That's all. But what do you want me to do? Knock? You'll panic. You just set a trap for me a couple of days ago. I didn't fall into it. You're going to be wary and paranoid for a while. Well, okay, actually you're going to be paranoid forever, but maybe a little less wary from time to time. So help me get in. Otherwise we have to go through a big scene, break down the door. Fight, even."

"Oh, all right," Germanicus grumbled. "Here, give me your sword. Don't get excited. You have the upper hand. Let's get this over with, without any violence. No?"

Corbo stifled a laugh. "No, I don't think so. What do you want with it?"

"All right. There is a big crack between the door and the wall. You just slide your blade in and you can lift up the bolt. That's why I remodeled it. The whole castle was built by churls who cared nothing about their work."

Ketoko surprisingly remarked in what was for him an even tone of voice, "Racist pig."

To which Germanicus replied, "I'm not a racist. Perhaps I might be considered an elitist."

Corbo, fiddling around with his blade, commented, "Same thing."

Suddenly a familiar voice from the inside called out, "Who is there? What is this? Guard? Where is my guard?"

"Oh my God, it's myself," Germanicus exclaimed, actually holding his hands over his chest.

"Calm down," Corbo said. "There, I've got it." He pushed the door open with his shoulder, then sheathed his sword.

"*O mine Gott,*" Germanicus muttered, trying not to look but obviously fascinated.

# 31

A FEW MOMENTS earlier, the other Germanicus sat inside his private room in the Great Tower of London, feeling safe on the one hand but troubled, too. The king gone, and this? He stared at the green guitar on the desk in front of him. What on earth did it mean? Surely it was from the twentieth century, wasn't it? He knew nothing about guitars, and this one did have a strange, rounded back like a lute. But the paint job. The plastic knobs—or were they really ivory or some such thing? They had brought him the body of King Rufus, and the guitar with it. Went hunting? Had he not ordered him to—

Then he heard something at the door. Something furtive. He felt uneasy, but not panicky. After all, this was the Tower of London. Who could reach him here? He carried the guitar over and stood it up in the corner of the room, getting it out of his sight. Walked back to his desk and forced himself to sit down at his papers. "Who is there? What is this? Guard? Where is my guard?" he shouted. No answer.

"I said, who is it? Who dares?" The door flew open. He hardly noticed Corbo standing in the doorway. His gaze was riveted on the handsome—no, more than handsome, godlike!—giant behind him.

Corbo opened up his paper bag and looked into it. "Well, what do you know?" he said. "I think my pineapple is finally ripe."

Germanicus Two was staring into and across the room at the man who was just now standing up behind the desk, holding a sword, when he realized what it was that Thaddeus had in his hand. "Oh no," he exclaimed helplessly as, smiling, Corbo pulled the pin and tossed the grenade casually yet expertly so that it bounced along the floor and finally rolled under the desk. Then he stepped back, reached out, and closed the door again.

"Get away from the door," he suggested helpfully.

And sure enough, the door was blown off its hinges.

He walked over and took hold of poor Germanicus Two by the shoulder and guided him over to the doorway. He did not resist.

"I, I'm still here," he muttered.

"I told you," Corbo reminded him. "Well, this is what I brought you here to see."

"Myself blown to bits?" Germanicus shouted, outraged.

"Exactly. That's how you will look the second time around if you piss me off. And you won't live through that one either."

"Is that true?" he whispered hoarsely.

"Oh, I don't know," Corbo said. "But you are the farthest forward of your selves. What you want most is to go on, see? You don't care about any of the others. So you just tell me everything I want to know, and then Ketoko will take you back to the twentieth century sometime after you disappeared, and drop you off so you can continue with your miserable existence. Forever, for all I care. But I will not let you live here. Stay out of England. And when you get back in the twentieth century, stay away from me."

"And me," Ketoko threw in enthusiastically.

"Careful, the two of you make me feel unwanted," Germanicus quipped, having regained control.

"That's because there're only two of us here," Corbo pointed out. "If there were more . . ." He smiled and shrugged.

Germanicus nodded, and then, strangely, smiled himself.

"Very well," he acknowledged, "you win this one. I would be a fool to waste any more energy on this. To be truthful, I should thank you. I've learned something."

"Don't get Corbo mad?" Ketoko tossed in.

Germanicus's smile now broadened.

"Besides that," he said. "I have learned about myself. What I am, what I am not. Memories lie to you. I am not those. I am only what's here now. It is, after all, rather liberating to learn that. But just a little scary, don't you think?"

"It will fade, though," the old man assured him. "With time, it will fade. It is a flame that will go out if you don't feed it. First your old habits will creep back in, and then you will forget for a little bit, and then for longer, and a month or two . . ." He shrugged. "You won't remember what you learned here now. You will fall back into your old painful, stupid ways, live out your constricted but vicious life, chained by the imaginary past. The flame will die."

"But not for you, eh?"

Corbo smiled. "I am that flame," he said. "Now, let's get down to business. William Rufus must die, and it must be as close as possible to when you last saved his worthless neck. How do I reach him?"

It was here that a trio of guards armed with battle axes charged into the room.

"You can see that I am still alive. Quite well, actually," Germanicus informed them sarcastically. "Not so much as a little ear on my head has been harmed, yes? You can see this?"

The guards nodded.

"Then get your useless stupid selves out of my sight. Go and guard your king."

The guards swiveled around, then turned back. "The king is dead," one of them said, obviously puzzled.

"Yes, well, who's the new king, then?"

The guards looked at each other. "Why, we don't know, either Robert or Henry, I suppose," one of them said.

"Henry's already got the money," one of the others tossed in.

"Then if Henry has taken over the treasury, he's going to be king, am I not right? Is he here?"

"No."

"Well, he will be. Meanwhile there must be someone here important that you can protect. Some duchess or famous priest. Go protect them. Now." They turned and charged out the door.

During this exchange, the old man had walked over and was examining the strange guitar in the corner. It was not only strange, but lucky. Somehow the grenade had missed it completely, while destroying almost everything else in the room.

"Isn't life odd?" Corbo muttered, turning back to Germanicus.

"Yes, I think we can safely admit that," Germanicus grumbled, then added grudgingly, "Well, it looks as though you have succeeded in your holy quest."

"It looks like that at the moment," Corbo admitted, "but that could change." Thought about it and added, "Maybe." Laughed. "But where were we? You were giving me the information I need to solidify this little twist of history."

Soon, satisfied with the info he had dredged up, Corbo snapped his fingers. It made a loud popping noise, and Germanicus actually startled from it, as if awakening from a deep sleep.

"I almost forgot," Corbo said. "The girl. Quickly."

Germanicus looked genuinely puzzled. "What girl?"

Corbo's sword moved so fast that for a few moments, no one but he was aware of what had just happened. Then Ketoko pointed to the ear on the floor. "I wonder if the stone will grow you a new one," he said in his awesome triple voice.

"Ow! *O mein Gott,* it hurts," Germanicus shouted, but he looked more fascinated than hurt.

"Well, what do you know?" Corbo said calmly, "Your little ear got hurt after all. Now let me ask you a different question. Do you think it would upset me a great deal to kill you?"

Holding his hand to the bloody side of his head, Germanicus groaned, "The girl is here. I will take you to her." He led them to a nearby room and, moving aside a tapestry depicting the ubiquitous triumphal hunt, reached into a recessed portion of the wall and turned a latch. The fireplace swung open, revealing a secret room.

"It's just the primitive stages of the Tower," he explained apologetically. "I haven't had any time to work on it. In fact, it's not even being used as a dungeon yet. But the walls are actually eighteen feet thick and, of course, riddled with secret rooms and passageways. There, you see, she has not been harmed. She is in fact quite comfortable, are you not, my dear?"

A fiery-looking woman with black kinky hair and a fierce hook nose, dressed like a harem dancer, sat on a large bed in the middle of her secret room, moving her hands in time to some music no one could quite hear. When she saw them enter, she sprang from the bed to her bare feet, and stood with hands on hips, glaring at them.

Germanicus had spoken to her in German, but her answer—

"So, what now? You finally found some guy not gay around here and dragged him up here to do me? Shit, the king's gay. This sorry dude, some kind of S-M freak, doesn't care if it's men or women as long as somebody gets hurt, right? So get this. Him and his buddy, the red-faced king, right? They make me watch. Can you believe it?"

Germanicus smiled noncommittally and shrugged.

"Anyway"—she advanced on Corbo—"you don't look gay. In fact, you're kind of cute. About a thousand years old"—a closer estimation than she might have imagined—"but, hell. But let me guess. No such luck. I get to do the other one, right, weird dude you can't even fucking see his face?"

Even Corbo was looking a little disoriented here. "You speak English, or I should say, you speak American, right?"

"Yeah, that's right. Donna. Who are you?" She held out her hand. Corbo

shook it. He found her absolutely gorgeous; her thin hook nose added that
extra touch of character and individuality that separated her from all those
even-featured beauties he found boring to look at. Not that he cared. Maybe.

"Corbo," he said. "No, you don't have to, uh, *do* anyone here. But how
is it you speak American?"

She looked at him and shook her head. "Ah gee, I wonder. Maybe it's
because I come from America, do you think?"

All the time she spoke, she moved. Her hands, her body, her head. She
had the lithe body of an acrobat or dancer.

"You are a dancer?"

She smiled, nodded, pirouetted a couple of times, and then writhed like
a snake.

"You bet."

"What kind?"

"Whatever pays. But if I had my choice, I prefer dancing in the nude.
You dig? You can see the body better that way."

Corbo nodded. "Good point."

So this was the woman that Theseus would do anything for? From
America?

"The world is a strange place," he repeated in awe.

"Boy, ain't it, though?" Donna agreed.

"Would you like to go back? Or would you rather return to Theseus?"

Donna laughed, pirouetted once more, and said, "Are you kidding? Return to what? You ever try dancing to Tiny Tim?"

Corbo grimaced and shuddered. Even Germanicus looked a little uneasy here. Only Ketoko, who was unreadable anyway, said, "Who's Tiny
Tim?"

"You would probably like him," Corbo remarked.

And soon the four of them were on their way back through the maze of
time, with Ketoko guiding, Germanicus docilely following, Donna moving
and grooving, and Corbo the flame, providing the necessary desire.

# 32

---

SAYETH NOT TO thyself, 'Oh, call me the most unlucky of all,' for hast thou not been blessed with, as cohort—friend, even—she who sees all, knows all, and even sometimes tells all? Namely me," Elspeth was saying to Tippi, who was practically cross-eyed from trying to sort through the language.

Tippi and Thaddeus shared glances and sadly looked once more back at the raised drawbridge. They were not about to scale those glassy walls.

"You mean you know some way to get in?" Tippi said. "Stop wasting time. What is it?"

Looking hurt but bewitching in her black commando jumpsuit, Elspeth said poutingly, "There is a secret way in and out of the castle known only to a few of the most high among the Wicca. In fact, there are many more than one. The nearest one starts from inside that little watch post on the hill. Thou canst not see it, because of the fog. But 'tis there. A path doth begin over there and leadeth up the hill to it. Hopefully, 'twill be deserted. After all, what use is surveillance when the war beeth this far along? If you can still call it a war at this stage."

She had a point. It was now at the pillaging, looting, raping stage, where little groups of berserkers wandered around in the fog looking for stragglers from both sides. Nobody had the faintest idea who was winning, but Thaddeus was willing to bet that whoever owned the posh little shops in North Wiccingham was losing right about now, in the worst possible way. And the horrifying thing about it was that this was a stage that he could picture going on for days.

The noble Crusaders, he seemed to remember, had trashed and raped Constantinople beyond all hope of recovery for three solid days and nights.

And now he realized fully what a fool he had been to take any part in this. Men's folly: war. Never women's. If only Violet or Tippi had been along, maybe . . .

But this reverie was broken by Mrs. Lim's observation, which as usual stopped him in his tracks with his stereotypical idealizing of women.

"You can call it war, all right," she said, "typical war. Many bad terrible thing occur. But, let me please assure you"—she pointed at Elspeth—"all you life is taking a nap. War is wake you up. Wake you up sad, or wake you up happy. But wake you up. You will always remember it. When you go back to sleep again."

Thaddeus shuddered. *Hope you're wrong for once, you vicious little warrior, but I doubt it,* he said to himself as they rushed their mounts along the path that led steeply uphill to the small deserted shack that overlooked castle and town. If there had been no fog and they had been cursed with the eyes of an eagle, they would not have liked what they saw happening down below.

Inside the hut, Elspeth began to falter. "It's been such a long time. I can't quite seem to . . ."

But Thaddeus did not. "It's over there on the far wall, one of those little protuberances. No, a series of them. Here, let me."

He strode over impatiently to the large open fireplace encircled with an arch of bricks, and pointed to the left of it.

"Starts there," he said. "But first—" He reached out and twisted a brick on the left side around the middle of the arch, but it would not move. "Ah," he said, "first you have to push it in." To the amazement of Tippi, Mrs. Lim—and who knew, maybe even Elspeth—this time the brick turned easily. He stopped it at exactly one-half turn around. When he let go of it, it clicked back into place, and since it was square, it looked no different from before.

"Then this." He reached up and ran his hand along the wooden mantel over the fireplace.

"Ouch, sliver," he said. "But here—" Where the mantel joined the wall, at each corner was a metal floral pattern that came up from the floor on each side of the fireplace.

"The rose knows," he said, reaching out without hesitation and twisting down one of the leaves on the right side until it pointed toward the ground.

"This be the tricky part." Back across the room to a hat rack on the front wall. Two fancy cloth caps were hanging from metal hooks there, and he impatiently tossed them behind him onto the floor.

"They don't turn 'less you do the other stuff first, right?"

Elspeth, who was just standing there with her mouth open, watching, said nothing as he twisted first the far right hook a quarter turn, the third from the right a half, and finally the hook on the far left a full turn. There was a clicking sound.

"There," he said, "that's it. Now just put everything back in reverse order, and . . ." He did so. "Then push here."

A door opened in the wall. He slipped through, followed by the others.

"We need torches," Thaddeus remarked. And then added, "Oh," as Elspeth flipped the switch, illuminating the long tunnel with fluorescent lamps embedded in the ceiling. The narrow passageway led parallel to the inside wall, and then to a flight of descending stairs. Once below ground, the passage widened out and led further down in a winding manner. There was now an eerie, low humming that added atmosphere, which Thaddeus recognized as the sound of the hidden generator that fed the lamps.

"Thou rememberest well what I did long ago. Indeed, much better than do I," Elspeth murmured in awe.

"There's a point to that," Theseus suggested, "that you should consider. Be this way. You thinking about fucking me over, I know about it before you do it. You dig?"

"Nay, nay, my heart beats pure beneath these luscious breasts," Elspeth assured him. "Verily do I dig thee in this matter. Am I then such a fool as to fall off a precipice jumping for the moon, when what I most desire is within a mere hop of my reach?"

"I don't know what you just said, but I believe you," Thaddeus answered.

From behind them, Tippi tossed in, "She'd cut your throat for a nickel."

To which Thaddeus replied, "Minute she think it, I'll know it. In fact, before she know she thinking it, I'll know."

Elspeth grumbled, "Surely if thou understandest thine own talk, thou canst understand me, or anyone else for that matter, even be they from LA, where everyone speaketh a dark, foreign tongue."

Finally the path leveled out and made a sharp turn, and they saw a door at the end of it.

"It leadeth into a big closet in the royal kitchen," Elspeth informed them. And sure enough, they came out into a great room where enormous pots of fragrant sauces bubbled slowly on four large stoves, with nobody there to watch them.

Through there, Elspeth led them swiftly down a hall and outdoors, through the courtyard, and back indoors again. Directly toward a room with the door smashed out and an aged guard outside in the hall who informed them in a trembling voice, "Don't go in there, sir and ladies, if you got any wish to live out yer life to its natural end."

Thaddeus rushed in through the open doorway and took in the scene that had been blaring at him psychically from outside in the corridor. Only now he fully understood it.

"Yellow Cloud," he said in a hoarse voice, and he stood there, riveted, fixated on the scene before him on the floor.

Elspeth and Tippi, followed by Mrs. Lim, who now had her sword out, moved past him, then pulled up suddenly, feeling the hair on their arms and the backs of their necks ripple and a cold chill hit their spines as they took it all in.

The swirling, agonized form hovered over the body on the floor. Billowing and shifting. A terrible stench issued from it, and now it made a noise, a sort of sigh. It sensed fresh food.

Suddenly it floated up and rushed at them eagerly. Tippi could see, inside of it, the form of what had once been human, could read the agony of what she knew had to be the essence of Raphael's enslaved father. But any empathy she was starting to feel was jolted out of her as the creature let loose its paralyzing psychic scream of unimaginable hunger, freezing everyone in their tracks. To this ghoul, the actual rending of flesh and spilling of blood was only secondary, a side effect, a celebration really, of the ecstasy that occurred as it absorbed life force. And when it zeroed in on its prey, it could not be distracted until it had fed, and it was zeroed in on Tippi, and she felt certain that all the powers of the stone would not save her from it. All of this she knew in a glance, in an instant, an instant which froze her as solid as if she were a cube of ice in a tray in someone's fridge. She could not even open her mouth to scream.

Though the thing that settled over her was more like some sickening form of corrosive acid fog than a creature, within the nauseating greenish-yellow swirl Tippi could make out only the faintest hint of human features. Someone from outside shouted, "Oh no, please no, not Tippi!" The billowing cloud hesitated and the features came clear for just one moment, expressing confusion and torment as restraint battled hunger. Clearly it was struggling against itself with unimaginable ferocity.

Then the instant was gone. It billowed and swept on past her and out the door.

Outside, someone screamed—the unlucky guard in the hall.

"It's liable to kill everybody in the castle," Thaddeus exclaimed. He leaped to the wall and threw the switch, lowering the drawbridge. Another scream.

"Let's hope it goes outside."

It was only then that they realized who had shouted at the creature to spare Tippi.

"Rafe's still alive," Thaddeus gasped. "But how . . . ?"

He ran to where Raphael, who had now lapsed back into unconsciousness, lay, and kneeled down, placing his hand over Raphael's forehead. Blackjack was already there, curled up at his feet.

"The Yellow Cloud must have kept him alive."

Another scream from outside.

"Sounds like that thing heading straight down the hall," Thaddeus said. "Let us pray, brethren, that he just keeps on heading that way till he reach Los Angeles or Detroit, someplace like that."

"Farther away is much better," Mrs. Lim added.

Tippi thought about it. "He's running away from me. He doesn't want to hurt me because Raphael begged him not to. I think he's going to keep going that way—get out of the castle, feed off of whoever's still left alive outside. How's Raphael?"

"That Yellow Cloud thing's got his daddy mixed up in there somewhere inside itself," Thaddeus said, thinking out loud. "His dad's got enough control to have kept Raphael alive, when the only thing the rest of it knows is 'kill and eat.' Kept it from killing you. But now it's out of control. Not likely stop till it eats the whole fucking village. Much as I hate to say it, we just got to go after it." Big pause, followed by a sigh. "You stay here with Rafe, and I'll go for it."

Tippi was just standing there, shaking her head.

"Got to," he said. He was now sitting cross-legged on the floor, cradling Raphael's head in his lap. "The war is horror enough without loosing that thing on these poor people."

"Better them than us," Mrs. Lim threw in, then added nervously, "I Chinese. We don't like nasty demons."

"I figure it knows us," Thaddeus continued, ignoring her, "because of the stones. I get it to settle on me and use my stone to try and control it. Take it into some other dimension and try to leave it there." His voice trailed off. "At least we got to try."

"Damn," Tippi whispered, fighting back tears. "You mean me. It knows who I am. And you're the healer. You have to stay here with Raphael. Besides, I'm the fighter. All of your powers are passive. I'm the aggressive one. I have to do it. Damn, isn't being a Guardian great?"

"You haven't even had time to get used to that stone, Tippi. This is no job for a beginner."

Tippi shook her head. "Right," she said, "no job for anybody. We're wasting time. We both know I've got to try it. Take good care of Rafe for me." She turned her back on them.

"How will you find it?"

Blackjack barked.

She turned back and looked into the dog's small, souped-up eyes. Had it answered her question?

"Okay, Fido," she said, "come on." The two left the room.

Then Mrs. Lim said, "I will go very cautiously out the drawbridge and see if I can find Mr. Smitty and his band of merry men, and lead them back here. But if I see ugly demon, I will run back here so fast so you can protect me." Then she, too, was gone.

For a while Thaddeus just sat there, monitoring Raphael's life forces with his psychic sense. The wound had already stopped bleeding, which was amazing. His breathing was shallow, but even. He was hanging in there.

So the Yellow Cloud, the most devastating beast of prey known to the Guardians, from any world, was capable of healing. Or was that somehow only the part that was Raphael's father, Brice? The old man, Corbo, had been able to control Yellow Cloud. But just barely, and at a price to his life force. But Tippi was not the old man. Nor was Raphael. Nor himself, for that matter.

"Good luck, Tippi," he said aloud. "You'll need it."

It was only then that he took a moment to wonder where the hell Elspeth had slipped off to.

# 33

───◈───

INSIDE THE MAIN room of the castle, there was little indication that a war was going on or that a monster was out there among the pillagers. Here everything moved in a slow, orderly fashion. Trumpets were blown, flowers strewn. The words that had been said over and over for hundreds of years and solidified into ritual were chanted by solemn-faced priestesses.

A small group of witnesses—five had been chosen to represent Sou Wiccingham, and five the north—sat in a straight line on uncomfortable wooden chairs, facing the center of the room. A ceremonial dais had been set up there, with a vermilion cloth draped over it. On top of this, the royal scepter lay waiting for Elena and William II, who faced each other from across the room, to meet in the middle.

And now, for the first time, as four young virgins sang in eerie high-pitched voices sacred hymns to the Goddess, Dame Beatrice, the ancient high priestess of the Wicca, standing at the right hand of the king, was startled to spot Elspeth. The upstart witch was staring at her from across the room, where she stood at the right hand of Elena.

The old witch scribbled something on a piece of paper and, as silently and unobtrusively as possible, summoned a young girl from a group of white-clad youths, and sent the child to deliver the message to Elspeth.

It said: *"Where's Diana?"*

Elspeth wrote on it, *"Dead. Long live Elspeth."*

Soon the girl was back again.

This time the note read, *"If thou art Wicca, then why art thou not at my side now?"*

Elspeth read it and smiled. She wrote, *"Alas, I do not find thee pleasant company,"* and sent the girl back.

But here she was again.

*"Dost thou realize what thou hast just said?"* the note read.

Elspeth answered, *"Thou art the one here who is senile, not I."*

Elspeth could tell from across the room that the message phase was over. She reached out and put her hand on Elena's shoulder and said, " 'Tis almost time. Thou shalt prevail. Verily I have invested much faith in thee."

Then she frowned. "For should thou be not able"—she ran her finger across her long white throat—"it surely shall be time for the world to kiss the lovely Elspeth good-bye."

# 34

THE SUN WAS finally going down on this most horrid of days. At least Tippi assumed that was why the light was fading from the fog.

She had worried about what she would do if she ran into stragglers. Thought of taking one of Thaddeus's handguns, but realized it would be worse than useless. she had never fired a gun at a moving target, and understood instinctively that it was very difficult to hit one, despite all of the bullshit she had seen in the movies.

She was now in possession of one of the three remaining stones of power (it was now three, since one of the original four had disappeared with Violet's brother William), but she hadn't any experience using it. She knew that she had a lot of natural wild talent, and felt confident she could misdirect, confuse, or control one or two people, but doubted she could do much if she ran into a group of four or five looters. From either army—it made no difference which one now.

But her fears turned out to be for nothing. She was following a trail of dead men. Burned-out husks, barely recognizable as human anymore. Somehow this did not comfort her.

Then she had sensed a riderless horse in the fog. Silently she called it to her, and it had come. The stone had no problem helping her perform that simple feat of psychic strength, anyway.

Once on horseback, she simply followed the joyful dog, who barked once and then took off as though he had been shot out of a cannon.

In no time she had crossed the field and reached the edge of the city, where she witnessed a charming little scene.

Ye Old Shaver Shoppe had been broken into. The woman inside, raped and killed—in which order, Tippi could not guess—and the five brutes, one of whom got caught with his pants down, had now become Yellow Cloud's prey. She heard or sensed the screaming, she wasn't sure which, through the fog. And now she pulled up her horse and watched through the smashed-out window as the creature killed and feasted on the last of the rapists.

She could feel the creature's agonizing hunger, and also the momentary remorse that must have been from the part of the creature which was Raphael's father's ghost. Then everything was swallowed up in a feeding frenzy.

*I am going to die here,* she thought. *The only question is, Can I survive long enough to get this ghost cloud somewhere else?* She shuddered.

Then she thought of the dog. "Blackjack," she said to him out loud, automatically adopting, without knowing it, Corbo's style of focusing her psychic sending, "go back. I don't need you anymore."

Blackjack whined and writhed.

"No, really, you go back. And do not under any circumstances attack this ugly beast. Now go on. Blackjack. Go on."

He whined some more and then turned and reluctantly trotted off into the darkening fog.

"Guess I won't need you anymore, either." She dismounted and swatted her steed on the butt, and it was gone. Then, quickly and effortlessly, she used the power of the stone to open a mystic doorway into a world she knew only too well: her world of gray shadows. The same one Violet had rescued her from an eternity ago. At last she turned back to the Shaver Shoppe and the hideous creature it harbored. *Okay,* she said to herself, and tried to send out a signal to it, but couldn't seem to get started. Tried to speak, but momentarily couldn't seem to. *Want to live, I guess,* she said to herself. Then she took a deep breath. *Come on, Tippi, let's do it.*

"Mi, mi, mi," she sang, finding her voice. "Maybe for the last time," she added to the song. Then shouted, "Okay, yellow fellow"—*most unmellow yellow,* she thought—"here I am! Tippi, the morsel of delight. Come and get it while it's hot."

Instantly the creature flowed out the window and darted at her, swimming through the air, fast as a great white shark. Then it stopped abruptly.

A voice that seemed to issue not so much from it as from someplace far away deep inside of it moaned, "Oh no, no, no, please no, please . . ."

"Hey, come on, big guy." She backed toward the dimensional doorway she had opened, which hung behind her like a tunnel into the fog.

And then it rushed her and flowed onto her, and all she could do was scream in agony, but it was muffled, and there wasn't any way to breathe because she was the hideous, stinking creature, part of it, but the part that was dying. She twisted around and stumbled in the direction she thought the doorway was, screaming in panic again and again, but nothing was coming out but a sorry, miserable, little mournful sigh, like the dying breath of a mouse in the bloody jaws of a cat.

# 35

---

I T WAS STARTING. Slowly, in time to the beating of ceremonial drums, the two elegant figures, he all in gold, she in white, moved across the floor toward each other. Elspeth's hand fell away from Elena's shoulder. She could only stand where she was and watch helplessly as the bag lady who would be queen moved out to meet the king in the center of the immense room. But at least the flashy witch in the black commando jumpsuit had been able to charge up her minor stone from Tippi's greater one, and one thing she could do now, the only thing she could do, was to shield Elena from old Dame Beatrice's surreptitious psychic attack. As for surviving the force from the scepter, Elspeth and her bag-lady protegée would both just have to hope that her original instinct had been correct, and that Elena was the one.

# 36

WHEN THE THREE time travelers finally arrived back at Corbo's hut in the desert, after dropping off Germanicus, things were found to be much as Corbo had left them. Young Elena, his apprentice, was still waiting inside the shack. Corbo could feel her stalking around the room restlessly, waiting for him to return. After all, to her, he had been gone for several minutes. She was already bored and upset.

He shook his head and looked around him. How could anyone find this place boring? The stark silence of the desert. The little shack. The old beat-up Chevy pickup parked out front. The stretch of empty blazing highway in the distance, and a couple of languid lizards, all shimmering in the heat, light, and silence. Corbo sighed: home sweet home.

After a moment or two of breathing in the silence, he said, "Ketoko, go your way, for now. Once I let Theseus know that Germanicus no longer has the girl, he will relinquish his control of you. You're free, except for me, of course."

In the bright clear light of the high desert, Ketoko was unbearable to look upon, and even Corbo avoided focusing his gaze for long while talking to him. "How did you find out it was Theseus?" he said in his hissing triple voice.

Corbo smiled wryly and held out his hands. "Who else?" he said simply.

"You always knew?"

"Of course," Corbo said. "The only thing I couldn't figure is why you would have been dumb enough to take Germanicus back there in the first place. Surely even you couldn't hate me enough to trust him."

Ketoko's silence was significant.

"Well, obviously you could and did."

"And once you knew it was Theseus controlling me, you figured it was her?" Ketoko dropped into a dramatic crouching position, pointing his arm as if his finger were a gun, at Donna, who was busy stretching her neck.

"Her or somebody like her," Corbo answered. "Sit around in a wading pool full of naked women with some fool for a while, and it's not too hard to figure out what makes him tick."

"Hey," Donna objected. "Someone like me? I don't think so, pookie. I'm one of a kind."

"Aren't we all?" Corbo remarked sadly. "Anyway, Ketoko, I'm not so much giving you leave to go as I am telling you to get out of here. I've still got things to do."

With a shout of rage, Ketoko simply disappeared, but the triple-voiced shout echoed in the empty desert for a long time. Finally it died away and was gone.

"At last," the old man sighed.

But of course the dancer was still there, standing behind him tapping her sandaled foot.

"So these guys was doing all this shit to you, that's what all this was about?"

He smiled a big full smile. "That's what they think," he said. "Let them think it."

He turned to face her, and smiled again: she was still moving and grooving, music or no music.

"This silence is kind of like music," she said. "I mean, you can dance to it."

He held out keys. "You can drive?"

"Does it have a radio?"

He nodded.

"Then I can drive it." She looked around as if making sure there were no missed clues in the empty environment. "I forgot to ask—*when* in America? Like Prince?"

The old man looked puzzled. "Which Prince?"

"Or the artist formerly known as . . ." Her voice died out as the old man shrugged.

"Maybe a little earlier?" she tried. "Like is all the music like Okie shit like Elvis Presley?"

The old man grimaced at the name. "English buffoons," he offered helpfully.

"Shit," she said. "Well, close enough, though. You did your best." She took the keys and eyed the old truck warily.

"Wait a minute." The old man took the paper bag, which he was still carrying, and tore off a piece. Then he fished around in the pockets of his shorts and dug out a little stub of a pencil, scribbled something on the piece of paper, and said, "You follow this little dirt road till you hit that highway over there, turn left and keep driving straight. You come to Joe's Filling Station, ask for Joe. Tell him that crazy old man Sanchez said for him to let you use his phone. Call this number. Someone will answer and say—I know, this is silly—but they will say, 'Why should we have to die?' To which you must answer, 'Because we are so boring.' " He shrugged. "I make up the passwords."

He made her repeat it.

"The operator will put on a man who will identify himself as Mr. Bucks. Tell him I gave you my little truck, and I need another one delivered here tonight. Just leave the keys in it. Maybe a lizard will steal it, but . . ." He shrugged.

Donna looked interested. "What kind of truck?"

"What kind do you think would be good?"

She closed her eyes, obviously thinking hard, but her hands were closed into fists, and she was circling them around along with her hips. "Does it have to be a truck?"

Corbo looked lovingly around him, as if for the last time. "No," he said, "I guess not."

"Some kind of Cadillac."

Corbo smiled again. "Okay, then, tell him some kind of Cadillac."

"Baby blue."

"A baby-blue Cadillac, then. And you need some money. How much do you want?"

She closed her eyes and thought about it. She had slipped her foot out of her sandal and was wiggling it in the hot sand.

"Two hundred thousand dollars," she said finally.

"Okay, then, tell him to leave two hundred thousand dollars in the trunk of the Caddie, and give an additional two hundred thousand to the woman waiting at the station."

She looked puzzled.

"You," he explained.

"Righteous," she said, and without another word got in the old pickup, started it up, and drove away. He never saw her again.

# 37

TIPPI WASN'T AWARE of where she was, or even who she was, for that matter. That she was walking, let alone why she was walking. Everything here was gray, shadowy, and indistinct. It seemed appropriate to her.

"Fading away," she said out loud. And then she finally hit that place (quite soon, actually) where she could walk no more, and went straight down. The cement, or whatever this gray unformed substance she was walking on represented, was far less punishing to fall on than the sidewalks back home, but it could hardly have mattered less to Tippi. Stone or no stone, she wasn't ready for this. Whatever it was.

She found herself standing at the end of a long, dark tunnel. She could see light up ahead, and she knew she was heading for the light. There was a figure waving toward her, but it was so bathed in light she could not make it out. No, two figures. She walked toward them. She was thrilled to see Violet waving to her, smiling. She was wearing some sort of lavender gown Tippi had never seen before, and no jewelry. She was so lovely. It wasn't really that she had changed at all, but somehow she had lost that "don't touch" look. She looked even better now that she was dead.

And the other figure, he was simply no different in death than he had been in life. Smiling that sweet smile, a beautiful, angelic-looking golden youth, so tickled to see her. As always.

"But, Raphael," she said, "what are you doing here?"

# 38

---

"WE GET OUTTA this, things gonna change." Thaddeus found himself talking out loud to Raphael from time to time, as though he were telling a child stories before he went to sleep, although Raphael obviously couldn't hear him.

"We goin' to work on our thang. Put our act on the road. Play us some sounds. Think I'll take up sax. Leave the guitar for you. You the one play it the best. It's natural for you, you know. For me, I just keep wishin' it was a horn.

"Guitar white man's tool. Blacks invented drums, reeds, most everything else except violin and accordion. Italian must have invented the accordion, or maybe the monkey invented it. Mexican invented the xylophone. Not much, but it drive you crazy.

"We buy one of those new minivans. Mercedes be the hot one. Throw yo ugly little white bulldog in the back and just go. Get away somewhere. Anywhere."

He closed his eyes. Unaccountably, he was drifting off to sleep. He seemed to see himself driving through a long tunnel. Up ahead, in that incredible light, was . . .

His eyes snapped open. He became aware that tears were streaming down his cheeks, and he was making too much noise for breathing to account for it. He knew why. He was afraid to look down at the man whose head rested in his lap. But he was aware that the breathing had stopped.

"Oh, hell and damnation," he said, startling himself. He had been a little boy and Mama had been put in the hospital for a while, just to catch herself up on some rest. But she must have needed a lot of rest, because a long time went by without his seeing her. He had had brief moments of incredible despair, but then he always believed them: "Home any day now. She fine as can be. Gettin' better."

Then one day his father came home, looked at him, and said in this wooden voice, simply, "Hell and damnation." Tears had been streaming down his cheeks, too, and what he said a few minutes later, when he was able to speak, had been lost on Thaddeus. He had already known what it would be. And he had never believed them again, always left that room for doubt, just as he had not believed himself when he made comments like, "You're going to make it, Rafe. You looking better already. Stone'll keep you alive, just hang in there." He had known all along that a dagger in the heart is, after all, a dagger in the heart.

"You fuckin' liar," he said to himself in that same wooden voice, as he looked down upon the best and brightest of them all, and found him—gone.

# 39

ELENA, THE REVITALIZED lady of the lake, was so beautiful that as she approached King William he almost had to avert his eyes. In the white, low-cut gown (bridal, sacrificial, is there a difference?, rich reddish-gold hair decked with bright blue and pink blossoms and green leaves, Tahitian-lagoon shade of green eyes, she was like an apparition, an angel from heaven. For the first time it dawned on him, incredibly, bizarrely, but undeniably, that there was a link between her and his new court Fool. The eyes, the hair. But where she was serious, inward, the crazy Fool was brimming with outward-spilling joy and energy, not at all unlike that white dog he kept.

But they were so much alike that once you saw it, it was virtually undeniable. Just one more amazing thing that had happened to the king since her arrival. And indeed, as they met in the middle of the great hall, yet another amazing thing became clear, shocking him even more.

Everyone was so tense that you could not really pretend that the war outside had not penetrated in here. Probably hardly anything left outside to be king of, yet here they were. He knew the Wicca were waiting on pins and needles for him to dominate the "queen" and thus South Wiccingham, so they could pull together and rebuild. And was also aware that Elspeth—always the wildest of the Wicca—had rebelled, and was somehow backing Elena.

But as he looked into those green eyes across the gleaming scepter, the new thing—not new of itself, but his awareness of it—became at first a pleasant pang, then a universe in itself touching everything he knew or had ever heard of. Changing everything.

"Wait," he said very loudly, startling everybody in the enormous room.

"I've got a proposition to make," he whispered this time, for Elena's ears only.

Elena's eyes opened even wider, searching his warily. Strangely, she smiled a nervous little smile.

"What is this proposition of yours, Your Majesty?"

His Majesty gestured imperiously back toward the crowd at his end of the room. Then at the crowd hovered around Elspeth. Then he used a word he had learned from his new Fool.

"Fuck 'em all," he said, causing Elena to actually take a step back and blink.

Moving with beautiful, liquid grace for a tall, rather plump man who was not an athlete, he rose up on one leg and kicked over the dais with the scepter on it. One enormous breath exhaled from the group beast in the room.

"I w-w-wouldn't hurt you for anything or anyone, so-so-so let them k-kill us or whatever they are going to do, but . . . Oh, and for G-G-Goodness's sake, don't call me Your Majesty. Just William."

He held out his hand. Outcries were coming from everywhere. A loud hum arose.

Elena stepped forward warily and put out her hand. "Well, William, you are just one wild and crazy guy, I must admit," she said, as his hand enfolded hers.

The buzz increased to a veritable roar.

# 40

THE TUNNELS WERE gone, but a dog was barking—Blackjack?—and Tippi was simply looking into beings formed of pure light.

What a dream! The Yellow Cloud creature was there, but no longer enveloping her. One of the light creatures seemed to be holding it with an arm that disappeared into the middle of it. Like it was casually holding a hand puppet.

"Take the Yellow Cloud creature back to where it came from," one of the others said. "But don't hurt him."

The two disappeared—imploded, really. Like turning off a lightbulb.

"We are talking out loud for you. Our thoughts are too vast for you to comprehend."

"I, uh, don't read thoughts anyway," Tippi said, although that wasn't totally true.

"Then, as always, our choice was perfect. We sense that, unlike the dog, you require information. So briefly, we will answer your questions." It gestured to her.

"You healed me." She sat up and groaned, but really, she was feeling better fast.

"You were what you human peoples called dead. But we removed obstacles that would have kept you from functioning."

"Thank you." She shielded her eyes. "You're too bright. Can you turn yourself down?"

Immediately they dimmed, and now she was surprised to see she could distinguish both males and females in the group.

"Same on every level," one of them said, in answer to her thoughts.

"But don't thank us. We don't care about you. We did it for the dog. Unlike you, he is perfect. Clear. He operates off the universal principle—love. He has no complicated motives. We could hardly turn him down."

"Who are you?" Tippi asked. Their features were definitely humanoid, but so delicate, so perfectly formed.

"Those of you who have been blessed with our presence refer to us by many names. The 'White Lodge' is a popular one. Though by 'white,' what is meant is lack of color. 'Light Lodge' would have been more accurate. Let us say simply that in all these myriad dimensions and universes, we are the most evolved beings."

Tippi stood up. She was already strong enough to stand up! Looked around her. Gray. Gray.

"What am I doing here?"

"You came here to carry the Yellow Cloud creature where it could do no harm. We appreciate that. Though we must point out to you that death is not real. There's no harm in it. Yet we understand you cannot possibly grasp this. Like the dog, you are doomed to live in fear of the unknown. Even though, ha ha ha"—spoken rather than laughed—"you wear one of the living crystals that guard your world, but will never understand what that implies, because"—it paused—"because your puny mind is like to us as the mind of an ant is to you. Ha ha ha. That is a good joke, yes."

"Not really," Tippi informed him.

"Nor is your heart pure like the heart of this fine dog Guardian. Ha ha."

"How did Blackjack find you?"

Another pause.

"Hard to explain this to so primitive a being. The crystals exist in every dimension simultaneously. They are reservoirs of power and information. But they are capable of volitional decision-making."

"They are alive?"

"They are more than alive. Like us. Yet, unlike us, they are also not really alive at all."

Tippi blinked, trying to clear her vision and see them better. But it hurt to look at them.

"I don't get it," she said.

"We told you you wouldn't. But let me finish. The crystal can find anything anywhere. The dog's purity of heart allowed the crystal to transport him to us.

"Then, since human beans are too stupid to understand, the crystal allowed us to communicate a few of its observations—things which obviously to more intelligent beans must be done."

"It's 'beings,' not 'beans.' The crystal transported the dog?"

"Ha ha ha, again you are too stupid. When you open a door to travel to another world, it is simply that you have removed certain obstacles so that the connections between the crystals can open. Surely even you can see that?"

"Yeah, sure, okay," Tippi snapped.

"You are beautiful when you are mad," one of them said, mimicking John Wayne's voice.

Tippi shook her head. "Spare me, will you, guys? No more jokes, please. I mean, have mercy."

"Ah, yes, I see," it said. "Jokes are a form of torture. Obvious, once it's pointed out. We were not sure what their purpose was. Sorry."

"Uh, that's okay. Look, White Lodge and all that—I thought you guys were supposed to be ascended masters?"

"If that is so," he said, "we are so far ascended that it would be impossible for anyone to tell."

"Including you?"

"Especially us."

Now Tippi glanced over at Blackjack. In their presence, he seemed to have converted the white of his body to the true light it was supposed to represent, at least partially. He gleamed, he wiggled, he pranced, and made a series of strange little ecstatic sideways hops. He shimmered, leaving psychedelic afterimages behind him in the air as he jumped and writhed. The only thing about him that had remained the same was the dull, opaque piece of black quartz he wore around his neck. Raphael's stone. Or was it? It was Blackjack's now, that much was for sure, and he was doing a good job of using it. That reminded her of Raphael.

"I've got to get back. Not that it wasn't a pleasure, but Raphael—"

The spokesman for the shining beings held out his hand to stop her.

"—is dead," he completed the sentence for her. "The dog is taking us there. We will take you with us, as the dog would be upset if you were hurt by some of your war heroes, who are out there pillaging. Oh, what a mess you feeble-minded Guardians have made of everything. Yet, you tried. You accomplished one thing that was very fortuitous."

"What?" Tippi couldn't resist, but knew she'd wish she had.

"Gave the stone to the dog so that he summoned us. And now we are here. Come."

He waved his hand and a large dark portal opened next to him. Barking happily, Blackjack led them through it into the drawbridge control room of the castle.

# 41

THE OLD MAN watched the truck drive away, then sighed and went in the house. Elena was sitting in her chair in front of the little table with a mirror over it, but she had turned it around so that she was facing the door.

"I'm back," he said.

"You've only been gone a few minutes," she answered.

"But Elena," he insisted, "that few minutes was an eternity."

"I see," she said, looking angry.

Corbo waited.

"I thought I heard talking," she said.

"Yes, there was talking," Corbo answered.

"I thought I heard the truck start up and drive off."

"Yes, the truck is gone."

"I see," she said again.

"You know, Elena, if you are so damn curious, why didn't you just go outside and take a look for yourself?"

Her eyes widened in furious disbelief. "You told me, no matter what, not to go outside."

Corbo clapped his hands three times. "That is a good answer, Elena. And that is exactly what I wanted to hear. Now that you have that down pat, listen to me carefully. I want you to go outside now, and no matter what you see or hear, don't come in here until I tell you."

"Fine!"

The door slammed so hard that it almost took the rickety old wall along with it. Corbo went over and calmly opened it and shouted after her. "And whatever you do, don't look in the window."

Then he went over to the old, worn Indian rug he liked to sit on and sat down, cross-legged. Closed his eyes. "Oh, Theseus," he whispered, "wherefore art thou, Theseus?"

"How could you do this to me?" The answer came flooding back to him from somewhere deep within. Deep within, but so loud it hurt.

"It was easy," Corbo answered inwardly.

Silence. Then Corbo projected, "Yoo hoo, still there?"

"She's all right? You got her free of Germanicus—I guess I ought to thank you for that."

"Not yet," Corbo informed him ominously. "She's in my little truck right now, tooling on down the highway. Playing the radio at full blast."

"So?"

"So you know how paranoid a man can get, mean guys like you and Ketoko and the big Nazi plotting against you all the time. I'm afraid I panicked and had the truck wired with explosives."

Silence.

Then, "Explosives?"

Corbo projected an image of a truck exploding.

More silence.

"Hello," Corbo projected. "Knock knock, I said I—"

"I heard you."

"And over there in that trunk in the corner, I've got the controller. All I've got to do is press a button."

More silence. Then Theseus insisted, "You wouldn't do it. I know you better than that."

"Listen to me carefully, you fool, because we don't have that much time. To save England, I would blow up a whole flock of Playboy bunnies, along with Mother Teresa. And I would throw in the singing nun, the flying nun, and—"

"Okay, I believe you, what do you want?"

"—Attila the nun," Corbo finished. Then he got up, went over to the chest, fished around until he came out with what looked to be some kind of remote control, or perhaps just a child's toy, and studied it. "Don't want to accidentally hit the wrong button. Tell you what, I'll just hold it here until she's out of range. That way I can't make an innocent mistake."

"I agree. I agree. How many times do I have to agree?"

Corbo sat back down on his rug and communicated to Theseus. "Just help me out with one more little chore here, and then we can both rest—me for a few hours' sleep on this mat, and you for an eternity in your little wading pool. I need you to guide me. And I need your power." It occurred to him that this sounded rather like a prayer, and he smiled again at the thought. Theseus was probably used to being the object of prayers.

# 42

---

A NOTHER TIME, ANOTHER place, far away, Thaddeus was also sitting cross-legged on a floor, only he was cradling Raphael's head in his lap. He was crying, but absently, vacantly, as if he were really somewhere else, away from all the blood that had been shed.

"I will remember next time," he said softly to Tippi, ignoring completely the beings of light that had materialized along with her. She was not sure what he was talking about, but one of the White Lodge answered, "Not necessarily, foolish, fragile one. Some damage to those delicate cells in your head would make you forget. Should another violent human stab you there with a pointed piece of metal, for example."

Thaddeus nodded. "Yeah, you probably right. Something probably happen, make me forget, and it just go on and on. But it got Violet and Raphael this time, and he was the best of us."

"No," the being of light corrected him. "The dog is the best. But the being you call Raphael is certainly the second best among you. The rest of you are all caught up in that fantasy game you think of as ego versus the world, and all the time conniving and scheming to win nothing at all. How can you be pure enough so that you can merit our concern? You are just so fortunate that you have the dog."

One of the others went over to Thaddeus, kneeled down, and began moving his hands over Raphael's head, causing a weird cascade of rainbows in the air.

"He will be easy to fix, but it will be necessary to make a few alterations in his brain cells. So many have been destroyed. We're going to change his heart a little, too."

"He's breathing," Thaddeus said in awe. "He's starting to breathe. Oh, thank God, he's breathing."

"Whom does he mean by 'God'? Advanced beings like us, or beyond-everything?"

Tippi thought about it. "Probably like you."

"Then the dog is welcome."

Tippi glanced at Blackjack, who was still jumping and jiving. Still had things to do, places to go, obviously. He barked excitedly.

"All right, all right. First I must talk to the Tipster. Then shall I attend to your doggie task."

Tippi smiled. He was obviously picking up expressions from Thaddeus's mind.

"Two things," he said. "One: You must now lead the Guardians. Not Thaddeus, not Raphael, but you, oh crazy one."

Tippi just stood there with wide-open mouth and eyes. After a moment of stunned silence, she said: "What? I'm the newest, and as you pointed out, the craziest. I don't even know how to use the stone. What is this, anyway, an order or advice? What?"

"Oh, Tippi, tsk, tsk, tsk," he said. The others joined in, and the room was filled with a weird insectlike chant.

"Everything that we say is advice, but obviously should be treated as the strictest orders from God. Considering our relationship to you on the evolutionary scale."

Something about the way he said it . . . "Is there also something beyond you on that scale?"

"Oh, of course. It is called . . . Lord God Jehovah."

Silence.

Then, "Just kidding. Just another good joke. Ho, ho, ho."

The others joined in with a wooden chorus of ho-ho-ho's.

Thaddeus commented, "Jesus, Tippi, where did you pick up these bozos, deep within?"

"Or it could be Jesus or Allah," one of the others sang in a rich African-American voice, "but his friends call him Duke of Earle."

"Oh, for crying out loud," Tippi groaned. "Look, getting back to the subject. It makes no sense. You said yourself that Raphael is the best. In which case he should be the one."

"We said the dog was the best. Raphael, second best. But the best should never lead. Nor should they follow. They are an example of how to behave outside the group action, in all the little things which determine the direction of the evolution of the race. In fact, they are what the masses are evolving to be. Inside the group, they should neither give orders nor take orders, but be left free to take independent action whenever they deem it necessary for the success of the group. Or otherwise . . ." he added ominously.

"At any rate, it's a meaningless question. Raphael will do what he wants regardless of who's in charge. But keep an eye on this one." He pointed at Thaddeus. "He will feel that he should be in charge because he is smarter than you, but he is wrong. You are the strongest. The strong should lead. It is nature. You can force him to think for you."

Thaddeus blinked and shook his head. "Yeah, thanks, man," he said.

"You are most welcome, O smart one. Now I have one more thing to say to you. But it is for you to hear alone, O leader." He continued to speak, but only Tippi heard the words.

Blackjack, clearly seething with impatience, barked once more in his powerful, shocking voice. To his credit, he didn't bark often, thank the gods!

"And now we leave you. The dog has one last request."

"Wait," Tippi said. "If we ever need you again, is there some way you . . ."

The White Lodge began to laugh again in unison. This time it was "ha ha ha."

"You already think like the leader," their spokesman said. "I will try to make the answer simple enough for you to understand: No!"

And then, quite suddenly, the White Lodge, complete with their white dog and his stone, imploded and were gone, leaving only the faintest hint of phosphorescent afterimages in the air.

# 43

---

IN THE THRONE room, the shouting had died down. In the center of the room, Elena and King William the Second stood holding hands in the midst of all the turmoil.

"Do not worry thyself," he whispered to her. "No matter what they all do, I will stand with thee."

"All right. Me, too," Elena answered, overwhelmed.

At first, the ancient witch, Dame Beatrice, had shrieked orders for the guards to arrest them in the name of the Wiccan overseers.

But Elspeth had shouted conflicting orders from the opposite side. "Pay no heed to the old hag. She has been set aside by the Wicca, and myself appointed in her place. I order thee to throw her in chains instead, and lock her in the darkest dungeon, and I will attend to her later." Much later, Elspeth figured.

The guards started to move, stopped, looked back and forth at each other for guidance as to what to do to whom, finally gave up, and stood there with everyone else, waiting for whatever it was that was happening here to clarify itself.

Almost everyone was shouting conflicting advice and orders at once, and then suddenly everyone went quiet, also at once.

Elspeth and the ancient Wiccan high priestess were momentarily locked in a silent struggle of psychic powers. Since Dame Beatrice's psychic attacks were of late somewhat blunted due to the disintegration of concentration that often accompanies living practically forever, and since Elspeth's powers were at an all-time high due to having unknowingly charged up her magic bauble from Tippi's vastly more powerful crystal, they were deadlocked.

Then, both at once, they broke mental contact. They saw. They rushed to conquer. The royal scepter was on the floor; the throne was up for grabs. They went for it.

Elena and William the Second watched in amazement, without moving so much as a muscle, as the two women raced to the middle of the room.

Elspeth was the quicker, but the ancient dame's feet wore the wings of greed, and she was a lot faster than one would have thought possible. And just as Elspeth got there, the old lady simply dived to the floor like an expert baseball player sliding home. They both grabbed the scepter and tried to stand back up. But they didn't make it.

The raw psychic energy coursing through the scepter proved far stronger than either of them had estimated. Neither of them could handle it.

For a moment they froze there, clutching the scepter and twitching as if in the grip of a massive seizure. Which they were.

When they hit the floor, the old high priestess was dead, and Elspeth lay there twitching and foaming at the mouth, while the two groups of stunned onlookers witnessed the tragedy in silence.

At this exact moment the White Lodge and their dog materialized in the middle of the room, entering through an instant doorway which appeared out of thin air.

"This one's still twitching. Shall we let her die? She looks quite lively."

"I've always been a sucker for a pretty babe," another one answered. He hovered over Elspeth, making passes with one of his humanoid but slender, translucent hands.

"What about the other one? She's dead. Should we bring her back?"

Elspeth moaned and managed, in a raspy whisper, "Methinks she's much easier to get along with this way. I would thou left her thus."

"That sounds like good advice," the spokesman for the Lodge of Light said sincerely.

Meanwhile, Blackjack ran to Elena, where he practically writhed himself in half with joy. He had completed all of his master's wishes.

But although she saw the stone wrapped around the dog's neck, entwined in his collar, she did not go for it.

"Just hold on," King William advised her, squeezing her hand to remind her.

"Big joke," the Lodge spokesman announced. "The royal scepter would have proved too strong for any of them. This old dead one must have been afraid it wouldn't do the job. I see her now, at midnight last night with other witches, drawing up a 'cone of power,' as they call it. They are all sitting around it in a circle, trying to charge it up. They succeed. But they are too successful. This power battery would have killed either of these two people. Or anyone else in the room, for that matter. Ha ha ha, stupid humans."

He went over to where the dog pranced.

"Is this the woman? Oh, who would have thought? Very well, I will do what's necessary." He reached out and put his glowing hand on Elena's head. Elena moaned and swayed.

"Just hold on," William repeated. She held on.

"And now we have finished our work on this gross, ugly plane. Fetch, Blackjack."

Immediately, Blackjack scampered over and picked up the royal scepter with his powerful jaws and, prancing happily, showing no ill effects whatsoever, carried it back to the Lodge spokesman, who took it from him.

"The dog is king," somebody from Dame Beatrice's crowd shouted. "Long live the dog!" A few others started to shout, "The dog is king!" then petered out, still trying to process the information overload but unable to.

"The dog doesn't want to be King," the spokesman—apparently for the dog as well as for the Lodge—said. "But I'll take care of this nasty toy for you. I guess that makes me the king. Good-bye, dog."

And just like that, they were gone, royal scepter and all.

"The king has disappeared," someone mumbled. "Long live the king, wherever he is."

Now Elena was crying. "They took away from me something beautiful. And I'll never even know what it was. Oh, William, what should I do?"

He squeezed her hand. "Trust me. Just hang on." Blackjack barked happily in agreement.

In the drawbridge control room, Raphael opened his eyes and sighed.

"You awake. That's good news," Thaddeus remarked. "Just relax. Tomorrow we look for your mama. But she probably be okay."

"Mama?" Raphael looked puzzled. "Who's my mama?"

"Well, you do have a mama, Rafe, just like everyone else, and she—" Tippi signaled to him to hush up.

"You know," Rafe muttered, "I've got to sleep. It's a weird thing, but I can't remember anything about my mama. My childhood. Just you, Thaddeus. You my mama?"

Thaddeus looked at Tippi, who said, "Just do it, Thaddeus. Take my word for it and do what I tell you to. At least till this is over."

Thaddeus continued staring into her eyes, then smiled a bitter smile. "Sure," he said. "You the boss. Obviously." He looked down. "Look at that, he's asleep again already. I could use me some sleep myself. Wake up in a few days, figure out who won the damn war."

"Everybody lost," Tippi reminded him.

"Oh yeah," he said, extricating himself from Raphael and then taking off his stone and carefully lifting Raphael's head, draping it around his neck, laying it on his chest. "Till the dog bring his back. If ever."

He stretched out on the floor and closed his eyes.

"I'll stand guard," Tippi said, "till my commandos arrive. Should be any moment now."

Eyes still closed, Thaddeus chuckled, "You got commandos already, boss? Figures. Well, good night, sweet boss."

"Yeah," Tippi said. "I know: farting is such sweet sorrow."

But Thaddeus was already asleep. Along with Raphael and the two guards, and even poor Morgan, the would-be conqueror of LA, who was sleeping the big sleep.

Tippi sat down and propped her back against the far wall, facing the doorway, with the shotgun across her knees, waiting for Mrs. Lim and Smitty to arrive. She wondered what was going on out there now. Wondering hard, because the door had been bashed off the hinges, and there was nothing there but open doorway, and the drawbridge was down. Soon, she, too, felt an almost irresistible urge to fall asleep. But she stayed awake. And when Mrs. Lim finally arrived, leading Smitty and his little band of commandos, Tippi had them go back out and bring in mattresses from somewhere or other and drape blankets over the doorway and windows. And then she waited until finally Thaddeus and Raphael were tucked in and breathing evenly and a schedule of guards was set up to watch the door, before she lay down on the other mattress, sighed, and slept.

She dreamed she was a queen. Which, in a way, was true. And in a way was not true. And that's what dreams are like. As confusing as what we think of as real life.

# 44

THE NEXT MORNING the sun came up, the fog and rain dissipated, and the fighting, which had continued sporadically over the long night, died out.

Officially, the north won the war, as almost any clear-minded person would have predicted from the start. But no one could have foreseen what a close and costly battle it had been. And in the end, many of the results were similar to those which would have occurred had the other side been victorious.

The fancy shops and inns of Nor Wiccingham had virtually all been broken into and looted, a large portion of its citizens raped and murdered, some by crazed soldiers from the south, but mostly by its own army. To top all this off, a legend had been born that all the violence and anger in the hearts of both sides had summoned forth a hideous demon who had issued from the castle, swept across the grassy plain from the drawbridge and into the town, devouring every human being within its reach. Then had the angels of light come forward at last to protect what little was left of order in a world plunged into chaos. For by now it was clear to all the citizens who had survived that the only thing worse than war was civil war.

So, while clearly the army of the north had been victorious, it was the north's city that wound up suffering the brunt of the damage. For not only was the southern town unreachable, the bridges having been destroyed, but the outlying farmlands lay quite a ways beyond the simple hamlet. The lands and properties of Sou Wiccingham were untouched. Only there were a lot of dead farmers.

Finally, out of desperation, the lands were united as the new king and queen, working together for the first time in history, set a great many formerly rich and idle titled landowners to work. Task forces were formed either to work on farms or to rebuild the towns. They were presided over by whoever seemed the most fit for the task, regardless of rank or geographical origin. Many a Nor Wiccingham nobleman found himself working harder than he could ever have imagined on a Sou Wiccingham farm, taking orders from a local peasant.

The first order had been the bridges, and by that afternoon, Tippi's commando forces, with the help of some of the peasant soldiers on the other side who had arrived too late to cross over, and some of the boats which had been hidden away, had built a makeshift bridge that could be crossed by one man at a time. It would be a week before they had a bridge you could ride a horse across.

But first, a series of ropes had been secured to what was left of the old bridges, and then a construction, more like a very long ladder than a bridge, was, with many mishaps, guided across and secured to the pilings. The ropes were then raised to provide guide rails, and a cheer went up. The real work could now begin.

That same afternoon, Raphael had awakened to find himself in a bed— his old room in the castle. Blackjack was there, curled up at his feet. He could feel the bed shake as the happy dog began to wag. But also there was, astonishingly, Tippi.

"Tippi," he whispered in a hoarse voice, "what's happened? Where's Violet? The war?"

Tippi sighed, took a deep breath, and said, "The war's over. Your mother's okay. We'll talk about the rest of it later. Okay?"

Raphael closed his eyes and mumbled something.

"What?"

"My mother? Funny thing, I don't seem to have any memory of ever having a mother. Must be some kind of temporary —sorry, I've got to . . ."

He drifted off to sleep again.

Tippi did not see it as a "funny thing." She remembered clearly the spokesman of the White Lodge informing them, "it will be necessary to make a few alterations in his brain cells."

But if that surprised her it was nothing compared to the shock she got when later that day she spoke for the first time in many long years to the queen, Elena.

Recognition had been instant. "Oh my God, Tippi, and you're wearing one of the stones. You must have won. It was so long ago. What happened to . . . ?"

The last time Elena had seen Tippi had been during a war. A different one, but a war nonetheless. They had been fighting over the stones, when the demon Ketoko had simply blasted Elena's brain away and deposited her, mindless, on the streets of Santa Monica. One more homeless wretch to deal with. But if she harbored any ill will over it, it wasn't showing.

"We, uh, lost," Tippi said nervously.

"But here you are anyway, wearing my stone."

"It's not your stone," Tippi said. "It's . . ." she faltered "Violet's. And his"—she gestured behind her toward Thaddeus—"well, it used to belong to Raphael. And now Raphael's got yours."

It was what Elena said next that threw her.

"Oh no," she said, and burst into tears. "Violet's gone. But who's Raphael?"

Tippi's mind reeled, but she had enough presence of mind to whirl and gesture to Thaddeus: not a word.

"He is my Fool," King William explained. "A witty fellow. With a heart. Unusual in a Fool, that. A brave man. Fought most v-valiantly in the war. G-G-Goddess only knows which side. K-k-kept raising and lowering the drawbridge for some reason. That white dog. That was Bl-Bl-Blackjack, his dog."

Elena stopped weeping for Violet. A strong, unnameable emotion swept her, and she seemed almost to remember something, but couldn't. Then she had it: a handsome man and his white dog, glimpsed on the drawbridge. And that in turn swept her with another strong emotion that again she could not place.

"His eyes," King William continued, unabashed, "remind me so much of . . ." But suddenly he began to stammer wildly, and simply could not finish that sentence. He never would have guessed that this incapacitating flow of confusion was issuing from the mind of the small but fierce-looking, ageless woman whom Elena called Tippi.

The next day, Tippi and Raphael set off on a small pilgrimage to the sacred lake, led by Elspeth the Almighty.

"At least, almighty for the time being," she explained. "Queen of the Witches of the North and South, high priestess, etc. Until the rest of the Wicca come from Los Angeles and take it all back."

"They will do that?" Tippi asked. She had cleverly used her newfound powers the day before to push the idea of the pilgrimage into Elena's consciousness. So Raphael was to be the first male to test the waters of the sacred lake.

Elspeth had at first protested, but once Elena caught the idea, she had liked it. And the king had backed her up. As he apparently intended to do in just about everything. Tippi wondered, was there something going there? The king was easy enough to read, but Elena, who could tell?

"So you think the Wic-Org will regroup in LA, come back here, and take over?"

"Indeed I do more than just think it so, I know it so. The sacred waters will bring them back, and they will want more control, not less. They will bring guns, and all the modern instruments of war. And they will initiate a new set of rules, more rigid than before, more rigorously enforced."

Tippi smiled at the phrase "instruments of war," as if a war were a symphony played by musicians instead of a bloody, mindless fight.

"So all this"—she searched for the word—"devastation will have been for nothing?"

Elspeth nodded. "So it would seem."

"And yourself?"

"I have a position here, the support of the king. I will use it to bargain with. Who knows? Elspeth hath risen from the ashes before, and, Goddess willing, will somehow do so again."

"And what about Elena?"

Tippi stopped moving up the path and turned back to face her.

"That one puzzleth me. Originally she was nothing but a figurehead, and now that her role had been fulfilled, one would have expected the king to cast her aside and reassert himself. Yet he does not. In fact, he does everything in his power to validate her position. Since bathing in the lake, she is indeed a luscious wench. Can His Royal Highness be scheming on her sexy bod?"

They started back up the path, which led uphill through a pine forest.

"I was wondering about that myself," Tippi said. And then as an afterthought, "How are you doing, Rafe?"

No answer. They followed the path back a ways, to find him sitting on a log alongside of Thaddeus. And Blackjack once again curled up at his feet.

"Sorry," he said with a wan smile, "the stone is healing me, but after all, I was clear dead."

"You two want to go ahead?" Thaddeus said. "Okay with us."

"No." Tippi shook her head. "We go together. But I still don't see why you're lugging around that ugly green guitar."

Raphael had the Custom Legend slung around his shoulder, and now, in answer, he took it off and strummed an ominous chord. It reverberated through the forest, echoing off the trees and eliciting a couple of outraged replies from the birds.

"I don't know," he said. "Somehow it seems right."

They continued their journey, only this time more slowly and with more rest stops in between, Raphael leaning on Thaddeus for help and Blackjack leading the way.

Then they heard him barking up ahead somewhere, obscured by trees, and found him at the summit, looking down a little ways on a clear blue lake shimmering in the light of midday.

The women rushed ahead down the path, and by the time Thaddeus and Raphael got there, Tippi and Elspeth were both naked, wading in.

"Come on, you sissies," Tippi shouted joyfully. "Wow, I can feel it already, tingling up my legs. It's wonderful."

"Indeed it is," Elspeth shouted back at them. "Take off thy pants, boys. I will not bite thee."

"I bet," Thaddeus mused, as Raphael took his arm from around his shoulder and simply waded in fully clothed.

"At least take off your guitar," he advised, unbuckling his belt. It struck him how medieval and archetypal Raphael looked, in his green tights and loose jerkin, with his round-backed green guitar slung over his shoulder, and his loose, shoulder-length red-blond hair, as the boy simply disappeared into the blue.

# 45

W<small>HAT RAPHAEL SAW</small> when he looked out into the lake was the two lovely, naked nymphs splashing in the water and giggling like ancient maenads. They were so lovely, Elspeth with her long witchy black hair, white skin, and red lips, her slender yet voluptuous body, and Tippi, small and childlike, but spicy as ginger, or maybe cinnamon. The beauty of the sunlight playing on them and on the clear water caused a surge of delirious joy to rise up in him out of nowhere and dispel the pain and aching in his heart. Just to see them like this, this simple moment, gave him rebirth. Despite all the terror, the struggle, the loss. These moments shouted to you that life was always worth living. Was always worth starting over. Now.

Then he looked directly down into the lake around his knees, and although he was not aware that it was odd, he saw the oddest thing there.

The sparkling water immediately sucked him into its playful dance, disorienting him, fascinating him. Was it alive? The patterns it formed somehow became more urgent and meaningful. The movement speeded up—hidden planes revealed themselves, shattered, re-formed, as the dance grew wilder.

And suddenly he found himself staring into a long dark tunnel that opened up into . . .

Everything lurched, and for a moment it was as if he were going to fall off the edge of the earth. But the earth revolved and everything righted itself. Never thinking about what he was doing, he simply walked down that long tunnel and into the room where the old man sat on the intricately patterned cloth rug in the middle of the dirt floor, waiting.

"Yawtlée," he cackled. "At long last we meet again. You seem to have jumped on down the gene pool. This young man's eyes are so like his mother's. I hope that doesn't mean anything, but it gives me the creeps." Followed by a burst of insane laughter.

"Now, what are you called? Raphael? I like that. Let me tell you what it is that you must do." His eyes grew narrow and, it seemed to Raphael, very like the eyes of a bird of prey, as he whispered his awful set of instructions into the innocent Fool's ear.

# 46

As if waking up from a nap, Raphael found himself in a forest, watching the light play, this time among the foliage dancing in the brilliant glare of summer, for though it was only late spring whence he had just come, it was indeed full summer here, in the deep forest.

Birds sang insanely in the trees, as if they were activated by the light—which in a way they were. For the first time in his life, Raphael felt himself on the verge of breaking through the great mystery: the answer was light. But what exactly was the question?

Then came the distant, excited barking of hunting dogs.

*I'm sweating,* he thought, *but not from the heat.*

*I will not do it,* he argued, as inexorably he slung the guitar from his back and found a suitable position under a tree and, seated cross-legged, began to play.

All at once the birds went utterly silent, as if they, too, were under the spell of the old man, and the weird music Raphael played reached out its tendrils among the trees and bushes, searching for prey.

And of course the worst part was that it wasn't the music; the music was simply the vehicle that transported his own terrible will.

Creatures began to come to him—at first just squirrels and chipmunks, finally deer, and a while later the dogs, who whimpered and lay down, panting, staring hungrily but helplessly at the stag and three does who stood so near, shivering but unable to run away. And at last came the two men on horseback.

"We've lost the damn dogs, and I can't control the horse," one of them shouted to the other. "Damn it, man, I'll skin him and eat him when we get back."

This had not been easy for Raphael to understand. In fact, it had been impossible at first, for though in England at this time and place Old English was finally giving way to Middle English, these men were Norman aristocrats and disdained them both as the language of losers. They spoke only Viking-influenced French.

In his semitrancelike state, Raphael felt the incredible, indomitable will of Corbo controlling him, impatiently dragging his psychic force into the consciousness of the red-faced rider of the horse, guiding him through the cellular dance of the man's knowledge of language.

It was easy once you knew how to do it. But it was subtle; he felt certain he would never have found it without Corbo's guidance. It was like discovering a brand-new sense of touch that you could apply mentally: eleventh-century French was clear to him all at once, and forever, now.

But he did not rejoice in this new gift. In fact, tears welled up in his eyes and overflowed as he continued to play the music which brought the horses to him.

The two men on horseback entered a sunny, enchanted glade where a handsome young man sat under a tree at the far edge, playing some sort of exotic lute, and all the animals had gathered to listen.

"By God's great toe," the ruddy one shouted. "Do you see that stag? I knew it. I just knew it. This afternoon, it was as if a voice came to me, whispering in my ear that no matter what that stodgy German advises, I am king. And the forest is mine, and every beast and bird in her. Why should I stay there slaving at my desk just because some cold fish of a German tells me to?"

"William, for God's sake, man, will you look at this? This is some sort of evil enchantment. We must get us away from here."

The whole scene suddenly came clear to William. Face red as a beet, he dismounted with such haste that he fell from his horse and tumbled on the forest floor. Scrambled up and started to run away. Back into the trees. But he turned back when he heard his friend calling him. Then he stood there, redder-faced than ever, swaying, gasping for breath. In the grip of full panic.

"Walter," he pleaded hoarsely, "don't aim that at me. I beg thee, Walter. As my dearest friend."

But his speech was cut short by the twang of a bowstring. And William Rufus, the Red King, crumpled and fell to earth with an arrow through his heart.

At last the man under the tree stopped playing his lute and stood up and walked over to where Walter Tyrell still sat astride his horse, holding his bow.

"Excellent shot," the man said in perfect French. "He looked as if he was about to die of a stroke anyway, didn't he?"

Strangely, the wizard was weeping as he spoke. Not loud, just sniffling a little. Tears flowing.

"Well," Walter said, "he's dead now. Whatever shall I do?"

He blinked as if awakening from a deep sleep.

"My God," he murmured reverently, "I've killed the king."

Still in the grip of the old man, Raphael advised him, "Ride for the ocean, head for France. Don't ever come back."

Walter Tyrell blinked again. "Of course. Thank you." And whipped his gelding around and dug in the spurs, and was gone.

Raphael looked down to find himself still holding the green guitar. "Fuck you," he said to it, and threw it down and walked away from it, but could not walk away from the voice in his head.

"Hey, blame me," the voice said. "That way you can still feel like the school safety, right?" Then laughter. Then, "Oh, come on, it's only death. Why make such a big thing out of it? Believe me, everyone's better off with that red-faced turkey gone. And I'm willing to take all the blame for everything. You name it, I did it. Or are you ready to step up and do the work my little stone has chosen for you?

"Don't you get it? Maybe it's you, no? Maybe that little stone chose you. All those years that I spent training Elena was to finally reach you."

Puzzlement crossed Raphael's face. "Who's Elena?" he said aloud. A bird hidden off in the trees tried to answer, but he couldn't understand it.

"Uh-oh," the voice in his head said. "Wait a minute and I'll fix that. Here, let me have a look at your little memory tapes, okay?" There was a momentary pause and Raphael felt a strange, dizzy sensation, as a flood of apparently unrelated images flipped through his mind. Then Corbo's voice was back.

"Uh-oh, no can do," it said. "Think I better just leave that one alone. Let's see, anything else? Well, then, that's it, I guess. *Hasta luego.* England thanks you."

Suddenly Raphael was aware that he was underwater. But he felt no sense of panic. Somehow it seemed ordinary, almost, holding his breath. Then it began to dawn on him.

He looked up toward the light and then gathered his feet under him and stood up.

He was standing waist deep in the waters of the sacred lake.

Someone shouted in wonder to see him thus appear. He smiled wanly, and as if he were a magician having performed a cheap trick, he gestured and bowed. He looked up to see Thaddeus approaching.

"What just happened here, Rafe? You know you disappeared for a solid five minutes?"

"Oh," Raphael said pensively, "five minutes? Ah . . . I went to merry old England to kill the king."

"Sure enough," Thaddeus answered in a wry tone. "I'll buy that. What happened to my guitar?"

"You still got the lute Jeremy made for you?"

Thaddeus blinked as tears welled up once again in his eyes. This was getting to be a common experience. "Yeah," he said hoarsely.

"Then fuck the Ovation," Raphael said, but he was starting to smile now despite himself. The mystical energy from the lake was pouring through him, energizing him, and charging up his stone to the fullest power it had ever been. In spite of everything, it was impossible not to feel joy. Every moment you were starting over, right? He smiled widely, like the Fool he was.

Energy was everything. It wasn't light after all, it was energy that created everything else, including life; it was energy that everthing was made up of, that you were, that he was. And when you had enough of it, everything was wonderful and new. And that was the secret. The big one that transcended good and evil and ran the world.

Something white and muscular came bursting through the water, shattering waves and fracturing the air with a fusillade of barks of ecstasy. Blackjack knew the secret. Everything starts now!

The lake did its job; it completely healed his ruptured heart, and his heart, that pounding clock of life, healed the rest.

And as the little procession at last headed back, he was not at all surprised when Tippi—who also seemed healed emotionally and also to have attained some new and secret form of strength—turned to him and Thaddeus and said in a no-nonsense tone, "Okay, that's it. We're leaving now."

Thaddeus and Elspeth stopped and looked at each other.

"And myself?" Elspeth ventured.

"You, too, babe. LA-bound, as of now."

"Uh, look, Tippi," Thaddeus started in. "What about Smitty and the—"

"I sent them back this morning. No more small talk."

"You can find it from here?"

"The White Lodge showed me how to find it. Programmed the directions in. Believe me, this is their idea. Let's go."

She waved her hand and instantly conjured up a doorway in the forest.

Still thinking up arguments, Thaddeus and Elspeth went through it and into a dark tunnel. Raphael and Blackjack followed.

Elspeth bit her lip and muttered, "But I pray thee, please tell me, why hast thou chosen me?"

"Must be your grasp of the language. Keep moving."

Raphael felt as though the old man would have approved. Hell, he probably was somewhere approving right now. Whenever right now was for him.

They progressed through the darkness toward an area where they were able to see three different lights ahead of them.

"This one," Tippi said, and led them toward the one to their right.

"Where the others go to?" Thaddeus wondered out loud.

"No idea," Tippi said. "They told me I wouldn't want to know, and I believe them."

"Those White Lodge dudes?" Thaddeus remarked. "Sounds like a racist trip to me."

"Sure," Tippi said, "only they're not really white, just like I'm not really white, and you're not really black either. The only one who's really white here is Blackjack."

"And his soul be pure to match."

"That's what they seemed to be telling me," Tippi answered.

They came out in an alley somewhere in LA. Its sole occupant was a drunk who sat leaning against the opposite wall in the shade of a trash can, watching with the nonchalant air of having seen everything.

"Spare some change?" he ventured.

Ignoring him, Tippi said to Raphael, "Okay, now destroy the connection. Don't ask me why it's got to be done. They said you could do it."

Raphael stared at her. There was no question that she was taking charge. He shook his head, but he didn't mean no.

He closed his eyes as if testing it out.

"Then we've got to make it to the Faire and close that doorway down, too."

"Just a quarter," the drunk said, but his voice died out as he got too interested in the weirdly dressed group to remember to beg. "Dressed up like a bunch of fucking elves," he mumbled.

"I feel like I can do them all at once, but I feel like . . . I don't know, I don't want to, you know?"

"Look," Elspeth cut in, "she's right. There is a huge, superpowerful Wiccan organization out here that will most assuredly desire to return to that innocent world and take over. It's the water. The sacred water from the lake. They've got to have it, and they will gladly kill or subjugate anyone they have to in order to get it. As much as I want to live forever, Tippi is right. Cut that world free from thine own. Let those simple people rebuild their lives in peace, on their own. Let them develop their own culture. Then maybe one day . . ."

But Raphael shook his head. "I cut it off, it's gone for good. We'll never see any of it again. I just feel so . . . I don't know, I feel this awful resistance—sadness, really."

"Just do it, Rafe."

Raphael looked at Tippi, their tiny leader, and smiled. "Tough guy, huh?" he said.

"Do it," Thaddeus added, "or Tippi kick your ass."

Raphael closed his eyes, and almost instantly they all felt some immense cosmic crashing of connections between worlds. It was a sad and awesome psychic spectacle, perhaps a mystical expression of empathy as the web between two of a myriad of worlds was torn asunder.

Raphael opened his eyes. For some reason he did not know, there were tears in them yet again.

"You can't get there from here," was all he said.

Tippi nodded. Now they would begin the enormous task of rooting out and destroying the Wiccan organization based in Los Angeles and Florida. Hopefully, Elspeth would provide them with the information they would need. They could always confiscate whatever "holy water" the Wiccan organization already had in storage here, or the products they had made with it, and give them all to Elspeth as a reward. Also, as long as her little crystal kept charging itself off their bigger, more powerful ones, who knew? Maybe the sexy witch would reap the same benefits Tippi herself had enjoyed from being with Violet. Maybe Elspeth would live forever, after all. For some reason the thought of all this made Tippi smile.

"Come on," she said, "we've got work to do," and led the way out of the alley into the sun. Raphael and Blackjack followed, then Elspeth, and at last Thaddeus tossed his coin purse full of weird coins to the bum and, with a wry expression, followed.

The bum looked at the coin purse, then opened it, and poured a couple of coins out. What the . . . ?

"May the god of the elves go with you!" he shouted after them. "I guess." But they were already gone.

# 47

THE OLD MAN went to the door and opened it.

"Come back inside, Elena," he called. Then, "Here, Elena. Here, Elena. Elena, come home."

With a sullen expression, she came back inside the little shack and went over and sat in her chair, looking in her mirror.

"Well, Elena, do you want to know where I went today?"

For a long time she was silent, but the old man patiently waited her out. He would, she knew, have waited forever.

"You went around back of the hut and you were gone for about ten minutes. Then you came back in and chased me outside for a half hour or so. So why should I care where you have been, when you haven't been anywhere?"

"Oh, but it doesn't take that long to be gone for days. For months, even. You see, Elena? Why don't you stop admiring yourself in that mirror and ask me?"

She turned her chair around and sat in it facing him, tapping her foot angrily. He was seated cross-legged on the floor on "his" rug, as usual.

"All right," she said, "where have you been?"

"I've been to London to kill the king."

Elena just sat there, staring. Tapping that foot. At last she said, "Isn't it supposed to be, 'Pussy cat, pussy cat, where have you been? I've been to London to look at the queen'? Or maybe 'to save the queen?' "

Corbo smiled. "Well, yes," he agreed. "I saved the queen, too. Only that was some kind of different London, Elena, and do you know who that queen there was?"

"Ah, let's see, was it Cinderella?"

"No, Elena, it was you."

After a long pause, punctuated by the foot tapping like a metronome, she said, "Gee, isn't that nice? Then I suppose I must owe you a lot. I wonder how may I ever repay you?"

"You know, Elena, give me that mirror, will you?"

Elena took the mirror off the wall and handed it to him, saying, "Gee, in payment for saving me, all you want is this cheapo little mirror of mine. What a bargain."

But as soon as she handed it to him, he threw it across the room, breaking it to bits.

Elena jumped up out of her chair, shouting, "What?"

"Well, it has served its purpose, you see. That's why I let you have it. That's the good part, see? Your ridiculous vanity served as a cover for me to have the mirror. So they would not suspect."

Elena, looking as miserable as she actually was, bit her lower lip and snuffled. "That mirror was the only thing I owned." Then, after a moment, "Okay, so *who* would not suspect? Who is 'they'?"

"One of them is that oaf Germanicus. Have I ever talked to you about him? No? Well, there are four of us who have these powers, Elena, and he is one of us. An ancient German, but a real Nazi, you see?"

"And he has the power to go to England in ten minutes and kill the king?"

"No, no, only I have that power, Elena. Besides, he liked the king. The king was his slave—you know, psychic slave—for a while."

"Like I'm yours?"

"Oh, come on, Elena, you know you are free to leave or do whatever you want. Don't you?

"Anyway, he spies on me. He wants to get control of my time demon so he can go back into the past and take over England. Then he plans to make England into Germany.

"But is that enough for him? Oh, no. So he goes back further, and he finds this weak man named Theseus who lives in a wading pool full of naked women. Yes, it's true, Elena, this poor fool is like Hugh Hefner. He's maybe the most powerful man who ever lived and all he does is sit around in a wading pool on his island and fall in love with all these beautiful women. His name is Theseus."

"The Greek god?"

"No, Elena, he's not a god, just a sort of . . . well, someone who lives for thousands of years and has a lot of powers—you know, psychic powers. Like me."

"Yes," Elena said in a clipped, repressed tone, "just like you."

"So Germanicus makes a deal with my time demon. Did I ever tell you about him, Elena? No? Well, he's only a minor imp really, not much to talk about. But anyway, the deal is, if Ketoko—that is the name of this demon—if Ketoko will take Germanicus back to where he can get at Theseus, then in return he will lure me back there and kill me. Then Ketoko will be free.

"So Ketoko is really not that stupid but"—here he paused and thought for a moment—"you know, maybe he is. Anyway, Germanicus uses my time demon to go back and steal Theseus's most beautiful slave girl, the one that this fool is the most romantic about, and he threatens to torture her if Theseus doesn't do what he wants. So now he can force Theseus to help him control Ketoko. Do you see? No?

"So anyway, Theseus has to reach across time and push me into going back to England so's I can kill King William Rufus. But it's a trap."

Here he paused and chuckled a little.

"I have to laugh, Elena, because these clumsy fools are all sneaking around plotting and spying on me, and I'm not supposed to be aware of it. So what do I do, Elena? This is the best part. Well?"

Elena shook her head.

"Oh, come on, Elena, damn it, use your head. What would I do? I act dumb, see? So Theseus is reaching across time, suggesting to me that I let you have a mirror, so that he can hypnotize me through it, see? So I let him do it because there is something I want that I think I can get out of all this. But I avoid the trap. Kill Germanicus. I used this magic helmet, see?" He held up the weird helmet with the swastika on it and gave her a confusing description of the helmet's supposed properties.

"So the silver in the helmet worked?" She looked slightly interested for the first time.

The old man shook his head in disgust. "Of course not, Elena. You are almost as dumb as Germanicus, and that is really saying something. I knew it wouldn't work— well, I was almost certain—I mean, 'Magic of silver, I call upon thee?' Oh, come on, Elena. It has to be something else, maybe like some kind of electrical wiring or something like that. Some kind of force field that the Wicca helmets generate. I knew this one probably wouldn't work, but there was a chance. I had to take it. Then when I sensed it wasn't working, I just bluffed it out.

"I think Germanicus could tell it wasn't really working, but, you know, what could he do? There was a lot of pressure on him. He didn't exactly have time to sit down and put on his thinking cap. He knew if he made a mistake,

I'd kill him while he was figuring it out. So, truth is, it didn't work, but it worked just as well as if it had worked.

"Let's see, then I set Theseus's girlfriend loose, and come back here, and chase you out so I can get someone else to kill the king for me. Know who that someone is, Elena?"

Elena thought about it. "No," she said.

"Well, you won't, then, either," he remarked cryptically, then added, "Poor Elena. But at least you get to be the queen." At this point he paused and blinked rapidly. "My eyes are tired, and you know what that means, Elena?"

Elena said, "No."

He shook his head wearily. "Poor Elena. It means that I am sleepy. Surely you have had experience with that."

She shook her head.

"Well, now you have. In the future if you see my eyes blinking a lot, like that, tell me to take a nap."

"Why, of course I will," Elena assured him. "That seems like a good little chore for me."

"And as for all these fools," the old man continued, "that think they are watching me and that I don't even know it, I say, 'Good luck, boys.' "

Then he broke into one of his wild bouts of laughter that just went on and on. Finally he said, "Uh-oh," and stopped. Then he looked up, as if he were staring through the ceiling, and shouted, "And as for all you members of the White Lodge, that includes you, too!"

A long, long silence. Then Elena said, "So that's how you spent the last half hour or so?"

He nodded. "That's it. Just the bare bones, you know? But that's it."

She nodded. "Okay. I'm leaving you. You are simply a crazy old man and I'm leaving you."

"Well, you know, Elena, that's too bad, because here we are out in the middle of this desert and that old Chevy truck of mine is gone. Besides, I wouldn't feel comfortable with you going to be queen and all, tooling around the desert in an old Chevy. Why don't you wait until morning and I'll conjure you up a new Cadillac so you can go in style? Hey, come on, Elena, it will have a mirror in it and everything."

"All right," she said tonelessly. "There won't be any buses to flag down anyway until morning. If then. If ever."

"Good, then," he said. "Oh, shit, there is no telephone, so I can't phone someplace and say, 'Hey, deliver a new Caddy out here in the desert for Elena.' What can I do?"

He snapped his fingers, which made a shockingly loud sound in the room, causing Elena to flinch.

"I know," he said, "I'll use me this here mirror trick that Theseus thinks he used on me. Here, how does it go?"

He leaned over, but could not reach any of the broken glass without uncrossing his legs and getting up.

"Hand me a piece of broken glass, would you, please? Yes, that's a good one."

He held it up in front of him.

"Let's see," he said, closing his eyes in thought, "how does that spell go?

> "Mirror, mirror on the wall
> Who's the fairest of them all?
> Not Elena, that's for sure
> Though, of course, I wish she were.
> Please bring a Cadillac for her."

"That sounds like it will work, don't you think, Elena? Doesn't that sound like a pretty good spell?"

Elena did not answer.

"Well, I guess we'll just have to wait until tomorrow morning and see, right?"

Elena nodded.

"And as for me, I know how early it is, but that was a tough little few minutes. I think I'm just going to eat a few beans and go to sleep. I plan to get up early tomorrow morning to see you off."

Bright and early the next morning, Elena, packed and ready to begin the arduous task of flagging down a bus on a practically deserted desert highway, headed out the door.

The sun was just coming up. There was sun and sand and cactus and highway. There was a brand-new big powder-blue Cadillac parked in front of their hut where the old man's truck used to sit.

"Well, my goodness, Elena, that little magic trick of Theseus's worked like a charm. How lucky. Know what? I'll bet you that the keys are in the ignition, and maybe there's some money in the trunk. Maybe thirty, forty dollars. No, I bet two hundred thousand dollars are in that trunk. So if you could give me a ride into town, I can buy myself some eggs and some coffee. Toast, too. I'll even treat you."

Elena nodded. She really couldn't speak just then. *I should leave him anyway,* she said to herself, *just run away and get a job as a waitress and marry some traveling salesman passing through, and live happily ever after.*

But she didn't. She just drove him into town and then on down the long lonely highway.

"You know," he said, "our work here is done, and now we are free to go. We are not going back, Elena."

"I thought you loved this place."

She did not have to take her eyes off the road to feel his eyes boring into her.

"What difference could that possibly make?" he said calmly. And she was sure that he was shaking his head. "And please don't ask me where we are headed, Elena. Just follow your star. Wherever that takes us will be home enough."

He sighed and slept, and Elena drove the big sleek Caddie on through the day and into the night, following her star.

# *Epilogue*

———◉———

F OR A WHILE they just lay there, Elena staring up past the stars into her own thoughts, King William not looking at anything, mumbling something to himself.

*So that's what it's like to drink too much wine,* she thought. *Not something you would want to do often, but . . .*

"What did you say?" She was over the main sweep of the euphoria now, and she was dizzy enough so that it became a little frightening to close her eyes.

"I said, life is s-o-o-o good."

Elena smiled up at the stars, so many stars, and said, "For some."

"And I do hope that you will be one of them. No, no, what I mean is that if you will just give me the chance, I will make it good for you. I swear to it, on my royal name."

"Not good enough," Elena said.

"No, you're right, it's nothing. I swear to it on my—what?"

"On your honor as a Boy Scout?"

"Why, yes, of course, only I don't know what a Boy Scout is. Am I a Boy Scout?"

Elena, who hardly ever smiled, smiled and said in a soft voice, "Yes, you are a Boy Scout."

"But what is a Boy Scout?"

"I'll tell you about it some other time. We've got lots of time."

"Oh yes, we do," he said ecstatically.

"If a tree don't fall on us, we'll live till we die." Elena had never felt so witty. Or for that matter, witty at all.

"Know what?" she said. "You're not stuttering."

"Yes," he said, "I-I-I no-no-noticed th-that."

Elena laughed, an almost unheard-of event.

"Thou dost not, I me-mean, you d-d-don't mind?"

"Of course not. I find it charming."

"Really?"

"Really."

"Then good gracious, what am I to do, stop it or cultivate it?"

Elena said languorously, "Do what you wish."

"But what if it hurts somebody?" he said earnestly.

"You don't want to hurt anybody, do you, William?"

"No, of c-c-course not."

"Then do as you wish, and everyone will be the better for it."

Emotion overwhelmed him and left him speechless for a moment. Then he said, "Thou art so wise."

For the second time Elena laughed out loud. "No one's ever said that to me before. Incidentally, you're pretty heavy. You have my royal permission to withdraw."

"And thou art so witty. But I will lose weight. I will. And then I shall lie on thee forever."

"Suit thyself," Elena said.

He rolled off her and lay on his back beside her, exulting in the cool, damp kiss of the grass, the stars, the dark.

"It's just all so wonderful," he said.

"That's true."

"And it's all so easy."

"That's true."

"But we make it so hard. Why do we do that?"

Elena thought to herself, *Me especially,* and said, "We are all crazy."

"Yes, that's it. We are all crazy." He rolled over, propped himself up on his elbows, and stared down into her eyes. He felt as if the very cells in his body were shimmering in an ecstasy of love. He touched her nose. The moon must have gone behind a cloud then, because everything darkened and a cool breeze teased his damp back. He sat up and pulled on his shirt.

"Wh-wh-what are we going to do without the guidance of the Wicca?"

Elena sat up. She was getting cold, too. She pulled on her blouse.

"Don't worry," she said. "It really isn't much of a problem. We've got a fair amount of technology here from the other world. I have some rudimentary knowledge of how it works. We have children. We simply put special emphasis on schooling them. We make it a priority that every one of them gets an excellent education. They'll take care of the rest." She shrugged.

"Why, that's fantastic. It can't fail. Is that how they did it in your world?"

Elena shook her head, causing her long silky hair to shimmer like the cells in William's body. "Hardly," she said, "The poor kids hardly get any education. About half the time they can't even read. Sometimes they don't even learn to speak English."

King William was staring at her in open amazement.

"Wha-what-what? Wha-what language do they speak?"

Elena stood up and pulled on her skirt. "The language of whatever country they originally came from. In the case of my ancestors it's Spanish."

"But how could that be? How do they communicate what they want? Need?"

"With great difficulty."

"But how does your society justify that?"

"Some bullshit about the past. Their ancestors all spoke Spanish, so— oh, I don't know. But clinging to the past is the cause of all suffering. I know that much because I had it crammed down my throat over and over again by an old man who raised me. And he was always right."

"Wha-wha-what happened to your parents?"

Fully dressed, Elena sat down next to him in the damp grass. What the hell. "Nothing happened to my parents, but you could hardly describe what they did as raising me. For years and years I was the apprentice to an old wizard. Anything I learned from him—and believe me, it was never easy—but whatever I learned from him, it raised me."

"Why, how marvelous," he exclaimed. Now he was up, pulling on his trousers. "No wonder you are so wise. A real wizard, real magick?"

"For real."

"Was he very powerful?"

"I think he was the most powerful and the wisest man who ever lived. He was also a clown and a fool."

"How can that be?"

She shook her head. "I don't really know. But it seemed to me somehow, I don't know, essential. Like you couldn't have one without the other."

"He must have loved you."

"Not at all. He thought I was a fool. He had no interest in me at all."

The moon had come out again and he could see that her eyes were filled with tears.

"How could that be? Why did he choose thee?" He put his arm around her shoulder, and she moved closer.

"Wizards don't choose," she said. "They simply do what they are told."

"Told by whom?"

Elena thought about it. "I don't know. But look up there. See all those stars? Once I said to him, 'Do you see all those stars?' He said, 'No.' I said, 'You see more than I do? Than an ordinary person sees?' He said, 'Less. I see less, Elena, that's why everything is so easy.' And I said, 'What do you see?' And he said, 'I see only myself, Elena.' And I said, 'I don't get it. You don't see all those stars?' And he just smiled and said, 'Of course I see the stars, but I see them only as myself. That's all.' Then he knocked on my head as if to see if it was really hollow. Sometimes I feel he must have hated me."

For a while, both of them were silent. Then he said, "Do you know what, Elena? I know I'm not wise or anything remotely resembling that, but I can tell you something here for certain. If I look at you and I see all these wonderful things in you, and I do, then how could this great wizard, this seer, if you will, not see them? No, believe me, Elena, he loved you. Probably more than I can ever manage to do. But, by the Goddess, I'm going to really try."

He kissed her on the cheek. She was crying, of course.

"Furthermore," he said, "it's cold, but it's not that cold. I suggest one more quick dip in the lake. I'll wager that it will wash away the effects of the wine. I want to make love sober."

Elena smiled and said through her tears, "Hey, I thought I was the wise one around here. But that sounds like one hell of a good idea."

King William said to her, quite seriously, "You know, I love it when you swear."

# *About the Author*

**Ronald Anthony Cross**'s short stories have been featured in *Science Fiction Age, Weird Tales, Asimov's Science Fiction Magazine,* and *The Magazine of Fantasy & Science Fiction.* His first novel, *Prisoners of Paradise,* was published in 1988.

Tor has published the first two books in *The Eternal Guardians* series, a jarring, fast-paced dance across the secret, true history of our world, led by the wit and style of Cross. With *The White Guardian,* Cross strikes up his unique song once again.

Cross meditates and practices tai chi. He dreams, but is aware that he is dreaming. He lives in Santa Monica, California, where he is currently working on the next book of *The Eternal Guardians* series.

## *Author's Note*

You may wish to hear the songs and instrumentals you have read about in this book. There is an hour-long tape of the music available, performed by the author.

Send check or money order (from a U.S. bank, U.S. dollars only, no credit cards) payable to Ronald Anthony Cross. $10.00 + $2 p/h (California residents add 8.25% sales tax. Outside U.S. please double the p/h.) Include the shipping address, and mail your order to:

**SONGS OF THE WHITE GUARDIAN**
**100 UCLA MED PLAZA**
**SUITE 150 PO BOX 6**
**LOS ANGELES CA 90024**